D1447229

Seducing the Spirits

Seducing the Spirits

LOUISE YOUNG

THE PERMANENT PRESS
Sag Harbor, New York 11963

For information, address:
The Permanent Press
4170 Noyac Road
Sag Harbor, NY 11963
www.thepermanentpress.com

Library of Congress Cataloging-in-Publication Data

Young, Louise
Seducing the spirits / Louise Young.
p. cm.
ISBN-13: 978-1-57962-190-2 (hardcover : alk. paper)
ISBN-10: 1-57962-190-2 (hardcover : alk. paper)
1. Ornithologists—Fiction. 2. Americans—Panama—Fiction.
3. Cuna Indians—Fiction. I. Title.

PS3625.O9665S43 2009
813'.6—dc22 2009026617

Printed in the United States of America.

I

In the uneasy hour before dawn, the jungle surrounding the research compound steams like the exhale of a sleeping, warm-blooded animal. Crickets mutter. Distance mellows the roars of a howler monkey into something vaguely human. Moths bewitch bats and are in turn betrayed by the lights of the jeep that waits in the clearing behind the dormitory. Their wings ghost at my hair as I heave the last of my duffle into the back seat, swing my leg over the rusted metal of the passenger's door, and hop inside.

Reilly's eyes, green like a bug's in the dashboard's glow, flash toward me. "I expected Calabrese to be out here to see you off."

I swipe my hand to chase the moths in front of my face but they ride the wake and return thicker than before. "Wouldn't that imply that he has some compassion, some conscience, some—maybe one ounce—of humanity? And balls too, for that matter. You think he has any of those?"

As if in response, the howler monkey lets loose with a full-throated bellow. Reilly glances at me again. "I guess you'd know more about that than I would—especially the last one. You don't want to wait?"

"I just want to get out of here. Now."

The road leading out of the compound is torn and rough, with walls of vegetation closing in at the edges. Reilly jerks the steering wheel from side to side as the jeep fishtails over ruts. Over the racket of the engine, I think I hear howlers again. I picture the bull male: thin-limbed, pot-bellied, with sagging, loose jowls and rheumy eyes.

"Listen, if it makes you feel any better, the last grad student Calabrese did the nasty with is in Coiba now."

"What?" I was in another place when Reilly spoke and I'm not sure that I heard him right.

"Coiba. It's an island off the Pacific coast. It's got the biggest population of scarlet macaws in Central America. It's also got a penal colony. So there sits sweet Colleen in the middle of the jungle with a couple hundred parrots and twice that many horny lifers."

"David's done this before?"

"What—humped grad students? Or sent them off into exile afterwards?"

"Jesus, Reilly, why didn't you warn me?"

"You were too busy telling me how disgusting I am. Besides, if I rat on Calabrese, he'd probably do the same to me and then I'd never get any."

The roadside vegetation melts as the jeep pushes into a clearing along the Chagres River. In the headlight beams, a swarm of nighthawks twists and darts as it pursues insects on the wing. There must be a hundred birds slicing above the ford where the river crosses the road.

"Yee-haw!" yips Reilly, flooring the jeep in the knee-high water.

"Reilly, for Christ's sake"—A muffled clunk interrupts me. A feathered body twists twice as it rolls up the windshield. Over the top it lands, limp, square in my lap. "Stop!" I shriek.

The battered jeep comes to a halt. Reilly's voice sounds annoyed. "I thought you were in such a hurry to get out of here."

"I don't want to leave a trail of dead animals in my wake."

"What kind of a biologist are you?" Reilly is using the pause to light one of his foul smelling, cigarette-thin cigars.

I examine the lump of feathers in my lap. In flight, the most obvious feature of a nighthawk is its long, slim wings, conspicuously banded and bent at the elbow. Nighthawks are sharp, precise predators. This pathetic thing I'm holding, softly mottled and still, looks defenseless and fragile. The eyes are open but glazed.

Reilly exhales a cloud of blue smoke. "It dead?"

"Yeah."

"Throw it in the back, okay? I'll wrap it in plastic and in two or three days, it'll be ripe enough to use as bait."

"That's disgusting."

"If I discover a new species, I'll name it after you."

"I don't know if I want my name forever linked with a dung beetle."

"Fifteen minutes of fame," he grins as he turns the key and the jeep's engine howls.

I smooth the breast feathers of the dead bird in my lap. I had never realized that nighthawks were so beautiful. "Please"—I'm surprised that my voice trembles when I say this. "Drive a little slower, okay?"

"Will do, babe." He tosses the still-glowing cigar butt into the darkness of the surrounding jungle. "What were we talking about before?"

"You and David. And how you like screwing grad students."

"Literally and metaphorically." When he laughs, I hear a rattle of phlegm in his chest and wonder if he's been checked for tuberculosis recently. "Every semester we get a new crop of you kids from up North in the States. Innocents, all of you. Seduced by the jungle. You have no idea what all this heat and humidity does to your hormones. I've set up experiments: keep beetles in the 'fridge for a few days, check their hormones. Nothing. Nada. Zilch. Get some live ones from a pile of fresh shit in the jungle and they're off the scale."

"How do you test for hormones?"

"Grind 'em up in a blender. Then centrifuge what's left."

"You test grad students the same way?"

Reilly cackles. "Don't have to test—I can see it in their eyes. It's all the fecundity down here. You can't help but be horny."

"But most of the grad students at the station are men."

"Everyone's got at least one hole."

"Reilly, you are truly disgusting!"

"I'm not the one sending you off to live the rest of your life in the jungle with nothing for company but a pair of overgrown chicken hawks and a bunch of Indians."

Even with the motion of the open jeep, the air around me feels like a thick, smothering blanket. I cradle the dead bird in my lap. Reilly fiddles with the cigarette lighter in the dash but when he can't get it to work, he brakes and uses both hands to shield the match at the cigar between his lips. I see him glance at me in the reflected flame. "You scared?"

I can't even fake bravado. "Shitless."

"David's an asshole for doing this to you. I told him that."

"I'm not even qualified to research eagles. All of my other work has been with songbirds."

"All birds are the same: they got feathers and they shit when they fly."

Lights from the Miraflores Locks of the canal shine through the vegetation on the right. My predawn brain balks at the transition from jungle to civilization. I wait until we've cleared the bustle of activity around the locks before I ask Reilly, "Did you know the guy who's been at the harpy eagle site until now?"

"Brian Geddes? Miserable little worm."

"You didn't check out his hormones?"

"I wouldn't even eat in the same room with that little shit."

"David said he's coming back because he caught leishmaniasis." Leishmaniasis is a disease carried in sand flea bites that causes living flesh to decay.

Reilly sneers around the butt of his cigar. "Probably just an infected zit."

When we get to the city there's a glow over the bay, the imaginings of dawn. I remember how confused I was my first morning in Panama by sunrise over the Pacific Ocean. We drive past the slums that were shelled during America's "Operation Just Cause."

Reilly finishes his second cigar, snuffs the ember on the metal door of the jeep, and tosses the butt. "Listen, I've run into some of those Indians from around where you're going. They're all little squirts. They'll go crazy over you—probably make you into their white goddess."

"And the sand fleas? Leishmaniasis? Vampire bats?"

"We're almost to the airport now."

"I thought the airport was way out of town the other way."

"That's the international one. This one's the local."

"But it's surrounded by skyscrapers!"

Reilly rattles another laugh. "Well, maybe you'll get lucky and your plane will crash into the side of a bank."

Through the glass door, the terminal looks like a Greyhound bus station. As Reilly hauls my bags out of the back of the jeep, I stroke the nighthawk's feathers one final time.

Reilly stands on the edge of the glare from the terminal, facing me like a lover. I'm not sure what to expect from him. "You know, babe, the part of Panama where you're going is famous for its snow."

I study his face to see if he's joking. "Snow?"

"I forgot—you're from some Podunk town in Montana. Cocaine, babe. The San Blas Islands are one of the main routes for cocaine coming out of Colombia."

"Like a migration flyway?"

Reilly throws back his head and laughs. "You can't give up that junior biologist shit, can you? Even when Calabrese is selling your ass up the river. Poor girl!"

"I don't need your sympathy."

"Well, since you won't take my sympathy, why don't you take pity on me and rustle up some of that Panamanian snow to ease my boredom here in this ever-lovin' hellhole?"

"And how am I supposed to get the snow to you before it melts?"

"Didn't they teach you anything in school?"

"I'm from some Podunk town in Montana, remember?"

Reilly sighs. With the backlight, I can't see his face so I'm surprised when he takes me by the shoulders and brushes his lips across mine. "Take care, babe." The stink of his cigar lingers even after the jeep's moans have been swallowed by the city.

I pull and drag and kick my duffels across the parking lot but when I peer through the glass door, the terminal is packed so tight with people that I decide to leave my luggage outside.

I open the door and the predawn stillness erupts into hot phosphorescence and voices—everyone speaking loudly, harshly, and angrily. I try to snake my way between a pair of colorfully dressed, incredibly short old women and am greeted with what I assume to be expletives. One is cussing me so emphatically that the ring between her nostrils jerks loose. When she senses the uneven weight in her nose, the old hen covers the front of her face with one hand while continuing to curse me with vehement gestures of the other.

I maneuver my way among bodies. The younger Indian men are about as tall as I am but compact and muscular, dressed in what look like hand-me-downs from Goodwill. The women are quite a bit shorter, with thick bodies and skinny legs. They seem to shrink as they age so that the really old ones are about the same height as my ten-year-old nephew. In contrast to the ragged appearance of the men, the women wear a uniform of incredible brilliance: red and yellow head scarf, multicolored blouse, navy and orange skirt, with the thousands of beads at their ankles and wrists accented by assorted gold jewelry, the highlight being a nose ring. The entire effect is dazzling, and makes me feel downright drab in my khaki shorts and beige t-shirt.

I worm my way to the ticket counter. A sleepy-eyed man, the only other white person in the room, has already begun to write my ticket.

"Porvenir?" he asks without looking up.

"Excuse me?" Disoriented by the ride and the hour, I use English.

"Destination?" The man says the word in Spanglish: half English and half Spanish.

"Sugatupu."

The man pauses with the pen above the ticket. As he raises his eyes to my face, I see his lips rehearse the English words. "What is your destination?"

I reply in Spanish. "Sugatupu. A one-way ticket, please."

His face remains impassive. This time he speaks Spanish, but slowly and clearly as if to a stupid child. "You will go to Porvenir."

I force a smile in an attempt to charm him. “Sugatupu. One way, please.”

He is nonplussed by my flirting and seems to address a point beyond my left shoulder. “They do not like outsiders in Sugatupu. There is no place to stay. Americans like you go to Porvenir and stay at the hotel. You will see lots of Indians there.”

“I am going to stay in the jungle.”

The sleepy-eyed man laughs—a “ha, ha, ha” that doesn’t touch his eyes.

“Sugatupu,” I insist.

He doesn’t look at my face again. When he finishes writing the ticket, he tells me the price.

“That’s twice as much as it should be!” I hear my voice rising with exasperation.

“I will not sell you a one-way ticket.” He straightens the papers on the counter. “The last white woman who tried to stay on Sugatupu didn’t even last the night.”

I’m dying to ask what happened to her but don’t want to admit ignorance.

“Your return ticket is for tomorrow.”

“I’m not coming back tomorrow.”

He shrugs. “You have the ticket. It is very difficult to buy an air taxi ticket on Sugatupu. I will note that you can use it for any flight in the next week.”

“I won’t be coming back in the next week!” I must sound like a spoiled little kid to him. I want to argue more but he’s already begun the paperwork for the man behind me.

I slink into a corner, trying to be as inconspicuous as possible with my lanky height and light hair. I notice another white person, taller than me: a man or maybe just a kid with tattoos up both his bare arms. He’s smoking a cigarette, looking bored. A little Indian girl—maybe six years old, maybe ten: I can’t tell because they all seem equally tiny—stares at the man with enormous eyes. The man smiles at her, a friendly smile, and I almost find myself smiling back but then he waggles his index finger to beckon the child. When she hesitates, the man pulls a piece of hard candy out of his pocket. The girl eagerly sidles up to the tall white kid. Even after I turn my head and squeeze my eyes shut, I can't erase the image of the jagged canine teeth the man exposed as he closed his fingers around the child's grasping hand.

The harsh, abrupt voices that surround me all sound as if they are holding back anger, or at least disdain. The Indians' language reminds me of the motion of David's head when he called me into his office yesterday: a short, quick jerk, more like he was dismissing a thought than summoning a human being. He'd hardly spoken to me since that night at the shabby hotel in the mountains where he promised me quetzals but delivered something completely different. In his office, I stand before him like a naughty schoolgirl.

"Your plane leaves at dawn. Reilly will drive you to the city." He looks everywhere except my face. "Brian has been on site for two years: he'll meet you at the airstrip when you arrive and fill you in on the progress of the research. It's pretty straightforward: a nesting observation study. You shouldn't have any problem with that."

David picks up a pencil and curls the fingers of one hand around it. With the other hand, he slides the pencil back and forth inside the tube of his fingers. I don't think he realizes that he is doing this, or that I notice.

"The main thing to remember"—he clears his throat and focuses his eyes on the base of my neck—"is that the observation site belongs to the Indians. Dr. Flemming had to work for months to convince them to let us set up on their land. Harpy eagle nests are hard to find, especially one this conveniently located. It's important to be able to continue this study: Flemming was planning on at least ten years. In order to do that, we have to stay on good terms with the Indians."

David's hand clenches around the pencil's barrel, gripping it tightly. "Whenever you're around the Indians, behave yourself. Follow their rules. And for Christ's sake, don't do anything to piss them off."

"Hainey Doonfray."

I hear the words above the generalized babble of foreign voices in the terminal, without recognition.

"Hainey Doonfray." The words hiss out again, closer and more urgent, and this time I realize they are a Spanglish corruption of my name. I glance up and see the sleepy-eyed ticket man glaring at me. His hand above his head twitches like a worm on a hook.

I hold up my index finger to him as an acknowledgement, then hustle outside to collect my bags. Loaded with three duffels and a knapsack, I can barely maneuver but the crowd in the terminal seems to respect my increased bulk. I follow the man through another door and outside to the tarmac of the airport.

Ashy streaks of dawn emphasize the lack of artificial lights on the runway. I'm led past idle aircraft of all sizes and shapes until we arrive at the smallest airplane I have ever seen. The plane is so small that it only has one propeller, on its nose like a kid's toy. There's a fist of people next to the plane's hatch. A short Latino man—shorter even than the Indians—orders people around using hand gestures. When he notices me, the man hurries to my side and slides one of my bags—the heaviest—off my shoulder. His body collapses from the weight but he smiles up at me, then tries to hoist the duffle into the cargo hold of the little plane. I drop my other duffels and help him lift the heavy bag. After we heave it into the hold, I reach for another bag.

"No," the man insists firmly but with a shy smile. He will not allow me to touch the two lighter duffels as he loads them. Once he is finished, he pulls a white handkerchief from the pocket of his pleated black trousers, wipes his hands and brow, then takes my elbow and guides me to the front of the plane. He points to the open door of the cockpit. Assuming that he is referring to the passenger's cabin, I mount the step to the hatch but am immediately cussed out by the four Indians filling every available seat.

"No, no," the slight Latino man corrects and when I turn to him, I realize that he is younger than me. "Here," he says in Spanish, sweeping his hand toward the cockpit as if welcoming a dignitary. I have to bend almost double to crawl through the pilot's door and am uncomfortably aware that my rear end is the last part of my anatomy to enter the plane. I slide into the copilot's seat petrified that I'll knock something out of position.

The pilot has to jimmy and jiggle the cockpit door before it closes but once he has it securely latched, he devotes all of his attention to me, fussing with the seat belt and checking to make sure that my shoulder harness is tight. He points once to the control panel in front of me and wags his finger. I acknowledge his warning with a nod although touching anything on the panel is the farthest thing from my mind.

"You speak Spanish?" he asks me in Spanish.

"Yes."

The little pilot smiles full and broad. Light from the control panel reflects off one of his front teeth and I realize that it sports a gold inlay shaped like a star.

The pilot adjusts his headset and begins flicking switches on the control panel, but he seems more interested in the contours of my legs than the readings of the instruments. I'm starting to sweat. Buildings rise steeply on every side of the airport except out toward the empty ocean.

Without a signal or a word, suddenly we're taxiing down the runway. The propeller spins. My stomach lurches. I haven't eaten this morning but still am afraid that I might throw up. I close my eyes. I hear the little pilot laugh once—a quick, triumphant "ha!"—and when I look out the window, we're flying over the ocean.

I glance at the pilot. He's already taken off the headset and is smoothing his greasy black hair. He grins broadly again, flashing me a "thumb's up." I must look green to him. I smile weakly and lean my head against the side window.

The cool of the glass quiets the throb in my head and I relax my shoulder into the door. The window is gray and streaked. When I blink, my reflection appears to dance across the dirty glass.

Once we've passed the lights of Panama City, the plane turns away from the featureless expanse of ocean. The day lightens. I crane my neck to watch the misty landscape unfold beneath me. The grassy hills and cattle remind me of eastern Montana. We fly so low that I can distinguish individual trails, eroded ridges of red soil. I see squatters' shacks with rusted tin roofs the color of dirt.

Ahead, the mist thickens as the mountains rise. The vegetation becomes deep and green, an abrupt jungle. The tiny plane slices into the atmosphere, the propeller on the nose dicing a route through viscous clouds. The windows fog over with raindrops so minute that they are not discrete but a film of moisture. The control panel glows green in the semidarkness of the cockpit.

The storm disorients me and although the pilot has switched on the wipers, all I see through the windshield is a thick, amorphous mass of nothingness. My breathing is sharp and tense. The pilot must sense my concern because he glances at me, grins, and nods to the control panel where a dime store compass points due east. Balancing atop the ball of the compass, a plastic statue of the Blessed Virgin meets my eyes with a serene smile.

As abruptly as the clouds appeared, they disappear like a rising curtain and suddenly we're flying directly into the sun. The pilot squints and shades his eyes with one hand. I find my sunglasses in my knapsack and offer them to him.

"Thanks." The gold star flashes and he smiles into my face so long that he has to jerk the plane back on course when he glances out the windshield.

Beneath us, the Caribbean Sea dazzles with its blue, a shade of turquoise I've known before only from postcards and dreams. The underwater topography paints coral reefs brown and teal against the darker blues. The mainland is deep green and smoky with the remains of clouds.

A river meanders out from the jungle hills and a minute later we pass over an island that reads an unnatural shade of gray. Squinting, I realize that the surface of the island is covered with an almost unbroken thatch of roofs. The houses of the Indians must be so tightly packed—like the bodies in the airport this morning—that there is virtually no space between them. In the turquoise water near the island, I notice bullet-shaped boats, some with billowy white sails, all pointed toward the mainland and the mouth of the river.

In his briefing—the emphasis was on "brief"—David described the Kuna islands as dormitory communities: like suburban families, the fathers commute to the mainland every morning to farm and hunt while the women stay home with the kids. In the afternoon, the men always return to the islands. "All of the Kunas sleep on the islands," he explained with a quick, sideways jerk of his head as he said the word "sleep." "The only time there will be people on the mainland around you will be during the day. You should always be in the blind—working—by the time the sun comes up, just to make sure—" His sentence ended abruptly and I wondered how he'd intended to finish it.

The plane continues on its eastbound course. To avoid the sun, I look straight down. The coast teems with human activity: airstrips, smoldering patches of jungle, boats maneuvering the tight oxbows of rivers. I see a few thatched buildings on the mainland but most of the construction is confined to the islands. Not all of the islands are inhabited: some are idyllic with white sand and palms while others crowd so many houses that they seem in danger of spilling into the surrounding sea. The pilot, noticing my interest, points to an island with huge water tanks dominating one end.

"What are those for?" I ask him.

"Hospital." We've already passed over that island and are steering inland. "It's the only one the Indians have. Except for their witch doctors."

Unsure of how I should respond, I widen my eyes like a dolt.

"You're only staying here one night?" He's studying my legs again.

I start to shake my head but then remember the insistence of the sleepy-eyed ticket man. "Yes. One night."

"You've got a lot of luggage for one night."

"I like to be prepared."

As we approach an airstrip, the plane banks. For a couple minutes, the pilot concentrates on positioning the plane above the narrow strip of blacktop hacked from the jungle. The landing is almost instantaneous: one minute we are skidding over treetops, the next we bounce to a halt at the very end of the runway.

"This isn't your stop," the pilot says to me as he unbuckles himself. He pats my knee when he rises from his seat.

We drop off three of the Indians here but pick up one more, a stale smelling albino man. When the pilot climbs back into the plane, he flashes me his star.

We taxi to the end of the runway, take off toward the ocean so low that we skim the water, then a wind gust catches the wings and the plane almost flips over. I hear loud shouts from the two Indians in the back. The pilot laughs, "ha!" but my eyes are closed too tight to observe what's happening.

A minute later, the pilot laughs again and tells me that I can open my eyes. When I do, the first thing I see is his face. I want to tell him to keep his eyes on the road, but there is no road.

"You were scared?"

I answer "No" as I nod my head.

"Where are you staying in the city?" He's begun circling, banking to approach another runway.

"The Hotel Costa Azul." That's where I spent my first night off the plane from the U.S., a lifetime ago.

Again our conversation wanes as he sets the little aircraft on to the runway. The kid seems to know what he's doing. I manage to keep my eyes open this time.

When the plane comes to a halt, the pilot touches my knee again. "Sugatupu."

He unbuckles my seatbelt and stands in the doorway to guide me out of the plane so that I have to shimmy against him to negotiate the steps down from the cockpit. I notice the remaining Panama City Indian muscling open the cabin door. He darts out of the plane and disappears into the surrounding forest like a scared rabbit. The pilot locates a stepladder in the cargo hold and we both struggle with my three big duffels. The albino hangs tight to his seat.

After my bags are piled at the edge of the runway and the ladder safely stowed, the pilot gives me his gold star smile. "Would you like to have dinner with me tomorrow?"

His proposal catches me off guard. I swat at an insect that's biting my leg.

"At eight. I will meet you in the lobby of the Hotel Costa Azul. And after we dine, we will go dancing."

"Of course." I can't think of any other response. I'm sweating again.

"You are a very brave woman," he says to me as he flashes his toothy star one final time. I'm not sure if he's referring to my stay with the Indians or my acceptance of his dinner date. On take off, the pilot dips a wing as the plane rises over the ocean, saluting me where I stand: alone with my three duffle bags on the edge of a jungle that breathes like a heavy-bodied animal, rich with the promise of unexplored life.

II

When Brian, the graduate student I'm replacing at the harpy eagle site, finally shows up at the airstrip, he greets me with a command: "You have to move those bags out of the way so that I can get my stuff ready for tomorrow." He's more concerned with shuttling and arranging his gear for the morning flight out than in orientating me on the details of the project. He doesn't ask questions and all of his sentences begin with either "I" or "you," those using "you" in the form of a command.

In all fairness, Brian probably has a hard time warming up to me since I won't look directly at his face. The lesion he believes to be leishmaniasis, an open, weeping sore on his upper lip, reads suspiciously like a chancre to my unpracticed eye. I try to ignore it when he talks but it's so lurid that I can't keep my eyes off it. I resolve to sanitize every eating utensil in camp as soon as Brian leaves, just in case his self-diagnosis is wrong.

Late in the afternoon, after dragging the last of Brian's six duffels to the airstrip and covering them with the project's waterproof tarp, we share an early dinner of baked beans, the same fare we enjoyed at lunch. Brian spoons his beans directly from the can. The sore doesn't appear to bother him; in fact, he favors that side of his mouth as he slurps runny orange sauce off the spoon.

After he gulps down the last of his beans, he wipes his lips with the back of his hand. "You have to change into long pants before you go to the island."

"The island?"

He sighs at my stupidity. "You have to go to the meeting tonight. It's Saturday."

My stomach tightens and suddenly I'm too exhausted to swallow. "Tonight? But I just got here."

"You have to go to their town meeting every Saturday night. It's the rules. They know that you flew in today so they'll be expecting you."

"Isn't there any way I can get out of it? I'm so tired now I can't think straight."

Even without looking at his face, I hear disdain in Brian's words. "I went to the meeting the first day I got here."

I want to cry from frustration but instead I swallow my self-pity with a mouthful of beans and ask, "Why do I have to wear long pants to the meeting?"

"I don't know. It's just one of their rules: no shorts. You'd better get going or you'll be late. I have to finish packing."

The island lies a couple hundred yards off the coast through the calm water of a bay. I paddle a little dugout canoe with a seat barely wide enough to accommodate my rump. As I approach, the details of the community resolve and I realize that the town is more complex that it appeared from the air. Irregular networks of houses are clustered in groups, often almost touching the sea. In some areas, canoes are moored to posts in shallow water while other beaches are tree-shaded and dim, and still others are hidden behind high stockades. The seaward side of the island butts against the reef, with breakers from the open ocean crashing so close that houses here are sheltered by a sea wall. I notice a tin-roofed store, a basketball court, and a concrete dock that rides a good three feet above the surface of the water.

On the leeward side of the island, isolated from the rest of the community by mangroves, a beach of white sand and palm trees stretches like a finger toward the mainland. Beneath the palms, a lone thatched hut squats like some kind of tropical dream. I beach my canoe in the shallows in front of the hut and wonder what member of the community lays claim to this isolated paradise: the mayor? the minister? the leper?

As I drag my canoe out of the water, I long to stretch out on this warm, white sand, so accommodating that it would shape to my body like a lover. My eyes closed, the sound of the surf would soothe and calm my tired brain while the sky slowly darkens to indigo and then freckles with stars like the spots on a meadowlark's egg.

But first I need to present myself at the town meeting. I grope for my sandals on the floor of the canoe, then remember that I left them on the mainland when I waded out to launch the boat. The realization that I will have to face an entire community of sharp-tongued Kunas barefoot like a beggar hits me like a physical blow. A sob bursts from my mouth but despite a shivery, broken ripple in my chest, my eyes produce no tears: I'm too dehydrated. I touch my cheek and feel a grit of dried salt.

To distract myself, I focus my thoughts on something concrete: the sound of the wind. It whispers through palm fronds like hushed voices, a babble as incomprehensible to me as the language of the Kunas at the airport this morning. Maybe among themselves, trees and wind communicate. Maybe if I stay on the beach long enough, I will be able to decipher the words that the natural world is saying to me.

Or maybe the Kuna who lives in this hut will show up and cuss me up and down the island for trespassing. So far, I haven't seen a trace of life: the owner either scared or absent or dead. Or waiting in ambush, I think as the sand mounds between my toes on each step I take toward the lonely, beautiful hut beneath the whispering palms.

The house is small—barely large enough for a person my height to stretch out full length. The walls are made entirely of upright bamboo sticks, a stockade of poles each as big around as a finger. The roof is gray, shaggy thatch that looks glamorous and exotic but I can't imagine the tattered leaves offer much protection from the weather, particularly during the rainy season. The door, the most substantial element of the entire building, consists of a single plywood board hinged with rope or maybe some kind of vine and held closed with a metal latch and padlock.

"Hello."

My voice sounds hollow and is immediately swallowed by the wind and the palms. Why am I speaking English? Probably most of these Indians don't even know Spanish, let alone English. How am I supposed to report to the community when none of them will understand a word I say?

"*Hola.*"

No one's home, that much is certain. I peek through the house's single window. The inside of the hut is Spartan, bare, lifeless. A pair of center poles, thick like palm trunks, supports the roof beams, and a hammock hangs between them. Against the far wall is an ancient propane range, the miniature kind made for apartments and trailers in the U.S. The range is hooked to a five-gallon tank. The stove and the hammock are the sum of the contents of the house. No dishes, no clothing, no furniture.

I'm about to turn away when I notice a dime store frame hanging on the bamboo wall next to the window. Only by twisting my shoulders all the way through the window's opening am I able to make out the image inside the frame. It's a black and white photo, grainy and stained yellow along the lower edge. Two people: a man and a woman. The man appears to be a Kuna but he's dressed formally, Western, in a suit and tie. The woman is blonde and a good head taller than the man. Both are smiling, their arms entwined.

The optimism and hope captured in the photo tighten my chest with sadness. The picture has frozen an instant of love, a love that, judging by the abandoned and forlorn state of the hut, no longer exists. I can squint my eyes and the young woman in the photo becomes me, flowers in my hair and a white satin gown. If I'd married Jack out of high school, by now I'd have three kids, an ex-husband, and belly boobs.

"*Ichegua.*"

The abrupt, distinctly human voice surprises me and my head jerks up, slamming into the window frame with a resounding clunk. When I spin around, a naked Kuna boy stands directly behind me. He is not smiling.

"*Ashna sugga nine olomedi?*" he says. Or something like it. To me it's a random collection of syllables.

I speak Spanish, hoping the boy might have picked up a few words in school. "*No comprendo.*"

He repeats—I think—the sentence he said a moment ago.

"*No comprendo* Kuna."

He pronounces the words again, this time slower and more distinctly, perhaps reasoning that I will understand his meaning if he repeats himself enough times.

Since the child does not respond to my Spanish, I figure I might as well use English. "I don't understand."

The boy's face breaks into a smile and he lunges in my direction as if he's going to embrace me but instead he grabs my hand and drags me away from the house, toward the mangroves and the village on the other side.

He leads me along a well-worn path, running so fast that I have to jog to keep up with him. His feet step securely but several times I trip: I'm not accustomed to walking barefoot, much less running. Even when I falter, the boy drags me forward without breaking stride. As we hustle along the narrow streets, houses flash past in a haphazard jumble. Women in doorways stare, dogs bark, chickens scramble. The boy ignores them all, twisting me through backyards and alleys, around fences. I become hopelessly lost.

Abruptly, his lithe body freezes at the doorway of a cinderblock building. Above the entrance is a painted inscription that seems to be in Spanish. As I strain to make out the words through the glare of the setting sun, the kid darts behind me and shoves—hard—so that I stumble forward. I'm propelled through the open door, stub my toe on the ridge of a sill, and sprawl into a dim room. Behind me, I hear a thud as the door slams shut.

When I regain my equilibrium, I look down at my throbbing foot and realize that I'm standing on concrete, damp and cool, instead of dirt. I also notice that my pant legs are still rolled up to my knees from when I hauled the canoe out of the water. I want to straighten the hems but then I glance up and see that I am positioned in front of a table and behind that table, like a panel of the Inquisition, four Kuna men sit as if they had been expecting me to stumble into their courtroom.

I stiffen my back, trying to establish as much dignity as I can after my ungainly entrance. The men do not acknowledge my presence. One—he has a weightlifter's chest and a thin mustache that droops to frame the sides of his mouth—writes in a spiral-bound notebook with the stub of a pencil. Another, an older man with his gray hair cropped tight to his skull, has both his bare feet propped on the edge of the table, his chair tipped backwards on two legs. He stares off to the side as if he's bored or sleeping.

The two other men sit close together, their heads bent, apparently arguing. Both speak at the same time in the clipped, emphatic, angry tone that I noted in the airport this morning. Neither man seems to hear what the other says. I recognize one as the man from the wedding photo at the house on the point. He's dressed less formally today, with his shirt opened to reveal a scrawny chest.

The man he argues with steals sidelong glances at me between his sentences. He does not look at my face. I sense that he's being discreet about it but I've been measured up in enough bars to recognize the appraising slide of his eyes down the length of my body.

I try to ignore the man's scrutiny but it isn't easy because he is one of the most handsome men I've seen in my life. His features are thinner than those of the other men, more sculpted, his nose almost aquiline. His high cheekbones and forehead give his face dignity, and his black eyes are quick and intelligent. As he studies me, his thin lips twitch into a tiny, unconscious smile.

The handsome man is dressed with more care than the others, in a clean polo shirt that stretches tight across his broad, well-formed shoulders. When he glances away from my body to check his watch, a fancy one much nicer than any I've ever owned, I notice that his hands are manicured and clean. He clears his throat and declares something in a calm, slow voice that commands the attention of the other three men.

The man with the gray hair glances at me once, his eyes cloudy with cataracts.

The weightlifter with the mustache says "Good" in Spanish.

The man from the photo speaks. "Mother's name."

The English words are so unexpected that their meaning doesn't register in my mind. I blink stupidly a couple times but can't formulate a response.

When he realizes that I'm not going to say anything, the man from the photo sighs heavily and levels his gaze directly on my face. His eyes resemble those of a snake. He repeats in perfect English, "Mother's name."

The naked hostility in his expression reminds me of the street bums in the reservation towns back home. I find my voice. "Amelia." One word, as abrupt as his question. I give the name the Spanish pronunciation.

"Father." The man has dropped his eyes to the notebook where the weightlifter carefully spells out "Amelia."

"His name?"

Snake eyes again meet mine. The man nods.

"Roberto."

"His mother."

I have to think for a moment. "Margarita."

"Father."

My grandfather's name was Chauncey. "Enrique." The secretary dutifully notes this on the next line.

We catalog my entire family: grandparents, brothers, sisters, and their respective spouses. The roll takes a long time because I am from a big family. After we note all my nephews and nieces, the snake-eyed man meets my eyes for the next line of interrogation:

"Husband."

I should have anticipated the question but I haven't been thinking straight since I beached my canoe on the point. The man stares at me, his viperous eyes half closed.

"I've never been married." Since I'm not sure how much English the snake-eyed man understands, I repeat the sentence in Spanish: "*Estoy soltera.*"

The snake eyes continue to dissect me without a flicker of acknowledgement for my words. I hear a low murmur as the handsome man says something to the others in Kuna. The secretary writes in his notebook, then he looks up at me with undisguised interested.

"How old are you?" he asks in Spanish.

The question is so naked that my mind goes blank. I manage to stutter out the Spanish word for twenty—"*Vente*"—but for the life of me I can't add five years to it.

The handsome man nods, then addresses the group with a few words in his official voice, the voice that called the interrogation to order. The secretary adds my final answer to the notebook while the old guy slides his feet off the table and drops the front legs of his chair to the floor. The snake-eyed man says something—he seems angry again—but the others ignore him. When they all stand I hope that the move signals the end of the inquisition but the secretary with the mustache touches my arm lightly and in Spanish says, "Follow me."

The welcoming committee marches me through another maze of paths and houses to a huge building, bamboo and thatch like the hut on the point but ten times as big. By this time the night is completely black. We duck inside the building. A pair of Coleman lanterns hangs from the center support beams, smoking and stinking and hissing. In the dim light, I see that the building is full of benches and the benches are packed with people. The whites of their eyes follow me through the gloom as I'm shepherded across the hall in a hurried procession.

In the middle of the building, two incredibly old men are stretched out in hammocks. At first I assume that the men are dead but then I notice a glowing ember in a pipe that one clutches between his teeth. The men in the hammocks are dressed like shabby businessmen: polyester pants and button-down shirts, drab ties and wool felt hats. The only incongruity is the lack of shoes: both are barefoot, the soles of their feet as white as mine.

My retinue comes to a halt in an open area beside the old guys' hammocks. The secretary points to a low stool, the seat barely elevated above the dirt floor. By this time, I'm so tired that all I want to do is get off my feet so I awkwardly lower myself down to the stool. My legs with their rolled-up pant cuffs extend almost into the first row of benches.

The secretary's mustache twitches as he addresses the crowd. I hear the names that I gave him during the inquisition embedded in a matrix of Kuna words. The three other members of the welcoming committee have dissolved into the mass of faces and smoky dusk of the cavernous room.

After the secretary completes his report, one of the old guys in the hammocks, the one with the pipe in his mouth, sits upright. The other speaks in a monotone from his prone position as if he addresses the thatched ceiling. His words, an incomprehensible, timeless drone, take me back to the Latin Mass of my childhood. I see Father Dopak, his vestments green as winter wheat, raise his arms above his head for the consecration of the host. Light-headed from the stale air, I am more concerned about fainting than the meaning of the muttered words.

In the Kuna meeting hall, the man in the hammock falls silent. I look up. Every eye in the room stares at me, every breath has been drawn in an expectant hush. The entire community waits for me to respond to what has been said. Somewhere in the mass of people, snake eyes glare with anger. The handsome man measures my body, a slight smile on his face. Beneath battered felt hats, the half-dead eyes of the two hammock men are heavy on my face. I twist my head over my shoulder to find the secretary but when I try to meet his eyes, he stares blankly into the flame of one of the Coleman lanterns.

Lost and abandoned, I shake my head, shrug my shoulders, and stretch my arms to the side with my palms lifted in a gesture of vacuous helplessness. I don't know what else to do. Behind me, someone hawks a gob of phlegm from his throat and spits.

After what seems like a silent eternity, the secretary clears his throat and addresses the crowd: a short speech, only a handful of sentences. Does he apologize for me, explain, or deride my stupidity? I have no way to know. But the old guys in the hammocks nod, and I have to kneel to collect my legs before I can stand. Then I'm stumbling between rows of benches as I follow the broad back of the secretary. I feel a tiny, tentative hand brush against my thigh, then another. I don't dare focus on anything but the white shirt in front of me: I can't bear to see their laughter.

In the farthest corner of the room, closest to the door, the secretary points to an empty bench and in Spanish orders me to sit. The night breeze is cool. I breathe deeply, close my eyes, and clench my fists against the spastic trembling I feel in the pit of my stomach.

After another hour of talking, the meeting ends without warning: abruptly everyone stands and begins filing out through the open door by my side. On his way to the exit, the snake-eyed man detours to my bench.

"You'll stay here tonight." He speaks better English than half the Americans at the research station.

After my long day, I'm dog tired and testy. "Excuse me?"

"Either here or at the cabin on the point."

"I don't remember anyone telling me that I have to spend the night on the island. Only that I have to go to the meeting."

"You see in the dark?"

"What?"

"There's no moon tonight."

"I have a flashlight."

The Coleman lanterns still hiss even though the building is practically deserted. In the half-light, the man rolls his eyes. "You know the ocean? You know the jungle? You've been here for what—about twelve hours—and you think that you can find your way to the mainland in the middle of the night?"

He's right, of course. The thought of navigating that little canoe across the ocean with nothing but the weak beam of my flashlight makes my stomach queasy.

"Is there a lock on the door here?"

He snorts. "To protect you? Or us?"

I'm too tired to argue. "Please." I hear my voice as a breathless whisper. "I just need to sleep somewhere. I've been up since before dawn. I'm so tired that I can't think straight. I didn't realize how dark it would be tonight. I must seem awful stupid to you."

"No stupider than the others. You want to stay here or at the point?"

"I don't know."

The man sighs. "You'll be in town here, with lots of people around. They wake up early and then they'll be in and out, milling around. At the point you'll pretty much have it to yourself."

"But?"

"But nothing. Some people don't like being alone is all. They get scared."

"Would it be a problem if I stayed at the point?"

The snake-eyed man shrugs. "You can sleep on the dock for all I care."

"But the house on the point is yours, isn't it?"

His eyes narrow. "I don't live there. I have a place in town."

All I want to do is put an end to this endless day. "If it's okay with you, I'd rather stay at the point. Could you show me the best way to get there?"

His lips twitch. "Can't even find your way across the island?"

"I already admitted to being stupid. What do you want me to do, wear a sign around my neck?"

As I speak, the Coleman lanterns abruptly go dim so I can't read the snake-eyed man's reaction. Over his shoulder, the man commands, "Follow me."

I'm lost as soon as we leave the meeting hall. The streets are narrow and cluttered and twist wildly in the darkness. I shine the flashlight at my feet to keep from tripping. The stars are out: a million stars, more stars than I've seen in my life.

I recognize the mangroves, the opening of sand and palms surrounded on three sides by ocean. At the doorway of the house, the man demands, "Give me your torch." He tucks the flashlight against his shoulder and holds the beam steady with his chin as he unlocks the padlock on the door with a tiny key. "There's a hammock inside, but no lights. I guess you won't need lights with your torch. You want the door locked?"

"To keep me in or other people out?"

He has to twist to look up at me—he's shorter than I am. The flashlight beam hits me straight in the eyes. "You want the door locked or not?"

"If you lock it, you'll have to come here in the morning to let me out."

"That's right."

"I'll be okay. I don't need it locked."

"And what about the rest of us?"

I can't tell if he's joking or serious. At least he's lowered the flashlight so that the beam doesn't hit directly in my face.

I find my voice. "Thanks for your help. I'll try not to mess anything up. I'll be out of here as soon as it's light in the morning."

For a moment, the snake-eyed man hesitates as if he intends to say something, but then he hands me the flashlight with an abrupt "Good night" and is gone before I can respond.

I close the plywood door behind me and, for the first time since I left the compound this morning, I am able to exhale. The inside of my mouth tastes like salt. I'm too thirsty to swallow.

The hammock is coarse and scratchy but I'm so tired that my muscles become jelly the instant they contact the rough cotton. I close my eyes. Images from the day flash like a slide show in the darkness: the mottled feathers of the dead nighthawk, the plane flying through white nothingness, Brian's chancre, the grainy wedding photo, the handsome man's subtle smile. Suddenly I realize that, out of the long list of relatives that the Kunas at the meeting used to identify me, my own name was never once mentioned.

III

The next morning, I'm paddling the little canoe toward the mainland when the air taxi banks gracefully overhead, skimming the tops of palms and mangroves as it swoops toward the landing strip. My breathing becomes shallow and expectant when the buzzing of the engine stills.

In my mind, I see the little pilot—his hair embellished with an extra dollop of Vaseline and the creases in his black slacks pressed to razor sharpness for the occasion—hop out from the cockpit and glance around the airstrip. The pilot's face clouds when he realizes there's no one on the tarmac but Brian. An argument ensues because the little man refuses to fly the plane without *la rubia valiente*—the brave blonde—in the copilot's seat beside him. Brian shakes his head, the sore on his lip spewing pus, but the pilot refuses to budge. Single-handed, Brian loads his six duffle bags into the cabin of the plane, then perches atop his luggage like Cleopatra on her barge. The pilot prowls the edge of the runway where I stood the last time he saw me, snapping heads from fruiting pampas grasses and gnawing at his lip. Through the window, Brian makes a show of tapping his index finger on the face of his watch. In a defiant gesture, the little man turns his back on the airplane and stalks into the bush.

The focus of my fantasy now shifts to a faint trail through the jungle where the pilot struggles with mangrove branches that impede his progress. A few whacks of his machete—twank! twank!—and the tangle of vegetation parts to reveal an open beach. The little man gazes across the water and spies me floating in my canoe on an ocean the color of my eyes. His face lights and the gold star in his front tooth shines like a beacon. I'm still twenty yards from shore but I leap into the water and dogpaddle toward him. The pilot wades out to meet me and we collapse in a puddle of Vaseline and sea water like Deborah Kerr and a diminutive Burt Lancaster, our limbs entwined, seaweed and dead minnows and sand gritting between our throbbing bodies.

I'm brought back to reality by the cough of an engine as it's forced into gear. A moment later, the plane spits out between trees and zings over the ocean. Gaining altitude, the wings dip as the pilot banks to the left, curling west toward the horizon. Too soon, the plane disappears and I am left alone, riding a hollowed-out log on the surface of a sea so deep that I could never touch bottom, not if I filled my lungs with oxygen, not if my heart burst from the pressure of tons of water against my soul. I am left alone on an ocean as blue as dreams with water as salty as tears.

When I arrive at camp, everything I own is soggy from a predawn drizzle. For breakfast, I open a can of beans and eat them cold. I locate my ensolite pad, my sleeping bag, and the pillow that I stole yesterday morning from the compound. My makeshift bed takes up half the floor of the tent. I zip the canvas window and door closed. The dim, stale air smells of mildew. I try to swallow the shivery tightness in my chest but, like the beans, it doesn't want to stay down.

I strip off my clothes, everything, even the watch that froze at 3:42 this morning, the stem locked so tight that it can't be wound. I stretch out on my stomach atop the clammy flannel of the sleeping bag. The shivery tightness in my chest becomes liquid, flows into my belly to mingle with the baked beans and the gallon of water I drank at the spring hole by the river, then bleeds into my muscles, my glands, my ducts, to finally escape in a choking stream so full of salt that it traces crooked paths of grit across the curve of my cheeks.

The observation blind is roughly the size and shape of an outhouse. Inside is a stool, a pair of binoculars worth more than the sum of everything I own in the world, and the odor of stale sweat. Through the viney slit of a window, I locate the tree—Brian calls it a Maria tree but it looks the same as all of the other trees in the jungle—that hosts the eagle nest. An elaborate structure of branches and dried vegetation mortared together with an unidentifiable substance (mud? decayed feathers? fecal matter?), the nest is not as massive as those constructed by eagles in the U.S., but it looks more substantial than most of the houses I saw on the island last night. Viewed from below, the nest appears abandoned and lifeless.

The legend of the harpy eagle project speaks of two nestings here. The first, observed by the illustrious Dr. Flemming, the founder of the project who has since moved on to the position of chair at some prestigious university in California, produced two chicks. Neither fledged, one apparently pecked to death by its stronger sibling, the other blown from the tree during a ferocious summer storm. The second nesting was reported by Brian only a year ago: two eggs, two chicks, and two weeks later both were dead. My erstwhile boss, David, described in vivid detail how, with total disregard for his personal safety, Brian braved fer-de-lance snakes, arborescent scorpions, and the wrath of the parent eagles by climbing the Maria tree to the crotch of branches that supports the nest. He found the two chicks, their meager white down damp, their pink skin withered and lifeless. Speculation was rampant both at the compound and at home in the States, but the cause of the chicks' death was never determined.

I have brought water with me to the blind, and a hard-covered copy of Ridgely's *Birds of Panama*. I arrange the stool so that I can lean into one of the upright posts that support the wall. A monkey ladder vine, contorted and woody and as thick as my wrist, trails along the floor. I use the vine as a footstool and prop my elbows on my knees. Training the binoculars on the harpy eagle nest in the crotch of the Maria tree, I brace myself for my day's work.

IV

I hurry along the farmers' path that angles away from the river through open plantations of banana bushes and coconut palms, my head low, my eyes focused only on my boots. I stutter-step over a column of leaf cutter ants, climb a slope with footholds grooved and packed daily by scores of bare feet. My boots are too heavy for this terrain: their waffle soles rip divots in the smooth dirt of the trail. Like my boots, I am ungainly and awkward: instead of slipping subtly through the jungle, I stomp around like an ox leaving ugly tracks everywhere I go.

For the hundredth time since I came here, I curse Brian for not giving me more background information about the Kunas before he left. I curse myself for my laziness, for not filling my water jugs last night when I knew that all of the Kunas would be on the island and there would be no one on the mainland. I curse my morning thirst. Most of all, I curse those four Kuna men I just surprised at the river, those four stark, buck naked men who probably were more embarrassed than me when I stumbled on to their morning bath. But no, they couldn't have been more embarrassed, not without dying of shame.

If I were a man, everything would be easier. Men have muscles and bulk and an attitude that declares that they belong no matter where they are, like that big white guy who showed up at the town meeting a couple nights ago. He didn't come cowed and submissive and subdued by a welcoming committee of officials, to humbly beg the community for its forbearance and to later endure endless Saturday night meetings of roll calls and arguments and lectures in a language that's impossible to understand. I sit on my bench alone, an anonymous contagion. No one here has ever spoken my name: the Kunas address me solely by the Spanish *tú*. The word translates into

English as you—not the regular form but the familiar. *Tú* is the word a person would use when speaking to a good friend, or a child, or an intellectual or social inferior.

I feel their eyes boring through me, although when I muster enough courage to glance around the meeting hall no one appears to pay me any mind except for that little boy with the harelip. He's hanging by his knees from the backrest of the bench in front of me. The kid looks like a little monkey: he wears nothing but a red shirt that his upended position has bunched around his neck like a collar. With his legs twisting and clinging, all he needs is a long tail to complete his monkey image. When he realizes that I'm watching him, the boy's face contorts into a goofy scowl. He arches his back so that his rear end slaps against the flat wooden plank that forms the bench's backrest, then rebounds off of it like a pendulum.

I shudder to think of how the meeting will be disrupted when this little monkey knocks over the bench he's hanging from, and that seems inevitable once his body builds up enough momentum. "Thwack!" As the boy's backside bounces off the board, the rear legs of the bench rise from the floor. I frown at the kid but my attention only incites him to grunt loudly.

With the next "thwack!" the bench rocks forward, and on the rebound the backrest leans precariously over my legs. Fortunately, no one's occupying that particular bench except for the little boy, who sticks out his tongue and crosses his eyes at me.

"Thwack!" On this swing the bench almost overbalances to the front. I brace myself for the back swing just in time to catch the monkey boy as the momentum of the upended bench deposits his wriggling body directly in my lap.

"*Ho-o-o-o-la*!"

The shouted greeting drowns out the clatter from the upended bench. The sinewy child in my arms raises his head, alert and unharmed, then bolts away from me, racing with every kid in the building to be the first to mob the stranger who stands in the doorway of the meeting hall.

Even adults turn and crane their necks to watch the man as he enters. His lower body is so engulfed by children that he appears to be human only from above the waist. Kids squeal as the man sweeps an armload of them up into the air and sings out, "*Amigos*! *Amigos todos*!" The two old guys in the middle of the room swallow their lugubrious mutterings and sit up in their hammocks. One of the shouters—the guys who stand in back during meetings and periodically yell out one or two words at the top of their voices—don't ask me why—one of the shouters calls out, but he's ignored because no one can hear him above the chaos.

The big stranger maneuvers through the shoulder-high Kunas in the meeting hall, every step hindered by scores of tiny bodies that cling to each of his legs. Men shake the man's hand, slap his back, women smile and nod. The man blows through the building like a wind: suddenly everything in the building seems fresher and more alive.

When the newcomer reaches the center of the room, the Coleman lanterns throw enough light so that his features become more defined. Surrounded by armloads and leg loads of wriggling kid-bodies, he's enormous. He's a white man but his skin is weathered and much darker than mine. With his baggy khaki pants and striped shirt, all he lacks is an eye patch and a parrot to be the model of a swashbuckler. His rakish swagger flutters my heart although when he turns toward the old men in the hammocks, I notice the stranger has a protruding gut and thick lips that make his face look slightly doltish. But those lips wear a jaunty, piratical smile, and he's the first man I've seen in almost a month who I can actually look up to.

The big white guy shakes himself loose from the kids and approaches the old timers in the hammocks, striding confidently and with a purpose. When he's beside the stool where I ingloriously plunked my rump a month ago, the pirate bows to the hammocks with a flourish, making an elaborate show of removing a non-existent hat. He slides a hand into each of the front pockets of his baggy pants, then his face breaks into an exaggerated pantomime of discovery as he pulls out two of the gaudiest men's neckties I've ever seen. With another elaborate bow, he presents one tie to each of the old timers, shaking hands and exchanging mumbled pleasantries. I hear "*Nuedi*," one of the few words I've been able to pick up from the Kuna language. It means good, or all right, or thank you: an all-purpose term expressing positivism. In the meeting hall, everyone—old timers, kids, adults, the pirate, even the shouters—is smiling to the sound of *nuedi*.

Everyone, that is, except me. I'm still seated, huddled, trying to go unnoticed and hoping that by doing so I will not, as David so delicately put it, piss anyone off. But no matter how inconspicuous I try to act, I'm still pale and blond and much too tall for a woman on this island. And in the meeting hall the Kunas add to my prominence by shunning not only the bench where I sit but all of the rows in my immediate vicinity.

I stand out like a sore thumb and I'm sure that the newcomer notices this. I see him glance toward me out of the corner of his eye after he's finished the presentation of the neckties and is shaking hands with the secretary and the guy with cataracts who was part of my welcoming committee. The shouters—all four of them—call the meeting back to order and the kids scurry off to the dark recesses of the room. The pirate's thick lips curve into a smile as he repeats "*Nuedi*" and claps the secretary's wide shoulders. When the stranger backs into the aisle, I assume that he's heading for the door but instead he sidesteps a couple benches, angles into my row and plunks down next to me without meeting my eyes. Once he's seated, the big man focuses all his attention on the activity in the center of the hall, apparently mesmerized by the two old men reclining in their hammocks and whatever the secretary reads from his spiral-bound notebook.

I steal covert glances up at the pirate. On the arm facing me, his shirt sleeve has been cut off. The ragged edge of fabric frames a crude tattoo on his shoulder, the design blurred and difficult to read. I keep glancing over, a second or two at a time, trying to make out what the thick blue lines represent. Finally, my curiosity gets the best of me and I turn my head to focus completely on his shoulder. The instant I realize what the picture on the pirate's arm depicts—a pair of naked, spread female legs with a curly beaver between them—the man turns his head and I'm confronted by the most suggestive pair of hazel eyes I've seen in my life.

Later in the starlight under the palms at the point, the pirate—his name is Ruiz—uses four cigarette papers to roll an enormous joint. Pedro—Snake Eyes—sits with us in front of his cabin, the ocean lapping like warm ink across the milk-white sand.

Ruiz slides the completed doobie between his thick lips, then hands it to me and strikes a match across the rough surface of a nearby palm tree. "The last thing I expected to find when I came to Sugatupu today was a beautiful woman." He laughs and winks at Pedro. "I should say, a beautiful white woman!"

After I inhale, I pass the joint to Pedro's slim, graceful fingers. I'm thinking that I could convince myself that Ruiz is handsome if only he didn't have such short hair, almost a crew cut. His beard and mustache are the same length as his hair, making him look like a dog that's been shaved because it has mange.

Pedro says something to Ruiz in Spanish and they both laugh. Ruiz's Spanish is different than what I am accustomed to, with the "s" sounds lisped into an affected "th" and the cadence slurred and liquid. I wonder if he's from Spain.

"So this mysterious lady of the islands—this incongruous blond beauty—does she have a name?"

I'm puzzling over Ruiz's use of "incongruous" when Pedro speaks out, in Spanish. I don't think he realizes how much Spanish I understand. "Don't ever ask her that!" he hisses to the tall white man beside him. "Don't ever ask her to tell you her name!"

Sometimes at night when the moon glows through the mosquito netting window of my canvas tent, I wake and feel myself, like some kind of gas or vapor, like breath, floating through the sky along the path of the moonlight. Above the ocean, soft and white as a whisper, I slide all the way up to join the stars in heaven. Without a name, do I have a soul? Am I a real person?

The trail to my eagle observation blind bends right, through a corn field. I continue straight ahead. I want to lose myself in the jungle, to keep walking until I arrive at a place so forgotten and so dense that I will not have to justify my existence to anyone, white or Kuna. I want to spend a day where I will be insignificant and unobserved, to find a place where I can own a name and my past and a future that doesn't involve incomprehensible words and deliberate, crowded silences.

In the hills, the river becomes rocky and shallow. I lie on the bank, on my belly, and suck water like a deer. Sunlight through the trees behind me paints the pool blue but my face is in shadow: the only reflection of me is an oblong outline. I draw a deep breath and drop my head forward until my entire face is underwater. I open my eyes but all I see is a milky gray light too undefined for detail.

For as long as I can stand it, I keep my head underwater. When I jerk up, sputtering and gasping and dripping, the first thing that I see is a frog frozen on a rock inches from my eyes. At first, I see two frogs, one beside the other, each a perfect duplicate. Even doubled, I realize that the animal is somehow extraordinary, but when I close my left eye the reality of the creature becomes crystal clear, like glass.

The frog's skin is completely transparent, a membrane that holds the animal together but allows light and who knows what else to penetrate to the delicate, visible organs within. I see the muscle of the heart clench like a tiny fist, then release. I see the lungs pump. I see the skeleton and the gut and the larvae that the animal ate for breakfast. The moist skin conceals nothing. I hold my breath, then purse my lips and blow a stream of air, very softly, toward the creature. I want to see muscles. I need proof that this delicate thing is actually alive.

No movement. I want to touch the frog but am afraid. How could I help but hurt it? That opaque green skin: there's no way it would protect the wan creature from something as huge and clumsy as my fingertip. The frog is so fragile I can't imagine it surviving more than an instant—one of Reilly's beetles could decapitate it with a wing. Life suddenly seems very sad and I dunk my face into the river again to keep from crying. When I come up for air, the frog is gone.

Water dripping from my chin produces rings that grow and expand and intercept each other on the surface of the pool. My faceless reflection ripples and contorts. Along the pale blue surface, I see another reflection. Dark and defined and also faceless, it glides purposefully across the sky beneath me. I recognize the top-heavy silhouette of a flying toucan, twist my head over my shoulder in time to see the bird land in a cecropia tree on the other side of the river. It's a keel-billed: the bright colors of the massive beak flash in the sunlight as the bird cocks its head to study me.

We face each other: bird and human. I see the bird as a member of a distinct species: *Ramphastos sulfuracus brevicarinatus*. I have no idea of the toucan's sex, its age, its breeding status, its place among other toucans. It's not an individual to me, it's a toucan like any of the hundreds of other keel-billed toucans I've seen in Panama.

And when the bird looks at me, it sees a human: no more and no less. I am no more an individual to the bird than it is to me. My name and my history are unimportant. I am a thing.

Having established my identity to its satisfaction, the toucan bobs its head several times then begins its harsh, croaking call: "Krek. Krek. Krek. Krek. Krek." As if my ears have suddenly unclogged, I hear the chatter and twitter and chirps of a hundred other birds, some totally invisible among the vegetation, others cryptic flecks of brown twitching in the shadows. A low, musical whistle: I've heard it every day but have never identified the singer. The machinegun rattle of a kingfisher. The croak of a heron. Locusts buzzing, an endless drone, and somewhere in the distance, felt maybe more than heard, the steady, white-noise rasp of wind through leaves.

I raise my eyes to the canopy. The sky is mottled with clouds, the trees still. The rustle that I hear can't be from wind. The sound continues, constant and confined: the distant roar of a waterfall.

Abandoning the trail, I follow the river downstream. The rocks are moss-covered and slippery. At the research station, workers were cautioned against walking along streambeds, where fer-de-lance snakes sun themselves between open boulders. *Campesinos* call the fer-de-lance the twenty breath snake because they claim that once it bites, the victim will draw only twenty breaths before death.

The midday sun is strong. I am shaky from the heat, from my diet of beans, from my sadness and exhaustion and loneliness. When I try to hop to the side of a boulder, my boot skids on a patch of moss and into the stream. Water rushes into my boots and my calf muscles tighten against the current. Unbalanced, I splash a couple of tripping steps before I regain my equilibrium.

Breathing slowly to calm myself, I slosh to the bank and plunk down on a rock. The knots in my shoelaces have tightened from the soaking but I'm able to loosen them enough to slip off my boots. I wad up my wool socks and push them inside the boots, then abandon both on the shore to retrieve on my return—if I return. The river shimmers with diffuse light.

Only a few minutes of downstream scrambling brings me to the place where the river drops into a canyon. I stand on a lip of jagged rock and look down. Water streams vertical, unbroken, to a quiet plunge pool at the bottom of the falls. Rock walls drip with vegetation, lush from the spray. The river canyon is so narrow that the plunge pool is in shadow even at midday. Above the falls, almost on a level with my face but highlighted by a bright shaft of sunlight, the oversized wings of a morpho butterfly flash their brilliant blue like a promise.

The canyon below seems virginal: a hidden retreat for dreams. Down there, I could forget the heat. I could forget the

Kunas and the eagles and maybe even myself. The only thing I need to enter that new world is the courage to jump from this cliff. A simple movement: one foot suspended in the air in front of me, a shift of weight to force the other foot to follow, and I will become airborne. Heights have always both frightened and fascinated me: I am drawn to the ledge but afraid to jump. To jump, you must abandon yourself, forsake your future. For a moment, for a few seconds, you will fly, you will become sky and wind and free.

And then it will be over. If you are lucky, the pool at the base of the cliff will be deep enough to cushion your fall and will harbor no hidden boulders. You will land with a lung-emptying whoosh! and when you sputter to the surface you will be laughing and crying at the same time. You'll be surrounded by cool, silky water, water that will wash away all of the loneliness and uncertainty of the outside world. The water will embrace you, will refresh you, will enter your soul like a sleeping lion and you will know that you will always have this place to return to, like a womb.

You will strip at the top of the cliff, stand naked on the jagged rock above the falls. Your toes will curl like a frog's hand as they attempt to create suction. You will be afraid. You will hold your fear in front of you: hold it out to the thin air above the canyon so that if it falls it will hit bottom before you do. Your fear will flutter weakly in your palm like a captured morpho butterfly: one side of the wings a vivid cerulean, the other dun-colored and marked with eye spots to distract predators.

When you turn over your hand to drop your fear, it does not fall but hangs in front of you like winter breath. Your fear becomes something that has no weight, no substance, no reality. Like memory or like a name. In a breath that fills my lungs with air as warm as my body, I step forward and fall.

My heart chokes my throat. Water closes over my head. In the blackness, my lungs swell and strain. I do not touch bottom.

I'm suspended in a world of heaviness, of coldness, an atmosphere I cannot breathe.

I flail to the surface. My arms and legs don't move the way they should. Above me, boulders swell and weep like something alive. My fingers claw at the steep, slippery rock but find nothing to hold. I whimper, and wonder whether this is death.

When I'm finally able to suction my body out of the pool and up on to the rocks, I curl in a tight ball, my knees to my chest, my arms encircling my legs, my whole body drawn together to keep my heart from shattering into a million brittle shards.

"I am alive," I whisper, a prayer. "I am alive."

V

I sit in front of the little thatched hut on the point while Pedro, who has accompanied me here after the town meeting, sprawls on a palm log next to the water. Reflected starlight glows on the ocean like a million drowned fireflies. Pedro bogarts a joint. A candle flame flickers with the breeze. I open the spiral-bound notebook in my lap. The ruled pages are covered from one end to the other with neatly printed words. Like his speech, Pedro's written English is precise and composed.

"When I was eleven, my father was visited by the Baptist missionary from the island of Ailigandi, a Kuna man who had married an American woman. I was scared of this stranger who spoke and dressed different from anyone I had ever seen so I ran away and hid in the mangroves. When I came home that night, I lied to my father and told him that I had been on the mainland all day with my friends. My father said that the man wanted to meet me because he had heard that I was a very bright boy who was always asking questions. The missionary said that I would find the answers to my questions at his school on the other island.

"I told my father that I was happy living here with my family and friends, living as a Kuna. But my father said that the missionary was offering me a wonderful opportunity and that I should think of others besides myself, that the things I would learn at the mission school would help all the people on Sugatupu."

The weekly town meeting ran late tonight, with arguing Kuna voices more vehement and acrimonious than usual. Whatever they were discussing, the issue apparently was never resolved to everyone's satisfaction. I overheard heated comments even as people were trailing out into the now-black night, the thin crescent moon having set sometime during the squabbling. I was surprised when Pedro suggested that we buy a six-pack of beer at one of the little stores on the island. On our way to the point, we stopped at Pedro's house in town and picked up this notebook.

I sip from the red and white can of Balboa. The beer is piss warm and tastes metallic, but it's the first alcohol I've had in over a month. I sneak a glance at Pedro. The joint dangles from his lower lip. His eyes are closed.

"Before the arrival of the missionary, I was a happy little Indian boy. I played naked and unashamed with my friends. We swam, flew kites, explored the mainland and the river. We canoed in boats and with our games we began to learn the things that a Kuna boy must know to become a man. But it never was work. We were naked and illiterate but wise and rich in happiness."

I'm raising the Balboa can to my lips again when I hear voices. Pedro jerks into action, snuffing out the red tip of the joint and slipping the roach into his shirt pocket. From the mangroves that separate Pedro's cabin from the rest of the town, two men emerge. I immediately recognize the broad shoulders of the secretary, who I have learned answers to the improbable name of Orestes. Beside him is the spectacularly handsome man from the welcoming committee. His features are even more beautiful by starlight.

The men each nod to me, then they position themselves on either side of Pedro and instantly, without an introduction or exchange of pleasantries, begin haranguing. At least Orestes does. The handsome man—his hand flashing a gold ring as he strokes his jaw—seems more interested in the proportions of my body than in the conversation. I bend my head over the notebook where naked little Pedro has fallen into the clutches of the missionary.

"The missionaries said that the Indian children at the school were happy. They said that we smiled and laughed all the time. I tell you, we smiled because we were terrified. We were convinced that something horrible was going to happen to us. We couldn't imagine being able to survive at the school, a strange place, without our parents or anyone we knew. We smiled because we thought that if we did, the people who were in charge wouldn't hurt us. We smiled because we thought we had to. All of us—every last one of us—we were so scared that we couldn't sleep at night. We would lie awake in the darkness and cry for our families, our friends, our real lives."

The babble of voices grows louder and I glance up. The group around Pedro has swelled to six or seven men, some seated on the log and some standing. Their voices are soft but sharp with an intensity I can feel even without understanding the words they say.

"The American missionary woman—she was an angel. I knew what angels look like because there were pictures in the Bible and I could see the resemblance between this white woman and the angels from God. The missionary woman was the most beautiful thing that I had ever seen. I would sit for hours when I should have been studying and stare at her. As I got older, I realized that white women were something very different from the coarse brown Indian girls, naked like animals, that I knew in the village. White women were holy and beautiful and smiled upon by God. Those skinny brown girls get down on all fours like monkeys. A white woman would never stick out her ass like an Indian. White women were"—

"My little beauty, why are you all alone?"

The Spanish is silky and sensuous and I just about jump out of my skin when I feel the whispered breath on the side of my face. As I translate the words in my head, I feel heat from a body leaning into mine. I smell coconut oil mixed with a musky male scent. With a shudder of anticipation, I turn my head to look at the face beside me.

The man's black hair is short on the sides but flamboyantly curled on top. A stray lock tips down his forehead above a pair of slanted, cat-like eyes. He wears a shirt like the other Kuna men but instead of trousers, around his waist he's wrapped the patterned blue fabric of a woman's skirt.

"Are all of these men too busy arguing to talk to you?"

In the flickering candlelight he is smiling, more open, more friendly than anyone on the island has ever smiled at me. Ignoring the man's unconventional attire, I smile back.

"So beautiful," he murmurs. He strokes my hair, his cat eyes closed in apparent ecstasy.

"What's your name?" I ask him.

"Carlitos. Litos." When he pronounces them, the words become a breathy whisper.

"My name is—"

He puts his finger over my mouth. "Hush, my love."

I want to argue but the man's fingertip, though gentle, pins my lips against my teeth so that I can't speak. I dart my eyes toward the group of men around Pedro and see the gray haired man with cataracts staring at me.

"You must let me comb your hair," Litos murmurs, his lips so close that I imagine his tongue flicks the rim of my ear.

"I didn't bring my comb with me. I thought I'd be able to go home tonight but the meeting went so long—"

"Poor little one." Both his hands are entwined in my hair now. I realize how lonely I've become because all I want to do is sink my head on to this man's skinny chest. Litos must feel the yearning from me because he whispers, "Lonely little girl." Do other men read me this readily? When I glance over at the knot of Kunas, they are too involved with their argument to notice.

"What are they talking about? Is something important going on?"

Litos shushes me again, his finger caressing my mouth so lightly that it tickles. I shiver, then jerk my head away from his hand. He laughs.

"Come." He stands and offers me his hand as if I'm his high school sweetheart. We stroll along the sand beach and when the sound of men's voices has faded, Litos leads me into the bathwater-warm ocean. Ankle-deep, he turns to face me.

"The men don't want you to know what's happening. They're embarrassed."

"Did I do something wrong? Something stupid?"

Litos laughs and snakes his arm past my elbow to encircle my waist. "Oh, no, no, no, no, no, my little love. You are perfect. It has nothing to do with you. It's just the men. They're embarrassed and they don't want you to know."

"Why?"

"Because men—all men—they want you to think that they are perfect, that they provide everything their women want. Isn't this true where you are from?"

"Of course. Men in the U.S. are probably worse than Kunas."

"No one could be worse than a Kuna man!" Litos laughs but I think I hear a note of sadness behind his words.

"But what's got the men all worked up?"

Litos is tall for a Kuna and his face in the starlight is older than I had imagined. "You don't know?"

I shake my head. "I don't understand your language. The only one who ever talks to me is Pedro and he doesn't tell me much."

Litos pulls me to his chest, laughing as he caresses my hair. "No wonder you always look so bored during the meetings. And Pedro—oo-la-la! He wouldn't be telling you anything because Felipa is one of the worst ones."

"The worst ones?"

"Oh, my dear, I will tell you the whole story but you have to promise me that you will never, never, never tell any of the men what I have told you."

"I promise."

"You must promise on something that you love. Something important."

Ankle-deep in the ocean, bioluminescent seaweed curled around my feet and my head resting on the shoulder of a man dressed in a skirt, I can think of absolutely nothing that I love. "The eagles?"

Litos grunts derisively. "You do not love the eagles."

"My friendship with you. I promise on my friendship with you."

"You are as kind as you are beautiful." He brushes my cheek with the whisper of a kiss.

"Now, you have to tell me what's going on."

Litos studies me for almost a minute, then he shakes his head. "Just like a female," he murmurs sadly. "Just like a little bitch dog. You know what you want and you want it now, don't you, little bitch?"

For some reason, the way he trills the double r in the Spanish word for "small female dog"—*perrita*—makes me all shivery inside. I decide that I'd rather be called a little bitch than be called nothing at all. "Please? Please tell this *perrita* what's going on?"

"It's all about Mateo," he begins.

"Mateo?"

"The *sayla*." He hesitates, apparently trying to translate the word into Spanish. "The chief."

"One of the old guys in the hammocks?"

"Yes, yes, yes."

I want to ask him which of the old guys is Mateo but then realize that I can't tell the two of them apart anyway.

"The *saylas*—Mateo and Ologuippa—they don't have to work on the farms on the mainland. The community takes care of them so that they have time to learn chants and visit other *saylas* to discuss the Kunas' problems and decide on solutions."

"So they get paid by the community."

"Yes. But Mateo also knows how to cure some diseases, so people come to him when they're sick. They pay him too. So he's got quite a bit of money from all his years as a healer."

"Of course."

"And he's got time—he's got all kinds of time on the island alone with the women while the men are away fishing or working on their farms."

I'm beginning to get the picture.

"So during the day, Mateo goes to the women, he says to them, 'I will give you a dollar if you have sex with me.'"

"And they do?"

"They like having the money. With Mateo, it's over quickly and then they have money to buy things—fabric and jewelry and beads."

"And Mateo's wife?"

"Oh, she doesn't care. She's happy to get him off her back." At first, I think he is using the American slang term—"off her back"—but then I realize that he means it literally.

"And the husbands?"

"They didn't know. For a long time, they didn't know. Then Jacinta—Orestes's wife—she shows up with this beautiful gold necklace that she had made special for her by the jeweler on Ustup and it must have cost her a month of monkeys with Mateo."

"So Orestes found out?"

Litos's voice is softer than before. "Yes."

"She told him?"

He doesn't respond. I think of Orestes's broad shoulders and chest. "Is she okay? Is Orestes's wife okay?"

Litos pats my cheek. "Yes, *Perrita*. Jacinta will be fine. Orestes did not hurt her."

"But now"—I want to say "the shit's hit the fan" but I'm not sure he'd understand. "Everyone on the island knows."

"Exactly. And the men are asking their wives, 'Where did you get the money for this new skirt? What do you do during the day while I am gone?'"

"And the women?"

"They tell the men that if they don't like it, they should give them more money so that they don't have to work for Mateo."

"Good for them!"

When Litos smiles, starlight twinkles on his teeth. "My *Perrita* is a liberated woman."

The phrase strikes me as oddly contemporary. "I don't have a man, Litos. There's nothing for me to be liberated from."

Again, I hear sadness in his voice. "And me also. It is the same for me."

The flame of the candle still dances on the palm log when I return although the sandy point is now deserted. I see that the men have left me three unopened cans of Balboa, one additional candle, and the notebook with Pedro's autobiography. I flip the ring on a fresh can of beer, light the spare candle, and press it into the puddle of molten wax from the previous stub. A breeze lifts my hair and I tuck a stray lock behind my ear.

"After seven years at the school, the missionaries told me that I was an educated, Christian man. I could speak English and Spanish. I could read—especially the King James Bible. I had those verses drilled into my head so often that I could recite them in my sleep. Even now, some mornings I wake with words from the Bible on my lips:

> 'The children of the kingdom shall be cast into
> outer darkness:
> There shall be weeping and gnashing of teeth.'

"The missionaries told me to go home and teach my poor, uneducated, heathen brothers on Sugatupu the truth about God. But my home was not the same place that I had left seven years ago as a naked little boy. I saw my brothers slaving every day in farms on the mainland, or fishing and hunting like the animals they sought. All that the Kuna men ever did was work to get food. They didn't think, or pray, or love. They were dumb animals—monkeys—and when they loved they loved like monkeys. I knew that things were different in other places. I knew that there were women in the world who were beautiful and holy—angels who put the scrawny brown women on the island to shame. Even my language—the sound of my brothers' voices—was horrible to me, the harsh barking of dogs. I would lie in my hammock all day because I could see no reason to get up, to waste my time grubbing in the dirt to bring home a few tubers for dinner.

"And what I dreamed about all day in the hammock while the men who were once my friends worked like slaves, like animals, what I dreamed about was those white women, those beautiful white women who are soft and downy, who smell like flowers and look like angels. I dreamed of what they would look like naked. I dreamed of what it would be like to touch an angel."

After moping around Sugatupu for a year or so, Pedro managed to scrounge up enough money for the trip to Panama City and from there he never looked back. The story gets confused once young Pedro hit the big city. I stop reading for a moment, sipping Balboa and imaging what Panama City would look like to a horny twenty-year-old who had never known any reality but life on the islands. I think of Pedro's snake eyes, half-closed as the smoke from his joint floats in the nighttime breeze. I remember the way he hissed at Ruiz, depriving me of my name, and try to feel sorry for that boy alone in a strange city with nothing but his wits and his lust.

In Panama, Pedro must have hooked up with some displaced hippies. In the notebook, he's written a lot about drugs and even more about sex: I get the feeling that for a while he was pimping and using the money to buy drugs. He certainly wasn't spending it for survival: he never once mentions what or how he ate, and his only comment on habitation was that he and his friends slept "in the trees," which conjures up images of a group of dissolute kids draped across branches like iguanas. After a while, he realized his childhood dream by partnering up with an Englishwoman.

"Katherine! Katherine was my angel! When I remembered that ugly old witch at the mission school, I felt that I would vomit! How could I ever have thought that she was beautiful? But Katherine is gentle and when she speaks her voice is music. I wake to the music of her voice and her soft white hands play across my body. They caress me between my legs and I realize what life is for, why I am a man. There is no beauty in merely coupling, in a man and a woman coming together with slapping flesh. That is what monkeys do, what dogs do in the street. Katherine is art, she is a prayer, she is a soul that transcends life."

What happened next was expected: Katherine became pregnant. At this point, Pedro's narrative is crystal clear, spare.

"We talked about our options, about the best thing to do for the child. We decided to go to my home, to my parents and my family and my people."

To me, this seems like a strange decision but maybe Katherine had idealized notions about noble savages. And Pedro, what had he expected? "The people on Sugatupu were not happy with us. The women hissed at me in our language, 'Why do you love this tall, ugly woman? She is so pale she looks like a maggot. She is soft and lazy. Aren't Kuna women good enough for you?' Katherine didn't understand their words but I know she felt their hate. We went to the meeting hall and the *saylas* told me, 'Once we thought that you would be a leader for this community. But all you care about is your pleasure. This woman is not one of us. You never should have brought her here.'

"That evening my sister said to me, 'There are plans to attack you and your wife while you sleep. The *saylas* have said that they cannot allow Kuna blood to mix with that of the whites.' I knew this was true because during the early days of this century, the Kunas had risen up against Panama and killed all of the mixed-blood children on the islands. Katherine and I had to escape. We borrowed a canoe from my sister and set out for Ailigandi, the island where the Kuna missionary lived with his white wife. We left at night, crossing the open ocean: the woman I loved most in the world, the woman who held my child inside her, and me. The swells were high. Katherine was sick. We arrived at Ailigandi at dawn, barely alive."

The candle sputters, the wick almost gone. I skim the remaining pages in the wavering light.

The lovers didn't stay on Ailigandi but instead traveled to Katherine's parents' home in England where their daughter, Marvel, was born. Pedro writes of her with love but soon the couple was on the road again, in Afghanistan. No mention of Marvel, but feasting on sheep and sex in tents with sand like warm water shifting to accommodate their bodies, absorbing the sweat and fluids of their love. Hashish with friends, sex with friends, and then across the desert to Cairo, to Casablanca. In Spain, the women had hair in their armpits: the taste reminded Pedro of the ocean, of his days as a naked Indian boy. The Black Forest was cold and in Norway people stared at him.

"Then I returned to my home here on the island, alone. I realized that no matter where I went, no matter how I tried to escape it, I was still that naked Indian boy. I have lost my wife—my love!—and my child. I have lost the respect of my friends, the affection of my parents, my ability to belong to a community. But I came back because this is the only place I have found where I am sure of exactly who I am."

The stars above have circled. Their configuration is different now than it was when I left the meeting house, than when I opened the notebook and began reading Pedro's story, than when I waded in the water with Litos. I blow out the candle and grope my way to the cabin.

When I wake in the morning, my eyes feel as if someone had rubbed sand in them the entire time that I slept. I shift onto my side and promptly tumble out of the hammock. On my hands and knees, I crawl to the door.

My eyes scrunch tight against the outside glare. The sun is up full, white on the ocean and on the pale sand surrounding the hut. My head pounds. I bend my face down like a dog, crack open my eyelids and try to focus on the hands splayed in front of me. When I am able to sort my fingers from my thumbs, I slowly raise my squinting eyes to brave the new morning.

Silently gliding off the point is a flotilla of canoes—hundreds of dugouts—all aimed toward the mainland. The entire male population of the island must pass this hut on its way to work in the morning. I see men's heads turn to study my abject form in the doorway, and I breathe a silent prayer of thanks that apparently I was too drunk last night to take off my clothes before passing out in the hammock.

Using the doorframe as a prop, I manage to ratchet my body upright. The motion brings a wave of nausea and for a few seconds I'm afraid that I'm going to vomit, but by swallowing a couple times and sealing my eyes against the glare of the low sun, I keep my stomach in place. I've never been this hung-over in my life.

I need to get to my canoe. I need to paddle to the mainland. I need to stumble to the spring hole and get enough water inside of me to counteract the dehydrating effect of the Balboa. A step-by-step process: I can handle each of the steps as long as I think of them in isolation. The canoe is close, only about twenty feet away on that little spit of sand at the end of the point. I take off my sandals first. I don't want to trip on my way out there. I don't want to have to crawl like a crab across the sand in plain, naked view of every Kuna man that I know.

The dugout rides low in the water and is tipsy at best but today it doesn't want to balance at all. On the open ocean, I try to aim straight into the choppy waves but the wind keeps blowing me every which way, always broadside to the motion of the sea. The farther from the island I go, the stronger the wind blows and the choppier the waves become.

I'm not a happy swimmer. When I was growing up—a million miles from the ocean—I made it a rule never to venture into water so deep that I couldn't touch bottom. On these canoe trips back and forth from the island I try not to think of how far beneath me the ocean floor lies, of the unknown creatures that lurk between me and a resting place on the bottom. Today, my head hurts so much that I feel as if it's bouncing off the jagged coral a hundred feet below me. The crash of the waves is so powerful that I freeze every time a new one breaks across the reef that shelters the island and this little bay.

No one else on the water seems to have any trouble: the men slide past me in their calm boats as if today is no different than any other day in their lives. Everyone ignores me, their eyes on the mainland. Their paddles slice silently through waves, propelling them forward without effort or mishap.

I mimic them, try to straighten my lopsided canoe with a flick of my paddle, but the wooden shaft is wet and slips out of my hands. A wave hits me from behind, broadside. Half the canoe fills with water. I lean over to recover the paddle. The motion overbalances the low boat and one gunwale dips below the surface. The hollow log of the dugout rolls over and I am spat into the roiling sea.

My nightmares here have often explored the act of drowning. The imagined sequence occurs in freeze-frame motion, a slow and studied slide into unforgiving water. Today is not like my dreams: it's a sputtery chaos of fear and confusion. I fight to keep above water but waves wash over me, driving the heavy, rudderless boat into my head. Salt water stings my eyes and my nose. I inhale it, I swallow it. I can't breathe. I sink.

My lungs explode from the lack of air. I try to fight my way upward but the water around me dissolves like liquid in my hands. For an instant, my head bobs above the surface in the trough of a wave—I manage to swallow a breath of air along with a gallon of ocean before another wave slams into me like a two-by-four. I know that I will never be able to swim to the mainland.

Even below the surface, waves attack me. I feel one wrap around my torso, tangling and binding me so that I can't move. The wave pushes against my chest so hard that my breasts flatten into my ribs. I feel my body rise, riding the motion of the ocean upward toward sweet, sweet air.

When my head pops out of the water, I realize that what propelled me to the surface is an arm, a strong arm, and that the arm is attached to a body that holds me firmly so that I and my savior move as one through the waves. I have no muscles, no strength, no will. The man who rescues me swims on his side to keep my head above water: smooth, confident strokes with one arm while the other holds me so tight against him that I feel his chest expand and then contract with his breaths. I face into that chest, the length of my body pressed against the front of his. The water and the closeness melt the clothing between us: I feel every contour of his chest, the tightness of his abdominal muscles, the rhythmic pumping of his legs. I feel something else down there too, something hard, and realize that this man's motivation for embracing me isn't entirely altruistic.

When he is close enough to the beach to get his legs beneath him, the man carries me in his arms. I keep my face buried in the folds of his wet shirt. Male voices call above the whoosh of the surf: voices speaking that damn Kuna language that I will never understand. The man who carries me is silent. He doesn't seem to feel my weight as he strides out of the water and up the uneven sand of the beach.

I inhale deeply and my shoulders shudder. I realize that I am shaking. I keep my eyes closed and try not to cry.

We enter the shade of the jungle. I am too ashamed to open my eyes but I feel the coolness surround me. I put my arm around the man's neck and nuzzle his shoulder.

Before he lays me down, he kneels. Dropping to his knees with my weight in his arms is the man's first awkward movement since he rescued me. He arranges with care, my back against the rough trunk of a tree.

"*Nuedi,*" I whisper with as much breath and voice as I can find in my lungs. I open my eyes and for the first time confront the man who saved me from drowning. The exquisitely handsome face does not smile but rises and turns before I can repeat my word of thanks.

VI

Mornings, after my breakfast of a banana and half a can of beans, I hike to the blind. In my knapsack I carry a change of clothing, two quarts of water, another banana, my notebook, and Ridgely's *Birds of Panama*. I wear field glasses around my neck although I no longer attempt to identify the birds that I see along the trail. In the early coolness, the men have not arrived from the island for their day's work and the world seems untouched and new.

I stop to study a pile of fresh scat in the weeds alongside the trail. The mound is soft, amorphous: something that would come out of a sick animal or a healthy cow. With a stick, I poke at the dark brown pile. While the main substrate is uniform and viscous, intact flecks of light-colored material are scattered throughout—maybe seeds, but they also could be tiny bone chips. I think I see embedded hair too, although those thin strands might be cellulose from stringy leaves or grass. I conclude that this dropping could have been made by anything: a monkey, a coati, an ocelot, even an owl. After my careful scrutiny and dissection, I have no better idea of the scat's origin than I did when the pile first caught my eye.

Squatting in the dust of the trail, I sigh and toss the stick into the weeds. The length and breadth and depth of my ignorance is beyond measure. I am an ornithologist surrounded by literally hundreds of birds: fairy-like shadows that flit along the ground or between leaves in the canopy; raucous, stubby-winged flocks black against the sky; haunting melodies from unseen singers at dawn and dusk. To date, I have identified only a handful of species. My field notes are populated by LBJs—little brown jobbies—and question marks.

It's not just the birds here that confound me: I am lost, adrift, stumbling through a world I do not understand. I hear a rustle in the undergrowth and can't decide if it's a jaguar stalking with ominous restraint or an LBJ scratching for worms. I find succulent globes of fruit but don't dare touch them for fear of poison. I recall lists of tropical diseases—yellow fever, Chagas, dengue, malaria—but not the symptoms. I hide from human voices, words I cannot understand.

I am as stupid as a child but unlike a child, I seem incapable of learning. I do not change or grow. I'm too big already: a huge, lumpish dolt, blundering and ungraceful. How can the Kunas do anything but laugh at me? Laugh or feel pity, but pity is reserved for things you can identify, things you understand, things that you name.

Abandoning the farmland and plantations, the trail enters the jungle. I feel the cool of shade and smell the rich, earthy scent of rot. By midday, the humidity here will be so intense that the air becomes opaque, a fog. On my way to the river in late afternoon, I will physically muscle my body through the atmosphere like a swimmer pushing through water. But for now the morning is soft and welcoming.

I train my attention to my boots as I walk: my heavy leather boots that are beastly hot but protect my tender soles from the bugs and fungi and other pathogens of the tropics. But not the roots. I'm forever tripping here, hooking those oversized, reinforced toes under things seen and unseen. In the jungle, along the river, on the island; half the time I'm not upright: I'm sprawling, stumbling, and off-balance.

So I watch my feet as I plod to the blind in the morning, to the river in the afternoon, to my camp in the evening. I eat beans and bananas and shit out more than I put in. I record with meticulous care every LBJ that I see although my watch is now officially defunct so I have no idea of the time and only a vague notion of the date. I study the Maria tree for a glimpse of the eagles. I curse and dread the passage of each day because every sunset brings me closer to Saturday, to the island and the meeting and the hundreds of Kunas who stare at me and laugh at me and judge me. I curse the Kunas but at the same time I know that I need them, that the Saturday night meetings are the one thing in this jungle that reminds me that I am still a member of the human race.

In the blind today I am restless and unable to concentrate. I give up on the absent eagles at midday, follow the faint path through the jungle to the river and the falls. Naked in the cool water of the pool, I convince myself that I am beautiful and sane and content.

Shadows dominate the jungle by the time I clamber out of the canyon. At the head of the falls, my clothes are damp and stink of sweat but I don't want to spoil the clean ones in my pack by wearing them on the hike back to camp. I wish I had the guts to stay in the canyon overnight but I am hungry and intimidated by the darkness.

I hurry along the path, straining to see through the gloom that's a daytime constant in this heavy jungle but even deeper now that the sun is low. Above the sharpness of my breathing I hear sounds of movement in the undergrowth. A small brown bird chatters, hopping about in the feeding frenzy that precedes roosting. The flick of a leaf, a flash of color: do my eyes record the creature or merely the ghost of its motion?

I'm about to plant my foot for another step on the long trail home when that ghost becomes reality: a winged creature that materializes out of nowhere to leap into my face. I fall backwards, jerk in my breath with a hiss. The apparition hovers for a split second in front of me, then in a whirring trill it disappears into the jungle.

Frozen, my body clenched, when I resume breathing my chest shudders so violently that my inhale proceeds in step-like stages. I expel the breath in a whooshing gasp.

A grouse. The thing that just flushed in front of me had to have been a grouse. I've never heard of grouse in the tropics but the bird acted exactly like the grouse do at home: hanging tight under the snow until you almost step on them, then exploding in a shatter of snow crystals and brown feathers and the same trilled wing whir I heard a moment ago. It had to have been a grouse, a creature that relies on camouflage, on surprise, on the startle of motion to protect itself. That's all it was doing: protecting itself. Like every animal in this world, it desired only to live.

Another deep breath and my legs are able to move again, more cautious this time. I cannot outrun the night. Even now, the chitter of birds is slowing. Soon the jungle will become a new domain, the haunt of moths and bats and owls and the thousand unnamed creatures that exploit the shadows of night. This new world will be cryptic, foreign, threatening. I do not carry a flashlight.

My breaths are light and shallow as if by not taking in much air I can keep my body fluid. I'm still shaking over my scare with the grouse or whatever it was that confronted me. I can't see into the forest past the first stanchion of trunks.

The path ahead detours around a huge, fluted buttress. On the other side of the tree, I'm startled—jump back, again frozen—by the figure of a man defining the trail. Like a living spirit, the man's white shirt glows in the gloom. I have never seen a Kuna on the mainland this late in the day. I never knew that any of them ventured this deep into the jungle.

The man hasn't noticed me, I think: as he stares at the undergrowth on the side of the trail he stands as still as I do. In the semi-darkness, the man has the features of virtually every Kuna man I've ever seen. I may have passed him this morning on my way to the blind or shared a bench with him during the town meeting last Saturday but today he is anonymous: a Kuna man. He's dressed with typical Kuna style: a ratty white t-shirt and formless pants that once may have been full length but have been hacked short until the fabric barely covers his knees.

The man seems so absorbed in what he watches that I feel I intrude on something private. I wonder if I am trespassing or doing something that will piss the Kunas off. I'm thinking that maybe I should try to melt into the folds of this tree's buttress. I could hide there until the man leaves, avoid an unpleasant scene by sneaking off before he discovers my presence. But just when I decide to back away, the man turns his head toward me as if he knew all along that I was here. He meets my eyes, covers his mouth with his hand, and jerks his head to the side. Is he beckoning me? I read the hand over the mouth as a signal for silence. On my toes, I sidle up to him.

At the side of the trail in a puddle of dead leaves and torn fern fronds, two spotted kittens wrestle. They are each about the size of a house cat but their paws and heads are enormous while their mouths bristle with the needle-tipped milk teeth of babies. The kittens are in constant, frantic motion: one moment they roll through the leaves in a tight ball, all mottled fur and spiked whiskers, an instant later one breaks off to attack a stray fern. A tail traces S curves as the kitten explores a scent in the litter until a pouncing leap by the other stills the tail and sends both into a frenzy of growls and tumbles and take-downs. One pulls its head away from its sibling with a mouthful of fur, one gnaws the other's paw as if it's trying to chew it off. Suddenly the kittens separate, bounding off in opposite directions, each distracted by a different shadow or scent or whimsy.

I glance sideways at the Kuna man and realize that he is watching me, his face as calm and observant as when he studied the kittens. I meet his eyes and he smiles, a kind smile, a smile that seems to indicate that he enjoys sharing this experience with me. I want to ask the man what kind of kittens these are: ocelots, pumas or—the thought brings a shiver—jaguars. I want to ask him how he found them here, how he knew that I was here, and if he knows about the waterfall. I want to ask him what he is doing in the jungle at this hour of the day. But the man hasn't said a word to me and although he's taken his hand away from his mouth, I feel that he desires silence. After his brief smile, he turned his attention back to the kittens.

We watch for a few more minutes, then he touches my arm, so lightly that it does not startle, turns his back to me, and heads down the trail toward the farmland. I follow. By now, the darkness makes me grateful for a companion. The man walks with a comfortable, even gait, so smooth that his white shirt seems to glide among the trees. He never glances back at me.

This is the longest silence I've experienced with a Kuna person. Many of the Kunas—almost all of the women, I think, and about half the men—do not speak Spanish. The lack of a common language does nothing to prevent them from addressing me, especially when I've done something that they decide is wrong or stupid. Considering how often I'm cussed out by Kunas, I guess it's fortunate that I don't understand their language.

Musing over the man's silence and the odd circumstance of his presence in the jungle at night, I don't register that he has paused in the trail until I slam right into his back. His arm reaches out and before I know what's happening, he steadies me against his body. By the way his mouth is open, I think he may be silently laughing. His eyes sparkle in the gloom.

I begin to speak but immediately he slaps his hand—the one that he was using to steady me—over his mouth, then he points to the ground at his feet. At first I see nothing. Slowly out of the shadows and vegetation, the outline of a bird emerges. Hunkered low to the ground, the bird is roughly the size and shape of a guinea hen but its cryptic coloration blends so perfectly with the surroundings that I have to blink my eyes to keep the outline of the bird from disappearing into the gloom.

The man beside me whistles: two clear, deep notes, musical and mellow. I have heard the song often at daybreak and dusk, a song as beautiful as any I have known.

The crouching bird raises its head, alert, and sharply surveys the vicinity.

The man whistles again, the same two notes, rich and deep.

The bird barely opens its beak as it calls, the notes more pure, more clear than the man's whistles, so lovely that my arms turn to gooseflesh.

Another whistle from the man, a heartbreakingly sweet response, then the bird rises and I realize why it was crouched so low and tight to the clump of dead leaves on the ground. Beneath the mottled breast are four oblong eggs. In the gloom, the shells glow like the blue of a morpho butterfly but buffed and polished to a richness I have never seen on a natural surface. I only glimpse the eggs for an instant while the bird executes a full turn; then it settles back to brooding and the nest.

The man whistles again but the bird does not respond. The Kuna's black eyes meet mine, then his fingertips brush my arm. Before he can turn, I tug at the sleeve of his shirt. When I have his attention, I raise my hand in front of my face, fluttering it like a wing, and trill the whirring sound I heard when the bird flushed at my feet along the jungle path. The man doesn't nod but with his smile he both acknowledges and answers my question.

Out of the jungle in the open farmland, daylight has lingered longer and the man quickens his pace. I watch the trail ahead of me, my eyes downcast. The man's bare feet touch the earth like hands, conforming to the surface so that he doesn't so much walk on the trail as caress it. He is totally silent as he moves: his footsteps, his breath, his clothes, his flesh.

When he stops abruptly again in the middle of the trail, I'm following so close that in order to avoid ploughing into him, I veer off to the side. Instantly, he grabs me across the shoulders and hurls my body behind him. The movement is so quick, so unexpectedly violent, that I stumble and fall backwards.

I lie in the dust afraid to rise, wondering what sparked this abrupt change in the man. He's speaking his own language now, not harshly like the others when they scold me but softly, a whisper or a chant. The words don't seem to be addressed to me: all of his attention is focused on the trail ahead. I see nothing but shadows and dirt.

Still speaking, the man lowers himself to a crouch, his knees spread, his eyes staring at the dust at his feet. A frightening thought enters my mind and I wonder if the Kunas get rid of troublesome madmen by banishing them to the jungle. The rhythm of his words is sing-song, like a child's rhyme.

Suddenly, the man's fingers streak out and he springs to his feet with the writhing body of a snake clutched in his fist. He holds the coiling, muscular whip for only an instant, as long as it takes to turn and fling the slithery thing toward the jungle behind us.

I'm still prone on the ground, propped on my elbows, watching him with wide, frightened eyes. The man smiles down at me as if nothing out of the ordinary has occurred, then offers his hand to help me rise.

Alone at camp, when I zip open the mosquito netting door of my tent, the first thing I see is a dead iguana lying at the foot of my sleeping bag. I want to cry out but I'm so conditioned to silence that I merely fall backwards with my hand over my mouth. The iguana's body, already losing its color so that it appears as gray as the fabric of my too-warm sleeping bag, is twisted and curled in death. The eyes are half-open, like Pedro's on the point as he watches smoke thread up from the joint balanced between his slim brown fingers.

I pull myself to my knees in front of the dead iguana. Someone took the time to kill this creature, to bring it all the way up here, to open my tent—my most personal space!—and plant this grinning death's hand at my symbolic feet. Why? Do the Kunas hate me that much? I remember Pedro's story about his wife, about how the community had planned to attack the couple while they slept. I resolve never to spend another night on the island with the Kunas, but then I remember my paralyzing fear after I dunked the canoe and the ocean closed over my head. At night, there would be no handsome man nearby, no dramatic, sexually-charged rescue.

I grit my teeth and lift the scaly, dead iguana by the end of its tail. The corpse is surprisingly heavy. The body hangs limp: it has not been dead long. Across the pale belly, I notice a slit, red with dried blood. When I lay the creature on the dirt in front of my tent, the slit gapes open. Someone has eviscerated this iguana, dressed it for use as meat. I check back inside the tent and find a half dozen green bananas—plantains—in the doorway. I had overlooked them in my initial shock over the iguana.

I have not built a fire for weeks, preferring to eat my beans cold rather than fuss with gathering wood. In the remaining daylight, I collect enough twigs to fuel a squaw fire. Even without salt, plantains are a passable substitute for potatoes and iguana meat tastes remarkably like chicken.

VII

I become aware of the silence in stages. At first, it is something barely sensed, something vague and amorphous, something I do not name. The world around me seems the same as it was a moment ago: the sky, the sunlight, the trees, the sweltering heat that rolls sweat down my backbone and behind my knees. I am naked, my hair pulled off my shoulders and folded on top of my head. I sit perfectly still but I sweat. I sweat in the stifling midday heat of the blind as if my skin bleeds, as if it weeps, as if the heat is a relentless lover probing every fold of my body with his tongue. But in my misery, above my misery, I feel the silence.

It's not a true silence: I hear wind rustling leaves high in the canopy and if I listen hard enough, I hear the heartbeat of the surf. The silence is not complete but it feels absolute. It feels as if the nerve connecting my ears to my brain has been severed, as if my head's plugged from a dive or a sinus-clogged sneeze. I open my mouth, flex my jaw side to side, with no effect. I feel the silence in my cavities and in my soul.

The birds have stopped singing. Here in the jungle, bird song has become white noise to me. Like the sound of the surf and the wind, it accompanies every waking moment of my day, every thought in my head. But every bird in the jungle seems to have been stilled. A moment ago, a hundred voices chirped and twittered and trilled and shrieked. Now: nothing.

A gray shadow: I know it is above me before I see it. The shadow, too, is silence, with wings as silent as death. How can something so huge be so utterly quiet? Even as it flies, it does not make a sound. At first, I assume it must be an owl. An eagle does not move in this manner: twisting between trees, massive wings never pumping or beating but stretched full in an effortless glide. The wraith of a shadow swoops through the jungle and comes to rest in the crotch of the Maria tree.

I train my field glasses to the gray outline beside the nest: upright, it's as tall as a Kuna. I anticipate the dish-flat face of an owl but instead view a beak bigger than my heart, precise and predatory. Eyes jagged as obsidian meet mine through binocular lenses. Eagle eyes read the world solely as motion and fear: the eyes of death.

I try to view the bird dispassionately, try to catalog diagnostic features for future reference, but then I realize that the gray shadow itself has a shadow. The shadow of the shadow glides to the Maria tree, the sturdy platform of twigs and vines cupped into the shape of a bowl. Talons thick as my jugular clench around a limb directly above the head of the first shadow. The branch tears with a crack like a pistol shot.

In the bald silence that follows, the shadow of the shadow swoops into the nest and plants the severed limb square in the center. Drafts from the flying wings catch the fresh leaves so that they flutter and dance. One quick over-flight, banking and circling in a tight spiral, then the second shadow vanishes as quickly as it appeared.

The original shadow watches morose, hunkered and still. The face is so massive that it fills the entire field of the binoculars. Above the humped shoulders, pale facial feathers articulate a predatory visage. When the gray shadow swoops to kill, the last thing that the rat or sloth or paca will see is a grimace: the gloss of the beak, the black streak across obsidian eyes, the feathered crest spiked above the head like the proud headdress of an Indian warrior.

The current catches my laundry and bobs it downstream on a raft of white froth. Crouched and rooted on the bank of the river, I'm too exhausted to chase after it. The flutter of leaves in the endless wind, the numbing cacophony of flowing water, the late afternoon heat: all of these combine to bring on a paralyzing lassitude. I cover my face with my hands and surrender.

"*Perrita*, what is wrong?"

The tentative whisper gropes its way past my damp palms. With an effort, I raise my head. Litos squats beside me, his eyes soft with concern.

"*Perrita*, what is the matter?"

"Nothing." When I inhale my breath jerks into a sob. "I'm just tired, I guess."

"My poor, poor little love. You must be sad out here all alone." He tightens his arms around me and whispers in my ear, "I know why you are sad, *Perrita*."

"You do?"

"You are not the only one who lives without love. Come now—you must shake away your sadness. There is someone here to see you."

"Here?"

"At your camp. We must go."

"I need—I was doing my laundry. It floated away."

"Is this it?" Litos holds up a dripping stack of shorts and t-shirts.

"Yes—thank you. How did you find it?"

"I found your clothes and your clothes told me where I would find you."

My panties are folded neatly on top of the pile. Embarrassed, I try to shuffle them into the middle but end up with a wadded mess. "Who would come out here to see me?"

"A very important visitor who needs to speak to you. You should not keep him waiting. You have your clothes now, and your beautiful panties with the flowers on them. We should go up to your camp to see your guest."

"Why would someone need to talk to me?"

"*Perrita*," Litos says sternly. "It is not polite to keep a visitor waiting."

On the path to camp, Litos calls to me over his shoulder. "You must hurry, *Perrita*. There is much to talk about and the sun is already behind the mountains."

"I'd be a lot more willing to hurry if I knew what this is all about."

"No time for that, my love. We must run!" He's halfway up the ridge. When he jogs, his body looks as if it's been broken and then hastily glued: everything hangs together but nothing seems to match.

I pause to catch my breath. Litos has disappeared above the ridge and I hear a faint murmur of male voices from the clearing. I can't imagine who Litos's important visitor could be. I try not to hope for the handsome man.

At the crest of the ridge, the trailhead is hidden by my tent so that I can peek unseen around the canvas to view the visitor's silhouette. A Kuna man—very short and very stocky—he sits on the log in front of my fire pit. Beside the man squats Litos, his head bent toward a brown felt hat that would only be worn by a shabby businessman or one of the old guys—Litos called them *saylas*—who apparently are the leaders of the Kuna community.

Behind the cover of my tent, I hesitate. Why would one of those old timers come all the way to the mainland to talk to me? Could this be the infamous Mateo? What should I do if he pulls a dollar bill out of his pocket? Flustered, I stash my dripping laundry in the weeds before I step into the clearing.

Litos rises, calling out, "*Perrita*—finally you are here!" He hurries over and leads me by the arm to the fire pit and the log.

The old man stands and offers me his hand. He is the shortest adult I have ever seen—the crown of his felt hat doesn't even reach my chin. Beneath his weathered skin, his features are strong and decisive. When I shake his hand, his grip is firm, his perfect teeth sparkle, and his eyes glow.

I've learned enough from the Kunas to offer basic hospitality—food and drink—but unfortunately all I have in camp are a few bananas and some water. The old guy—Mateo?—accepts graciously. I apologize for the meager fare. Litos translates.

Through Litos, the man asks if this is all the food I eat. Sheepishly, I explain about the canned beans.

The old man asks why I don't eat real food: rice, yucca, and fish.

I am stupid, I explain. I am too stupid to know how to prepare foods like those.

"Didn't your mother teach you how to cook?"

"She tried. Both of my sisters can cook but I never learned. I was always too busy watching birds or studying plants."

After Litos translates this, the old man smiles warmly at me. I am struck again by his vigor and apparent intelligence. The man says something in Kuna.

Litos translates. "He says that these are all good things to know."

"Maybe. But they don't help much when I'm hungry."

The old guy laughs easily when Litos tells him what I said.

"He says that you must learn how to cook. If you eat only canned food, you will become so skinny that the eagles will catch you and feed you to their babies." I laugh at this, probably more than the joke deserves but I am as nervous as little Pedro at the mission school.

"Tomorrow before the meeting, my wife will teach you to cook. Litos will be there also, to tell you what she says. You can come to our house in the afternoon and Irina will show you how to make good food, Kuna food. Irina has only sons—no daughters—and she has no one to nag at in the kitchen. If I am nearby, she scolds me all afternoon. You come to our house tomorrow and Irina will spend the afternoon bossing you around, then you will know how to cook and my wife will be happy for a change."

It's awkward talking through a third party. As Litos translates, I feel the old man's quick eyes study my face. I smile and nod, wondering if the phrasing comes from Litos or the *sayla*.

When Litos finishes, I reach over—I'm squatting in front of the log—and shake the old man's hand. "*Nuedi. Nuedi.*" I'm scared as hell about what I'm getting myself into, but at least for now everyone seems happy.

Abruptly, the *sayla's* face becomes more serious and he speaks again, a group of sentences without breaks.

"Mateo wants to know what religion you are."

When Litos says this, my elation over handling the cooking issue melts into pure fear. How am I going to talk about religion without pissing someone off? Buying time, I question Litos: "He said more than that, didn't he?"

"Sometimes it takes many words for one idea."

I brace myself with a stiff inhale before I venture into the quagmire. "I was raised Catholic."

"*Catolica.*" Litos speaks the single word rapidly, then the *sayla* repeats it slowly as if he mulls over each syllable. The man asks me directly, "*Cristiana*?"

"*Eh-yea.*" I answer with the Kuna word for yes and nod for emphasis.

The old man is silent for almost a minute as he gazes toward the ocean. My mind races, imagining every possible reason why the Kunas would want to know my religion and devising a strategy to deal with each potential land mine.

Finally the man speaks. "He wants to know why you never try to convince the Kunas to become Christians like you."

This was not one of the land mines I had anticipated. I ponder—maybe for as long as the *sayla*—before responding. "I believe that religion is something very important and individual. Every person chooses his religion based on experience, family, and community. Most people think long and hard about what they choose to believe, and their decision should always be respected. I am young and my experience and background are very different from any of you on Sugatupu. It is not for me to tell you what to believe."

Litos translates this more easily than I had assumed he could. As Litos speaks, the elder man studies my face with his ageless eyes. When the translation of my Spanish is complete, his next question is only a handful of words.

"Don't you believe that Christianity is the only true religion?"

Sticky sweat slides down my sides. My mouth is dry. "The man who started Christianity, Jesus Christ, said that religion is not as important as the way you treat other people. He said that it doesn't matter what religion you are as long as you love your neighbor"—I want to add "like yourself" but when I try, I get tangled up in the Spanish reflexive verb.

Litos rescues me. "I understand what you mean."

I watch his face as he confers with the other and suddenly I'm very tired. These two men seem kind but their presence emphasizes how alone I am, how friendless and stilted my life has become.

Litos shoots me a quick glance, never pausing in his speech. He goes on much longer than my simple, stuttered response would warrant. The way the *sayla* watches me leads me to believe that they have abandoned their discussion of religion and now the focus of their conversation is me. I bow my head.

Immediately, the older man rises to his feet and offers me his hand.

"He says that you are tired. You work all day and don't eat good food. You are still a child. You need to rest. He is sorry that he has bothered you for so long."

I feel that I should stand but if I did I would tower over the old-timer. I shift forward so that I am on my knees in front of him. "*Sully*. No. You didn't bother me. I appreciate you asking my opinion and respect you for not laughing at the stupidity of my ideas."

The hand that shook mine opens to gently pat my cheek. "Roberto and Amelia did a good job raising their daughter."

"Even if I never learned how to cook?"

When Litos translates this, the old man throws back his head and laughs. With a springy stride, he swings around the tent to the head of the trail and waves once before he disappears. Litos follows after a whispered, "Goodbye, *Perrita*."

Alone in the growing darkness, I try to choke down a can of cold beans but only finish four spoonfuls before tears again overwhelm me.

VIII

Mateo's wife Irina, the woman who in one afternoon will try to reverse my twenty-five years of culinary incompetence, is the skinniest living person I have ever seen: a creature composed entirely of bones, loose skin, and a nose ring. By my side, Litos stands ready to be my tongue and my ears, but Irina doesn't say a word. Instead, she hands me a coconut.

I stand in the baked, bare yard, the wind blowing strong and fresh through the leaves of a spreading mango tree that shades the house but not the yard or the open cooking hut. The sound of breakers off the reef is refreshing but distant. In the full, midday sun, sweat soaks my t-shirt and pastes the thin fabric to my back.

When she realizes that I have no idea what to do with the coconut, Irina, who moves with the velocity and precision of a wasp, snatches the heavy thing from my hand and zips off to the edge of the yard. On a palm log striped with scars, she centers the hard husk under a machete as long as my arm. One quick whack and a good-sized chunk of the husk breaks off.

Litos nudges me from behind. When I glance over my shoulder at him, he shoos me toward my teacher. She hands me the machete and the coconut. I center the coconut on the palm log and aim the blade. When I bring down my arm, the kickback rips the machete out of my hand and sends it twirling into the air behind me.

"Careful!" Perhaps anticipating a mishap like this, Litos has remained on the far side of the yard.

Wordlessly buzzing and clucking, Irina retrieves the machete, closing her hand over mine to guide me in the proper grip. When she removes her hand, I raise my arm to attempt another cut but before I can hack, Irina jerks the machete from my fist.

Her bony fingers curl around the wooden handle and she brandishes it in my face for emphasis. After her demonstration, Irina again centers the machete handle in my palm and twists her fingers around mine. Her grip is like a vise: I don't understand where she gets her strength since the woman doesn't appear to have one ounce of muscle anywhere on her stringy body.

Finally, she is satisfied with the way I hold the machete and I begin to hack at the coconut. Each impact shudders through my arm all the way to my shoulder. The fibrous husk peels off in miniscule increments. Irina watches with her cloudy eyes but offers no assistance.

After about a hundred hacks, I'm glowing from exertion, the hairy coconut shell is completely exposed, and my arm is rubber. Before I have a chance to congratulate myself, Irina's skinny hand snakes out and plants the hard-shelled coconut square in the center of the chopping block. I hear a titter and glance over my shoulder. A peanut gallery of women and children has gathered in the shade under the mango tree. As I search the faces to see if any appear familiar, Irina stamps her bare foot sternly in the dust to regain my attention. She motions for me to deliver one firm hack directly in the center of the shell. Harking back to my girl scout training, I imagine the coconut as an unsplit lodgepole log, take aim with the machete, squeeze my eyes firmly closed, and slam the blade into the chopping block with as much force as my skinny arms can muster. A cheer rises from the audience and when I open my eyes, the coconut shell has been cleaved neatly in two.

After the coconut meat is dug out of the shell, it is grated using a tin can roughened with nail holes. The resultant meal undoubtedly is supposed to be white but mine is pale pink from blood off my scraped knuckles. The spectator's gallery has swelled to include a few men: I see a handsome, sculpted face along the edge exchange words with the gap-toothed woman who stands nearby.

Next, I'm taught to arrange and light a fire inside the open cooking hut, then peel some kind of tubers—they look like potatoes but are covered with hair—and slice plantains. By this time, the water over the fire is boiling and Irina indicates that I should put all of the food I've prepared into the pot. At least I think that's what she means, but when I try to empty the banana leaf that holds the grated coconut, she snatches it out of my hand. The audience explodes with laughter.

"I'm sorry. I am so stupid." Litos translates for my teacher and for the crowd.

My next task is to clean and cut up fish. Fortunately, Irina replaces the machete with a smaller knife for this chore. The silvery bodies of the fish are slim and scaly and as long as my hand. Their flesh is firm and very pink but I have difficulty extracting the Y bones. Irina whips the knife away from me and demonstrates how to scrape the flesh against the grain to raise the tiny bones from the meat.

The fish, then the coconut, are added to the stew. Before Irina hands me the wooden spoon, she demonstrates how to grip the handle and the proper motion for stirring. After all the mistakes I've made, she must assume that I lack even the most rudimentary skills.

The soup is thick and fragrant with coconut. As it bubbles around the spoon, I sneak a few glances at my audience. The kids have lined up in two rows: little ones, most of them sitting cross-legged or squatting, in front of the older children. Their silence and concentration is amazing: they don't seem restless or fidgety and all eyes appear to be glued to me. Behind the children, the mothers and grandmothers are more relaxed, chatting and joking with Litos and the few other men interspersed among them. In their bright, colorful dresses, the women always appear elegant, even when hauling water or chopping wood. The children and men—at least most of the men—are another story. They seem to dress in snatches, in whatever they can rummage: dirty, torn, or completely absent. Kids may wear only a waist-length shirt, or underwear so big it reveals more than it conceals. As often as not, zippers are either dysfunctional or ignored.

Among the men, there are expectations. Pedro, exchanging jokes under the mango tree with a woman who seems to suffer from pink eye, always wears a clean shirt although I have never once seen it buttoned over his chest. And the handsome man—how does he manage to keep his khakis so impeccable? I notice a flash as the silver band of his wristwatch catches the sun and wonder how he protects the metal from salt and humidity, not to mention all the sand here on the island.

I hear laughter as Irina stamps again. The sole of her foot is milk-white and her big toe sticks out so far to the side it seems almost prehensile.

"Sorry." I make a show of focusing my attention on the soup, stirring vigorously and rapidly. Everyone—even Irina—laughs.

The soup turns out better than I had expected. Irina has me ladle a serving for each of the kids, who have come prepared with bowls in hand. As I move among the audience, I see a couple of albino children with squinty eyes and stringy yellow hair. One, a naked little boy, has red sores all over his body. I wonder how albinos manage to survive the long-day glare of the tropical sun.

In the deep shade, I notice a young girl who is not albino but whose skin is lighter than the other Kuna children. Instead of the lank, jet-black hair of the Indians, her hair is wavy and brown. She meets my eyes with a pair of hazel ones. Am I imagining that she is not as shy as the other children? "*Nuedi,*" she politely tells me when I serve her the soup.

There are more lessons: I have to grind corn using a rock, then add the meal to a pot of water to make a thin gruel. The gruel simmers while with that same rock I crush a shriveled, dried fruit pod into dust. The odor of the fruit is vaguely familiar and makes my mouth water. When I think that no one is looking, I touch my tongue to the brown flesh. The meat is so bitter that my face scrunches into an involuntary grimace. My ears burn with the sound of the audience's laughter.

Irina storms over and stands directly above me. Huddled as small as I can make my lanky body, I hang my head. "I'm sorry. I'm sorry that I am so stupid."

Litos barely finishes with the translation of my sentence before Irina launches into a tirade, the first words she's spoken since my arrival. I'm shocked by the vehemence in her voice. Brandishing the wooden spoon in front of her like a weapon, she shakes her bony finger in my face for emphasis. At first, I imagine a translation of the words she uses to scold me, but soon her anger becomes so overwhelming that I stop thinking and try to transport myself somewhere—anywhere—away from this too-public humiliation. I bow my head, hunch my shoulders, and fight back tears. Everyone stares at me, everyone is silent in the face of my shame. For what seems like an eternity, the woman berates me with more energy and passion than her poor withered body seems capable of producing.

After the violence of Irina's speech, Litos's voice is soft and soothing. "Irina says that she does not like it when you say you are stupid because it's not true. You are very intelligent to know about eagles and other animals on the mainland. And you are brave to come here all alone, so far from your home and your family and your people. But most of all, she says you should not say that you are stupid because you are the only white person who has come to Sugatupu who has not told us that we—the Kuna—are stupid, who has not tried to change us and teach us other ways to live. You try to understand the Kuna and because you don't learn right away you say that you are stupid, but you are not. Irina says that your parents, Amelia and Roberto, must be very good people, and that all your family must be very, very proud of their beautiful, brave, intelligent daughter."

I raise my eyes. I can only focus on Litos's face. "Is that really what she said?"

"*Perrita*, I swear by my love that every word I just spoke is the truth."

Some of the men—I guess the ones who know Spanish well enough to understand what we just said—laugh, and I hear whispers as words are passed from person to person. Soon everyone is laughing. I hug myself, keeping my head down so that the Kunas will think that the shaking of my shoulders is from laughter and no one will notice the tears that slide down my face.

The corn and fruit gruel is finished just before we leave for the town meeting. With the first sip, I recognize the bitter brown flavor from the fruit as unsweetened chocolate.

In the meeting house, Litos leads me to a bench close to the stage-like center of the room. "So now, *Perrita*, you know how to cook like a Kuna woman."

Pedro is talking with the *saylas* in the hammocks but he turns his head to glare at us when Litos speaks. A moment later, he storms over to our bench. In Spanish, he rebukes both Litos and me: "You shouldn't allow him to call you that! '*Perrita,*'" he simpers in a mocking imitation of Litos's affected speech. "That name is totally inappropriate! He is not giving you the respect that you deserve!"

I've never seen Pedro so animated. His words are loud and I have the distinct impression that they are intended more to be overheard than heeded.

I answer Pedro in Spanish so that Litos understands, but so softly that no one besides him and Pedro can hear. "At least he calls me something. He gives me a name instead of taking my own away from me."

In the dim light I see Pedro's snake eyes flash, but he turns and stalks away without a word. Litos whispers to me, "You shouldn't say that to Pedro. He didn't take away your name. It was all of us—we all agreed that it was best."

My voice catches on the lump that has suddenly clogged my throat. "Everyone? You all decided to never call me by my name? Why? Why would you do that to me?"

"Hush, *Perrita*. You wouldn't understand."

"Why would you want to hurt me like that?"

"Sh-h-h, my little love. The meeting is beginning."

I pout while Orestes calls the role—my name conspicuous by its absence. A slim, very pretty young woman slides onto the bench beside me. She carries a small child, maybe a year old, in her arms. Glued to her side, the light-skinned, brown-haired girl from this afternoon plays with a piece of string. When the child realizes that I am watching her, she crawls onto my lap. She demonstrates her game for me: like cat's cradle, complicated designs are formed by twists in a loop of string. While she plays, the girl sings to herself in Kuna.

The weight of the child in my lap calms me in a way that I'm not sure I understand. The child's head rests against my tanned arm and I'm startled to realize that her skin is lighter than mine. I remember the girl's hazel eyes and glance at the young woman beside me. The baby in her arms is pink.

Litos whispers in my ear. "The missionary—the *evangelico*—he wants to talk to us about Christianity. He has been on Usdup for several weeks and now would like to come to Sugatupu to teach the people here about the one true god."

I realize that Litos is translating what Orestes says into Spanish for me. I whisper, "*Nuedi.*"

With Litos's translations, the meeting becomes fascinating. One by one, townspeople approach the stage presided over by the two old men—I recognize Mateo because his face is less square than the other's—who lie in their hammocks seemingly oblivious to the proceedings. The people voice their opinions and concerns and everything is recorded faithfully by Orestes. In translation, the Kunas sound rational and reasonable although when I listen to their voices all I hear is contention and argument.

After a half dozen people have spoken, the handsome man approaches the center of the hall. His appearance commands attention: his bearing is straight and dignified, his clothing impeccable, his gaze direct. Even I, knowing virtually nothing of the community's politics, can see that he is an important figure.

"Who is he?" I whisper.

"Eulogio. He is one of the leaders of the younger men. His father is a healer. He will probably become a *sayla* in a few years."

I try to imagine the handsome man's well-formed, muscular body slumped semi-comatose in a hammock, his direct eyes glazed, but can't. Litos whispers to me, "Eulogio tells the story of his grandfather. He says that long ago, the grandfather found a strange object in the jungle—it was shiny and cold and had lots of different parts. The grandfather, a young boy at the time, showed the object to everyone in the community but no one had any idea what to do with it. The Kunas had never seen anything like it. Years later, a boat with some white men on it—a boat like Ruiz's—came to Sugatupu, and Eulogio's grandfather decided to ask the white men if they knew what the object was. One of the strangers took the object from the boy, pointed it at the sky, and killed a bird. That was the first gun the people of Sugatupu had seen, but by themselves they didn't know how to use it. The gun was worthless until we knew its purpose.

"Now, Eulogio says, the people of Sugatupu use guns all the time for hunting. The white man's object has given us a way to improve our lives. We are not so weak that we should fear the world outside: it will always be there, like that gun my grandfather found. We need to know about the people and things from other lands. Without knowing, how can we decide what is good for the Kunas? We should listen to this man first, then decide whether to accept him."

I'm impressed—Eulogio is more than just a pretty face. I wonder why he has never spoken to me although he invariably seems to be somewhere near.

A stocky woman has the floor now. "Elena worries about a white man on the island at night. She has fear for her daughters and their daughters."

Another woman, almost as old as Irina, speaks next. The nose rings on the women seem to grow as their owners age. Many of the older women have nose rings so massive that they hang down below their lips. "Yarilista says that other missionaries have forced Kunas to abandon their traditions. On islands with Christians, many of the women do not make traditional blouses or wear arm and leg beads, and there are no parties to acknowledge girls becoming women. Christians want Kunas to assume all of the habits of white men."

When Pedro claims the floor, I hear a murmur of excitement that stills as soon as he opens his mouth. "You are fools—fools!—to believe that you can take what you want selectively from this man. He will not rest until everyone—every woman, man, child, every dog and cat and bird and fish—on Sugatupu believes exactly what he wants you to believe. He will play with your children, offer them toys and candy, but all the while he will be telling them that their parents are heathens, are bad people, are ignorant because they do not believe in the white man's religion."

Pedro's words hiss with anger. "I know these people. They will not give up until they have converted you to their beliefs. They will not allow you to take a little of their religion—the parts that you think would be good for you—and reject the rest. No! They will insist that you swallow it all: all of the lies and hate, all of the white man's poison. It has killed the Indians in the rest of America and it will kill us too, kill us as sure as with bullets, if we accept this man into our community."

Eulogio rises again. He appears calm and collected, the soul of reason after Pedro's impassioned outburst. "We have had others in our community before. Flemming"—he nods toward me to acknowledge my predecessor, the man who began the harpy eagle study seven years ago. "And Ruiz also. These men are white but they are men like us. There is good and bad in all of them, just as both exist in us. We accept the failings of others but we do not declare that Mateo or Pedro or Flemming is evil because of what he does. And it's the same with the missionary. If he does things that we do not approve of, we will respond in the appropriate manner. But we should not fear him. He is just a man."

Pedro does not give up the floor easily. "You are wrong, Eulogio. A missionary is not merely a man. He is a devil. He has the power of a devil because he believes in god."

I hear a disembodied voice, slow and almost languid. My eyes search the faces in the center of the room until I locate one with moving lips. It is the final man from my welcoming committee, the gray-haired guy with cataracts. Unlike the other Kunas, he sits as he speaks, directly beside the hammock of the second *sayla*.

"Is he an official?" I whisper to Litos.

"Anselmo, the *arkar*."

"*Arkar*?"

"It's—it's one step below a *sayla*. Anselmo used to be a *sayla* before Mateo. He was the *sayla* when Pedro first returned to the island."

"But he's been demoted?"

Litos shifts but doesn't respond.

"What's he saying?" The man is still droning, an almost whiny sound with no inflection or intonation.

When Litos doesn't respond, I turn to look at his face. He lowers his eyes. "Nothing. Nothing really. Don't worry about it."

In his hammock, Mateo shifts and clears his throat. The man with the cataracts raises his voice for a couple words, then ends abruptly.

Orestes, who has been feverishly writing down all of the arguments, rises to his feet. "There is one other person here tonight who can talk to us about the Christian religion. Perhaps her explanation will help us decide about the missionary."

As he translates, Litos nudges my shoulder, and I realize that the person Orestes refers to is me.

"Please, Litos," I whisper in panic. "I can't get up there and talk."

"It's very important. Just say what you told Mateo yesterday."

"I can't."

Litos continues to whisper as he rises to his feet. In order to hear him, I have to stand also. I catch his last words, "—I will be at your side the entire time."

I still hold the little girl in my arms: she fell asleep during the talking. Stalling for time, I pass her limp body over to her mother. Every eye in the meeting hall is trained on me except for those of the second *sayla*, who has closed his and appears to be sleeping. My mind is as blank as the face of the moon.

Mateo's gaze flashes out for a moment to meet mine and he smiles without raising his head. The gesture is so subtle that I don't think that anyone besides me—not even Litos—notices it. I remember Irina's words and straighten my back.

"I shouldn't be up here speaking at your meeting. I'm an outsider, a stranger. I'm sure that before I came you went through this same discussion about me." In the pause as Litos translates, I remember Eulogio's story and decide to try a similar tactic.

"My family is Christian, which means that we follow the teachings of a very wise and kind man, Jesus Christ. He taught that all people are equal, that the most important thing in a person's life should be love for other people. He told a story—I'm sure Pedro knows it—about a man who was robbed and beaten and left to die in the jungle. A stranger, a man from a faraway community, finds the wounded man. He takes him to his house, feeds him, and takes care of his wounds. He stays with the man until he is strong, then the stranger gives the wounded man money to return home. He helped the man in spite of the fact that he didn't know him. He helped him not expecting anything in return, just because the man needed help.

"That's the story that best describes what it means to be a Christian. That's the way my parents taught me to live and how I should treat other people. I guess that's what I want to say about being a Christian."

While I was speaking, I was too nervous to make eye contact with anyone, but as Litos translates my last few sentences, I glance up. Eulogio's proud, handsome face seems to approve. Pedro is nowhere in sight. The audience sits stone silent, without acknowledgement. Litos shepherds me back to the bench where I slide in beside the young mother and reclaim the sleeping child.

After an almost imperceptible nod from Mateo, Orestes rises. "We should hear from Ceferino."

In the generalized buzz that follows, I whisper to Litos, "Who is Ceferino?"

"Eulogio's brother. He's the doctor."

"I thought Mateo was the doctor."

"He's just a healer. There are a lot of healers. But Ceferino is special. He knows more about medicine than anyone else on the island. He was born with the cape of knowledge."

I'm intrigued by this phrase—"the cape of knowledge"—but before I can question Litos, a figure rises from the shadows in the rear of the building. As he approaches the brightly-lit center of the hall, I immediately recognize the man I met in the jungle the night I returned from the waterfall.

The doctor, Ceferino, looks nothing like his handsome brother. While Eulogio's features are sculpted and firm, his brother's face appears soft, relaxed, and almost pliant. His body too: Eulogio is triangular, with broad, well-defined shoulders tapering to thin hips, while his brother is slim and lithe throughout. Both are tall for Kunas but in a crowd of people, Eulogio would dominate while the doctor would not warrant a second glance.

In the center of the floor, I see the doctor exchange nods with Mateo—is that old-timer orchestrating this entire debate?—then the man's eyes flit through the room as if evaluating the health of each of his patients. For quite a few moments, the doctor does not speak. I remember his silence along the trail, how the lack of words actually made me feel more at ease. Ceferino's silence seems to trivialize all of the words that were spoken earlier.

I hear a voice and for a moment I'm not sure where it comes from, then I notice Mateo's lips move.

"He is asking Ceferino what he thinks we should do about the missionary."

Ceferino's response is brief—incredibly brief compared to all of the other speeches—and delivered in a soft, almost musical voice.

"Ceferino says that many wise words have been spoken tonight. He thinks that we should all go home and consider what has been said before we decide anything."

Even before Litos finishes translating Ceferino's simple response, the meeting hall begins to empty. The woman beside me stands, her arms heavy with the body of her younger child. I glance at Litos. "I can carry this girl home if she wants me to."

When Litos explains to the mother, she nods and responds, "*Nuedi.*" I leave with the sleeping child on my shoulder and Litos's arm around my waist. As we pass the hammocks, Ceferino catches my eye and smiles.

The mother lives on the far side of the island, closest to the breakers. I want to ask where the children's father is but then I remember the other pair of hazel eyes I saw on Sugatupu, and an obscene tattoo, and decide that I really don't need to ask. As soon as we leave the woman's house, Pedro appears at my elbow and without a word Litos vanishes. Recalling the dignity and power of Ceferino's silence, I say nothing.

On the path through town, Pedro and I walk side by side without speaking. Soft voices flit through the thin walls of houses, a few candles or oil lamps glowing between cracks in the bamboo. With every step, I feel Pedro's anger.

When we're surrounded by mangroves on the deserted part of the island, Pedro pauses to light a cigarette. The moon shines full on his face as he speaks. "Do you believe what you said at the meeting tonight?"

We face each other like two mangrove shadows. He inhales twice from the cigarette before I respond. "No." The word seems flat, final, naked.

"Then why did you feed them that load of crap?"

I let him inhale again, then exhale, before I reply. "My boss only gave me one directive before I came here. He told me not to piss anyone off."

"And you're afraid of pissing off the missionary?"

I pluck the cigarette from Pedro's fingers and inhale deeply. When I try to hand it back to him, he growls, "Keep it."

"I don't want it. I just needed a nicotine buzz to get through this."

"Get through what?"

"This. Everything. I'm scared shitless every time I have to come to this island, but it's better than staying on the mainland because I'm so lonely there I think I'm going crazy."

"So you want the missionary around for company?" I hear sarcasm in his voice.

"I just don't want to piss anyone off."

"What about me?"

"You're pissed at me?"

In the moonlight, I see disdain on his face. "So what exactly do you believe?"

"You mean like god?"

This time he makes me wait: an exhale of smoke and then he crushes the cigarette under the sole of his rubber flip-flop. "Yeah."

"Nothing."

"You don't believe in anything?" His astonishment is obvious and I congratulate myself for blindsiding him.

"No. I believe in absolutely nothing. You know, Camus, Sartre, Kafka. The chess game in *The Seventh Seal* that the goody-goody knight always loses." I don't know if he'll understand any of my references but I'm so edgy from what's happened today that I really don't care. "What do you believe?"

I see him smile. "More than you, I guess. I believe in love."

"How sweet."

"Have you ever tried it?"

"The last guy I slept with sent me out here as punishment."

He draws his breath in sharply. We walk the rest of the way to my canoe in silence.

The ocean is black except for glints of moonlight on the broken water, isolated slivers like dreams or words or hope. Pedro steadies me as I push the small dugout off the beach and step in.

He continues to clasp my forearm. For the first time, I hear sincerity in his voice. "I'm sorry."

"And I'm sorry for you, *amigo*."

"*Anai.*"

"*Anai*?"

"It's *amigo* in Kuna."

"*Anai,*" I repeat. The canoe catches a current and drifts so that Pedro is forced to release my arm. I wave to him once, then drop to my knees to paddle.

IX

Sometime before dawn, I wake to the drone of an airplane flying so close that the engine's roar drowns out the white noise of the surf. I lie on my back atop the clammy flannel of my sleeping bag, remembering Reilly's parting shot about drug smugglers and wondering if I can think of any other plausible reason for a small plane to be flying so low so early over a deserted stretch of coastal jungle so near to the Colombian border.

When I realize that I am not going to fall asleep again, I crawl to the mosquito netting of the door. My tent faces the ocean, north and east. Outside, the sky is overcast—a few drops of rain fell last night but nothing like the downpours of a month ago. A thin strip of blue defines the horizon where sky and water meet. The air cloys with the heavy perfume of a night blooming tree. As the insect whine of the plane recedes, the emptiness swells into something tangible, something I can almost taste in the back of my throat before I swallow a sigh.

Later, on the trail to the blind, I stumble over a loaf-shaped bale wrapped in brown paper and tied with a string. Slightly to the left, I see a similar package, then another. The hillside is open here: a few scraggly palms but mostly a low, thin growth of corn and squash—Kuna farmland. An ideal location for an airdrop, easily spotted from the sky and equally accessible on foot from the coast.

I'm not sure who enforces the law around here besides the Kunas. I've never seen Panamanian police or any sign of a government presence. For that matter, I'm not sure that what is contained in these packages is illegal, in Panama or anywhere else. That pre-dawn flight may have merely signaled the latest shipment of ratty old clothes for the kids on Sugatupu. I leave the packages where they lie and head up the trail to concentrate on the job I'm being paid to do.

The eagles have been active around the Maria tree the past two days. They arrive soon after I do, in tandem, accompanied as always by an abrupt and complete silence. One eagle glowers from a nearby branch while the other reinforces the nest. With its talons, the working eagle weaves vines into the old framework of branches, then fresh mud is packed into cracks with the smooth weight of the breast. Since I have no way to distinguish between the two eagles, I cannot tell if the same eagle always supervises while the other works, if the bulk of nest maintenance is performed by the male or the female bird.

Now that I've overcome my initial euphoria over seeing eagles, I am able to concentrate on establishing an accurate field identification. For the hundredth time, I open Ridgely's *Birds of Panama* to the line drawings of hawk and eagle species and train my field glasses on the gray form that hunches, still and brooding, in the shadows below the canopy.

After I carefully study and compare the features of the birds in the tree with diagrams in the field guide, I conclude, as I have the ninety-nine other times I have performed this exercise, that the pair of raptors on the nest are not *Harpia harpyja*, the harpy eagle, the most massive avian predator in the world and the national symbol of Panama. As far as I can determine from the description and drawings in Ridgely's guide, these are a different species entirely—crested eagles—a species of absolutely no interest to the Republic of Panama, the primary source of funding for my research here in the jungle.

I lower the binoculars and—again!—read Ridgely's descriptions of the two species. Several diagnostic features are comparative: harpies are bigger, heavier, and more massive; their tails are shorter and their legs stubbier. The text explains that differences between harpies and cresteds are subtle and difficult in the field, that many individuals cannot be identified with certainty. But Ridgely is definite about the harpy's "conspicuous two pointed crest," while the crested sports but a single "pointed blackish occipital crest." A mature harpy also wears a black collar of feathers, contrasting strongly with the lighter chest and head and completely lacking in either of the two eagles on the nest.

I close the book with a snap and a sigh. The rapid and frequent jump in focus from printed page to the magnified image in the binoculars has made my head ache. I close my eyes, rub my temple. I find my canteen and drink deeply. The monkey-ladder vine that twines along the floor of the blind distracts me, and I kneel in the dirt to study it. The twists and contortions of the thick stem are random and undeniably grotesque. I lower my haunches to my heels and press my throbbing forehead against the weird wood of the vine.

I wish I had access to references other than Ridgely, background information on the site, a directive, a prospectus: anything that would make me feel less alone in my decisions. Brian took every bit of data from the project with him in those six huge duffels, every damn note beginning with Flemming's first scribbles years ago. I have nothing to guide me except the memory of David's words: "A nesting observation study. You should be able to handle that."

Without harpy eagles on the nest, I have no justification for the continuation of this study—or do I? Ridgely says that crested eagles are as rare as harpies, their numbers declining, their habits imperfectly known. A nesting study of crested eagles would be every bit as valuable to science as a nesting study of harpy eagles. According to Ridgely, the known habits of the two species are similar. The difference lies solely in charisma: the harpy eagle is a figurehead for the Republic of Panama, the crested is merely a big bird.

The presence of crested eagles at a known harpy nest poses a host of intriguing questions. Did harpy eagles build this nest originally? Have harpies and all of their progeny died out in the area, or were they chased from the site by the smaller cresteds? Or did the harpies have another motive—maybe Brian's interference or the lack of nesting success—for willingly abandoning this area, the cresteds merely taking advantage of the unoccupied site?

I am here to perform a nesting observation study. Those are the words that my superior, Dr. David Calabrese, used to describe my duties. I now have eagles actively nesting on this site. It doesn't matter what species: these are undeniably eagles, and I have been assigned to observe nesting eagles. I raise my field glasses to focus on the Maria tree, open my notebook, and settle in for another day on the job.

When the sun sinks to a point a hand's breadth above the nest, I leave the blind—the eagles long gone—and head to the river to wash. The cool water assuages my doubts about the validity of my work and assures me that I can survive another day in the jungle. On the trail to camp, the paper-wrapped bales that I observed this morning have disappeared. Halfway up the ridge, I smell wood smoke.

The first thing I see when I crest the hill is a shirtless white back towering over my pup tent.

"*Amiga*! My beautiful American *amiga*!" With two strides Ruiz sweeps me into a swirling embrace. As he lowers me to my feet, his hands—both of them—linger on the curve of my breasts.

I look up at his face—his thick lips framed by dark stubble, his mangy-dog haircut, his wide, expressive eyes—and decide that he is the best thing that I've seen in weeks. "Do you always grope at the breasts of your *amigas* when you greet them?"

"Only the ones over fifteen. And you—do you always not wear a bra?"

I return his expansive hug. Between our bodies, near my groin, I feel a hardness similar to what the handsome man had when he rescued me from drowning, only with Ruiz the protrusion is off to one side. I push away from his hairy chest and glance down. Something appears to be nestled in the pocket of those baggy white pants. I'm pretty sure it's not part of his body.

"It's too hot in the jungle for bras. I never wear one when I'm working."

Ruiz's hazel eyes bulge. "So it is true what they say about you American women!"

I glance again at his leg. By the length of the barrel outlined through the thin fabric, the gun in Ruiz's pocket isn't some little .22. "I don't know. What do they say about us?"

Ruiz waggles his finger in my face. He's so clownish that I can almost forget the pistol in his pocket, and the paper-wrapped packages along the trail, and the two half-white kids on the island. "They say that you are so hungry, Ruiz might not escape from you in one piece!"

"Who says that?"

"I have my sources," he murmurs as he turns his shoulder so that I'm confronted by the female crotch tattooed on his arm. "But see, I have brought something for your hunger!"

He squats next to the fire, licks his fingers and jerks the lid off my aluminum pot. Through clouds of steam, I glimpse a huge, blood-red claw.

"Oh my God! Are those lobsters?"

"I have no butter."

"Ruiz, where did you get those?"

"The Kunas. They dive for them sometimes, very deep in the ocean. Very dangerous. Very expensive."

"So what am I going to have to pay you for these?"

He slides both his arms around my waist and squeezes. "Ah, you American women. So suspicious."

The lobster meat is sumptuous, so rich that I can barely finish the juicy flesh that Ruiz digs from the claws and spiny torso for me. Ruiz eats another lobster on his own, and a third he strips and piles the meaty orange shards in a bowl for later.

"You need a good feed. You look almost as skinny as a Brit."

"That bad?"

"You do not see how thin you are?"

"I don't have a mirror."

Ruiz pauses, the rock in his hand suspended above a claw. "You do not have a mirror? I have never heard of a woman without a mirror! That must be like—"

"Like a fish without a bicycle?"

He laughs, a laugh as big and open as he is. With a whack, the claw cracks open and Ruiz extracts a hunk of meat from the splinters of the shell. Grinning, he pops it in his mouth and leans forward to kiss me. His tongue forces my lips apart and presses the salty meat into my mouth.

Although I enjoy the titillation of being fed this way, I'm almost too full to swallow. I hop to my feet when I see Ruiz prepare another bite. "*No más*!"

"But you are so thin. What have you been eating?"

"Beans."

"Beans?"

"Brian left ten thousand cans of baked beans here in camp. It's about the only thing that he left for me."

"Besides the tent."

"Yeah, besides the tent."

"And that is where you sleep?"

I think I'm picking up on Ruiz's train of thought. "It's pretty tight in that little tent—not near enough room for two people. Besides, I sleep on the ground."

His eyes widen. "You sleep on the ground?"

"It's pretty hard."

"I imagine. But if you slept with someone, you would lie beneath him, right? Because you are so used to sleeping on the ground."

"If I did, that would put me somewhere that we Americans say is between a rock and a hard place."

"And you do not think that you would like Ruiz's rocks?"

"I think that everyone would be a lot happier if you went back to the island and slept with the mother of your children."

His big body stiffens, and when he grabs me by the shoulders I mentally kick myself for getting too comfortable around a man with a gun in his pocket. But the look on Ruiz's face is not angry and his tone is light when he demands, "And what do you mean by that?"

"That one Kuna woman on the island has two half-white kids."

"And you think that I—" He presses his hand to his heart in a ridiculous pantomime of innocence.

I can't help but grin. "Who else is there?"

"Flemming."

"Flemming?" This time it's my voice that becomes high-pitched with astonishment.

"Why is that so hard to believe?"

"He's—he's a full professor, a chair at Stanford or someplace like that. And he's married. And he's really, really fat."

"Is all of his equipment in working order?"

"I don't know. I never met the man. And even if I had, I wouldn't know that kind of stuff about him."

"Then why are you surprised to learn that he has fathered children with a Kuna woman?"

"Everyone at the research station talked about him like he was a god or something."

Ruiz throws back his head and laughs. It's such a comfortable sound that I sink back into his chest.

"I suppose next you're going to tell me that Brian was doing Kuna women too."

"Ah, Brian. That boy had a weakness for chocolate milk."

"Chocolate milk?"

The arm around me tightens. "The first month, after he gets his paycheck he says to me, 'Ruiz, you must take me to Cartagenia. I am going stone shit crazy here.' He gives me $20 and I drop him off on my way home. I come back two days later to find him sitting on a barrel of wallpaper paste on the wharf, and he begs me to lend him $100. When I ask him why he just rolls his eyes like a sheep that has eaten too much hay. I cannot get him to budge off the barrel so I give him the money. Snap! He vanishes like a rabbit. That night I see him in a whorehouse with a *negra* twice his size—I swear that woman had breasts as big as watermelons!"

"Brian?"

"He is a friend of yours?"

"He's a little prick."

"That is what I thought also. So I made him sleep on the deck of my boat for two weeks and do my laundry and cleaning to pay back the money he owed me. But the next month as soon as his pay comes, there he is, begging me to take him to Cartegenia."

"So what did you think of Flemming?"

"He was a prick also. No, not a prick: a pompous ass."

"You don't like any of us, do you?"

"I like you."

"That's only because I have breasts and don't wear a bra."

"That is a big part of it. But you are not like the others. How did you end up here?"

I rub my face in the hair on his chest. "I'm starting to wish that my tent was a little bigger."

"You can come with me to my boat. I have rum on my boat, and a bed also."

"That's how I ended up here."

"The rum or the bed?"

"I slept with my boss."

"You must not have given him a very good time."

I'm drunk on the rich food and Ruiz's attention. "I was great. I'm always great. But he was all hung up about someone finding out what happened."

"So he shipped you out here? He is the worst of the lot! Why do you work with dogs like that?"

I play with the curly chest hair near my cheek. "You know, the worst part is that he didn't tell me anything about the Kunas or how I'm supposed to act with them. All that David—my boss—told me was: 'Don't piss anyone off.'"

Ruiz's ringing laugh makes the stars dance. "That is hard when you have no idea what pisses them off. I wish I could help but I do not know much about them either. The one thing I do know is never try to get inside their women. That advice would not help you much."

"But you said that Flemming was screwing around."

"He married her."

"And then he just left?"

"Like a sailor in the night."

"And now she's got two kids and no husband—"

"And no one will give her any help because they think that she was bad for marrying a white guy and then not satisfying him enough so that he would stay."

"How does she support herself?"

"Her parents help her, I guess. She is very poor."

I'm ashamed that I didn't notice her poverty the night I went home with her, but the Kunas have so few possessions that I have a hard time judging relative wealth. "How much does it cost to live on the island? For a month or so?"

"Depends on how much you like chocolate milk."

I slap the flat of my hand on his chest. "I'm serious."

"Twenty dollars is a lot of money around here."

"For a month? For a mother and two kids?"

"You are just going to go to the island and give her money?"

"I'll tell her it's from Flemming."

"You do not have anything better to do with your money?"

"I don't like chocolate milk."

"What about Spanish fly?"

X

In the sober light of a new day, I'm glad that I kept my clothes on last night and chased Ruiz back to his boat after the moon rose over the ocean. I breakfast on cold beans and lobster, then head to the blind. The eagles continue their construction until the high heat at midday convinces them to retire for their afternoon *siesta*.

One of the few pieces of information about the Kunas that Brian shared with me was this: "Don't trust the Indians. They may seem nice but it's all just an act to get your guard down. They'll go through everything in camp as soon as they know you're not watching. You wouldn't believe how many things they stole right out of my tent. Make sure that you hide anything valuable—jewelry, letters, especially cash—someplace good and safe, somewhere those noisy Indians will never think of looking."

I'm ashamed to admit that I followed Brian's lead and buried my money in a jar under the stool in the blind. I don't think that I hide my cash because I mistrust the Kunas—at least not in the way that Brian did. To me, keeping my money stash private seems the best way to avoid pissing anyone off. I know that the Kunas have been in my camp and at least one went inside my tent to drop off the gift of the iguana. Ignorance may not bring bliss but it does tend to discourage discussion in matters of religion, politics, and personal economics.

Not that I am wallowing in cash. The project pays me $200 per month with an additional $100 stipend for living expenses. The money is delivered along with the latest instructions from the project's *de facto* director, David, and any personal correspondence from my family and friends in a big manila envelope via air taxi on the first of every month. At home, that salary would amount to starvation wages, but judging by what Ruiz told me last night, cash flow is more constricted here than in the U.S.

I use my bathroom trowel to unearth the mason jar. After only a couple months in the soggy tropical soil, the metal screw ring on the jar has rusted so tight that I can barely twist it off. The money inside smells like worms. I peel three twenties off the wad of bills and muscle the rusty ring tight.

By midday, the banks of the river are deserted, the Kunas preferring the cool of morning for bathing and chores. I wash the dirt and sweat of the blind off my skin, dress in a fresh set of clothes, then make a beeline for the beach and my dugout canoe.

On Sugatupu, I find Pedro sunning himself on the palm log near the hut at the point. He doesn't offer to help me with the canoe. "Did you come to the island to meet the preacher?"

"He's here?"

"At the dock. I left town to get away from all his noise."

"That bad?"

"He hasn't shut up all day."

"Pedro—*anai*—I need to do a couple things in town. Do you think that you could help me? I still haven't learned my way around the island, and I have a hard time communicating with people who don't speak Spanish."

Pedro eyes me up and down before he responds. "I'll go with you as long as you don't make me listen to the preacher. And I'd just as soon avoid the dock—or anywhere near there, for that matter."

We go to one of the little stores first. I buy rice, corn, plantains, yucca, chocolate, and a couple coconuts. The bill is less than $5. We drop off the food at Pedro's house in town, and then I explain that Dr. Flemming has sent money for me to give to his wife and kids.

"That doesn't sound like something Flemming would do."

"Maybe he had a change of heart. I don't know. I never met the man."

Pedro heaves a sigh like he's got a hundred better things to do.

"Listen, I know this is a real pain for you, nurse-maiding me around all the time. Here, why don't you take this for helping me?"

Pedro looks at the $5 bill in my hand as if it's something unclean and makes no motion to touch it. I glance over at Felipa, Pedro's wife, and see her eyes bulge. I set the $5 on a shelf near the door when I leave.

On our way to the other side of the island, I ask Pedro, "Where's Litos?"

"Hiding from the preacher. That self-righteous prig lit into Litos the minute he got off the boat from Usdup—couldn't stop ranting about how Litos is an abomination in the eyes of the lord and that we should purge this filthy pervert from our community before he corrupts our children. You know, the usual hellfire and damnation."

"He sounds horrible."

"What did you expect, the Good Samaritan?"

"You're still mad at me, aren't you?"

Pedro doesn't answer. He's walking so fast I have to skip to keep pace with him.

Flemming's Kuna wife is named Iris. She cries when I give her $50, calls her mother over. The mother—a woman much too young to be a grandmother—holds my hand in both of hers. Her fingers are calloused and bony.

I am about to leave when Iris stops me with a few quick words in Kuna. "She says wait," Pedro translates. The young woman hurries to a basket in a corner of the hut. She returns briskly, snapping a woman's traditional blouse.

After she's turned it right-side out, Iris presses the garment into my hands. The body of the blouse is made of several layers of fabric, cut and sewn into an intricate design of flowers, butterflies, and birds. The sleeves and yoke are blue but the design on the bodice packs so many snippets of color it looks like a carnival or a kaleidoscope. The overall impression is rhythmic and pleasing, the workmanship incredibly precise. "It's beautiful," I whisper and try to hand it back to her.

She holds her hands palm forward, refusing. "It's for you," Pedro says. "A gift."

"I can't." Again I try to hand back the blouse. "It's much too beautiful."

"She wants you to have it. She knows Flemming better than you think. I'm sure she has no doubts about where that money came from."

I glance over at Pedro but he's exchanging words in Kuna with Iris's mother.

"Okay. I mean, *nuedi, nuedi.*" I smile and nod. "How do I tell her that it's beautiful?"

"*Yer dailege.*"

I repeat Pedro's words as accurately as I can. The women laugh and smile and pat my hands, then Iris again scurries off to the basket in the corner, returning with a length of the navy blue fabric that women wear for skirts and a red and yellow headscarf.

"She says that now you can dress properly for town meetings."

"Tell her that if I wear this on Saturday, I'll be the best dressed woman at the meeting."

Pedro translates and we all repeat "*nuedi*" several times with smiles and nods.

Outside, Pedro tells me, "That is her most intricate blouse. It's probably the best blouse on the whole island."

"It's incredibly beautiful. I feel guilty taking it from her."

"She wouldn't have given it to you if she didn't want you to have it."

Pedro must be as distracted as I am by the gift because we follow the main street straight into the center of town. A knot of people, mostly men, has gathered at the dock where a strident voice rises above the yapping of gulls.

"Shit!" Pedro hisses under his breath. He grabs my arm to steer me toward a side street, but the missionary has already zeroed in on the blond height of me.

"Oh, sister," he calls out in English. "Oh, sister, won't you help me? Won't you help me spread the word of the Lord to these poor, heathen children?" He opens his arms to encompass the cluster of men around him.

I'm tempted to deny any knowledge of the English language. From the few words of his preaching that I have heard, the missionary's Spanish is so broadly accented that even the Kunas who are fluent probably can't understand what he's saying.

"Come forward, sister! Come forward and testify!"

Everyone on the dock has turned and now I'm the center of attention. Pedro has vanished. The missionary is a little guy, not much taller than the Kunas, red-faced, stocky, and hairy. Since I've made no motion to meet him, he strides toward me with such determination that I'm afraid he's going to plough right into me. I speak to halt his momentum. "You should wear a hat if you're going to be out in the sun all day. You're really sunburned."

"Praise the Lord! Another American!" He grabs my shoulders with both hands as if he intends to embrace me but the movement ends there, appearing detached and mechanical compared to the ardor of his words. "You must help me, sister. My soul is heavy with the word of God but my tongue cannot form a language that these heathen souls understand!"

"I'm afraid I can't help you with that."

His pale blue eyes flash, but when he speaks his voice is that of a salesman, loud and theatric. From his accent, it sounds like he is from down South somewhere, Texas or Oklahoma. "You speak Spanish, don't you? That is the language I learned to teach these heathens the words of our Savior."

"I speak Spanish but most of the people on this island don't. They only speak their own language."

"On Usdup almost everyone knows Spanish."

"There's a school on Usdup. There's no school here. Kids learn from their parents."

"And these forsaken children have nothing—not even a language! Oh, my sister, your presence here is surely a sign from

God that we should work together to save these souls from eternal perdition!"

"Sorry I can't help you with that. I'm here to study eagles."

"Eagles! Of what importance are birds compared to the glory of bringing new lambs into the flock of the Good Shepherd?"

"The Kunas aren't sheep. They probably have their own beliefs and religion and feel as strongly about them as you do about yours. How would you like it if they came to your town and tried to convince you to give up Christianity?"

"I would drive them as far from me as possible! I do not accept false idols before my Lord, Jesus Christ!"

"Maybe these people feel the same about their religion. Did you ever think that other people have the right to believe what they want to believe?"

When the man in front of me raises his arm as if to strike, I assume that he is bluffing, putting on a show for the audience. I think maybe I even smile a little, daring him to go further.

I hear the blow before I feel it: the flashing whap! of his wide, beefy palm flat against my face. The sound is loud, as abrupt as the crack of a gunshot. I stagger backwards: I'm not sure if I instinctively try to duck out of his reach or if my body absorbs momentum from his hand. My face is wet: tears jerked out of my eyes by the unexpected strike.

As if through water, I hear his voice: "The hand of righteousness will smite my foes, and the Lord will defeat mine enemies because they are evil and unholy in his eyes. Go now, thou blasphemer! How can you deny the power of the Lord, your God?"

I try to focus my eyes but all I see is red. I'm more startled than hurt, dizzy and confused. I realize that the red I see is blood dripping from my chin down to the packed dirt at my feet.

The preacher continues in English, a language that only Pedro and I understand. "Verily, I say to you children: unless you repent, unless you drive the evil devils—the blasphemers, the sodomites, the whores—from your midst, you will never know the kingdom of heaven. You will burn for all eternity with the fires of damnation!"

His words fade as he moves away from me. The puddle of blood at my feet grows wider, deeper: a pool like the one in the jungle under the waterfall. A cool pool to wash in: washed in the blood of lambs. My body sways and I close my eyes to keep from falling. An arm slides around my waist to steady me. I lean into a chest broad and male, a man about as tall as me. I feel his breath in my hair, on the side of my face.

"Are you okay?" He speaks Spanish but uses the American term "okay."

I nod, "*eh-yea*," before turning my head to look at the face beside me. It is Eulogio, the handsome man.

"Can you walk?" he asks me, again in Spanish.

"*Eh-yea*."

Blood drips from my nose as Eulogio guides me down a narrow lane. He doesn't let go until I am safely seated on a hammock in a dim house somewhere far from the noise at the dock.

In front of me another Eulogio appears, almost an exact duplicate, only older. The second Eulogio says something in Kuna. I hear a voice—Eulogio's?—answer with a single word, "*Evangelico*."

The older man's hands are gentle. He wipes the blood from under my nose with a rag, then washes my face in water that smells cleaner and fresher than any I have ever known. He takes a small clay pot from a shelf, licks the tips of two of his fingers, then swirls them around inside the pot. The square-tipped fingers emerge coated with brown dust. Steadying my head with his other hand, he inserts the fingers, one at a time, into each of my nostrils. On contact with the brown powder, my membranes burn like a hot pepper on the tongue but the bite lasts only an instant. When I wipe my nose, the bleeding has stopped.

"Are you okay?" Eulogio again uses the American word.

"*Eh-yea. Nuedi*."

The younger man purses his lips as if he is going to say something but the other motions with his head toward the door.

When I stand, my blood pounds and I feel dizzy. Eulogio wraps his arm around me, strong and protective. "*Nuedi,*" I mumble.

Eulogio escorts me to the point where Pedro has already loaded my food into the dugout. In the bottom of the canoe, three slim fish shimmer like metal beside the neatly folded blouse and my new, navy blue Kuna skirt.

XI

Saturday afternoon, when I beach my canoe at the point, Pedro is nowhere to be found. Alone, I head toward town on the path through the mangroves. I feel conspicuous and uncomfortable in the Kuna clothes that Iris gave me. The intricately worked layers of fabric in the bodice of the blouse constrict like a too-tight bra. The scarf keeps catching the wind and ballooning off my head. Worst is the skirt, a simple length of cloth that Kuna women—apparently by magic—fasten around their waists. The ends won't stay together for me without a hard knot and the seam over my thigh gapes with every step.

I no sooner pass the first house when I am ambushed by ten or twelve women, gathered from every direction to completely surround me. Most of the women are young, with a baby on their hip and a toddler or two at their heels. My head towers above the crowd as the women talk among themselves. They touch the blouse as if it is something apart from me, running their fingers along the appliqué ridges, heedless of the body parts beneath the fabric. Someone grabs my shoulders and roughly turns me half-around so that she can study the pattern on my back. I smile and nod and try not to flinch when they poke me.

One woman—thin and slightly cross-eyed—notices my skirt. She stabs at my crude knot with her finger, then waggles that same finger in my face. All of the women now focus on my skirt. With so many hands tugging at the knot, the inevitable occurs and I feel the cloth around my waist loosen.

Keeping David's admonition about not pissing anyone off firmly in mind, I control my impulse to snatch the fabric out of their hands and twist it securely around my hips. Instead, I grit my teeth and laugh nervously. Maybe because my face is so far above their heads, the women ignore me as if I am a statue. Before I know it, my skirt has been removed entirely and I stand in the middle of the street wearing nothing but a blouse and my yellow bikini panties.

I know that it is a mistake to look up at this moment—shame always should be kept as private as possible—but the clutch of women around me has grown so tight that I feel claustrophobic. When I glance over the shoulder-high black heads that surround me, the first thing I see is a figure standing to the side, just far enough away so that the women don't notice. I recognize him immediately as the man that I met in the jungle dusk, the man who saved me from the snake and showed me the wild kittens, the man who is the brother of the most handsome man I've ever seen.

When I look at the doctor, Ceferino, I see his black eyes dance as if he is laughing. He acknowledges me by slapping his palm over his mouth with the same gesture he used to signal silence when we were in the jungle. I'm not sure why he expects me to obey him now but before I can react, the cross-eyed woman turns her head to see what has distracted me. When she catches sight of the doctor, she lets out a whoop that gets the attention of all the other women. Ceferino claps his hand over his eyes, his shoulders shaking from stifled laughter. As the pack of women bears down on him, clucking and wagging their fingers, the doctor beats a hasty retreat.

Now that the cluster of women has broken up, my bare legs seem even more exposed than before. An intensely beautiful girl with a smiling, heart-shaped mouth snaps my skirt to straighten it, then circles the fabric around my hips. She tucks the excess firmly under the waistline and steps back to admire her work. Amazingly, the makeshift skirt stays in place. The woman loosens the edges, taking care that the cloth remains over my hips. With one corner in each hand, she pokes me in the stomach to make sure that I pay attention, then re-tucks the fabric ends into the waist of the skirt.

The crowd has reassembled around me. Another woman—short and plump—undoes the skirt, then grabs one of my hands and closes it around the loose fabric. Understanding—I think—her intention, I take the other corner and try to arrange the skirt the way the first woman did. My attempt is greeted by laughter. The proper technique is demonstrated again and finally I display enough proficiency at dressing that I am allowed to proceed down the path. "*Nuedi*," I tell the women who follow and flank me. "*Nuedi*."

My entourage grows through town until by the time I arrive at the meeting hall it seems as though half of the women in the community have gathered around me. I feel a hug at my thighs, look down, and recognize Iris's little half-white girl, the one who slept in my lap at the meeting last week. I lift her into my arms and she snuggles her face against my chest. Iris slides her slender body through the crowd.

"*Yer dailege*," she says.

Her words are picked up by other women until the entire gathering echoes. I think I recognize the phrase as the one Pedro had me parrot to tell Iris that her blouse was pretty.

Litos materializes at my side. "Ah, my beautiful little love."

"Litos, what are they saying?" I'm not sure why I whisper because I don't think that any of these women understand Spanish.

"They are saying that you are beautiful, *Perrita*. *Yer dailege*. You are beautiful."

I feel that I might burst the seams on Iris's tight blouse. I squeeze the child in my arms.

"You are beautiful, you know that, don't you? In that blouse, you are the most beautiful woman on the island. You are the most beautiful woman I have ever seen."

"*Nuedi*," I say to everyone and no one.

In the meeting hall, Litos sits on one side of me, Iris on the other, the child in my lap. Flemming's daughter plays at outlining the figures in the blouse. She runs her finger across the fabric in the same way the older women did, as if the picture is more important that the person inside.

The initial business at the meeting is trivial. A pair of teenage boys asks for permission to attend school on another island. The *sayla*—not Mateo but the other—gives them a stern lecture as they sit cramped together on the low supplicant's stool. A woman wants to go to Panama City to retrieve her husband. When Mateo asks why, the woman says that he is sleeping with other women. Everyone laughs but Mateo allows her to go. A man reports that his daughter is now a woman. I'm dying to know the significance of his announcement but decide that Litos is not the best person to consult on the subject.

At this point, a murmur arises near the doorway and Orestes, Eulogio, and several other men enter with the ruddy missionary between them. Pedro is not among the guard and I smile to myself: at least the Kunas gave me the benefit of English during my interrogation by the welcoming committee. Orestes marches the missionary to the center of the hall, to the supplicant's stool, and in Spanish orders him to sit.

The white man's eyes dart around the room. The hall is dim and I don't think that he notices me, dressed as I am like the other women. The missionary does not sit. Instead, he strides between the hammocks—completely ignoring the two old *saylas*—and throws his arms wide.

"Oh, my children," he begins in his mangled Spanish. "How can you expect me to be still when I am bursting with the word of the Lord Jesus? Every moment I remain silent may be an eternity for some soul, an eternity of torture in the fires of hell. How can I ignore the voices of sinners crying out for salvation?"

Orestes says something in Kuna, curt and brief, and Litos whispers in my ear, "They want you to translate for them. No one can understand his Spanish because it's so bad."

"Please Litos, I can't"—I'm halfway through the sentence before I realize that Litos has abandoned me and slinks toward the doorway like a cat.

Orestes glares at me, his calf-roper shoulders barely contained by his tight white t-shirt. Beside me, someone spits. Orestes makes an impatient gesture with his hand. I bundle Iris's daughter onto the bench before I rise.

The missionary pauses in his preaching to shoot me a look so venomous that the Coleman lantern above his head hisses.

I address him in English. "They want me to translate what you're saying. They can't understand your accent."

"I thought you had no time for this." Light sparks off bits of spittle that flick from his mouth as he speaks. "I thought you were only here to look at birds."

"The leaders have asked me to help them."

"And you will act at the bidding of these heathens but have no time to help me spread the word of the Lord? It that why you are dressed in those ugly rags like some kind of godless savage?"

"What is he saying?" Orestes demands of me in Spanish.

"He says that he wants to save you all from the eternal fires of hell."

Orestes announces a few sentences in Kuna, apparently translating the words I just relayed to him.

"Tell them more," the missionary commands. "Tell them everything I said."

"He says that the only way you can be saved is if you rid your community of the evil that exits here now. You need to remove the sinners. They make everything dirty and God will punish your entire town for what the evil ones do."

"More!" the missionary demands of me. "I can understand everything you say. You're not telling them all of it!"

I feel cold and detached in the face of this man's passion. I glance over to Iris and her daughter. The little girl stares at me with wide, frightened eyes.

Mateo says something to Orestes.

In Spanish, Orestes says to me, "Mateo asks where is the love that the man Christ spoke of in his teachings? This man speaks of nothing but hate."

The missionary launches into his tirade—in English—before Orestes can finish speaking. "For the good and righteous, for the holy, no love is too great. They will enjoy the wonders of paradise for all eternity. But sinners are an abomination to God and to man. They must be cast out from your midst as you would cut off a finger which is diseased. Those who whore, those who miscegenate, those who perform unspeakable, godless, perverted acts with other men—"

"I'm sorry but I can't translate that. I don't know the Spanish words."

"Whore!" Somehow the missionary manages to cross the length of the room in the space of that single word. Directly in front of me, his face is red and contorted with rage. I bow my head so that I won't have to look at him.

"From woman comes wickedness!"

A low murmur passes through the crowd. Four bare feet enter my field of view, one pair on either side of the missionary's wing-tipped shoes. I glance up. Two men—the community guards whose main duty seems to be to wake up anyone who falls asleep during meetings—flank the preacher. One of the guards raises his hand to the man's shoulder.

When he feels pressure from the hand, the missionary jerks away from the guard and butts his chest against mine. I stumble backwards. He curses me. "Be gone, thou godless slut! Hellfire and damnation are too good for you!"

The broad shoulders of Orestes impose themselves between the missionary and me. His single word rings through the hall like a gunshot. "Quiet!"

There is an instant of stunned silence while the missionary measures the secretary's weight-lifter physique. Orestes says something in Kuna and two more men join the guards. All five Kunas escort the missionary down the main aisle of the meeting hall and out into the now-black streets.

The atmosphere for the remainder of the meeting is restrained. Since Litos has disappeared, I have no idea what is said during the discussion that follows. When the meeting is over the brothers, Eulogio and Ceferino, fall into step on either side of me as I negotiate the maze of narrow streets on my way to the point.

Eulogio's Spanish is adequate but not as fluid as Litos's. "Your face looks like it is still hurt from where the *evangelico* hit you the other day. Does it pain you?"

"I'm all right."

"Your skin is so white, the bruises are obvious."

"Really, it doesn't hurt at all."

He falls silent beside me. His brother—does he even understand Spanish?—makes no effort to speak.

I wonder where Orestes and the others have taken the missionary. Apparently he is not fully contained or these brothers wouldn't have felt the need to escort me across the island. I don't think that I've ever had one man—let alone two—go so far out of his way to protect me. We pass a house livened by oil lamps and a murmur of low voices.

"It is very dark tonight. You will stay on the island?"

"The moon will be up in a little while. It's still pretty big—almost half-full."

"Be careful on the water."

My face burns in the darkness as I remember Eulogio's firm chest and the hardness between his legs. "*Eh-yea.*" We're almost to the mangroves. "*Nuedi.*"

"And don't worry about the *evangelico*. He won't bother you again."

I can't raise my eyes to look at him. "Thanks. *Nuedi.*"

On the log near his "vacation home," Pedro smokes a joint. He and Eulogio exchange a few words in Kuna. In English, I say to Pedro, "You don't have to stay up and take care of me. I'll be okay here."

As he inhales, the red glow from the joint illuminates Pedro's face. His eyes are closed. He answers in English, "I'm not doing this for you. When Ruiz isn't around, I don't have anyone to get high with. I feel like an addict smoking by myself. Kunas don't do drugs."

"You're a Kuna."

He glances up at me and flips the roach into the water. "More or less."

Eulogio shakes my hand formally and tells me goodbye—"*Tegi malo*"—in Kuna. His brother merely touches my hand. I cannot see his face but imagine the slow smile in his eyes and on his lips.

After the others leave, Pedro rolls another joint. His graceful fingers balance the cigarette paper and crumbled leaves, then manipulate the mass into a tube. He speaks without looking up. "You going to stand there showing off your long legs or will you sit down and join me?"

I settle onto the log, barely close enough to Pedro for the joint to pass between us. Even that seems too tight.

He strikes a match on the rough wood between his legs. In the flare, I see his eyes study me. "I'm not going to yell at you if that's what you're scared of. I guess you had enough of that at the meeting."

"You were right." He hands me the joint and when I inhale I realize how tense my body is, my insides knotted up so that I can barely breathe. "I was wrong about the missionary. I don't know what I was thinking when I said all those things at the last meeting." I exhale with a cough.

Pedro inhales, studies the joint between his fingers for a good half minute, then takes another hit before he hands it off to me. "Why did you just stand there and let him say those things to you?"

"It doesn't do any good to argue with a crazy person."

Pedro snorts. His features are dark against the glow of the ocean. "I thought that you were turning the other cheek."

"If I did, he'd probably hit me there, too."

Pedro barks a quick laugh. "He probably wouldn't pick up on the biblical allusion either."

Suddenly, I'm very tired and very stoned. I sigh. Pedro finishes the joint, then flips it toward the sound of the surf. There's a glow in the east: the moon will be up soon.

When I speak, my voice is a little girl's whisper. "I don't understand why he hates me so much."

Pedro laughs, not a happy laugh. "You sound even stupider now than when you were preaching universal love at the meeting last week."

I hug my arms to my chest. "You're mean."

"He hates you because you're beautiful. Any fool can see that."

"So he hates all women who are good-looking?" I can't bring myself to say that I am beautiful.

"No. He just hates you because you are a beautiful, blond, white woman. That gives you power. You could go anywhere in the world and stand up and talk nonsense and people would pay attention to you because you're blond and beautiful."

"That's not true." I use my little girl whisper again, but haltingly because I am afraid of what Pedro says.

"You know it is. Why do you think everyone here likes you so much? Why do you think that Iris gave you that blouse? She knew it would look good on you—better than it would ever look on her. And everyone would notice it—they did, didn't they? Why do you think women and children want to touch you all the time?"

"I don't know."

"Because you're beautiful."

I expect him to say more but he doesn't. We're silent for a moment, then I feel the need to speak even though I can predict exactly what Pedro is going to say, even though I'm certain that his response will hurt me. "The women and children want to touch me. What do the men want?"

He tilts his head and twists his lips into a smile. "If you have to ask that, you're even stupider than I thought you were."

"And you, *anai*—what do you want from me?"

He rolls another joint before he answers. When he strikes the match, his face becomes a map of light and shadow. "I have two balls like every other man on this island."

I refuse the joint when he offers it to me. Pedro shrugs and takes another hit. "You pouting because I'm telling you the truth?"

This time I accept the weed, and hold the smoke in my lungs until I think I'm about to explode. "So the missionary wants to screw me."

In the red glow of the lit joint, Pedro's lips stretch. "Probably. But it wouldn't be pleasant. It wouldn't be as nice as if I did you."

"Then why does he call me names and yell at me?"

Pedro mashes the glowing tip of the joint on the palm log before he speaks. "Listen, you don't know these kinds of people. All of the missionaries at the school were like this guy. They don't care about love or sex or anything that normal people care about. All they think about is counting souls and converting sinners.

"So this *evangelico* comes here to gather up all of our wayward souls. He's short and ugly and can barely speak Spanish. Everyone laughs at him. Then he sees you and immediately thinks one thing: power. He sees the way that people on the island respect you. He knows that if you help him, he can gather up all of the godless heathens here—at least the ones who are worthy, not the incorrigibles like Litos and Iris and me—and bring them into his holy flock.

"But you won't have anything to do with him and when you say that, he feels the others turn against him too. So he needs to diffuse your power. He has to convince the Kunas that you are unworthy. He figures they'll respect him then, for being the first to see through to your evil soul. That's why he says all those things about you."

"And he won't stop saying them, will he?"

"Mateo and Ologuippa have kicked him off the island for now. But he'll be back. Those kind never give up."

"And he'll still hate me."

"He'll do anything he can to turn the community against you."

As I stare out over the ocean, a sliver of the moon cracks the eastern horizon. The concentrated light seems to intensify the darkness that surrounds us.

"When I was young," Pedro begins. I turn to him and see moonlight in his eyes, making them appear milk-white and blind. "I used to dream about being beautiful. I thought the world would be perfect if I was beautiful."

"But not now?"

"You have power when you're beautiful but you also become an object, something for people to use. There are men on this island who would use your beauty."

"They want to have sex with me?"

He waves his hand impatiently. "People like Mateo and Eulogio. Anselmo too. They want your power."

"You're telling me not to trust them?"

"You do what you want." His voice is flat, final. I feel his eyes bore through me though I know that from where I sit I am only a shadow to him. "Are you too stoned to find your way back to the mainland tonight?"

"I'll be careful," I whisper, and swallow hard.

XII

Above the canopy of jungle trees, the pair of crested eagles soars in formation, measuring the pale morning sky. Their ghost-gray bodies glide without effort, without a single flick of those huge, archaic wings. Through the binocular lenses, I bring the black-scarred faces into focus and discover that the eyes are trained straight ahead. Oblivious to the earth-bound creatures below—creatures imprisoned by chaotic vegetation, by gravity, by their own fear and lack of ambition, by this makeshift blind of canvas and dead branches—the eagles soar until they disappear into the thick clouds that cloak the crest of the San Blas Mountains.

Bolt upright in the blind, I recite by memory every one of Hamlet's soliloquies, then Tennyson's "Ulysses" and Eliot's "The Love Song of J. Alfred Prufrock." I flex and point my toes a hundred counts. I bite—hard—on the inside of my cheek. When all else fails, I plant my hands palm down on the stool and sit square on top of them. But no matter how I try to distract myself, I can't stop my fingers from clawing at my burning, itching hide.

I'm guessing that what's deviling me are chiggers, parasitic insects that crawl inside clothing to find the warmest, fleshiest places on a human body. This batch seems especially fond of the groin area. Once they've located a promising site, the chiggers set up housekeeping inside the host's skin: burrowing out little nests, laying eggs and raising their families. The itching that this domestic activity produces is overwhelming—far worse than mosquito bites or poison ivy—but when scratched the welts burn as hot as the missionary's promised hell fire.

I must have adopted these little bastards yesterday afternoon when I got bored by the inactivity at the blind and took off to explore the other side of the river. The eagles have flown the coop. I had assumed that their spectacular aerial display of a few days ago was a prelude to mating, but ever since that gliding flight when they vanished into the mist I haven't seen hide nor hair of them. I try to convince myself that this is a good thing, that the departure of the cresteds will open the nest again to harpies, but the fact remains that at this moment there are no eagles in the nest. I have nothing to observe. I have nothing to do all day except remind myself not to scratch those pox-like welts that fester over every inch of my body.

I abandon work in the lazy mid-afternoon heat and head down to the river for a soak. The cool water alleviates some of my misery and reminds me of one of Reilly's jungle cures: he claimed that the best way to get rid of chiggers is to burn them out. Reilly used the lit end of a cigar but most people prefer hot—almost boiling—water.

I'm so eager to try something—anything!—to get rid of this infernal itching that I break a sweat as I climb up the ridge. The increased warmth excites the chiggers in my skin to a frenzy. I bite my cheek until I taste blood but still can't keep my fingers from digging at the welts. At camp, I divert myself by building a fire and then I fill my battered aluminum pot with water. I crawl into my tent, find a clean bandana to use as a compress, and strip naked.

Back at the fire, I dip one corner of the bandana into the boiling water and immediately press the hot fabric into the welts at my groin. Stifling a yelp of pain, I count: "One thousand one, one thousand two." I make it to twenty before the burn stings so much that I have to pull away the bandana. I repeat the process on those same bites to make sure that the chiggers inside are sufficiently parboiled. Three down, a thousand more to go.

I work along either side of my groin, then start on the bites at my waist. If I don't think and move automatically, the rhythm helps me ignore the pain. As sweat slides down my back, I pray that Reilly wasn't bullshitting when he told me about this cure.

Facing the fire, I am bending forward, my back to my tent and the trail, when I hear a voice—a male voice—call out, "*Na—*"

The greeting ends abruptly and I spin around in time to see a black head disappear behind the tent. My first impulse is to call out but pride instantly overrides: I am stark naked and covered head to toe with welted chigger bites. Whoever came to visit me must be halfway to the beach by now, running as fast as those short Kuna legs will carry him. His vision of my naked rump undoubtedly will be the butt of conversation in every household on Sugatupu tonight, and for many nights to come.

I plunk my itchy rear down on my only piece of furniture: the smooth log in front of the fire. Last Saturday night when the preacher was cussing me, I thought that I had reached the nadir, that I could never possibly be more miserable. Apparently I was mistaken. Along with my name, my history, and my personal comfort, I now have relinquished any semblance of pride or dignity.

I want to cry but instead I laugh. I laugh until my body shakes, until I can no longer sit but fall to the ground and curl in a fetal position. I roll in the dust and laugh until trails of sweat and tears add stripes to the red polka dots that already adorn my burning white skin.

By sunset, I've applied hot compresses to all of the bites that I can reach. I feel as exhausted as if I've spent the past hour making love. I almost convince myself that the urge to itch is gone, but I know that tonight my sleepless mind will be focused on keeping my fingernails away from those welts. Abruptly chilled, I throw a handful of sticks on the fire and crawl into my tent to dress.

The last rays of golden sunlight bathe the ridge when I emerge. I sit near the fire, too tired to eat, too uncomfortable to sleep, and too stupid to have packed anything to read. What was I thinking: that I would spend eight hours a day sleeping and the other sixteen studying birds? I open Ridgely's *Birds of Panama* and, for the thousandth time, read Alexander Wetmore's one-page foreword.

A pop—loud, like the report of a varmint gun—makes me jump. I cast my eyes away from the fire into the surrounding twilight. After the abrupt appearance of that man in camp my nerves, already irritated by the chiggers, flare at anything, even a stick that explodes in the fire with a shower of sparks. I stare at the yellow flame for a minute, turn the page, and begin to read Robert Ridgely's introduction. "The Republic of Panama comprises an area of 75,648 square kilometers—"

The evening bird songs begin. I share camp with an owl—never seen, only heard: his voice a nasal and repetitive "blah, blah, blah, blah, blah, blah." An osprey flies along the coast with his series of brief, ascending whistles. Nighthawks wake with chirps and chatter. In the distance, I hear the song of a tinamou, the bird Ceferino spoke to on the nest that evening in the jungle. The tinamou's rich, quavering notes are the most beautiful sound that I have heard in Panama. The first note is clear and steady, the second slides down the scale with a slight, hesitant hitch. A tinamou sings every evening somewhere in the jungle, and every evening I wonder if it is the same individual that sings. I picture the subtle colors of the bird, cryptic and almost invisible among the understory plants, the feathers on the breast pressed low to hide the brilliant blue of the eggs.

The song sounds again in the distance and then the sweet, plaintive notes rise from below the ridge, somewhere very near. I've never heard a tinamou so close to my camp: Ridgely says that they are shy birds of the deep jungle. But there's the song again, those two clear notes indicating that the singer has settled somewhere just below the hill, perhaps crouched on the trail that leads up to my camp.

I stand and step away from the fire, cock my head to listen. My mouth is open, my breath soundless. I'm barely breathing anyway: waiting, concentrating, the fragile image of the bird like a ghost in my mind. When the notes sound again, they are startling in their fullness and clarity. I set the book on the log and tiptoe to the other side of my tent.

With every step out of camp, my eyes search the dry mud of the trail and the tangle of weeds beside it. I'm so intent and focused that when the bulk of a man rises in front of me, my heart stops and I trip backwards with surprise. The man grabs hold of my shoulders before I can fall. I look into his face and recognize the doctor, Ceferino.

I want to tell him that he startled me, to explain that I was expecting a tinamou, but I'm not sure that he understands Spanish and don't want to embarrass him. I decide to use the standard Kuna greeting: "*Na.*"

He doesn't answer with words: instead he purses his lips and whistles the two notes that drew me from camp. He still holds my shoulders.

I smile and nod. I'm not sure what to do next: apparently he called me from camp for some reason but I can't for the life of me imagine what that reason might be. His movements almost a dance, Ceferino turns me around until I face the direction from where I came. With his hand on my arm, he leads me up the trail.

At the top of the ridge, he releases my arm and wordlessly follows me to the log in front of the fire. He wears maybe the same clothes he had on the last time I saw him, the white t-shirt a little dingy, a string bag like a field hand's slung over his shoulder. Pausing at the fire, he crouches to examine the pot and sniff the steam.

The silence between us has grown into something so ponderous I feel compelled to speak. "It's water."

He glances at me, then studies the pot again, a self-contained smile on his lips. When he rises, he takes a few steps toward the log so that we stand face to face, closer than most Americans would find comfortable. I notice that the string bag on his hip bulges with leaves.

Without a word, he sinks to his knees at my feet. The movement is startling and inexplicable and I don't know if I'm supposed to follow his lead or remain standing. Once he's on his knees, Ceferino seems to forget about me. He lifts the string bag over his head and sets it against the log, then rummages through the leaves inside until he finds a coke bottle, half-full of dark liquid and sealed by a banana leaf tied with a vine.

The bottle in hand, Ceferino raises his eyes so that he can look at my face. His actions have me almost as nervous as when he talked to the snake on the trail but his smile is so kind that I feel I should trust him. When he finally speaks, his Spanish pronunciation is flawless. "*Con permiso.*"

The phrase is a polite term, a way to ask a person's pardon. Literally, it translates to "with your permission." The kneeling doctor holds my gaze, the outside corners of his eyes creased by his smile, apparently waiting for my response. I decide to trust his eyes. "*Eh-yea.*"

His hand is very gentle: he doesn't touch my skin but still my stomach jumps when his fingers reach for the part of my body that's directly in front of his face. He unbuttons the waistband of my pants and zips down my fly. I fight a sudden urge to urinate. Ceferino spreads open the front of my khakis—fortunately, the pants are tight enough so that the waistband balances on my hips instead of sliding down my legs. When I dressed after the hot water treatment, I deliberately left off my panties, reasoning that the lack of pressure from the elastic would soothe the inflamed bites on my groin. Exposed, the upper tufts of my pubic hair curl from my open fly.

I try to keep as still as possible, hardly breathing, crazy with fear that the slightest movement might dislodge my pants and expose even more of me to his face, which isn't more than six inches from my crotch. He fusses with the Coke bottle, untying the vine and pulling off the banana leaf, then pours some green liquid—it's thick, almost gelatinous—onto his fingertips.

"*Con permiso,*" he murmurs again, but doesn't wait for my response. About twenty bites have been exposed along my waist. Ceferino's fingers massage the oily gel into them. As soon as the ointment comes in contact with the welts, my skin becomes cool and soothed.

"Is that better?"

The relief from the itching is so sweet that my throat clogs with tears. "*Eh-yea. Nuedi.*"

When he removes his hand from my stomach, I shiver.

He ties the banana leaf back over the mouth of the bottle. "This is for the others." Again, the Spanish words are pronounced with a perfect accent. Their arrangement, however, is just a little disordered, making the sentence seem stilted and awkward.

"*Nuedi.* Thank you."

Before he stands, he conscientiously re-zips my pants and buttons the waistband.

As he's lifting the string bag back over his head, I belatedly remember the first rule of Kuna etiquette. "Would you like something to eat or drink?"

His smile crinkles the edges of his eyes. "Hot water?"

"No, no." After the man practically undressed me a minute ago, I don't know why I'm embarrassed now. "I have some bananas."

"Bananas," he muses as if considering. "Litos calls you a little dog, but in town you buy so many bananas that I think you must be a little monkey."

I wish I could laugh but my hands are suddenly so big that I can't figure out what to do with them.

"You need to take care of the rest of those bites. I will eat bananas with you another time. *Panni malo.*"

"*Panni malo*?"

"*Panni malo*. Until tomorrow, little monkey."

The green liquid smells earthy and clean, and during my blessed sleep I dream of monkeys.

I'm so hungry in the morning that I open a can of beans and try to eat them cold. Halfway through, I remember the bellyaches that made my first month here so miserable. I dump the rest of the beans in the fire pit and settle for a banana. Remembering Ceferino's *panni malo,* I prepare a huge batch of the corn and chocolate gruel. I've been experimenting with a solar oven, jerry-rigged with a black plastic garbage bag and some aluminum pie plates that I found in a wooden crate labeled "Harpy Eagle Project." The plates focus the sun and the plastic concentrates the heat on my cooking pot. If I set up the stove in the morning, my meal usually is cooked by the time I get back from the day's work. I leave for the blind confident that I will be prepared for any company that might turn up at my camp this afternoon.

Still no sign of the eagles. To kill time, I unearth my money jar and count my stash. I am amazed to discover that I own over a thousand dollars—probably more than the sum of all the cash on Sugatupu. I wonder what kind of good time Ruiz could show me for a thousand dollars, if he'd find anyone as delicious as Brian's chocolate milk mama for me. If Brian had that much money, he probably would have abandoned the project entirely. Or Mateo—if he had a thousand one-dollar bills, he might buck himself right into the cemetery on the other side of the river.

I stuff my wad back inside the jar. Without a watch or a calendar, I've been losing track of time. Near the equator, every day seems identical to the one that preceded it, to the one that will follow. Mornings are sweet and warm, afternoons cloudy, hot, and humid. The path of the sun through the sky does not vary, unlike home where every day is a different sunset as the seasons and the sky shift. I remember how confused I was when I first arrived in Panama, accustomed to warm summer days that stretched sixteen or seventeen hours. When the sun slid beneath the steaming horizon at 6:30 sharp, I was convinced that my watch had stopped.

The empty work day finally ends. At the river, I inventory my chigger bites and discover that they are barely visible, my skin smooth and the welts receding. I dress carefully, donning a bra just in case Doctor Ceferino decides that he needs to check on the progress of his cure.

I haven't even started to climb the ridge when I hear male voices coming from my camp. Curious but more than a little apprehensive, I consider scurrying back to the river and hiding there until dark. The memory of Ceferino's dancing black eyes convinces me to brave whatever and whoever I may find on the ridge.

When I crest the hill and get my first view of the clearing, I barely recognize my camp: it's been transformed into a construction zone. The ridge top is now dominated by a wooden frame roughly the size of Pedro's hut on the point. Piles of building materials—bamboo poles, sturdy logs, thatching for a roof—are scattered throughout the rest of the clearing. Several men mill around the site in the organized chaos of work.

I recognize Orestes first: impossible to overlook his massive torso. Over one of his wide shoulders, he drags a log toward the rudimentary frame. Eulogio and a man I don't know brace a support upright against the roof joists while another man balances overhead on the cross beam and lashes the log to the frame with vines. Using a machete, a fifth man hacks at the ends of bamboo poles.

Eulogio notices me almost immediately. He shouts something to the man on the roof joint: I imagine, "Get your butt in gear and tie that thing off!" The man on the roof responds with a laugh and by his smile I recognize Ceferino.

When the post is finally secured, Eulogio strides toward me, brushing dirt from his hands and the front of what appears to be an impeccably clean shirt. A broad smile makes his face even more handsome. "You like it?"

For a moment I'm speechless. "This is for me?"

"Of course."

"My God, this is incredible. It's beautiful. I can't believe it."

"We were all thinking that it's not right for you to live in a little cloth cave that you can't even stand up in, sleeping on the ground. It's not safe."

The man who was helping Eulogio now holds one side of the center pole, Orestes opposite, as Ceferino ties it to the frame.

"This is the nicest thing anyone has ever done for me."

By the way Eulogio stands, I half-expect him to put his arm around my waist and give me a hug. "You need a real house. A *nega*."

"*Nega* is house?"

"A Kuna house. Not like ones in the city. They're just houses."

Ceferino must have finished attaching the center pole because Orestes comes to join us. For an instant, Eulogio's face registers annoyance but he greets the other man with a few words in Kuna.

"*Nuedi*, Orestes, *nuedi*," I say. "*Mil gracias.*"

He mumbles something in Kuna to Eulogio and I realize that the beefy secretary is actually shy. The only times I've seen him have been in his official capacity where he appears as imposing as his physical presence, self-assured and in control.

To ease the moment I ask him, "Who are the others?"

Orestes points to the man with the machete. "Esquivel is married to Pedro's sister. Raul"—who at the moment is passing bundles of thatch up to Ceferino—"runs the store next to the meeting house. And Ceferino is Eulogio's brother."

"They don't speak Spanish," Eulogio adds. I wonder if he denies his brother's language skills in order to emphasize his own, or if he thinks Ceferino's Spanish is too limited to acknowledge.

I ask, "Is there anything I can do to help?"

Both men burst out laughing as if what I said is the most preposterous thing they have ever heard.

"You just sit in the shade and relax." I think I detect a patronizing note in Eulogio's voice. "We'll be done for today in about"—he consults his watch with an official air—"two hours or so. Then we'll finish up tomorrow."

"Well, thank you again so much. *Nuedi, nuedi.*"

Orestes goes to help Raul with the thatch, but Eulogio makes a show of escorting me to a shady spot under a palm tree and arranges a seat from the stub of a log. I feel awkward sitting alone once Eulogio leaves. He works with Pedro's relative, Esquivel, measuring each bamboo stick against the others and hacking them to length accordingly. Both men stand in the full glare of the afternoon sun. After a few minutes, Eulogio pauses to squint up at the sky. He straightens and with what seems a casual motion, grabs the hem of his white polo shirt and stretches his arms over his head, pulling off the shirt in the process.

The movement makes me realize that, even though various body parts are often displayed through holes in their clothing, I have never seen a Kuna man without a shirt. I have the distinct impression that Eulogio's gesture was executed entirely for my benefit. Since he has gone through so much effort to display his upper torso, I figure that the only polite thing for me to do is sit back and appreciate the scenery.

The scenery is remarkably attractive. Eulogio's chest, while not as massive as Orestes's, is well proportioned and extremely male. His skin is absolutely smooth, without a scar or blemish or blush. Not one hair to be found anywhere on it. His two dark nipples are tight and erect as if he's only just emerged from a cold bath. I suppress a shiver when I think of another reason his nipples would be erect, when I remember the length of his body pressed against mine in the skin-baring water of the ocean. Reilly's experiments with dung beetle hormones stab into my mind and I feel my face burn. When I look up, I see Ceferino grinning at me from the crossbeams of the roof.

A few minutes later, Orestes decides that he, too, feels the heat, so off pops his shirt. The two other men on the ground soon follow suit. Every time I glance at Ceferino, he's laughing so hard that he seems in danger of falling off the roof.

Before my hormones have a chance to get totally out of control, I remember my solar oven and the corn and chocolate gruel. Under the black plastic, the pot is so hot that I have to use my bandana as an oven mitt. I scrounge through my makeshift kitchen to find enough jars and mugs for everyone. When I hand Orestes a mug of the gruel, he accidentally slides his fingers over mine. He blushes deeply and whispers, "*Nuedi.*" The two men I didn't know before are equally shy: they won't even meet my eyes. But Eulogio smiles broadly and cups his hands around the mug as he brings it to his nose to sniff. "How did you cook this without a fire?"

I grin at him. "Magic."

Eulogio samples the gruel. "You cook well with magic."

"Irina taught me how to cook."

"Did she also teach you the magic?"

"What do you think?"

"I think I need to learn more about your magic."

The men on the ground—all shirtless—retire to the shade, sipping from their cups and talking among themselves. I fill my final mug and stand under the half-finished roof, calling up to Ceferino, "You look like a monkey climbing around up there."

He glances down at me with a grin.

"I've got something for you to drink if you want to take a break."

"Hot water?"

"Better. And no bananas in it, either."

He crawls like a spider to the beam directly over my head, then lies on his belly with his legs wrapped around the pole. From this position, he could rest his hand on my head.

"*Nuedi,*" he says as he reaches down for the cup.

"You don't have to stay up there. You can come down and take a break."

His eyes dance the way they did in town when the women were teaching me how to tie my skirt. "You would laugh at this skinny monkey."

"Why would I laugh at you?"

"Because if I come down, I will have to take off my shirt like the others. And you will laugh because I am so skinny I look like a monkey."

"You're the one laughing at me. Every time I look at you, you laugh at me."

"I haven't made a sound."

"You laugh with your eyes. You're doing it now."

"I'm not laughing. I'm just wondering why a monkey like you didn't put bananas in this drink."

"But you are the monkey today."

"*Eh-yea.* You are right. I am a monkey. You are a paca." A paca is a jungle rodent whose Spanish name—painted rabbit—refers to its fawn-like, mottled coloring.

"Why am I a paca?"

Ceferino hands down the empty cup. "I have to get back to work. The boss is coming." I glance over my shoulder and see that Eulogio has risen and is making a show of stretching the muscles in his shoulders and chest.

"Ceferino, why do you say that I'm a paca?"

With perfect balance, he stands upright on the narrow beam, tight-ropes a few steps to the cross-bar, and then turns back to me with a laugh. "Because only a paca could have as many spots as I saw on your ass last night."

XIII

I lower the field glasses, lower my gaze to the open book in my lap, to the detailed comparative sketches of a crested eagle (light phase, adult) and a harpy eagle (adult) that appear on page 104 of Ridgely's *Birds of Panama*. The harpy is shown in profile, his roman nose of a beak huge and threatening, while the crested's face is as delicate as a falcon's. The black and white drawing diagrams differences so extreme that any confusion between the two species could only be the result of inexperience on the part of the observer, or stupidity.

I raise the binoculars again. The eagles have returned—at least one of them—and she is brooding on the nest. Her face juts fiercely from the rubble of sticks in the crotch of the Maria tree. I fiddle with the focus on the binoculars, hoping to clarify the shape of the beak, the number of feathers in the topknot, the shading of the plumage around the bird's neck. The powerful lens provides just enough detail to frustrate.

The eagle on the nest appears to be an amalgamation of the two species pictured in Ridgely's diagram: a perfect blending, a hybrid. The instant I convince myself that the live bird is definitely a crested, shimmering heat morphs the single topknot into a double pointed crown. My eyes flick down to the illustration and a shift in posture causes the eagle's neck plumage to darken into a contrasting collar.

I stare through field glasses at what now appears to be a harpy eagle and question—not for the first time—my powers of observation, my years of ornithological research, my master's degree, my sanity. What is real? A harpy eagle has appeared on the nest. She is brooding. The eggs will hatch. I will record every detail of the nestling phase, the fledging, and the eventual adulthood. My research will result in a groundbreaking paper on the ecology and life cycle of harpy eagles; but when the TV cameras arrive at the blind they will find only a few broken egg shells, an abandoned nest, and a faint trail of boot tracks leading to the lip of the waterfall.

In the clearing around my new *nega*, an overcast sky has brought early darkness. My soup of tubers and coconut is well-cooked and steams from the solar oven but still I build a squaw fire. I am not cold but crave company. By the yellow light of the flames, I review my notes from almost two months of observation and wonder what value these pages could hold for anyone. My monthly report is due soon. I imagine the almost imperceptible jerk of David's head as he motions me into his office. "How could you have accepted this position when you knew that you were grossly unqualified for the job? Do you realize how seriously your ignorance and lies have compromised the research?"

The research: it should be my god. I should worship at the altar of science. If I were true to my study, I would scribble an immediate note to David confessing my doubts, my incompetence, my stupidity. I would prostrate myself on the dung heap of my failure, expose my uncertainty to the ridicule of true believers. And through contrition and penance, the research would be redeemed.

But the missionary is right: I am a whore. I will compose my report to David carefully, the wording deliberate in its ambiguity. I will describe the process of nest modification, the mating ritual, and date the beginning of the brooding period, but I will never mention by name the species that I observe. My subjects are eagles. Any more precise identification exists only in the mind of the reader.

I tear a sheet of paper out of my spiral notebook and pick up my pen. "Dear Mom and Dad."

Is today Thanksgiving? No, today's Friday so that means yesterday was Thanksgiving. I'll date this letter from yesterday—

November 27—so they'll think that I remembered them on the holiday.

"I miss you all very much and hope that you are enjoying a wonderful Thanksgiving together. How is Diane's baby? I can't wait to hear news and see pictures of my new niece or nephew. You should have a lively Christmas this year with so many grandchildren coming to visit!

"I am fine. The weather here is hot—as usual—but the rains have slacked off so my clothes are finally drying. I thought that they would rot from being wet so long! Now some days I even get to see the sun which is a mixed blessing since it makes everything much hotter."

My hands are sweating—I rub them on my thighs to dry. The spiral notebook serves as my desk as I sit on the log with the nearly blank sheet of paper angled to gather light from the fire. "A couple of weeks ago, the wife of the Indian chief gave me a cooking lesson. Mom, I'm sure you can imagine what a disaster that was! Everyone was laughing so hard they could hardly swallow the food—although I don't think my cooking was as bad as it used to be at home! I'm eating lots of coconut here and things like potatoes and rice, and lots and lots of bananas!"

It's cold in Montana now, and dark. Maybe tonight my parents—alone since Jill married over the summer—have built a fire in the fireplace. Dad reads. Mom knits. The wind rattles the front door. Mom glances up, sees her reflection in the blackness of the window, a white rime of frost around the edge. She sighs and turns her face toward the fire, watches the flames finger and twist above the furrowed bark of the quartered cottonwood log.

I bend my face back to the paper, read over the words that I have written. My pen poised, I can think of nothing else to say. Distracted, I glance into the darkness on the other side of the fire.

A man stands in front of the door to my *nega*.

I drop my pen and notebook and jump to my feet. The loose page of my letter catches the updraft from the fire and floats lazily back and forth like a pendulum. An instant before the paper describes its final arc into the flames, the man, who has been as frozen as me, lunges abruptly into motion and snatches the letter in midair. As he hands me the paper, I recognize Eulogio. He fusses over me, gathering up my notebook and pen, apologizing. He almost touches my arm: the motion draws up a split second before he makes contact with my shirt sleeve. "I'm sorry," he repeats.

"It's okay." My breathing doesn't want to return to normal after the scare. "You surprised me. I wasn't expecting anyone to be here."

"You were writing?" He holds my notebook, open, in his hand.

"A letter." I don't know why I'm embarrassed to have him see what I wrote.

"I can read." I can't tell if his words express pride or a challenge.

"It's to my parents." He's studying the writing. "It's in English."

"Your parents speak English?"

"*Eh-yea*. That's the only language they know." I'm wondering why he is here, on the mainland, after dark. We face each other awkwardly.

"It is difficult to learn another language."

"You speak Spanish very well. Where did you learn it?"

"In Panama City." He sits down on the log in front of the fire.

"You lived there?"

"A couple of years. I was working."

He seems to be establishing himself in my camp. I'm not sure how welcome I should make him at this time of night. I settle on the log an arm's length away from him. "Did you like the city?"

He thinks for a moment before he replies. "There were many different people there: whites, blacks, Chinese. I liked all the different people. There are different people where you are from?"

"Not like in Panama. I'm from a little town and it's mostly just whites there. And Indians."

"Indians? North American Indians with feathers?"

"*Eh-yea*. My brother's wife is part Indian."

"Really?" Eulogio appears totally astonished, as if I'd just told him that my mother was from the moon.

Abruptly, he looks up and meets my eyes. "You are okay?" As he did the day the missionary hit me, he uses the American word, "okay."

"*Eh-yea.* Why?"

"When you didn't come to the meeting tonight, everyone was worried. We thought you might be sick or hurt."

"The meeting? The meeting was on Friday this week?"

"Today is Saturday," Eulogio says with a smile.

"Oh my god—I can't believe I'm so stupid." I cover my face with my hands.

He does touch me now, a whisper on my upper arm. I barely feel the pressure of his fingers through my shirt sleeve, but a quiver of electricity tingles inside of me from the closeness of his skin.

"You are not stupid. It's hard to keep track of time when you're alone."

I glance at the man beside me and in the fire his expression is so intimate that my breath catches in my throat. I rise abruptly.

"Where are you going?"

"To the meeting. I'm supposed to be there now, right?"

Eulogio's handsome face breaks into a smile. I try not to look at his eyes again. "Sit down. You don't have to go to the island tonight."

"I thought I was supposed to be there every Saturday."

He pats the log beside him invitingly but when I sit I am farther from him than before. "The meeting isn't important tonight. They're just talking about repairing the runway—there's a big crack in it and the pilots are complaining. The community is trying to figure out how to get money to repair it."

"But I'm supposed to be there, right?"

"The only reason they want you to be at the meeting is so that they know you're not sick or hurt."

I must look astonished because he continues. "When Flemming said that he wanted to live in the jungle to study eagles, we all thought he was crazy. It's dangerous in the jungle for anyone, especially a fat white man who doesn't know what he's doing. We were worried that something would happen to him, that he'd get sick or hurt and wouldn't know how to take care of himself. So Mateo said it would be best if we told the white people living in the jungle to come to one of our meetings every week. That way we'd be able to keep track of them and know if they needed help."

"And that's the reason you came here tonight—to check on me because I didn't show up at the meeting?"

"*Eh-yea.*"

I'm still uncomfortablc about the intimacy I saw or imagined in Eulogio's face. I stare at the fire. "So did the other researchers go to the meetings every Saturday?"

Eulogio snorts—I'm not sure if he's expressing disdain or chuckling. "Flemming lived mostly on the island with Iris. Sometimes he never even left his hammock."

"He didn't go to the blind?"

"He didn't do much of anything except—" Eulogio pauses here and I feel his next words are carefully chosen—"lie in the hammock with Iris. He got money from Panama and paid for food with that. He didn't go to the meetings but we knew he was well—he made enough noise when he—" He stops abruptly. I can't help myself and glance over at him. This time it's his body, the casual physicality of a man, that pulses inside me like a current.

I speak quickly to distract myself. "And the other?"

"Brian?" The dislike in his voice is obvious. "He was always off with Ruiz on his boat. A *pajaro*." *Pajaro* is the Spanish word for bird.

"A *pajaro*?"

Eulogio shifts as if he's uncomfortable. "A man who likes other men. Like Litos."

"Ruiz also?"

He rolls his eyes at my question but doesn't respond.

"So Brian didn't go to the meetings either?"

"Sometimes. Then he complained that we were stealing things from him."

"That's what he told me, too."

"You believed him?"

I hear a challenge behind the measured words, something strong and hostile, and realize how alone I am in the jungle here with this man. I shiver.

"You are cold?" Eulogio asks in his halting, careful Spanish.

"*Sully.* No."

The conversation stalls. After almost a minute of silence, Eulogio shifts on the log, then asks me: "Your parents live in the town where you were raised?"

"*Eh-yea.*"

"And when you lived there, you knew all of the people around you?"

"It was like Sugatupu. Everyone knew everyone else."

"You knew the men in your town and none of them wanted to marry you?"

"*Sully*. No one ever asked me to marry him."

Eulogio digests this information for several moments as he stares into the fire. His voice is abrupt when he speaks again. "The wife of my brother died two years ago."

"Ceferino? His wife?"

"*Eh-yea.*"

"How did it happen?"

"After she gave birth to a son, she didn't stop bleeding. No one could stop it."

I wonder if Ceferino loved her, if he still grieves. "Did the son live?"

"*Eh-yea*. Ceferino has two sons."

"Who takes care of them?"

"His mother-in-law. Ceferino lives with his in-laws. His father-in-law broke his leg and the bone never healed right so he can't work. Ceferino works for them."

"That's nice of him."

I'm thinking of Ceferino's smile when Eulogio's next words break into my thoughts. "You don't want to have children?"

The question is so naked that I need a moment to frame my response. "I—I guess I always figured that I would have to find a man first."

"I don't understand why you would have to look for a man. I would think that they would come to you. The men in your country must all be crazy."

The fire has burned down to coals. I toss on a couple of sticks to brighten the flame. "Well, you've met one of them. The *evangelico*."

"And all of the men in your country are like him?"

"Some are like Flemming, and others are like Brian."

"Now I understand why you are here."

A twig burns with a blue flame. Everything else is embers. I turn my head to face Eulogio but can't make out his features in the darkness. "I'm here to study the eagles."

Eulogio's teeth flash white. "Of course. You are here to study eagles."

XIV

I meet the air taxi in an early morning drizzle, a manila envelope tucked under my shirt to protect the inked address from the rain. Along with my monthly update on the project and a letter to my family, the envelope contains $50 and a note to Reilly asking him to pick up a present for my parents in Panama City. He's heading back to the U.S. for Christmas. Since I always assumed that like his dung beetles Reilly crawled out from under a rock somewhere, the notion that he might actually have a family inspires novel, at times frightening, images in my mind.

The air taxi pilot—not the sweet, diminutive kid from my flight a couple of months ago but a surly older man—cusses in Spanish at no one in particular as he rummages through freight in the cargo hold. When he emerges with a suitcase-sized box that has my name scrawled across the front, I want to throw my arms around his sweaty neck and kiss him.

I can barely wait until I'm in the blind to rip open the package. Before I slit the tape with my penknife, I check the eagle through the binoculars to make sure that nothing has happened at the nest during the night. The mother's stoic face, fierce and proud and resolute, points toward the ocean, the same direction she gazed when I closed down the blind last night. As far as I know, this eagle has not left the Maria tree, not eaten or drunk, since she began brooding the eggs a week ago.

I bite my lip, pick up my notebook, scribble the date—December 1—and SOS—same old shit. The cardboard carton dominates the floor in front of my stool. I lower myself to my knees, close my eyes, and inhale. In my imagination, I smell spruce trees.

At the mouth of the box is the mandatory envelope from David. A curt note: he found a way to cash the check I received from the U.S., something about independent research last May and June. He's including that money along with my month's wages and stipend. The project's funding has been renewed for the next two years. An end-of-the-year summary is due January 1. Best wishes for a happy holiday.

Clipped to David's note is another sheet of paper. I scan the university letterhead and skim to the signature: Dr. Roger Flemming. He's thanking me for the sacrifice I'm making in the interest of science, encouraging me to persevere despite the hardships of field work, holding himself up as an example of what can be accomplished through hard work and determination. "And a very merry Christmas to you—and to all of my Indian friends in the village!" No mention of Iris or the two little girls.

At the bottom of the envelope is a thick wad of bills—at least David had the sense to send nothing bigger than a twenty, but how in the blue hell can I be expected to dispose of over eight hundred dollars in the middle of the jungle?

The carton contains two smaller boxes, one—my heart jumps into my throat when I recognize the handwriting on the address—from home. The other box is unlabeled, a mystery. I open that one first. Inside is a roll of toilet paper, a box of tampons, and a Christmas card featuring Santa in a union suit with the trap door open, his bare pink behind filling half the face of the card. "Checking it twice." Reilly's signature is scrawled across Santa's rear. I can't decide if Reilly's gifts are disgustingly crass or sweetly considerate: the stores on Sugatupu stock neither of these two essentials.

The box from home, wrapped in heavy brown paper, is weighty with promise. I cut the tape at the corners so that the paper unfolds complete and intact. When I glimpse what's inside the box, a convulsive shudder tightens my muscles. I hug my arms against my heart to still my shaking, to keep loneliness from overcoming me.

In the blackness behind my closed eyelids, the contents of my mother's box dance: bright presents swathed with images of pine trees and snowmen and reindeer, the ribbons and bows crushed from the transit. On top is a card picturing the nativity: Mary and Joseph on their knees, the baby Jesus so well-formed and beautiful He couldn't possibly be newborn.

I open the card. Love from all. They hope that I am well. They know I am working hard, they are proud of their adventurous daughter and trust that I won't be too lonely this year over Christmas. Diane had a baby girl on October 27—they named her Erin. Dad doesn't like the name but Mom thinks it's pretty. Jill is expecting already, due sometime in May.

More news: Dad got the snow plough contract. Weather's been unseasonably cold. There was a big accident on the highline, five Indians killed. Lucia the cat died in her sleep, poor thing. She was over fifteen and had had a good life. Aunt Ruth says hi.

Mom is a master at this: empty news and vacant chatter. When I was in high school the sound of my mother's voice—a teacher's precise and measured cadence—used to set my teeth on edge. I vowed that every word I spoke in my life would be important, that I would never subject myself or others to idle babble. I had never been alone in those days, never known how silence can transform a single word—no matter how trivial—into a lifeline.

Before I leave the blind, I load the unopened Christmas presents from home back into the packing carton, along with the tampons and toilet paper and letters. I unearth the money jar and stuff in the wad of bills that David sent, setting aside a handful of twenties to take with me to the island.

It must be dinnertime in the village—when I beach my canoe at the point Pedro is nowhere to be found—but I think I know the community well enough now to navigate the maze of streets by myself. I give my wrap skirt an extra twist to make sure it's tight, straighten my headscarf, and set out for the far end of the island.

Was Iris expecting me? Her father is home today, with deep eyes and a tired face. And her beautiful mother—with Iris, the house holds two beautiful mothers, each too young for the role she plays. Why in God's name did this delicate young woman shack up with that pig Flemming? The family sets a plastic lawn chair under the low overhang that provides the only shade in their yard. As soon as I sit, they push a cup of banana soup into my hand.

"*Maskunne*," they say to me. I think they're telling me to eat.

I swallow a mouthful of soup and nod. "*Nuedi.*" Everyone smiles. Iris's older girl, Katrina Maria, crawls into my lap. Litos materializes out of the low sun like a smiling, skinny wraith. He touches my shoulder and whispers in my ear, "They say that you are much too thin. That you do not eat enough."

I swell my stomach with air, then make a show of patting the bulge. Katrina Maria squeals with laughter. I have to drink another cup of banana soup before Iris will accept three twenty-dollar bills from me.

On the street, Litos walks with me in silence until we are out of the family's sight. Then he abruptly stops and places one hand on each of my shoulders, squaring me in front of him. He stares at my face until I meet his eyes. "*Perrita*, what is wrong?"

"I'm so stupid I forgot to keep track of the days and missed the meeting."

"No *Perrita*, not Saturday. Today. You've been crying."

"It's nothing, Litos. I got a letter from home in the mail and I'm just a little sad—they're so far away."

He pulls me to his bony chest. "Ah, *Perrita*, you are so alone out there on the mainland. You should come to town more often. I will comb your hair and hold your hand and we can talk and laugh like old friends."

"Thank you, Litos. That would be nice. You are a good friend, *anai*."

"I wanted to go to you on Saturday to make sure that you were all right, but I was afraid. The mainland is dangerous, especially at night. Nobody wants to be there after dark except Ceferino. He was going to check on you Saturday but then Eulogio said that he should go because his Spanish is better."

"Thank you Litos, for thinking of me. I appreciate everything that you do. Everyone on the island is so good to me. I'm sorry I make problems by being so stupid."

"I don't think Eulogio minded at all that he got to sit with you alone in the dark."

"What about Eulogio's wife?"

Litos laughs. "She has a present for you. We will see her later, I'm sure."

We stop at Raul's store near the meeting house and I pick up supplies. I ask Litos to tell the man that I appreciate the *nega* he helped build for me. Raul, like most Kuna men, is so shy that he will not meet my eyes. I again wonder about Pedro's report that all the men on the island are hot for my body.

"*Perrita*, you picked a good day to come to the island. The *evangelico* is gone to the mainland."

"To the mainland? Why?"

Litos laughs—affected, like a girl. "We only hope to bathe and wash his clothes. His smell is now much louder than his voice."

"That must be awful! Does he have a boat?"

"He borrowed one. Everyone wanted to get rid of him. Everyone is hoping that he bathes. Now you will come to my house and I will comb your hair?"

"First, Litos, I have to see Orestes."

"Orestes?"

"On business."

"I will take you there and while you are doing business with him, I will take your food to your boat."

"*Nuedi, anai.*"

"For you, *Achugoa,* I would do anything."

"*Achugoa?*"

"*Perrita. Achugoa* is *perrita*. And here is Orestes's *nega, Achugoa*."

Orestes's astonishingly beautiful wife greets me with a smile. Her husband is away but she sends someone scurrying off to find him. Again I'm given a chair in the shade and fed banana soup. At my feet, a small boy plays with a broken flip-flop, pretending it is a boat, while a withered, gray-haired woman watches with glazed eyes. She's dressed only in a length of skirt fabric wrapped around her like a bath towel.

When he appears, Orestes is flanked by the older man with the cataracts—I think Litos said his name is Anselmo. The man's cloudy eyes seem cold when they meet mine.

Confronted with the two town officials, my resolution falters. "I'm sorry about last Saturday. I made a lot of problems for people."

Orestes waves his hand—I wonder if he picked up that gesture in Panama City along with his Spanish. "It's nothing. Eulogio explained it to us. Don't worry about it."

"But people on Sugatupu have done a lot for me, building me a house and looking after me and all. It must be a pain to have this stupid white person to worry about all the time."

Orestes betrays a hint of a smile. The other continues to stare at me with his almost white eyes.

"Eulogio told me that the meeting I missed was about the airstrip, that it needs to be repaired. I want to give the community money to help pay for the materials."

Orestes waves his hand again. "You don't have to do that."

"You didn't have to build me a *nega*, either. But you did."

Orestes exchanges a couple of sentences with the other man, who shakes his head and motions toward the mainland with his chin. The beefy secretary shrugs and says one word. With a grunt, the older man abruptly turns and walks away.

Orestes shakes his head as he watches him leave. "We'll have to talk to Mateo about this. He's at home now, I think. Come with me."

When we pass the dock, the missionary is tying a canoe to a post. Orestes glares at him and mutters "*waga*" under his breath.

Mateo is not home but Irina greets me with an embrace and another cup of banana soup and another throne, this one an intricately carved stool under the mango tree. When Mateo arrives, I'm struck again by his energy: his face seems ancient but his gait and gestures are those of a vigorous young man.

Orestes and Mateo argue in Kuna for what seems like several minutes. Irina smiles and nods every time I look at her. Finally, Orestes addresses me in Spanish: "Mateo says that you are a guest in our community. You don't have to pay us."

"It's a gift. To help with expenses like the airstrip repair, or if there are orphans or old people who can't work, or kids who want to go to school on another island."

Orestes translates.

Before the two men can crank up another argument, I continue. "We have a saying in our country: 'Fish and visitors smell after three days.'"

Orestes gives a shout of laughter. He looks different when he smiles, smaller and less imposing.

I add, "I don't want people on Sugatupu thinking that I smell like an old fish."

Orestes grins as he translates and when he finishes, Mateo also laughs. Orestes says to me, "One stinking white person on Sugatupu is enough."

When he holds out his hand to take the money, the gesture seems awkward. Because the Kuna skirt I wear has no pockets, I have been carrying the money folded tight in my fist. The bills are damp from sweat. Both men's eyes bulge when they realize how much I'm giving them.

Mateo recovers first. "*Nuedi.*" He says the word only once, simply and gracefully, and I can almost forget the image of him dangling dollar bills in front of all the pretty young Kuna wives.

Orestes insists on escorting me back to the point, I assume to ward off a possible assault by the missionary. We're almost to the mangroves when I hear a sharp "whit!" like a catcall. Orestes turns to look back. Behind us is a group of six or seven women, all young, all giggling with their hands in front of their faces like a bunch of high school girls at a sock hop. I recognize Orestes's wife: she darts her eyes to my face but every time she meets my gaze she dissolves into helpless laughter.

The women act as shy as the men, exchanging nudges as if they dare each other to take the lead. I glance at Orestes but all I see in his face is a slow smile of pride as he watches his beautiful wife. The way the women jockey and feign, I wonder if they will ever get up enough courage to address me.

Finally one woman, taller than the others and with a proud, intelligent face, steps forward. As she approaches, I see her straighten her back as if she's trying to bring herself up to my height. She seems ready to deliver a speech, but then I meet her eyes and her serious veneer crumbles into such a fit of giggles that she hides behind her headscarf. When she raises her hands, I notice that she is carrying something that looks like a magazine: on the folded front page, I make out the glossy photo of a sports car. Orestes's wife shoves the tall woman from behind and she stumbles into me. I catch her and she slips the magazine into my hand, then scurries back to join the others.

Orestes says something in Kuna and all six women respond at once, each with different words.

The tall woman hushes the others and begins her speech, but then she glances at me out of the corner of her eye and laughs too hard to finish.

"This is Disrelita, Eulogio's wife. That's a present from her," Orestes explains.

I look down at the glossy paper in my hand. Below the photo of the car is a grid titled "*Noviembre*," and I realize that what I had assumed to be a magazine is actually a calendar. When I flip to the next month, I see that every Saturday in December has been highlighted with a bright red circle.

XV

During the blackest part of the night, a whining drone intrudes into my dreams. The sound becomes identifiable as it increases: a plane flying so low that, now fully awake, I worry about the thatching on the roof of my *nega*. After one quick pass overhead, the buzz fades. I imagine the pilot banking out over the silver sea, wagging his wings as he climbs toward the stars.

In anticipation of Ruiz's visit, I mash three extra bananas and arrange my solar oven to slow-cook a soup. I now think of my morning walk through the farmland as a commute, my hours in the blind as work. My job here is most like my stints as a waitress in that activity accounts for only a small fraction of my day. The majority of my time in the blind I am restless and bored, distracting myself with busy work while I wait for something—anything—to happen.

Today the male eagle brings a half-eaten sloth to the nest. When presented with the limp bundle of hair and bones, the mother becomes more animated than I have seen her since she began brooding. As soon as the male retires to a separate tree—he's shown absolutely no interest in the eggs—the female attacks the sloth as if it were still alive. She tears at it with her talons and beak, she shakes it, at one point she even lifts the entire carcass into the air and then impales it on an upright branch. Her actions are painful for me to watch: they seem senselessly violent. The sloth is long dead. My only explanation is that the female is venting the excess energy and frustration from her idle days of brooding—she's got to be just as bored sitting on those eggs as I am watching her.

Finally, mercifully, the mother eagle exhausts her fury and settles down to eat what remains of the sloth. Her beak and talons are bright red from blood. She tears slabs of flesh from the carcass and gulps them down whole. Once, she gags on a chunk so big that she is forced to retch the entire wad—a part of the skull?—up from her craw.

Later, when I leave the blind under cover of dusk, I creep to the base of the nest tree and locate the fresh, discarded remains of the sloth. The eagles have left no bone unbroken.

By pale moonlight, I bathe quickly. I expect that Ruiz is waiting for me. On the hike up the ridge, I finger the twenty-dollar bill in my pocket and rehearse imaginary conversations. My voice seems foreign to me as I mutter the English words: "Hello." "Don't touch me there." "Holy shit!"

I crest the ridge and the glow of Ruiz's fire makes the twilight seem as dense as a memory. I announce myself—"Hello, Handsome"—and Ruiz bounds over to sweep me into the circle of pallid light. He spins as he crushes me against his body. We're both laughing. I rub my face into his chest and smell garlic.

When he sets me back on my feet, Ruiz slides his hands across my t-shirt, cupping my breasts with his palms as he plays his thumbs across my nipples. "Yum," he murmurs, licking his lips. "I must visit your country soon. I hear that none of the women in the U.S. wear bras."

"You might not like what you see, Ruiz. Some women really need to wear a bra."

"Yes, but if even a quarter of them—just an eighth of them—have breasts like yours"—

"Do men's nipples get hard when they're excited?"

"How would I know?"

"From what I hear, you're an expert in the field of male sexual response."

Ruiz's face is as expressive as a clown's. "What do you mean by that?"

"Just something someone told me." I turn away from him demurely.

He spins me around by the shoulder. "The Kunas said something, right?"

"It's not like my social sphere encompasses a whole lot of other people."

He nuzzles the top of my head with his cheek. His stubble is scratchy.

"So why do they think that you're a—how did he put it—a *pajaro*?"

"Is that the word they use for faggot?" He's got his arm around my waist and shepherds me toward the fire. With the toe of his dirty canvas shoe, he pokes at a burlap bag. "Look, I brought you a present: crabs!"

"The last time a man gave me crabs, I had to go to the health clinic because they itched so bad."

Ruiz's face falls. "You are allergic to crabs?"

"Not the kind you eat—a different kind. These are great. But tell me, why do the Kunas think that you're a *pajaro*?"

"Probably because I will not poke their women. And I suppose it is because of Litos, also. It is a long story. I will tell it to you after we eat. I wanted to have the crabs ready when you got here but could not find a pot to boil them in."

"My pot's out back," I say over my shoulder as I head for the solar oven. I try to ignore the implication that Ruiz was snooping around my camp looking for a pot, in the same way I ignore the gun barrel I feel on the outside of his thigh when he hugs me.

He flicks on his flashlight and follows me. "How can you see in the dark?"

"You get used to it." I pull the black plastic away from the aluminum pot. The metal is almost too hot to hold.

"What is that?" His voice sounds suspicious.

"Banana soup. It's good."

"You are eating Kuna food now?"

"Ceferino says that I eat so many bananas I must be a monkey."

"You have a tail hidden somewhere inside those pants?" His hand is a little too familiar as it explores my rump.

I twist out of his reach. "Don't touch me there."

Ruiz makes a show of crossing his wrists behind his back. "You do look a whole lot healthier these days—you were half-starved the last time I saw you."

I shudder. "Too many of Brian's beans."

"But this is hot. How did you cook it when you were not here?"

"With the sun, a reflector oven. They taught us about these in girl scouts but I never thought I'd find a use for one. You can even use them to bake bread."

He examines the pie plates with his flashlight. "You really are an amazing lady."

"You're just saying that because you want to grope my breasts again."

"Can I?"

"I'm starving, Ruiz. Let's get dinner ready."

When Ruiz pulls the crabs—there are three of them—out from the burlap sack, he makes an elaborate show of one pinching his hand although I think the animals are long dead. I pour the banana soup into two mugs, then rinse out the pot and fill it with water to boil. Ruiz hefts the burlap bag. As he lifts it off the ground, it's obvious that something's still inside.

He burrows his upper body into the sack, then pantomimes astonishment when he emerges with a fifth of rum. "How did that get in there?"

I laugh. I discover that banana soup tastes even better when seasoned with *añejo* rum.

"How do you like my *nega*?"

Ruiz adds another shot of rum to my mug. "They just came here and built it for you?"

"Eulogio said they built it because it's dangerous for me to sleep on the ground."

"They have a lot of superstitions like that, especially about the jungle."

"You think that's why they won't call me by my name?"

Ruiz sits back so that he can look at my face. "I forgot about that."

"I haven't. You don't know what it's like—like I'm so insignificant that I'm not even worth naming. Like I'm not a real person."

"For some reason they do not want anyone to know your name. Pedro made me swear that I would never ask you what it is."

"Pedro," I grumble.

"He is nowhere near us tonight. Forget about him and smile at me instead. I brought you a housewarming present."

"Really? What is it?"

"I will give it to you after we eat." His arm is wrapped around my waist and I lean into his shoulder as we sit on the log.

"You want a tour of my *nega*?"

"I went inside to look for a pot." I'm glad he admits this.

"It's pretty nice, isn't it?"

"What are those presents in the corners?"

"They're from home. My parents sent them for Christmas." I sit up straight. "That reminds me: could you do me a big favor?"

"For a beautiful lady, I would do anything. What do you need?"

"I want to get some Christmas presents for Iris and her girls. Just little things—maybe a stuffed toy for each of the girls and something pretty like a necklace for Iris."

"And you will say they are from Flemming?"

I place my palm on his hairy chest. "Please?"

"I said that I would do anything for you. I will not do anything for Flemming."

I pull the money out of my pocket. "I'll pay you, of course."

Ruiz jumps up so quickly that he spills the rest of my bananas and rum. He stands with both his hands palm forward as if to form a barrier between us. "This is not about money. It is about you paying for something that asshole Flemming did."

I'm too startled by his abrupt change to answer. A few moments pass but Ruiz does not relax. He towers over me, his face harsh in the shadowed light of the fire.

I find my voice. "You're right—Flemming is an asshole. But Iris isn't, and those two baby girls aren't, either. I'm not doing this to get Flemming off the hook. I'm doing it for Iris and her girls."

Ruiz's shoulders slump and he lowers his arms from their defensive position. Bending forward, he cups my chin with both his big hands. "You are a very, very good woman and I am not worthy to lick your feet. Of course I will buy the things you ask me for."

"Take this money."

"I will not take your money."

When he sits down on the log and pulls me against him, I slip the $20 into his pocket.

"So tell me"—his arm encircles my shoulders so that the tip of his index finger brushes my nipple—"how are you going to celebrate Christmas?"

"I have to stay here."

Ruiz's hand jerks from my breast and grabs my shoulder. "You have to stay in the jungle for Christmas?"

"Where else would I go?" My voice is timid again—his grip on my shoulder hurts.

"Flemming is making you stay here all alone on Christmas?"

"I have to watch the eagles—they're brooding now and the chicks could hatch any time. It's important."

"But you cannot spend Christmas all alone here. It is obscene!"

"It's my job."

His voice becomes tender. "No, no, no, no, no, no. You are not going to spend Christmas day alone. I will take you to my house in Santa Marta. I swear that I will not touch you—I have an extra bedroom that you will use. I will buy you a dress as blue as your eyes and we will go to midnight Mass at the church, then we will dance in the plaza for the rest of the night and all of the next day."

"What about the eagles?"

"They will survive a couple of days without you."

"But the study!" I realize how hollow these words sound as soon as I say them.

"Forget the study! You are a beautiful young woman. You deserve a beautiful Christmas. You think that Brian and Flemming were slaves to the eagles?"

"Brian and Flemming were slackers. I want to be better than either of them."

"You already are better than both of them, *Perrita*. That is what Litos calls you, right? *Perrita*?"

"Last time he called me *Achugoa*. He said that means *Perrita* in Kuna."

Ruiz throws back his head and laughs. "You see, you do have a name. They even translated it into Kuna for you. That means they like you a lot."

"Pedro says that the only reason the Kunas like me is because I'm pretty."

"Pedro is a cynical old pissant."

"So you think they like me for other reasons?" I hear myself saying this like a vulnerable little girl.

"We must eat now. The crabs are ready and we need food in our bellies to soak up all this rum."

After we polish off the crabs and the rum, I feel sleepy. The fire is down to coals, a red glow of shadows. I lean into Ruiz.

"Tired?" he asks.

"Mmm."

"I need to get up."

Through half-closed eyes, I watch the glow of his white pants at the edge of the clearing. When he turns away from the fire, I hear the "zrup" of his fly. I close my eyes.

"Wake up, my love." His voice is a whisper, his face lit by the flame of an oil lamp as his big body crouches beside me. "This is for you, for those long nights when you do not have Ruiz at your side to amuse you."

He carefully hands me the lamp. I set it on the ground and throw my arms around his neck. "Oh Ruiz, thank you. *Mil, mil gracias*." My face is so close to his that when I lean forward our mouths meet. His lips are full and sensual. Tonight, he keeps his tongue to himself.

Too soon, he pulls away. "That is enough of that, *Perrita*. You will make Ruiz forget that he is a gentleman."

"You're a *pajaro*, remember? You promised to tell me that story about Litos."

"First you have to tell me why you are so curious about the nipples of men."

I'm hoping that the darkness hides my blush. "Oh, I sit by myself all day in the blind. Sometimes I get bored watching the eagles and think about all kinds of things."

"You are not a very good liar, you know. Even by the light of this little lamp, I can see that you are lying."

"It's not polite to look that close at people."

"I will tell you about Litos but only if you first tell me the truth about your interest in men's nipples."

"I guess that's fair." In the weak firelight, I notice that a few of Ruiz's chest hairs are gray. I wonder how old he is.

"Well?"

"I'm sorry. I got distracted by your hairy chest. Kunas don't have hair there."

"You speak from experience?"

"When they built my *nega*, all of the men took off their shirts."

"And their nipples were hard?"

"Not all of them. Just one," I murmur.

"So which Kuna man had tight nipples because he knew you were looking at him?"

"I shouldn't tell you."

"You should tell me everything. What man on the island lusts after you?"

"Eulogio," I whisper.

Ruiz whistles. "I should have guessed."

"You won't tell anyone?"

"It is a small island. I imagine everyone knows already."

"Even his wife?"

"I am sure that she is accustomed to it by now."

"You're saying that Eulogio—"

"That is none of your business. Let me tell the story I promised you about Litos."

"Mmm." I close my eyes and snuggle against him.

"You will not fall asleep?"

"I won't. I promise."

"Litos was living in Barranquilla when I first arrived there about ten years ago. He was—I guess you would say he was a mistress to one of the big *politicos* in the area, a guy with a whole lot of power. When Litos found out that I worked the coast, he started giving me things—money and presents—to take to Sugatupu. I found out later that he was supporting his parents the whole time he was in Colombia. Anyway, about a year ago something happened—I never could follow the politics down there—and Litos's boyfriend got into trouble. When that happens in Colombia, they do not just vote you out of office."

I'm afraid to ask. "What do they do?"

Ruiz points his index finger to the side of his head and mimics a gun.

"That night, I was getting ready to leave and Litos showed up at the dock. He was hurt very bad. Those kind of guys, they do not last long on the streets—all of the punks in the area want to beat them just to show how *macho* they are. I got Litos on board my boat but the next morning I saw that he was a lot worse than I had thought. He was very weak and also coughing up blood. I wanted to take him to the hospital in Cartagenia but Litos said no, that there was a doctor on his island who knew how to take care of Kuna problems."

"Ceferino?"

Ruiz nods. "I did not think that Litos would live to get to Sugatupu, but I left him there and the next time I came through he appeared to have completely recovered."

"Litos told me once that he has a broken heart."

"He is a good man, one of my best friends. If that makes the Kunas think that I am a faggot, I guess that is their problem."

We're silent for a while, then Ruiz sits up straight. "I almost forgot the most important part of your housewarming gift." From the shadows behind the log he pulls out two paperback books. "The last time I saw you, you said that you were bored. I thought that these might help."

"Oh Ruiz, you're so sweet."

"I hope that you can read Spanish."

"Better than I speak it."

"I like your Spanish. It is so soft it sounds like every word you say is a question, but your accent is perfect. Most Americans have terrible accents."

"Like the *evangelico*?"

"You need to watch out for that guy. On Usdup, there was a lot of talk about him. There are two towns on Usdup and they kept sending the *evangelico* back and forth between them because no one wanted him near their women. I think that man is more dangerous than anyone on Sugatupu realizes."

"So now you're warning me about the missionary. A few days ago, Eulogio warned me about you. And Pedro's warned me about Eulogio."

"And the missionary warned you about Pedro," Ruiz says softly. "They all are right. You should not trust any of us. In the jungle, no man is what he pretends to be."

XVI

As I haul my canoe through the knee-deep water off the point, Pedro's words bring me to a stop. "Litos won't be at the meeting tonight."

I straighten but still have to lift my chin to look at him, high and dry on the sand under a palm. "Why not?"

"He's sick." Pedro folds his arms across his chest and eyes my skirt as if the seam gapes open.

"Can I see him?"

"No."

By the tone of his voice, I can tell that he's trying to intimidate me. I drag my dugout out of the water and climb onto the beach so that I am able to stand next to him, looking down. "Can I at least send him a note?"

Pedro sighs heavily. "He's sick. He shouldn't be disturbed."

I soften my tone to a wheedle. "A little note won't bother him. Please?" Since Pedro doesn't turn away, I assume he's relented. "And can I borrow a piece of paper? And a pen?"

He mutters under his breath—I can't tell what language—and shoots me a dirty look, then turns and stalks toward the abandoned hut.

I sit on the palm log to write, a spiral-bound notebook in my lap.

"Don't take too long." Pedro's arms are again tight across his chest. "We can't be late for the meeting tonight."

His disapproving presence makes me self-conscious and my mind is suddenly blank. I'm not even sure that Litos can read. I sketch a big cartoon heart and in the center add a jagged line like a crack. Along the crack, I place a series of short, perpendicular slashes, the last connected to a longer, wavy thread that ends with a pointed needle. I want the picture to represent a broken heart being sewn together but I'm not sure that my artwork is good enough. On the bottom of the page I write "I love you, Litos" and sign it "*Achugoa*—your *Perrita*."

"That looks like something a kid would draw," Pedro sneers.

"You're really mean sometimes. Do you know that?"

In town, he finds a boy to take the note to Litos—or at least I hope that's what he tells the kid to do.

"One good thing—we won't have to listen to the missionary tonight."

"Why not?"

"He's decided to hold prayer services every Saturday night. I don't know who he expects to come to them since the meeting's going on at the same time. Mateo and Ologuippa were glad to get rid of him even though it's a direct challenge to their authority."

"Is he really that stupid?"

"Of course he's that stupid," Pedro snaps. "He's stupid and crazy. All of the trouble in the world comes from people like him: stupid, crazy people." He doesn't wait for me to respond but turns and disappears through the door of the meeting house.

Iris and her two daughters have already settled at our usual place near the center of the hall. When she sees me, Katrina Maria jumps up on to the bench. I lift her into my arms, relishing her warm weightiness and her little-girl smell.

Even as people arrange themselves through the hall, I become aware that Mateo is talking. Or maybe talking isn't the best word for what's coming out of his mouth: chanting, singing, or melodic mumbling. After he drones out a handful of syllables, his sidekick, the old guy in the other hammock, hums a response, something like "wee-oh" with a marked drop in tone at the end so that the sound segues into the next sentence that Mateo has already begun. The two voices overlap and intermingle: sometimes they merge into a single sound and I wonder which of the old timers is actually doing the singing. Neither appears to move his lips or expend any energy. The monotonous chant is the complete opposite of the emphatic, almost violent rhythms that characterize normal Kuna conversation.

The chanting becomes louder as the community assembles. The Coleman lanterns are lit. A few women sew, others breastfeed. Katrina Maria dozes in my lap, thumb in mouth. Under the hypnotic spell of the droning voices, I feel my body relax, my muscles loosen. The past week has been difficult: I worry too much about the project, about eagle identification, about home and the missionary and men in general. And then Pedro gives me a hard time at the point this afternoon: sometimes he seems to want to hurt me just for spite. I miss Litos. If he were here now, he would tell me what this ritual is all about. The sound is really very soothing. The rhythm reminds me of Ceferino's hands when he spread that goop on my belly and massaged it in. I don't see Ceferino anywhere on the benches—maybe he's with Litos. I hope that he's with him. I hope that Litos is not alone. I hope he's not in pain. That was a sad story Ruiz told about Litos, about his broken heart. I hope Litos is strong enough to survive whatever's wrong with him. Ceferino will help him. He will bring green goop out from that string bag and rub it into Litos's heart. That will make him all better again so that the next time I see him, he will laugh like a girl and call me "*Achugoa*" and play with my hair while he whispers in my ear.

A shout from the back of the room knifes through my thoughts. I realize that I have been dozing. Katrina Maria is fast asleep. Her little hand—so clean, not even any dirt under those tiny fingernails—rests on my right breast. I wonder what it would be like to nurse a baby. Would the teeth be sharp and bite like a puppy's? Or would the feeling be more sensual, like when Ruiz played with my nipples the other night by the fire?

Another shout. I straighten my back and bite my lip.

After the chanting Anselmo, the guy with the cataracts takes the stage for a long speech. His cadence is less musical than Mateo's, basically a low, toneless mumble. For a while I listen to see if I can pick out any of the handful of Kuna words I recognize, but I don't hear any. I try to appear interested.

Pedro escorts me back to the point when the meeting is over. The moon already hangs low over the mountains on the mainland.

"On Tuesday we'll be having an *inna* here on the island."

"An *inna*?"

"It's the ceremony when a girl is introduced to the community. It's an important part of Kuna culture."

"On Tuesday?"

"Tuesday, Wednesday, and Thursday. Three days."

"And am I supposed to be on the island those days, or stay away?"

Pedro stops walking and I see him study me in the moonlight. "Sometimes," his voice is too casual for the expression on his face, "I can't tell if you are really, really smart or really, really stupid."

I shrug my shoulders and continue through the mangroves toward the point. "And which am I being now?"

"You should stay off the island those days. And be careful. A lot happens during an *inna*."

"And that's all you're going to tell me, right?"

"That's all I'm going to tell you, *anai*."

"Well maybe, *anai*, you can tell me why I'm the only person around here who doesn't have a name. I'm just 'you' to everyone, except when Litos calls me *Perrita* and that pisses you off. Everyone talks about Brian and Flemming and uses their names. So why won't anyone use mine?"

Pedro continues walking as if I haven't spoken.

"You're not going to answer me, are you?"

"No."

"Why not?"

He doesn't break stride and he doesn't turn toward me. "Because you have no right to demand anything from me."

"How about if I ask you as a friend? *Anai*?"

"If you were a friend, you wouldn't ask." He bends to push my canoe into the water, then holds it steady while I wade out and step in.

I settle onto the low seat. "In other words, sit down and shut up."

Pedro smiles, the first time I've seen his teeth by tonight's moon. "You got it, *Perrita*."

Sunday morning: the ninth day on the nest for the brooding eagle. Today the male brings her another sloth, this one apparently still alive. After a couple minutes, I can no longer watch as the female tortures the poor creature. Sloths are pathetic things anyway, so inoffensive and helpless that I feel an ache of pity every time I see one. They are natural victims, like the new kid at school who showed up with a fleshy pink hearing aid clipped to his ear. God must be a sadist; he must get pleasure out of creating life just to watch it suffer. I think of Litos and those damn *macho* punks who beat him and whisper a prayer for the broken heart of my poor friend.

At dusk in the doorway of my *nega*, I discover two small sacks of grain, a couple hands of bananas, and a chocolate pod. A piece of paper is tucked between the sacks and when I unfold it, I recognize Pedro's firm, precise handwriting. I squat on my haunches to read but as my eyes sweep down the page, my vision becomes blurred and unfocused. The paper shakes in my hands. I swallow and come back to the top of the page, to the four stark words in the first sentence of Pedro's note: "Litos died this morning."

XVII

In the days that follow a choking mass lodges in my throat, midway between my heart and my tongue. Every time I close my eyes I feel the whisper of Litos's breath in my ear, the soft tug of his fingers in my hair. I see his knobby knees and elbows, his ribs washboarding under his thin cotton shirt, the flapping tangle of his skirt.

I never said goodbye to him. That last time I saw him, I got involved with business, with Orestes and Mateo and the money for the community. My best friend died and I never told him goodbye.

In his letter, Pedro details a multitude of taboos for me to observe. Everyone in the community is in mourning, he says, so I should stay away from the island. As an outsider, I am forbidden to enter the cemetery until after the burial. For the next three nights, I am not to go outside after dark. "Stay inside your *nega* with the door securely latched," Pedro commands.

By day, I sit in the blind and never move from the stool and the field glasses but I don't see much because my eyes can't seem to focus. I work at working. I convince myself that I am accomplishing something but in my field notes I enter only the date and three letters: SOS.

I don't eat. I lie in the dark in my *nega* and shake. I light Ruiz's lamp and try to read but cannot concentrate. I kneel on the dirt floor and pray that wherever Litos is now, he is not in pain. I think of his heart torn open by those brutal punks who beat him. Litos was dying when he met me but he was kind to me. He felt my pain—so minor compared to what throbbed inside his own chest—and the pieces of his broken heart were generous enough to name me when no other would: *Perrita,*

Achugoa. I lean forward so that my forehead rests on the packed dirt of the floor, and sob.

After a sleepless night, with red eyes I face the humid yellow glare of a new day. SOS in the blind. My mouth is dry but I do not drink. The sky is washed out, featureless, white. I knock off work early, abandon the blind and the statue-like creature on the nest, hike to the river. I want to wash away my sadness but as soon as I arrive at the bank I remember how Litos retrieved my laundry that one afternoon, comforted me when I was lonely and homesick. I barely have the energy to dress myself after a half-hearted rinse.

At camp, a few hours of daylight remain but I'm too weak to do anything. The walk from the river has exhausted me: all I can do is shiver. I slump on the log with my thighs supporting my elbows and my head cradled in my hands. If my body weren't braced in this manner, everything that's inside of me might bleed out into the packed, raw dirt at my feet.

Gradually, I recover the strength of my sorrow. The shivers become shakes and the shakes become sobs. I remember the way that Litos laughed: so free, like a delighted child. My tears begin to flow and I cry as if these are the first tears that I have shed.

I don't know when I become aware that I am not alone, when the pressure of a hand between my shoulder blades penetrates the wall of my sorrow. The hand is firm, still, and it feels as steady as the trunk of a tree. A thigh appears next to mine, long bones parallel. Two arms tuck me into an embrace.

I recognize Ceferino by his silence. He is absolutely still: the only movement is my gulping sobs. I drag my palms away from my eyes so that I can fist handfuls of his shirt to wipe my face. His body absorbs everything—my shivers and sobs, my tears and snot—but remains unchanged, untouched. He is like the earth. I push my face against him, seeking the source of his peace.

"Listen to my heart," he murmurs.

I press the side of my head into his chest, swallow my wracking gulps so that I can hear. At first, I'm shaking too hard: even when I push against him, I don't hear anything. I bite my lip and swallow a sob, concentrating on the stillness of the two arms that encircle me, of the thigh that braces against my own. When my body quiets, I feel it: the steady, strong "thup/thum" of Ceferino's heart. The rhythm is slow, decisive, defined: a sound so elemental that it seems older than fear or sadness or longing, older than thought. The beat of Ceferino's heart is the sound of life, as solid as the earth, as infinite as the surf.

As I listen, my sobs school themselves to the rhythm of his heart. My tears slow, my breathing becomes less forced and more measured. Eventually, I am able to stop crying altogether. I draw in a deep, shuddering breath. "*Nuedi*," I whisper.

He answers by stroking my arm twice, then he is still.

I don't know how long we sit in silence. I listen to his heart. Once, I nuzzle my face against his shirt, wiping my tears, breathing the smoky, outdoor scent of his skin.

When he finally speaks, his voice is as hoarse as if it were he who had been crying. "The paper you sent made Litos very happy."

I push myself away from his chest so that I can look into his face. "You were with him?"

"*Eh-yea*."

"Did he suffer?"

"He is not suffering now."

I look hard into his black eyes. He does not turn away. "Thank you for not lying to me."

He pulls me back against his chest and does not speak again for several minutes. Finally, he says, "I brought you some food. You must eat."

When I do not answer, he loosens his arms. "You are stronger now?"

"*Eh-yea*," I nod.

He slides away from me so gently that my body is barely aware of his absence. I watch as he arranges a few sticks in the fire pit. He shaves off kindling with his machete, sparks the blade with a small stone that he pulls from his string bag. He blows on the punk to nurse the flame, then feeds the tiny fire with a few more sticks.

I try to ignore the twigs popping in the fire so that I can hear the last evening calls of birds. A few gulls yap along the coast and an osprey soars with ponderous wing beats into the horizon. The smaller song birds have fallen silent, already bedded down against the unseeing night. In the distance, probably along the river, I hear the toneless rattle call of a kingfisher.

Ceferino pauses, his head cocked to the side as he listens. "*Sinna*."

"*Sinna*?"

"The bird of death. My people believe that when *sinna* cries, he is calling the spirit to leave the body and join him."

"Litos's spirit?"

Ceferino centers a small pot over the growing fire. When he glances up, he doesn't look at me but out to sea. "Look. The moon."

At the point where earth and sky meet, the sea has begun to glow. Underneath the lead gray water, the moon's light could be made of a hundred thousand creatures of darkness—bioluminescent fishes and boneless bottom dwellers—that coalesced in the depths and rose through the sea like souls bound for glory. Thick-bodied with life, the moon lies ready to be released from the amniotic ocean.

The whisper of a touch on my wrist pulls me back to the clearing. Ceferino hands me a spoon and the aluminum pot swaddled in a banana leaf. The soup is unpleasantly spicy but I force myself to eat. Ceferino busies himself with the fire. When the flames flare, he adds more twigs, then waits until the fire has burned down to embers. He sprinkles some powder onto the coals. The acrid smoke smells like burning sage.

Abruptly, the ridge is awash with white light. I look to the east and see a thumbnail of the moon above the horizon, silver, so bright it seems to concentrate all of the life and energy of the past day into a single core. Ceferino swings one leg over the log, straddling it so that he can face the rising moon, and slides toward me. He pulls my body tight against his. I would never allow Eulogio to hold me between his legs like this. But Ceferino seems to notice only the moon.

Searching for his heart, I nestle my ear into his shirt. When I locate the rhythm, the beat provides a cadence for the moon's ascent. The moon is not torn from the sea smoothly but with the pulsing thrusts of a woman in labor. The sound is a steady inhale and exhale, the surf, a thup/thum that calms my soul and numbs my mind. Once it's free in the sky, the moon traces a fish-scale path across the now-black sea.

I find my voice. "Where is Litos?"

"He was buried today."

"Not his body. Where is his life, his spirit? With the *sinna* bird?"

Ceferino shifts.

"Please tell me, Ceferino. I miss Litos so much. I just want to know where he is."

"The Kunas believe that everyone has a *purba*."

"And the *purba* lives after a body dies?"

"He stays here on earth for three days." Ceferino's words are slow and measured as if he thinks them through before he speaks. "He will visit his friends and places that he loved. And then, tomorrow morning, he will begin his journey to the next world."

"How does he travel?"

"He has a boat. His *purba* has a boat."

"Is the trip hard? Or dangerous?"

"Sometimes. If a man has been bad in life, the trip can be hard. But Litos was a good man. He will not have any trouble."

"And then he will get to a place where he will be happy?"

"He will be happy there."

"While he is here, those three days, is that why I'm supposed to be inside at night? What if I want to see him before he leaves?"

"That is not good. His *purba* might forget about the journey and decide to stay here instead. Then he will not be happy."

"But his *purba* will visit me before he leaves?"

"A *purba* will visit everyone he knows. The more a *purba* knows about a person, the easier it is for him to find you."

"That's why you are here, and making the fire smoke tonight?"

"*Eh-yea.*"

"Are there many *purbas* who don't travel to the next world?"

"*Eh-yea*. Some are from good men who don't want to leave the people they love. Some are men who died in the jungle or at sea and weren't buried properly, with a boat for their spirit to use. Some are bad men who know that they will not survive the journey so they refuse to take it."

"Where do these *purbas* live?"

"They are all around us."

"Everywhere?"

Ceferino sighs. "You should be in your *nega* now. It is dark."

"Please? Just a little longer?"

"Everything has a *purba*. Not just people but animals. Plants, trees, rocks, and rivers."

"So the world is full of life."

"*Eh-yea*. My people believe that the spirits of the jungle—the *purbakan* of rocks and animals—these are all men. But the jungle trees are women. During the day, the trees are straight and rigid and rough. Their *purbakan* are sleeping deep inside the trunks. But at night the hard shell that confines them falls away and the *purbakan* of the trees reveal themselves. They are naked and smooth and graceful. At night in the jungle, the trees that are women dance in the wind and the moonlight shines silver on their smooth bodies, and the *purbakan* of the trees are very beautiful. At night, they open their fingers and the tips become white flowers so the tree women smell beautiful as they dance in the moonlight. And the restless male *purbakan* trapped between worlds, they see the beautiful tree women and come to the jungle to be with them, to dance with them, to enter their bodies."

"So at night, *purbakan* are all in the jungle?"

"*Eh-yea.*"

"Are they dangerous?"

Ceferino pauses before he answers. "They can be. They want to—they want to get inside a woman. They are excited by all the beautiful, naked tree *purbakan*. Once they get inside, they try to control your *purba* because if they can become a living person, when that body dies they will have another chance at making the journey to the next life."

"How do they get inside a body?"

Ceferino hesitates again. "They enter a woman the way a man enters a woman."

"What about men? Can they get inside of them, too?"

"*Purbakan* can enter a body in many ways. It is easier for them to enter a woman, but they enter men, too."

"But if you stay here tonight, outside, won't the *purbakan* try to get inside of you?"

"I have lived with *purbakan* all my life."

"But I haven't, right? And it's dark now, and dangerous, and I should be in my *nega*."

"*Eh-yea*."

"And you'll be all right out here alone tonight?"

"*Eh-yea*."

"*Nuedi*, Ceferino."

"*Pani malo*." His arms tighten around me, then relax.

"*Pani malo*."

I don't know if my grief has run its course or if Ceferino's company comforted me or maybe it was the soup, but in my hammock, I am asleep before I have time to think.

I dream that I am naked, dancing, my hair curling in vine-like tendrils around my face. When I hold out my hands, the wind pushes against my fingers and they sway as if they move outside my will. My breasts are taut and the moon with its cold light paints my nipples dark blue. My hands, my head, my hair are all wreathed with white flowers, small and fragrant. The scent makes me dizzy, makes my hips circle and flex with a pulse that comes from inside my chest. I sway with the strong, steady rhythm of a heartbeat—thup/thum—as the wind lifts my hair and the musk of my sweat mingles with the perfume of the flowers. My naked skin glows. I become a tree woman, seducing the spirits of the jungle night.

XVIII

The morning stripes through gaps in the bamboo wall of my *nega*. I close my eyes to prolong my waking dream, rubbing my cheek against the thick cotton of the hammock and pretending that it is Ceferino's shirt. I even manufacture the wood-smoky scent of his skin. Fully awake, I inhale and realize that the odor of smoke is too strong to be a product of my imagination.

I hear the crackle of burning sticks and a mutter of voices. I slide out of my hammock, creep to the wall, and peer through one of the more substantial gaps between the uprights. Ceferino crouches in front of a small campfire stirring a pot while his brother sits sprawled on the log. Eulogio speaks softly. Ceferino straightens and walks to the edge of the clearing. I see the string bag in his hands, see him pull out a tin cup. Back at the fire, he dips the cup into the pot, then hands it to his brother. Eulogio continues talking.

I smile. I'm not surprised that Ceferino performs woman's work—cooking and serving—while Eulogio watches. When his wife was alive, did Ceferino relax like a king while she worked?

My observations on the difference between siblings are interrupted by a more compelling sensation, this one originating in my bladder. The door of my *nega* faces the fire pit, making it impossible for me to sneak out for a quick trip to the trees without first addressing the two men in my camp. I dress, hoping to distract my mind from my full bladder but now that I've acknowledged the obvious, my body demands relief. I take a deep breath and open the door.

Eulogio sees me first. "*Na.*"

Ceferino rises, a wooden spoon in his hand.

"*Con permiso,*" I mumble. My face must be beet red. The last thing I see before I bolt for cover in the woods is a faint smile playing across Ceferino's lips.

I linger behind the trees longer than necessary, but when I return to the clearing neither man seems to have noticed my awkward departure. Ceferino hands me my red enamel mug, full of the corn and chocolate gruel. "You are better this morning?" he asks.

Eulogio appears concerned. "You were sick?"

"*Sully.*" I settle onto the log a comfortable distance from both Eulogio and the heat of the fire. "I was just sad."

"But nothing happened last night?"

"*Sully.*" I sip the gruel. Ceferino's recipe is much better than mine.

Ceferino's tone is soft and he speaks to the fire. "Litos has begun his journey now."

At the sound of his voice, I realize that Ceferino is the only one who doesn't have breakfast. "Here." I try to hand him my mug. "You must be hungry this morning. Take mine."

"*Sully, sully.*" He holds his hands palm-forward. "You have to go to work soon. I'll have some later."

"You're leaving to watch the eagles?" The two brothers have totally different faces. Eulogio's, so strikingly handsome, sometimes appears cold and calculating, or maybe it's just the angled light of morning.

"I should leave soon. I like to set up before the sun gets too high."

"Where is the nest?"

"Over the next rise, about three quarters of the way from here to the river."

"In a big tree that stands out from all the others?"

"*Eh-yea.*"

"My father told me about that nest. He said that there have been eagles there since before he was born."

Eulogio's words shame me even more than my bathroom visit to the trees. I never thought to ask the Kunas if they had any information about the eagles. "The eagles have been using that same nest for years?"

"That's what my father said. He was on the mainland a lot when he was younger."

"It's always the same eagles?"

Eulogio says something to Ceferino in Kuna. Ceferino, using the hem of his shirt to protect his hand as he slides the cooking pot off the fire, answers with a handful of words.

Eulogio translates Ceferino's Kuna into Spanish. "The eagles on the nest now have been here for fifteen years. The pair before them was only here six years—the female was killed in the ocean and her mate left the area soon after that."

"But it's always the same kind of eagle?"

Eulogio again consults with Ceferino, who answers with a couple sentences. Eulogio's response is a single word, "*Eh-yea*."

"Do you know how often they raise a new batch of babies? Every year? Every two years?"

After asking Ceferino, Eulogio explains, "Every three years they nest. Always in December or January."

"But the nests aren't always successful, are they? They don't always have babies that survive?"

Eulogio confers with Ceferino and listens to the other's response. "Unless there are late rains or heavy winds, usually one of the babies will live. Last time there were two but the larger one killed the smaller when they were about three months old."

I can't believe I'm getting so much information. "How long are the babies in the nest?"

As Eulogio translates, I wonder why he acts as if Ceferino can't understand my Spanish, especially since we were all talking together just a few minutes ago.

Ceferino answers—in Kuna—and Eulogio translates. "After the eagles lay the eggs, it takes about forty-five days for the chicks to hatch. The babies learn to fly about nine months later but they stay around the nest until they're two-and-a-half years old."

"And then where do they go?" I want to ask Ceferino this directly but it's not my place to interfere with the two brothers.

Eulogio translates. "The eagle that left the nest in August is up the coast near Ailigandi now. Several people have seen it there."

"An eagle just left the nest in August? Brian said that the last nesting lost all of their babies."

Eulogio doesn't translate this but instead asks in Spanish, "You believe him?" I hear contempt behind Eulogio's words.

"I don't know."

"Brian is your friend?" Eulogio's eyes are half-closed and he won't look at me directly.

"I never met him until I got off the plane at the airstrip down here."

"You didn't know him before?" From the position of Eulogio's body, inclined forward with his hands on his knees, I know that my answer is important to him.

I glance at Ceferino. His face is serious, but when our eyes meet he gives me a tiny smile.

"*Sully*. No." I say the word in both languages and shake my head for emphasis.

Ceferino still wears that slight smile on his face. He says in Spanish, "Brian said that he had been inside of you."

When I spring to my feet, I spill most of the remaining gruel. "What?"

Ceferino laughs.

"You were not his lover?" Eulogio is serious.

I try to come up with the most emphatic way to convey my disgust. "I'd rather have my eyes pecked out and fed to baby eagles."

Ceferino laughs again.

"When did Brian say that I was his lover?"

"There was an *inna* ceremony about a week before you arrived." Eulogio has relaxed and seems to be enjoying his gruel.

"And Brian went? Pedro told me that an *inna* is the initiation ceremony for a girl. He said that it's something really important to your culture."

"*Eh-yea.*"

"That doesn't sound like something Brian would want to go to."

Eulogio appears focused on the mug in his hand and again is not meeting my eyes. "Whenever there was an *inna* on the island, Brian went. Flemming also."

"Pedro said that a lot of things happen during an *inna*. He said that it would be best if I stay off the island when there's an *inna* going on."

Ceferino laughs and Eulogio shoots him a haughty look. "Pedro is right."

"So what happens at an *inna*?"

Eulogio hesitates and Ceferino answers for him. "Brian drops his pants and bends over so that everyone sees his ass."

"What? It sounds like he went crazy!"

"At an *inna*, everyone is drunk."

"They get drunk for three days? That's the ceremony?"

"*Eh-yea.*"

"And everyone is drunk?"

"*Eh-yea.*"

"Mateo? Irina?"

"Everyone."

"And you?"

Ceferino smiles broadly but doesn't reply.

"Sounds like fun."

Eulogio says with dignity, "There are many things that happen at an *inna*. The entire history of our people is chanted. And the duties of women are discussed and established."

"But while they're discussing and establishing, everyone's drunk?"

"It's an important part of our culture."

“What happened with the *inna* that was supposed to start on Tuesday? Did they have to cancel it because of the mourning period?”

“It was postponed until Saturday. There won’t be a meeting this Saturday night.”

“Because you’re all going to be drunk.”

“Because we will be observing a very important part of our culture.”

“You’re having a party and I’m not invited.”

Ceferino grins. “Poor little one!”

Eulogio shoots him another dirty look. “The last time, when Brian did that act, everyone on the island was very angry because they thought that he had insulted the community.”

“And you’re afraid that I might insult your community the same way?”

Ceferino lets out a bark of surprised laughter. Eulogio leans back and studies me, a slow smile spreading across his face. By the way he catches his lower lip under his teeth, I can tell that he is forming a mental image of my potential insult, and that anger is nowhere near the reaction that this vision provokes.

XIX

The quiet out here is driving me crazy. The *inna* started yesterday morning and today the mainland is so deserted I feel that I'm the only person on the face of the earth. I didn't realize how accustomed I'd grown to the presence of Kunas nearby: the daily traffic on the river and in the farmlands, the Saturday night meetings, and my occasional jaunts to the island. This silence wears on me like a churchless Sunday morning. I keep thinking that I should feel free, remote from any obligations, but instead I'm consumed by a vague hunger that has nothing to do with food.

I know that I am better off sober in the blind than drunk on the island. I'm so lonely now there's no telling what I would do if I were to let my guard down around the Kunas. Litos was a good safety valve: I could relish his physical contact without getting myself into trouble. Since he's gone, I'll have to be content with Katrina Maria—funny how a child's touch on my breast, the weight of her body against mine, can be as gratifying to me these days as sex. If I were to be caressed by a man right now, I'd probably explode from all those dung beetle hormones that Reilly is so eagerly cataloging, all of the longing that's grown like a fatherless fetus inside my soul.

I bite my lip to focus my attention on the eagle in the nest. The male brought another sloth to the brooding female this morning and now, sated, she dozes. I train the field glasses to the precisely patterned head that juts out from the nest. In my lap, Ridgely's field guide flops open to the well-worn page that features the harpy and crested eagle comparisons.

The information that I received from Ceferino and Eulogio has only further clouded my understanding of the eagles. I still cannot reconcile the harpy eagle sketch in *Birds of Panama* with the pair at the Maria tree. From what I see, the eagle on the nest is not a harpy—at least not by Ridgely's definition. But then, who is Ridgely? A Princeton boy who bragged in his introduction that he first came to Panama during a stint with the military: a former army grunt!

Flemming, on the other hand, is the world's foremost authority on avian raptors. He's chair at one of the most prestigious universities in the United States, his ground-breaking research in eagle behavior recognized throughout the world. All of his unsavory personal features aside, he's considered the ultimate source for information on terrestrial eagles. If Flemming says that this is a harpy eagle nest, it's not for me or Robert Ridgely or anyone else to question the identification of the inhabitants of the nest.

According to Eulogio and Ceferino, this eagle is the same one that Flemming declared to be a harpy when he began this study seven years ago. But the brothers also told me that, contrary to Flemming's reported results, the pair of eagles on the nest has reproduced successfully at least two times since the study began. Sugatupu gossip implies that Flemming rarely visited the mainland and the blind but spent most of his time on the island screwing Iris.

I lower the binoculars and sigh. My head aches. Maybe I should abandon my research and run off with Ruiz, put on a blue dress and dance all night in the village—barefoot. I flex my feet and enjoy the cool, dry whisk of skin as my toes brush against each other. At least one good thing happened in the past week: I finally got rid of my athlete's foot. The itching between my toes deviled me so much that I'd almost asked Ceferino if he could spare any more of that green goop, but then I noticed how clean and healthy his own feet look. The Kunas hardly ever wear shoes: once in a while a pair of rubber flip-flops but even that's rare.

So I experimented by going barefoot myself. At first, my feet were so tender that I was hobbled, picking my way along the trail like an ill-shod horse. I couldn't forget studies I'd read about skin parasites that live in tropical soil: toe fleas, burrowing mites, disfiguring fungi. But even as I fretted, the soles of my feet toughened, the nasty white mold flaked away and the itching disappeared.

Now, as I walk the trail from the river to my camp, my big toe sinks into something unexpected: a sudden patch of moisture in the dust of the trail. I glance down. Beneath my toes, the gray mud shines with slime, and when I crouch to examine the area a foul odor hits my nose. Something, probably a good-sized mammal, has been sick here. Judging by the contents of the vomit—nothing solid, only mucus and stomach fluids—whatever puked here had been puking for quite a while.

As I squat in the dust, the steamy afternoon silence is broken by a gagging retch. I cock my head to listen. A pained grunt follows the retching, and then this sick creature spits and moans in a very human, very American voice, "Oh my God."

I find the missionary curled in the fetal position, clutching his stomach and groaning. I recognize him by his leather wing-tip shoes: the rest of him is so filthy I can't even tell that his skin is white. He's dressed in a Kuna woman's blouse—ragged and oversized, also filthy—and a wrap skirt. The knot in the skirt has come undone and the fabric isn't doing its job of covering his legs. Underneath, he wears only a pair of dirty white jockey shorts.

I poke at his back with my bare toes. "Hey."

The missionary curls his body as if he's being attacked by a grizzly bear.

I poke at him again. "Hey. You're not going to die. You've puked up everything that was inside your stomach so whatever was making you sick isn't in there anymore. You'll live. Just relax."

The man manages to crack his eyelids and twist so that his face points up to me. What I can see of his eyes is blood-red, and I realize that the streaks on his cheeks are from tears.

I kneel beside him. "You're okay. I know you feel horrible right now but you're going to be okay." I dribble a little water from my canteen onto a bandana and wipe the dirt from his face. “Here, rinse out your mouth.” He has trouble when he tries to sit so I put my arm around his shoulders. Immediately, I wish I hadn’t—the man stinks like a roadhouse bathroom.

After he spits, I tell him to drink some water.

“No. It’ll make me sick.”

“You need water right now. Alcohol dehydrates. The main reason you get sick when you drink too much is because you need water.”

He takes a couple of gulps from my canteen but his hands shake so much that most of the water ends up running down his chin.

“We’ve got to get you cleaned up. Can you walk?”

He looks so miserable that I actually feel sorry for him. “You’ll feel better once you get a bath. Come on.” I stand and offer him my hand. I guess he feels lousy enough to accept help from an infidel because he takes hold and I haul him to his feet. The skirt immediately slides off his hips and he dives for it, losing his balance and falling face-first into the slime that he just heaved out of his guts.

The missionary’s shoulders shake and I realize that he is crying. I kneel next to him and put my hand on his back. “It’s okay,” I murmur. “It’s okay. I know you feel like hell right now but you’re going to be okay. People have been getting drunk for thousands of years and they hardly ever die from it. We just need to get you cleaned up. By tomorrow you’ll be your old Bible-thumping self again.”

He still sobs.

“Calm down, calm down, it’s okay. Can you roll over? I’ll wash your face.”

I get him to sit and clean him up a little. The whole time, he clutches that filthy piece of fabric in front of his groin as if he’s afraid I’m going to rape him.

“Let’s try to stand up again. Forget about the skirt.”

He turns his face away from me. “No. You’ll see me.”

“I’ll keep my eyes closed, okay? Take my hand and I’ll pull you up and you can lean on me for balance while you tie that skirt on tight. Okay?”

"Close your eyes." His voice is both surly and vulnerable.

"Okay, they're closed."

This time he makes it to his feet in one piece.

"Let me know when I can look."

"I can't get this thing fastened!"

"Just tie it in a knot."

"I can't!" he whines.

When I open my eyes, he's fussing with the skirt like a little old lady. "For Christ's sake!" I grab the ends of the fabric and twist them a couple of times, then tie a firm knot.

"It won't stay together when I walk." He sounds close to tears again.

"At least it won't fall off. I promise I won't look at your hairy legs."

He shoots me a look as if I'm unclean.

"If it makes you feel any better you can call me a godless sinner."

He doesn't say anything but his body sways as if he's dizzy. I put my arm around his waist.

"I don't want you to touch me."

"You don't have a choice. Come on."

The river is just on the other side of a low hill but it takes us a good half hour to cut through the farm plots and banana plantations. I'm glad that the missionary doesn't throw up in anyone's vegetable garden.

At the river, I tell him to wash up and his face instantly loses its color. "In front of you?"

"I need to go back to camp. I think I have some clothes that will fit you. And I'll get some more drinking water, too."

"But what if you come back and I'm—"

"It's not like you have anything I haven't seen before."

"You are a whore." Even in his disgraced state, he manages to sound self-righteous.

"I'm a biologist, remember? What do you think I studied all those years in college?"

"Blasphemy and fornication."

I heave a huge sigh and cross my arms. "I'm going to camp to get those clothes. I'll leave the canteen here. Try to drink as much as you can: your gums are almost as white as your teeth. I'll be back in about an hour."

That's how I end up playing hostess to the missionary man. He bitches about everything: the clothes I lend him, my cooking, the accommodations. He claims to be claustrophobic so he commandeers my *nega* and hammock while I'm left with "the cave made out of cloth," as Eulogio labeled the tent. The worst part about spending the night on the ground is that the next morning I have to crawl out and face the missionary.

"Don't you have any coffee?"

"Where am I supposed to get coffee?"

"The Colombians sell it." He's referring to the illegal boats that ply the islands, trading things like coffee and underwear for Kuna coconuts.

"The Colombians also sell cocaine. Am I supposed to pick that up for you, too?"

With virtually no prodding on my part, I'm treated to the entire story of how my reluctant guest ended up drunk and abandoned on the mainland. On the first day of the *inna* he got wind of the party and he "confronted those heathens in their place of sin." Knowing the Reverend Mister Hellfire, I don't suppose that he was cxactly diplomatic in his arguments. After a few minutes of listening to his rants, some of the men, including "that big one who looks like a common thug," physically removed him from the party.

"They took me to this prison—it was totally dark in there, just one little candle to see by. I thought they were going to kill me. They all reeked of alcohol—godless, drunken heathens! I got down on my knees and prayed for their salvation."

You got down on your knees and begged for your life, I want to say.

"They stripped me—they stripped me naked, like Christ before he was crucified."

Christ in dirty white jockey shorts?

"They were all drinking and laughing—coarse, demonic laughter! The sounds of Satan! They pushed me onto a chair. The big one held me by my shoulders. He pulled my head back and another forced me to drink their cursed alcohol!

"They dressed me in those heathen rags—women's clothes! They kept me in that room all night, pouring liquor down my throat, mocking me with their laughter, cursing me in their foul language. After a while I couldn't even sit, I could only lie on the ground. That made those Indians laugh even louder and they kept pouring more and more liquor down my throat until I prayed to die!"

"You've never been drunk before?"

"My lips had never touched alcohol until that night."

I want to tell him that maybe he should look at this as a lesson in humility but decide not to waste my breath. "Then what happened?"

"At dawn I was half-dead"—half-dead drunk, I want to correct—"and they dragged me out, paraded me in front of the whole godless bunch of them—all of the women, everyone, all pointing and laughing. By this time I was so weak I didn't care what happened next. They sat me down with the women and made me drink again, then I must have passed out. Next thing I knew, I was on a boat in the open ocean. They abandoned me on the beach without checking to see if I was dead or alive. I managed to crawl on my hands and knees to where you found me. I could have easily died there."

"You didn't though."

"No thanks to any of them!"

"So what are you going to do now?"

"I'm going to return to the island and confront those infidels!"

"You must be feeling better."

"I cannot sit idle while sin flourishes!" The story of his near martyrdom seems to have energized him: he's no longer focused on my lack of coffee.

"How are you going to get to the island?"

His face clouds when he realizes that I'm not sympathetic to his plans. "How do you go back and forth?"

"I have a canoe. But it's not mine—it belongs to the project. And I need it for my work."

"But you can take me to the island."

"I'm not going anywhere near the island today. Everyone's drunk."

"All the more reason to confront them with evidence of their sin."

"You've never been around drunks, have you? They're not easy to reason with. And they can get really mean if you piss them off. Wait until tomorrow when everyone's hung over. You'll get lots of converts then."

"And what should I do in the meantime?"

"Sleep. Eat. Find some Colombians and buy cocaine. I don't care what you do. I have to go to work."

I wait until dark to return from the blind. I was hoping that the missionary would steal my canoe and paddle back to the island but apparently the commandment that forbids theft is a powerful one in his mind. After dinner—banana soup for me, canned beans for him—I discover that another factor influenced his decision.

"I can't go to the island dressed in these clothes."

"Why not?"

"They're women's clothes."

"They are women's clothes because they belong to me. But they're just khaki shorts and t-shirts—guys wear those as much as women."

"They are not appropriate for a man of God. Tomorrow you can go to the island and pick up my clothes."

"And?"

"And then take me back to the island."

"So you've got this all planned out. I'm supposed to paddle to the island, pick up your clothes, paddle back here, wait until you get yourself properly attired, escort you to the island, and then I'll have to paddle all the way back here. When am I supposed to work?"

"After what they did to me, you can't expect me to go back to the island wearing women's clothing!"

He's so irrational that eventually I give in and agree to his plan. I crawl into the tent cursing altruism in all of its pernicious manifestations. The missionary keeps me awake all night with his snoring.

XX

In the white sand at the point, Pedro lies on his back with a damp cloth over his eyes. I nudge his arm with my toe. "Hair of the dog?"

He doesn't respond.

I prod him again. "Hair of the dog."

Without moving or taking away the cloth, he demands, "What the hell are you talking about?"

"Hair of the dog that bit you. It's a hangover cure."

"Dog hair?" He sits up and removes the cloth from his eyes. His face is ten years older than it was a week ago.

"Booze. The dog that bit you. You drink a glass of whatever you got drunk on and it'll take away your hangover."

Pedro shudders. "Sounds like some kind of barbaric American superstition."

"It works. I think the only reason I'm alive today is because of Bloody Marys."

"Bloody Marys?"

"Vodka and tomato juice. For breakfast."

Pedro lies down again and covers his face. "Savages."

"I need your help, *anai*."

"So what else is new?"

"I ran out of bananas."

"You're always out of bananas."

"And I need to pick up some clothes for the missionary."

"I told Orestes that if they dumped him on the mainland, he'd end up on your doorstep. He give you any trouble?"

"He was too sick. Who do these belong to?"

Pedro removes the cloth and squints up at the blouse and skirt in my hands. "I think they're from Eulogio's mother-in-law. Leave them here and I'll find out. You washed them?"

"They were pretty foul. Oh, and he must have torn the blouse when he got out of it. I sewed it up the best I could."

"So he's been in your camp for a couple days?"

"He wanted me to bring him back yesterday but I thought I'd better not, with the *inna* still going on."

"Lucky one of you had some sense. He sitting around naked?"

"I had some clothes that fit him."

"And you probably fed him and let him sleep in your hammock. You know what happened to the Samaritans from that story in the Bible?"

"No, what?"

"They were slaughtered by the Crusaders. For being infidels." He closes his eyes and folds his arms across his chest.

"Ruiz says that you're a cynical old pissant."

Pedro doesn't open his eyes. "I'm younger than Ruiz."

"Maybe he's not referring to chronological age."

"So you and the missionary are good friends now."

"Oh, yeah, best of buddies." I'm tired of talking down to Pedro's prone form so I plunk on the sand beside him.

"What's his name?"

"The missionary? I don't know. I didn't ask."

"I thought names were so god-almighty important to you."

"I didn't ask him because I thought if I did he might ask what mine is. And I wouldn't be able to tell him because if I said my name, that would make it easier for *purbakan* to find me in the jungle."

Pedro props himself up on his elbows and twists his head to face me. For the first time, he fully opens his red eyes. "That's just a stupid superstition."

"Like hair of the dog?"

"Stupider."

"Is that why you didn't tell me about it when I was so mad at you for taking away my name?"

"Who did tell you?"

"No one. Well, Ceferino told me about *purbakan* that night he stayed at my camp, the night after Litos was buried. And I figured out the rest."

"Aren't you clever."

"So if you think that it's a stupid superstition, why did you go along with it?"

"I live here."

"You don't live here. You live in town."

"Yeah, you know why? Because Kunas are afraid of this point. They think it's haunted. I built this *nega* to show them that it isn't but Felipa refused to live in it with me. None of them will come out here alone at night, not even ones like Eulogio who should know better. They're all scared."

"And that makes them stupid."

"Yeah. Like believing that spirits can get inside of you just because someone says your name."

"You like judging things, don't you, *anai*? You hold them up to the measuring stick of what you think is true and if they don't fit you say that they're stupid."

"So you don't think that those are stupid superstitions."

"Shakespeare said something like, 'There are more things in heaven and earth than are dreamt of in your philosophy.'"

"He said that about ghosts, didn't he?"

"A lot of white people believe in ghosts."

"A lot of white people are as stupid as Kunas."

"Like the missionary?"

Pedro lies down and covers his entire face with the cloth. "I take that back. A lot of white people are stupider than Kunas."

XXI

Wind-blown rain hisses on coals. I kneel close to the fire as I grate the remains of a chocolate pod and then brush the crumbs into my pot of gruel. These few shreds represent the last of my chocolate: tomorrow and the day after I'll have to settle for plain cornmeal mush for breakfast. No matter how low I am on food, I refuse to go back to the island before the meeting on Saturday night. Yesterday when I returned the missionary to Sugatupu, the Kunas in town were so curt and rude that I actually felt bad about abandoning that stiff prig to be alone with them.

Another gust of wind shakes a shower of drops from the leaves above me. As far as I can tell the rain has stopped, but in the chilly dampness everything seems to be sleeping late this morning. Not one gull plies the coastline like a skipper, not one voice pipes from the shadows under the ferns, not one unseen creature rustles through the litter at the edge of the clearing. I stir the gruel and inhale the earthy scents of corn and chocolate.

Out toward the jungle, a clear, sweet whistle pulls my attention away from the fire. The second note quivers as it ascends, pure and mellow. I smile. On its nest of enameled eggs, the tinamou has wakened. Does the bird sense the life flickering inside those shells, the color almost too beautiful to be real? The delicate blue is like Easter eggs from when I was a child, so full of enchantment and promise that I never could be convinced that they were only hard-boiled hen's eggs.

The tinamou whistles again, too close: it is not the bird on the nest. The call comes from the farmland, the trail below the ridge somewhere very near my camp. With a bandana over my hand, I slide the pot of gruel off the coals. When the notes sound again, they ring so clear that my soul swells with memory.

Ceferino waits at the base of the ridge. "*Na.*"

The sparkle in his eyes tugs at my feet. I take a step toward him but catch myself before my hands reach his arms. Standing awkwardly close, I work through the words that Pedro taught me, the Kuna sentence I've rehearsed for days. "Will you share a drink with me, friend?"

He's so near that I feel the quick intake of Ceferino's breath. His smile deepens and the corners of his eyes crinkle as he tilts his head to study my face. When he speaks, I'm almost as startled as if a tinamou has spoken. "*Eh-yea.*"

At camp, I try to act like I know what I'm doing as I reposition the gruel on the fire and add enough water to stretch one serving into two. Ceferino watches me with so much intensity that I almost upset the pot.

"You're cooking on a fire."

I must look puzzled because he explains, "When we built the *nega*, you had soup that you cooked without fire."

"I use the sun to cook during the day."

"You cook with the sun?"

The gruel is so thin now I don't have to worry about it scorching. "Come, I'll show you."

Ceferino squats beside the solar oven as I pantomime how sunlight reflects off the pie plates and heats the black plastic. To avoid distracting him with translations, I speak as little as possible. When I'm finished with my demonstration, he examines the pie plates carefully, fingers the black plastic garbage bag as if it is something of value. "You are very intelligent."

Embarrassed by the sincerity in his voice, I shake my head. I want to tell him that I learned how to set up a solar oven from Mrs. Mallick, our girl scout leader in seventh grade whose husband died of cancer that next year and the funeral was the first I'd ever been to. I want to tell him how much I appreciate his kindness to me the night when Litos was buried, how much he has helped me to be comfortable with my life here among the

Kunas. Instead I say, apropos of nothing, "I don't cook as well as you."

"But you cook with the sun so it is better."

"You are very kind to say that." I hide my embarrassment behind the too-formal words.

"You are very kind not to laugh at me."

"Why would I laugh at you?"

"Because my Spanish is so bad."

"Your Spanish isn't that bad. I always understand what you say."

"How do you know?"

"What?"

"How do you know"—We're close again, so close that I feel his exhale when he speaks. His breath smells like menthol.—"what I say, if I don't say it right?"

I want to assure him that what he says always makes sense, that his Spanish isn't as bad as he thinks it is, that I understand how difficult it is to speak in a language so foreign that you know you constantly make mistakes and sound like an idiot, but the only thing I can think of is how playfully his black eyes dance when he smiles. "I know what you say from your eyes."

"You will go to work now?"

"*Eh-yea.*" I pack the rinsed mugs in a canvas sack. During the day, I hang my supplies from a branch to keep animals from getting into the food.

"You work too much." Ceferino's words surprise me and I glance at his face. He is not smiling.

"My work is important." As soon as I say this, I realize how pompous I sound.

"You need to rest. Everyone needs to rest sometimes."

"What about the eagle mother?"

"She rests on the nest. The eggs won't hatch today. I need to go to the jungle. Come with me."

His invitation catches me off guard. To buy time, I hoist the canvas sack into the tree and tie off the rope, then rinse my hands. Ceferino watches from the palm log. I comb my damp fingers through my hair, pull a barrette out of my pocket, and fasten a ponytail on top of my head. I wonder how long Ceferino would sit there, his eyes following my every move, his body as still and patient as the eagle on the nest.

"I'm ready," I announce.

As before, we are silent in the jungle. I walk barefoot and measure my stride directly to Ceferino's. As his body glides along the trail, it disturbs nothing, touches nothing. I think of him as a spirit, a *purba*, but I know that he is flesh and blood: I have felt his heartbeat and the warmth of his living body. But in the jungle he has become a liquid that flows without motion. Behind him, I am clumsy with life.

I am not surprised when he abruptly stops in front of me. His eyes study the canopy to focus on a point about halfway up to the crown of one of the tallest trees. The overcast of the sky melts into the rising mist, softening distance and color into amorphous outlines. I see nothing.

Ceferino must sense my frustration because he extends his arm toward the tree, pointing. I try to align my vision with the tip of his finger. Maybe I see something there, something big and hulking, a featureless gray silhouette crouched on a branch near the trunk.

"Eagle," Ceferino whispers.

"The male?"

"*Eh-yea*."

"He comes here to hunt?"

"To sleep. He is sleeping now."

"He is here often?'

"*Eh-yea*."

"You know a lot about the eagles."

"I watch them like you do."

"The things you told me about the eagles—that you and Eulogio told me—they were very valuable to me. They help me understand the history of the nest. You are a very good observer."

Ceferino has been focused on the sleeping eagle but now he turns and meets my eyes. The look on his face is so warm that I am surprised when he doesn't kiss me. His breath flicks across my cheek. "*Nuedi.*"

Later, we stop at an enormous tree with buttresses so deep my entire body could disappear between them.

"Wait," Ceferino says simply.

Wedging himself between two flukes of the buttress, he ratchets his body six or seven feet off the ground to where the ribs unite to form the trunk. From here, he uses woody vines as handholds to climb the tree. As I watch, I feel that he follows a familiar route: philodendron, monstera, monkey ladder, ficus. In the time it takes for me to say the names, Ceferino has climbed to the first branch that supports a horizontal garden of epiphytes.

Wrapping his legs around the limb, he pulls a machete from the sheath at his side and sets to work. He's selective about what he harvests, examining several specimens before choosing a particular plant. After he shaves it off the branch, he carefully stows it in the string bag that he carries over his shoulder. On its way to the bag, a glossy, deep green leaf slips from his fingers and Ceferino twists nearly upside-down to catch it.

Startled by his acrobatics, I must let out an audible gasp because once he's regained his balance, Ceferino grins down at me. "Even monkeys fall sometimes."

Back along the trail, he stops to collect at other sites until his string bag bulges. At one tree he gathers a half-dozen hard fruits the size and shape of wild plums; beneath another he scrapes a handful of dirt from an anthill and wraps it in a folded leaf. The midday air under the trees is visceral and dense, a living thing that pulses against us as we move. We stop at a small stream to drink.

"You are tired?" he asks.

"*Sully*. It feels good to be in the jungle, walking like this."

We push on. I follow Ceferino like a trusting dog. As he examines a flower that must have fallen from the canopy, I'm startled by a loud jabbering overhead. Ceferino glances at the sky. About a dozen fat birds flutter past on stubby wings, squawking. He mimics their call. Three bright green parrots flit toward us, chattering noisily. Ceferino whistles another call, softly this time, and one of the parrots lands on his outstretched wrist.

The bird is about the size of a jay, with a slate blue head and bright red feathers under its tail. The eyes are black and beady. When Ceferino jiggles his finger, the parrot shrieks shrilly.

Ceferino extends his arm toward me so that I can study the bird. "*Waga*."

"Isn't that what you call the *evangelico*?" The colors on the parrot are so clear and defined they seem artificial. I wish I could touch the elegant green feathers but I am afraid of startling the bird into flight.

"Finished?" Ceferino asks.

"*Eh-yea*."

He tosses the bird in the air and, squawking and flapping, the parrot flies off to rejoin its flock. "The *evangelico* is a *waga* because he makes as much noise as those birds do."

"Am I a *waga*?"

Ceferino chuckles softly. "*Sully*. You are a *sule*."

"A *sule*?"

"A paca."

"But I don't have spots anymore."

"Not even on your ass?"

"Nowhere. Really."

"But you are still a *sule* because you are gentle and quiet. When a *sule* moves, it barely makes a sound."

As the afternoon grows, clouds boil overhead. Sweat trickles down my sides. Ahead of me, Ceferino's white shirt clings to the small of his back.

When we come to the river, I flop on my belly, drink, then drop my face into the water. Heat streams out of my skin.

When my lungs are about to burst, I yank up my head, shaking like a dog and spraying water droplets that ripple in concentric rings on the surface of the river. The ripples dominate my unfocused vision. Even after I blink, I still see rings, not just in the water but in the air above it. The circles in the air are an iridescent blue that sparks with green and gold like the head of a hummingbird.

The blue circles are not fixed: they flit from one side of the river to the other, from rock to rock, from leaf to fern to dirt. They travel downstream, away from me. My eyes follow the spots as they float and dance, weightless and unsubstantial in the thick jungle air.

The iridescent dots alight on the tip of a fern that drapes over the pool. The circles separate: one rests on the frond while a second forms a mirror image in the water. I barely breathe as I creep toward them. I am a scientist now, a biologist examining the phenomenon of the dots. Their motion indicate direction, will, and desire—all attributes of a living being—but I have yet to encounter a life form that consists solely of disembodied circles.

The blue rings remain frozen. As I approach, I make out the glistening outline of a wing, almost transparent. Beneath that wing is another, this one blushed with pink and sporting an eyespot of blue along its margin. A slim insect body, soft and furry like a moth, anchors the wings to reality. I inhale deeply, too enchanted to speak.

"It's beautiful." How long has Ceferino been standing at my side?

"It is beautiful," I repeat. "*Yer dailege.*"

"You do not have these where you are from?"

"We have butterflies but not like this. This one is so beautiful it made me forget where I was."

"Forget that you were with me?"

I glance at his face but his eyes are fixed on the butterfly.

He continues without turning his head. "Your eyes speak to me in the same way that you say my eyes speak to you.

Your eyes tell me how much love you have for everything that you see."

Water from my hair drips onto my shoulders. I imagine the sizzle when the droplets come in contact with the heat of my skin. I'm on fire, much hotter than the afternoon and the exertion. I flick my eyes across Ceferino's face but can't look at him directly for more than an instant.

"The animals and birds in the jungle. The people—everyone on the island. The river, the trees—at night the stars and the moon. When I look in your eyes, I see how much love you have for all of them."

I want to tell him that he is wrong, to disabuse him of this notion that I am a good person, but I seem to have left my voice with the glass-winged butterfly. I open my mouth but can't make a sound. Ceferino's hand reaches out to me: his fingertips slide along my jaw, his palm cups my chin and raises my face so that my eyes are level with his. I know that he wants me to look at him but I am afraid of what he will see. I lower my gaze. Somewhere not too far away, I hear the white roar of the waterfall.

A breath of menthol tricks me into glancing up. Ceferino's lips are pursed to blow. I shiver, dislodging my chin from his palm.

"Your eyes are so beautiful because every place they look, they see something that they love."

I start to shake my head to deny what he says but he's so close that when I move his lips meet mine. I taste the salt of his sweat, the silky pressure of his smooth skin. Everything inside of me becomes a hundred iridescent blue dots rimmed with pink, dancing just beneath my skin. Does he feel them pulse when he puts his arms around me? His lips are a *purba*, a beating heart. They slide into me to touch a place that has been asleep, dreaming, yearning for as long as I can remember.

As he pulls me tighter against him, the energy inside of me explodes into a restless tension I cannot control. My breathing become jerky and shallow. I dig my fingernails into the flesh on his back, suck his lips between my teeth and bite. Ceferino moans and I jerk away from him. My body acts outside of my mind's control. I race without thinking along the bank of the river, heedless of the rocks and slime, heedless of the fer-de-lance snakes and the heat that rises from my flesh like a shrill, demanding yelp.

On the rocky lip above the falls, I yank off my soggy t-shirt, step out of my shorts and panties. The heat inside me is unbearable. I don't look behind. I don't look down. I close my eyes and fall.

When I hit the pool, the impact is a doctor's hand against a newborn's bottom: suddenly the world becomes ordered and under the administration of my mind. No more dancing dots, no more racing pulse, no more hot softness inside of me that I was afraid might melt into a puddle between my legs. The bracing cold tightens my skin, wakes me from a dream. How long have I slept?

An instant, a splash, and I am joined in the pool by another, cool and smooth and slippery but conscientious, cautious, aware. Even before his black head surfaces, I feel him measure the distance between his body and mine. He makes no attempt to touch me. Ceferino's eyes meet mine for only an instant and then he is gone: a brown otter sliding through the water, quick and sure and desperately alive.

He swims around the pool a couple of times, then dives and comes up directly under the falls, sputtering and whipping his face from side to side in the spray of falling water. Buoyant and sleek, he glides backwards into a protected cove and then vanishes beneath the surface to reappear in the calm, still water near the outlet. I watch him as I cling to a submerged rock, crouched low to hide my nakedness. When he leaves the pool, Ceferino climbs onto a smooth, round boulder. Stretched flat on his back and pillowing his head on his forearm, he closes his eyes.

I remain crouched and huddled. The water is cold. I cannot move.

Ceferino makes no attempt to cover himself. I don't want to look at his body but my eyes won't stay away from him.

I have never seen a man so naked. From here, I cannot see even one strand of pubic hair. I shiver. My teeth chatter against themselves.

My fingers are wrinkled and blue, my arms and legs numb, before I can bring myself to release my hold on the rock and dogpaddle across the pool. Almost all of the shore is undercut. The only path out of the water is the boulder where Ceferino lies. I crawl onto the sloping bank and perch there, my legs tight against my chest, my arms twisted around my knees. Water streams down my body and snakes back into the pool.

I have not seen Ceferino open his eyes so I am startled when he speaks. "You don't look very comfortable all knotted up like that."

I'm shaking too hard to trust my voice. I hug my legs tighter and swallow. "I'm sorry."

He hasn't moved, his eyes still closed. "You didn't do anything that hurt me."

"The *evangelico* is right."

I hear him shift and when I peek up, Ceferino has twisted on to his side, one leg bent, so that I am confronted with the entirety of his nakedness. "The *evangelico*?"

"He said that I am a whore."

"I don't know that word."

Ceferino's voice is so gentle that I glance over at him, but when I catch sight of his genitals I bury my face in the cup formed by my thighs and arms.

"How can the *evangelico* know anything about you?"

"He said that I am a bad woman." I speak to my breasts, my belly, my genitals.

"Because you are here?"

I lock my head in place against my knees so that I won't be tempted to look up again, so that I can't see Ceferino's face to determine if his question is deliberately vague or if he's just confused by my Spanish. I hear the sound of movement and become aware that his body is now very close to mine.

"The *evangelico* says that a woman is bad if she is lonely?"

I hug my knees tighter so that they push against my forehead. I thought that I was shivering but by the shattered glass inside my chest, I know that I am crying.

"Can I touch you?" I feel the whisper of his breath on the back of my neck, the warmth of his thighs beside my hips. But he doesn't make physical contact with my body until I am able to sob out a reply. "*Eh-yea.*"

In his arms, my muscles relax. I stretch my legs and shift my hips and try not to think about the parts of his body that press into my flesh down there.

"Why have you never married?"

"I never found anyone I wanted to marry."

"So you've been alone since you left your family?"

"Not—not completely alone. I mean, I've known men." I try to think of some way to explain with the limited words we share. "I've let men—I've let men inside of my body. But I've never let them touch my life."

"Why not?" His question is simple, anticipated, but his tone is not: from the way he says those three Spanish words, I know that he understands more than my awkward, stuttered sentences.

I swallow and the sound of Ceferino's heartbeat is suddenly strong against my cheek. "I am afraid," I whisper.

Ceferino sighs and for a while neither of us talks. When he finally speaks, it is as if we have both just wakened. "Let me lie on my back. We'll be more comfortable that way." He shifts. On my side, my body rests almost entirely on top of him. "Is that better?"

"*Eh-yea.*"

"Are you afraid of me?"

"*Sully*. No. Never."

"But you are afraid of other men?"

I want to shake my head in denial but realize that I can't. "I've never been comfortable around other people. I'd always rather be by myself in the woods, studying the trees and birds.

I guess I'm afraid that if I get close to someone, they'll realize that I'm not worth knowing."

"Because you like trees and birds more than people?"

"Because—I don't know—because if I tried to love him, he'd be disappointed in me, and I'd be disappointed with him. I don't think I'm strong enough to love another person."

Ceferino slides his hand along my thigh until it comes to rest near my knee. The gesture seems protective.

"But maybe," I speak in a whisper and I wonder if Ceferino can even hear my words, much less understand the muttered Spanish. "Maybe I'm afraid to lose myself. I'm afraid to lose the little bit I have now, the few things that I believe in, that I love."

For several minutes, Ceferino says nothing. Then, "Listen," he whispers.

"All I hear is your heart."

"The birds."

"They're singing. They sing all the time down here, all day long. It's very beautiful."

"They don't sing all day where you are from?"

"*Sully*. Mostly just at dawn and dusk."

"It's like that here, too."

"Then why are the birds singing now?"

"The birds sing whenever they are around *Sulegoa*."

I lift my head so I can look into his face.

"During the day, I always know where you are in the jungle. All I have to do is follow the singing of the birds. I know that wherever they are singing, there I will find *Sulegoa*."

"Really?"

My face is so close to his that he only has to lift his head a fraction and our lips join. With his kiss, I feel a loss of will and power. My body slides to lie full on top of his: I do not know if he pulls me into that position or if my muscles respond to a force outside of thought. At first I struggle to regain control, but Ceferino's touch flows like a current down my back. One hand on each of my hips, he pulls me firmly on to his body. He is no longer slack. I shudder.

He turns his face to the side so that his lips pull away from mine. "You are frightened?" he asks.

"*Sully.*"

"You are sad?"

"*Sully.*"

His mouth forms his response, "*Nuedi,*" but the word is swallowed by our kiss.

At the foot of the trail up the ridge to my camp, Ceferino reaches into his string bag and pulls out a handful of thick, fleshy leaves. "You must soak these in water, then use the water to wash inside you."

"So that I won't get pregnant?" The Spanish word for pregnant sounds like "embarrassed."

"So that you won't get pregnant."

"You will come to my camp with me?"

"It's better if I don't. You need to wash yourself soon. Tomorrow also. And you must go inside your *nega* and stay there all night until you hear the birds sing in the morning."

"Why? Is something wrong?"

Ceferino wraps his arms around me. "I think tonight the *purbakan* may trouble you. For months, the birds have been singing about *Sulegoa*, about how beautiful this golden woman is, but because you were so sad, so closed, the *purbakan* didn't notice you. Today your body opened like a flower and now the *purbakan* can see how beautiful you are. They will not be satisfied with tree women tonight."

XXII

Early sun whitens the uppermost branches of the Maria tree, while the understory vegetation—and the blind—remain shadowed and chilled. By slow increments, the morning filters downward from the canopy. The jungle awakes: snake-like lianas of monstera and philodendron writhe in the swelling warmth, passion flowers unfold, and songbirds chitter from hidden perches. A ray of light finds the crotch of the tree that has been the focus of my attention for the past two months. The silver sun shines into an empty nest.

For a few hours, I convince myself that the mother eagle is sleeping, that she has hunkered down low inside the bowl of sticks and mud to better protect her eggs. But by midday when I have yet to observe one sign of activity or life, I am forced to conclude the obvious: the mother has abandoned the nest. Until today, the male eagle visited the Maria tree every morning to bring food to his mate. His continued absence confirms that the female is nowhere near the eggs.

A sigh wells up from my chest. The mother eagle has gone. The wait was too much for her: the confinement, the inactivity. She lost her focus, couldn't see past these long, dull days to the satisfaction that surely all mothers must realize in procreating and fostering a new generation.

I guess it's better now than later, better for those still unborn eaglets to have never tasted life than to die of exposure and hunger and neglect after the eggs hatch. Better to remain unborn, to be flushed away in a stream of water fragrant and bitter with the infusion of leafy sap. Better for the eagles, better for me, for Ceferino, better for all the Kunas who believe that their blood should never be tainted by contact with an outsider.

I pull away from the binoculars and lean my head against the wall of the blind. Through the narrow slit of the window I see the sky, not cloudy but not exactly clear, the rusty blue that characterizes midday in the tropics. I see the Maria tree, a few small birds flitting among the epiphytic bromeliads and orchids. I even see the air, thick with the humidity of dreams, ambition, and desire.

I close my eyes. Ceferino says that he sees love in my eyes but it is an illusion: he sees what he wants to see. Flemming saw harpy eagles on the nest in the Maria tree.

The next morning, in the strongly defined light above the blind, the brooding outline of an eagle dominates the nest and the Maria tree. The returned mother's eyes glisten as bitter and astringent as my empty womb.

The day that follows is like any other—the eagle motionless and precise on the nest—as if my observations from yesterday were a heat-induced delusion. I do not understand what is happening. Do the eggs still live? How can a mother be the soul of devotion for weeks on end, disappear cavalierly one day, and then return as dedicated and obsessive as ever?

I leave the blind early to bathe and prepare for the Saturday meeting. For once, I will be glad to spend the moonless night surrounded by people and conversations, even if I remain anonymous and mute. Along the river, I hear the rattle call of a kingfisher.

I have no idea why I glance down at this point, what compels me to pause with my foot suspended a hand's breadth above the dirt on the trail. Low sun through thick weeds—mostly cutgrass and some kind of small-flowered composite—produces stark contrasts: yellow diamonds of light and velvet shadows of creamy brown. Woven together and crosshatched with the nondescript gray of dirt, the result is a gleaming apparition so luminous it almost appears alive.

I twist my head and my breath catches in my throat. The pattern of yellow and brown and gray is too defined for mere physics: it is alive. My eyes widen as the texture at my feet resolves into a pebbled network of scales, a series of muscular coils as thick as my wrist and ending with a massive, wedge-shaped head. Movement: the flick of a black tongue, slim and almost insect-like, the rhythmic swell and compress of breath.

I stumble backwards. Yellow eyes follow my movement, unblinking. Two words—pit viper—drum through my brain like a pulse, defined by the snake's triangular head and the hollows on either side of its nose, the pit-like organs that sense the warmth of life, that lead a predator to its prey. Fer-de-lance: one of the most dangerous snakes in the world, its venom so deadly that a single drop can kill a full-grown man. The poison acts by necrosis, decomposing tissue around the bite. Fast acting, once the venom enters the bloodstream it produces spectacular, almost instantaneous rupture of membranes. Death occurs within a matter of minutes.

The fer-de-lance is frozen. I am frozen. Who will make the first move?

Ceferino spoke to this snake when he encountered it on the trail, calmed it with his words and his voice. I do not know what language this fer-de-lance understands. I whisper out of respect.

"The missionary would say that you are evil, that you are Satan, but I know that you're just an animal like any other, an animal like me. The only reason you're here now is because this trail is a good place to soak up the afternoon sun. You're a predator: you sense the heat of my body in those pits on the sides of your nose. You know that because I am warm, I am a potential meal. But you also see with your eyes and you know that I am too big to swallow, that to bite me would be a waste of your venom. I know that you are not evil, you're just a guy looking for a meal. *Anai*, you listened to Ceferino when he spoke to you. My words aren't as wise as Ceferino's or even in the right language, but I respect you and I do not intend to do you any harm. I hope that you can respect me. You always have in the past. You've allowed me to walk this trail every day so far. Please, *anai,* allow me to pass by you again."

The snake's yellow eyes hold mine. His pupils are black, slotted upright like an owl's or a sheep's. They hold no hatred, no anger, no innate evil. This snake is not a threat to me. He is not the missionary, not Eulogio or Ruiz or—despite his eyes—Pedro. With a muttered "*Con permiso,*" I hop over the coiled body and continue along the trail. After two steps, my breath collapses. I close my eyes and whisper, "*Nuedi.*"

Attendance has already been taken and business begun by the time I arrive at the meeting house. Trying to be as inconspicuous as possible, I creep past the back benches. I'm almost at the empty seat beside Iris when a slim, beaded ankle juts into the aisle and blocks my path. Fortunately, my downcast eyes spare me the humiliation of tripping and falling on my face. I glance over to identify the owner of the ankle.

Eulogio's wife flashes her perfect, self-assured smile and holds up her wrist. With the tip of her finger, she taps the face of her fancy gold watch. In response, I extend my arm and point to my bare wrist. Eulogio's wife laughs so hard that she has to cover her face with her headscarf.

I slide onto the bench beside Iris. She nurses the baby: a zipper in her bodice permits access without sacrificing modesty. The other child, Katrina Maria, apparently was sleeping but as soon as I sit on the bench she crawls into my lap as if she has been waiting for me.

In the center of the hall Anselmo—the man with the cataracts—seems to be talking to himself in a low, barely audible monotone. He stands upright, stiff—I never realized how rigid he is, his feet planted as if he is rooted in the dirt floor. His cloudy, almost white eyes flash toward me. I wonder what he sees, if he even recognizes me in the shadows beside Iris.

The man continues his speech, so low, so monotonous that I cannot understand a single word. If Litos were here now, he would whisper in my ear an explanation of everything that has gotten this man up in front of the community to speak. Litos would pepper his narrative with frequent, caressing purrs of "*Perrita*" and maybe I'd shiver from the play of his fingers through my hair.

I inhale raggedly and stifle a sob. In my lap, Katrina Maria opens her eyes and with a child's unashamed curiosity twists to look at my face. I smile and wonder if she notices the tears in my eyes.

Anselmo's gaze flashes out again, then after a few more words he focuses on me for a longer stretch of time. By my side, Iris shifts the baby to her other arm and zips her blouse closed.

I glance around the dim room. Under the hissing Coleman lanterns, Mateo seems more detached than usual, stretched in his hammock with his eyes closed as if he's asleep. Orestes, ever official, takes notes from his designated chair: a student desk like those we had in grade school with a flat support for the right arm that flares into a writing surface. Unfortunately, Orestes is a lefty so he has to sit almost sideways and curl his hand awkwardly over the spiral-bound notebook as he writes.

I see Eulogio, well-dressed as always, lean forward with his fingers laced between his knees, his handsome face focused on Anselmo. Near the back door, Pedro speaks in a low voice with his brother-in-law, the guy who helped build my *nega*. From the smile on Pedro's face, I know that he is faking unconcern. Even across the room, I see intensity in his eyes.

I feel that intensity now in the meeting hall, an intensity that seems to be directed toward me. Anselmo's eyes flash often and once he even gestures at me with his arm: a small movement, tight and restrained. The kids in the hall follow his lead and openly stare. The adults are more subtle: a quick head turn, a shadowed glance, a hand in front of a mouth. Maybe because they try to disguise it, their attention seem hostile. Iris squirms on the bench beside me.

The white eyes of the speaker settle on to me, the face that holds them as blank as its pupils. The voice slows so that every word is precise and defined. Iris shifts again. I try to hold Anselmo's gaze but his eyes are so veiled that I can't distinguish their irises from the surrounding white. Directly behind me, someone spits.

Mateo still seems to be sleeping. Eulogio—he's leaning back now, his arms crossed over his chest. Ceferino is nowhere in sight. Pedro stands in the doorway. Is that a smirk on his face? Anselmo executes another deliberate swing of his arm toward our bench, then ponderously shuffles his rooted feet.

The animosity in his gesture causes something inside me to snap. As deliberate as Anselmo's voice, I pass the sleeping body of Katrina Maria to her mother. When I stand, I hear a strangled gasp as the man in the center of the room chokes on his words. Ignoring him, I turn, making no effort to conceal my purpose. I angle between the rows of wooden benches until I come to a halt in front of Pedro.

In full voice, in English, I demand, "What's going on?"

Pedro gives a quick head shake.

"You can't brush me off on this." I know that everyone in the building is listening to me, even if they can't understand what I say. "What is Anselmo saying about me?"

Pedro's whisper hisses. "Let's go outside."

"No." I haven't used this tone since my uneasy first dates in college. "I'm not leaving this building until you tell me exactly what is going on. I'm going to stand here speaking English and making a scene until I find out."

When Pedro glances up at me, I'm surprised by a grin.

"What's so funny?"

"You standing there saying that you're going to disrupt the meeting until you get what you want. That's a Kuna tactic for winning arguments. It's the same strategy Anselmo used to get Mateo to let him take over the meeting tonight."

My voice still has an edge of anger in it. "Why is that funny?"

"Because Anselmo's up there claiming that you're corrupting the Kunas, but the way you're acting it's the Kunas who've corrupted you."

"I'm corrupting the Kunas?"

"Let's take this outside, okay? Anselmo wants to get back to his rant and he can't do that while you're shouting at me in English."

With his words, I become aware of how ridiculous I must look: my blond head brushing the rafters and anger distorting my features. Without waiting for Pedro, I duck out the door.

It's full dark outside until Pedro lights a cigarette. I follow him meekly. He waits to speak until we're almost to the mangroves. "Anselmo's a racist."

The statement is so flat that I can't formulate a response but simply parrot Pedro's words: "A racist?"

"Whites don't have a monopoly on hate. Anselmo thinks that you're a menace to the purity of the Kuna people."

"Me?"

"All whites. He hates all whites."

"Why?"

"I'm not Freud." Pedro flicks his cigarette butt toward the swamp. I follow the orange arc until it disappears, then realize that Pedro has resumed walking. I hustle to catch up. "The point is that he doesn't want you around. It's not just you—it's the missionary and Ruiz and Iris's two kids—and Katherine, of course."

"Katherine—your wife?"

Pedro snorts but when he speaks his voice is more human, more vulnerable than I have ever heard it. "Anselmo was *sayla* back then. I think he was the one who turned the community against us."

"You must hate him."

In the starlight, I see Pedro shrug. "Maybe he was right."

XXIII

I blink my eyes and the world becomes sharply focused: the eagle's face glowering from the platform of sticks and detritus, the lush green of the epiphytic gardens halfway up the trunk of the Maria tree, and the tree itself, broadly swaying against the gray smudge of the sky.

I must have dozed off. These long afternoons always challenge my concentration. It doesn't help that everything else in the jungle sleeps in the midday heat. What is that old saying? The only things stupid enough to try to get anything done during a tropical afternoon are mad dogs and white people. And mad dogs eventually get put out of their misery.

As I unfasten the barrette on top of my head, I'm surprised by a shiver that traces across my skin and leaves goose bumps on my arms. I check the weather through the narrow slit of the blind's window. The sky is the angry gray of a bruise, the wind winnowing the upper reaches of the canopy. Above the tree tops, a swallow-tailed kite rides effortlessly along a growing clot of clouds.

There's a storm coming—soon, if I'm any judge—and I don't want to be trapped in the blind when it rains. This roof leaks like a sieve. I must have written twenty letters to David that first month, pleading with him to send canvas to fix the top of the blind. My begging stopped with the rains but David never did send that tarp. One more glance at the sky, the clouds boiling behind the Maria tree, and I decide that the mother eagle will have to weather this storm by herself.

I throw on my clothes—they're still damp from the morning hike from camp—and toss my gear into my knapsack: clean clothes, soap, towel, water bottles. I squirrel Ridgely's field guide under the stool, the most protected place I can think of in the porous blind. After I duck through the canvas door, for the first time in months I tie the flap closed behind me.

The lowering clouds hurry me along the trail and despite the cool wind and drizzle I break a sweat before I'm halfway to the river. I'm anxious to get through with my chores—laundry, bath, and hauling water—before the storm hits. I've been nervous about high winds ever since I found that huge downed tree on the trail near the waterfall. Someone—was it David?—once told me that the biggest threat to tropical research is loosely-rooted trees in a storm.

I glance at the sky: if I'm lucky, the main part of the storm will pass to the east, curving along the valley and up into the mountains. I follow the trail as it turns right and descends steeply to the river, the footing already muddy from the drizzle.

The Kunas are all on the island now, safe from falling trees. They never come to the mainland this time of day. In the morning, the river bustles with human activity: women bathing, doing laundry, collecting water; men puttering around their farm plots or hunting for whatever small game they can find. At noon, returning traffic flows downstream, back toward the island. The late afternoon heat finds the banks populated only by iguanas, kingfishers, and white-faced capuchin monkeys.

I encounter one lone capuchin on the bank opposite from me, swinging back and forth through the thin branches of a cecropia tree. As soon as the monkey sees me, it grunts loudly and bares its teeth, but after that brief display of aggression it melts into the shadows. Capuchins usually are not so skittish: I've had entire troops of them watch from trees while I bathe, the monkeys hooting and jeering like a gang of construction workers.

I peel off my clothes, grab my soap, and slide into the current. The river is shallow here but the gravel bar keeps the water cleaner than in the deep, muddy sections. I kneel in water to my waist and soap my upper body.

A shriek startles me and I almost lose my grip on the soap. I study the trees along the bank but see nothing. A second cry focuses my attention beneath a palm where the capuchin bobs up and down like a dipper. The monkey screams once more, its head raised as if to enhance its voice, then on all fours it scampers back into the jungle.

I crouch low, my arms crossed in front of my breasts, and listen. Something more immediate than the weather has upset that monkey. There's not a bird singing anywhere, not a sound. Why didn't I notice this silence before? Mouth open, I strain my ears. Barely discernable above the roar of the river comes the sound of a human voice: "Oh Lord, we pray that you will welcome this child into your fold—"

I find the missionary at a sharp bend in the river where the current has undercut the bank into a wide pool. The man stands waist deep in water, his hands on the shoulders of a teenaged Kuna girl wearing a white robe. Their movements have stirred the mud on the river bottom so that the water is the color and consistency of barn paint. The missionary's voice rises and falls in a sing-song of prayer.

"What the hell—?"

Without taking his hands from the teenaged girl, the missionary whips his head around to face me. "Blasphemy!" he shouts. "How dare you sully this sacred place with your curses?"

"What in God's name are you doing?"

"It is in God's name that I perform this act!"

"Are you baptizing that girl?"

"I am opening the gates of heaven to this wretched, heathen soul. Don't try to stop me, you infidel!"

"For Christ's sake—" When I step toward the river, the missionary forces the girl's shoulders forward. She squeals, then ducks her head underwater. I see her legs kick as she swims out of his grasp. "I guess you didn't set the hook cleanly. She got away."

The missionary throws his arms open. "She will be welcomed into the fold now—baptized a true Christian. She is my first convert among the Indians."

"You think that little girl understood one word of what you said to her?"

He shoots me a withering glance. "The Lord has opened her ears to my teaching. A non-believer like you cannot comprehend the rapture that comes with the acceptance of the word of God."

"Is that why she swam away?" The girl's head has popped out of the river about ten feet from where the missionary stands. She treads water in a deep pool. "Listen, right now there's something more important than the rapture—"

"Nothing is more important than the rapture!"

"—like getting that girl safely back to the island before this storm hits." The girl giggles. I glance over at her and realize that her arms and shoulders are bare. "What's she wearing, anyway?"

"I dressed her in the purest white linen to welcome her into the flock of the Lord Jesus Christ."

"Yeah, I noticed that—but it doesn't look like she's got it on anymore."

When the missionary finally takes notice of the girl swimming beside him, his face blanches.

I call out to the girl, "*Dónde está tu ropa*?"

She laughs and ducks under the water again.

"What did you say to her?" the missionary demands.

"I asked her where her clothes are. Does she understand Spanish?"

"I think so—Oh dear God!" The missionary claps his hand over his eyes as the girl, stark naked, emerges from the river in front of me.

She's a little sprite of a thing, her head barely reaching up to my chin, with pipe-stem limbs but precocious breasts. She responds to everything I say with identical, bubbling giggles. My t-shirt fits her like a shift. Once she's dressed, I grasp her hand firmly and hustle down the trail to the ocean.

On the empty beach, the wind pushes into us like the hand of God. It whips up swells on the water—I've never seen the ocean so rough. A gray sheet of rain blurs the horizon.

I tug the girl toward my beached canoe but she snakes her hand away from me. "No."

"Come on—we have to get to the island before it rains."

The girl plants her feet in the sand and shakes her head mulishly. "No."

"It's dangerous here—it's going to be night soon, and with this storm who knows what will happen."

"No!"

The squall line over the ocean engulfs the island. The wind on my sweaty shirt is cold. I try to keep my voice level. "Why? Why don't you want to go back home where it's dry?"

The girl says something that doesn't sound like anything I've ever heard in Kuna or Spanish.

"What?"

She repeats her response, and this time I recognize the English words. "Blue jeans."

"Blue jeans?"

"Blue jeans," the girl nods vigorously. "The *evangelico* said that if I went with him to the river, afterwards I would get everything that I want."

"He didn't"—I look at her eager face and realize that she's not ready to accept a theological explanation of the afterlife. "And you want blue jeans."

"Blue jeans." Her body wiggles as she nods. "Like in *Cosmopolitan* magazine."

"Where in the world did you get hold of a *Cosmo*?"

"Blue jeans," she insists.

Lightning cracks open the sky to the north. Angry swells, white-capped, are so high they obscure the island—from this angle they're even taller than the palms around Pedro's *nega*. The chances of me delivering this girl safe and dry to the island are about as high as the missionary gaining additional converts once this incident is broadcast through the village.

"Blue jeans," the girl repeats.

"You know, I have a pair of blue jeans in my *nega* that would fit you just perfectly. Let's go up to my camp and I'll get you dressed up right—I have a really foxy shirt in my bag—it'll look great on you. I swear that when we're done, no one on the island will even recognize you—they'll think you're one of those models from *Cosmo*."

XXIV

Saturday afternoon, two men stand under the palms near Pedro's cabin. They watch, motionless, as I hop out of my canoe and drag the dugout on to the beach. One of the men is young, probably about my age. The other could be his father. When I draw up beside them, I smile and try to meet their eyes. The younger man flinches and turns his head away. The older man wears the same look of studied indifference, almost boredom, that I recognize from Anselmo.

Without a word, the men fall into step, flanking me on either side. Neither man looks at me as we walk. The younger one says "*Cuidado*"—Spanish for "careful"—when I stumble over a mangrove root.

The village is deserted: no fires crackling in outdoor kitchens, no low voices filtering through bamboo walls, not even any kids flying kites at the edge of the surf. As we follow the now-familiar route to the meeting hall, the silence grows oppressive.

"Where is everyone?" I ask in Spanish.

Neither man responds.

It's early—still full daylight—when we duck through the door of the meeting hall, but as soon as my eyes adjust to the dimness inside, I realize why the town is deserted. The hall is packed: I've never seen so many people in the building at once. Every bench is crammed—men, women, and there must be a couple hundred kids in here. The room is close and humid with exhalations and body heat. When I was outside I heard a comforting hum of voices, but the instant my outline is silhouetted in the brightness of the doorway, the babble stills.

The two men—my police escort—lead me to the center of the hall. Ologuippa and Mateo, nearly identical in their hammocks, lie still and expressionless. The supplicant's stool, basically just a block of wood, squats in the dirt to the left of Mateo's hammock.

The Coleman lanterns have not been lit and the hall is thick with gloom. The two policemen position themselves on either side of the stool. I look into their faces. The one I assume to be Anselmo's brother gazes over my shoulder, refusing to acknowledge me. The other motions with his head to the stool. I lower my rump awkwardly, knowing that every eye in the room watches me. It seems to take forever for my butt to make contact with the smooth wood of the seat. The policemen remain, standing, on either side of me. My head is on the same level as their crotches.

Apparently the Kunas were waiting for my arrival because as soon as I sit, a woman in the front row of benches begins talking. At first, I don't bother to listen because she's so far to my left that I can't see her. But after a couple of minutes she's still speaking and I tune in to what she says. I can't understand the Kuna words but the woman's voice is amazingly animated. She acts as if she's telling a story. The woman has risen and strides back and forth in the center of the hall, ducking under the hammocks. I can see her plainly now: she seems to be about forty, trim and self-assured. She pauses in her pacing for a moment. Standing directly in front of me, her eyes flick down from her superior height as if she's only now realized that something insignificant crouches at her feet.

When she resumes her narration, the woman circles one finger through the air as if she's signaling to an airplane, then lisps out several sentences in a squeaky falsetto. As soon as she uses this voice, a low laugh swells through the audience.

In spite of my awkward and exposed position I'm enjoying the show. The narrative has a cast of three or four different voices: a low, deliberate male, a couple of young, frisky ones, and that goofy falsetto that never fails to inspire laughter. As the story approaches a climax the woman's voice becomes faster and louder, her gestures more emphatic. Her pacing brings her back to the bench were she was seated when the meeting began. She uses that falsetto voice again: a speech delivered with such emphasis and elaboration of certain words that the entire hall explodes with laughter. Then the woman claps her hands once and abruptly sits down.

Now Anselmo speaks. I was getting a crick in my neck from following the theatrical woman, but with Anselmo I don't have to move a muscle: he stands directly in front of me, facing outward so that his back fills my entire field of vision. With the two policemen on either side, I feel claustrophobic.

As usual, Anselmo speaks in a monotone, slow and deliberate. Since his words hold no interest for me, I use the time to consider my predicament. I assume that I am in some kind of trouble, probably because of that girl the missionary was trying to baptize. Anselmo must be angry about it: the way Pedro talked, the man wanted both me and the missionary off the island before this happened and he's probably even madder now.

A voice speaks up from behind me. I think it's Ologuippa, the alternate *sayla*: his tone lacks the calm intelligence of Mateo's. He speaks for several minutes and then there's a brief intermission as the lanterns are lit. Almost immediately the old guy resumes talking, a steady drone of incomprehensible words. Around me, the standing men form a cubicle the size of a confessional.

I'm being scolded. The tone and the cadence of the speech are obvious even if I can't understand the words. As the evening wears on and the rebuke continues, I conclude that scold isn't a strong enough word for the dressing-down that the *sayla* is giving me. From the way he's going on, the Kunas must think that I'm a major criminal, a menace to their society. I cross my arms, chew my lip, and try to remember what David told me about not pissing off the natives.

When the voice behind me pauses, probably mustering righteousness for the next round of admonitions, I twist my head so that I can look directly at Orestes. Speaking Spanish, I attempt a casual tone: "It doesn't do much good to lecture me when I can't understand a word that he's saying."

Orestes was writing—he must have a terrible time keeping up with these long-winded speeches—but at the sound of my voice the pencil slips out of his hand.

I try to keep the annoyance out of my voice. "I haven't understood one thing that's been said to me tonight."

Orestes says something, his tone as testy as mine, and suddenly Eulogio pops into the center of the hall. After a murmured conversation, Anselmo and Eulogio exchange positions. Eulogio bows his head to look down at me.

I've used the quick break to compose my next remark: "I feel like a six-year-old kid who's been caught watching dogs have sex in the alley."

A few of the men, including Eulogio, laugh.

"This stool is really uncomfortable. Can I stand up?"

Eulogio measures me, a smile playing with the corners of his lips. For the first time, I notice a resemblance between him and Ceferino. Eulogio waits almost a full minute before he responds. "*Sully*."

"Are you at least going to tell me what this is all about?"

His grin widens. "They've decided to fine you $25."

"Why?" The two Spanish words sound much gentler than I intended.

"For keeping Esmelia on the mainland all night. And for dressing her in your clothes."

I bite my lip to give myself time to frame a diplomatic rebuttal. "And you're declaring me guilty without knowing any of the details of what happened? Without letting me explain why I did the things I did?"

"Do you deny that you did these things?"

"*Sully*."

Eulogio launches into a speech in Kuna—a long one—and after he's finished Anselmo and several of the others put in their two cents. When the discussion is over, Eulogio turns to me again. "We've raised your fine to $30."

"What?"

"We've decided to raise your fine because you're being so uncooperative."

"This is totally unfair! You're crazy if you think I'm going to pay that!"

"You don't have any choice. You have to pay it."

"No I don't—I don't have to do anything!"

"Now you are acting like a six-year-old."

I gather my legs beneath me and rise as gracefully as possible. Standing, I outsize both policemen and come up roughly even with Eulogio. "Do you still think that I resemble a six-year-old?"

"If you leave the island without paying the fine, it'll go up another $5."

"I don't have any money with me. These skirts don't have pockets, you know."

"I guess that's why white women always wear blue jeans." He says the last two words—blue jeans—in English.

"You're a son of a bitch. Do you know that?"

Eulogio throws back his head and laughs.

XXV

My exile days pass slowly. I tell myself that life now is no different than it was a week ago. I rise with the sun, eat a quick breakfast, pack water and a couple of bananas for lunch at the blind. In late afternoon I return to the *nega*, eat, then stretch out for the night in my hammock. I have enough food to last another week—more if I swipe a few bananas from the local farms. No one should notice the loss: monkeys must eat more bananas in a single night that I could steal in a week.

I shake out my shoulders and sigh. Nothing has changed at the nest: the midday heat yawns over the living green of the jungle. The sky pales as the daily byproducts of photosynthesis—carbon dioxide and water vapor—coalesce in folds above the slumbering spirits of tree women. The mother eagle broods in her Maria tree, stoic and immobile, as she has nearly every day for the past month. But today isn't any day. Today is Christmas Eve and I feel even more alone and hungry and pathetic than this sad eagle that I watch squatting on her nest of dead branches and cold, stone eggs.

A bath revives me a little. I lie in the pebbled shallows as clear water ripples over my torso. My skin is as white as fungus. Under the crystal lens of the river, my whole body looks parasitic, like something that can't live on its own but instead sucks nourishment from others. I wrap my arms over my breasts and focus on the cecropia leaves that spread above me. The lobed shadows ghost across my body like the hands of invisible *purbakan*.

"Merry Christmas," I whisper to the spirits in heaven.

I have to stop feeling sorry for myself. I need to haul my skinny, white butt out of this river, put on some clean clothes, and hike the mile or so of trail back to my *nega*. I need to get a fire going so that I can cook up a decent meal: I was so depressed this morning I didn't even set up my solar oven. I'll feel better once I get some food in me. When it's good and dark tonight, I'll pretend it's midnight and by the light of Ruiz's little oil lamp I'll open all of those presents that Mom sent from home.

Forcing cheerfulness, I sing a Christmas carol—"O come all ye faithful"—as I climb up the hill to my camp. I'm trying to remember the words to the second verse when a figure leaps out from behind the *nega*.

I scream and jump backwards but the movement tangles me in the clothesline that's strung from the palm trees along the edge of the clearing. My feet trip under me and I end up in a heap, face down on the ground. A body—someone heavy—lands gently on top of me, more deliberate than a fall. Something cylindrical and hard pokes into the fleshy part of my rump.

"Ruiz!"

The weight lifts off my back as he props himself on his elbows. "I am sorry. I was worried about all the noise you made coming up the hill. The way you were shouting, I thought that something was attacking you. I covered your body with mine to protect you."

"I was singing."

"That was singing?" Ruiz's hands have snaked around beneath me to grope at my breasts.

"You've got a lot of nerve, feeling me up at the same time you insult my singing."

"M-m-m-m." When he touches my nipples, my insides become liquid. I had no idea that I was this lonely. "This almost makes up for the fact that you stood me up this morning."

"I stood you up?" I've managed to squirm out from under him, but both his hands remain inside my shirt.

"We had a date, remember?" He jiggles my breasts with his palms. "Christmas in Santa Marta. I got here as early as I could but you were nowhere to be found."

"I was working. I can't just sit around all day waiting for people to come"—I swat at him to get his hands out of my shirt—"and feel me up."

Ruiz rises and waggles his finger at me. "Be nice. Remember, I am the only friend you have right now." Once I'm standing, he pretends to brush dirt from the front of my body but his big paws keep coming back to my breasts.

I twist away from his groping. "You've been to the island?"

"There is still time for us to celebrate Christmas together. If we leave right now, we will be in Santa Marta in time for high Mass at the Cathedral."

"Religion is the last thing I need tonight."

Ruiz laughs and throws his arms around me. The kiss that follows is rough and assertive. After a few seconds I try to escape by pushing against him but he won't let go. He pulls his lips away just far enough to whisper, "Be nice or I will abandon you the way the Kunas did."

"Is that a threat or a promise?"

"So why are the Kunas mad at you?"

Ruiz refused to tell me what this stew is made of: there's some kind of meat in it but not from any animal I've ever eaten. "It's a long story. Where did you find this bread?"

"You always change the subject when I try to get serious with you."

"It's just that I haven't had bread in ages. I've been dreaming about it ever since I came to the jungle."

"It sounds like you have developed an unhealthy obsession."

"Like your obsession with my breasts?"

"That obsession is perfectly healthy. And now my little love, are you going to keep talking about bread or will you answer my question and tell me how you managed to get the Kunas so mad at you?"

"So they're really mad? They had this trial for me but I got the impression that the whole thing was kind of a joke."

"Wait—start at the beginning. They had a trial for you?"

"It all started with the missionary."

"I should have guessed that. I knew he would make problems for you."

"It wasn't all his fault. There was this teenaged girl, too. She probably had as much to do with it as the missionary."

"A teenaged girl and a missionary? And a beautiful lady scientist living alone in the jungle. This sounds like it belongs in a *telanovela*."

"It gets better." I wipe the last of the gravy from my bowl with the heel of the bread. "The missionary was trying to baptize the girl but I think that she had other ideas. He'd given her some kind of baptismal robe to wear but as soon as she got in the water she stripped it off."

Ruiz throws back his head and laughs. "Those Kuna girls are a bunch of little tramps! They're always trying to trick men into marrying them."

"That girl was trying to get the missionary to marry her?"

"They do it all the time—get a guy caught in a compromising situation so that he has to marry her."

I'm so shocked that I forget about the rest of the bread. "She wanted to marry the missionary? Why would anyone want to do that?"

Ruiz shrugs. "Once upon a time, Iris thought that Fleming was worth getting married to. And I have had Kuna girls who wanted to marry me."

I hug Ruiz's waist. "They'd have to be really desperate to want that. Or crazy."

"And blind too, right? But what I cannot understand is how the beautiful lady scientist got involved in all of this."

"I showed up just in time to see the girl come out of the river wearing nothing but her birthday suit. The missionary was too embarrassed to do anything so I threw some clothes on the kid and tried to get her back to the island. But she wouldn't leave until I gave her a pair of my blue jeans."

"Blue jeans?"

"Yeah—she even asked for them in English. I guess she'd seen some pictures in magazines."

"But I do not understand why the Kunas would put you on trial and not the missionary."

"Who knows? They really didn't seem serious about it. Eulogio was smirking like an idiot the whole time he was explaining it to me, then at the end he made some crack about blue jeans as if he understood everything that had happened."

"The girl's father must have felt humiliated by you. Kuna men are obsessed with their women. They always want people to think that their wives and daughters are totally satisfied with their lives, even when the evidence indicates otherwise."

"Litos told me that too, a long time ago. I think it was the first time I ever talked to him."

"And then they fined you $35."

"No, they fined me $25. The price keeps going up."

"Just like the Kunas. They will keep raising the fine as long as you do not pay it."

"They can raise it as high as they want but I'm never going to pay it. I didn't do anything wrong."

His voice is suddenly gentle. "You cannot live all alone out here with no one to look after you."

"I don't need the Kunas."

"You do not have money to pay the fine?"

I snort angrily and jerk away from his arm. "Of course I have enough money! But they don't have the right to fine me for what happened!"

Ruiz slides me onto his lap. "All of these words about what is right, I feel as if I am talking to the *evangelico*. You are much too pretty for that."

"For what?"

"To talk about foolish things like justice and right and wrong. Things that do not exist anywhere except inside your own head."

I open my mouth to reply but Ruiz kisses me, lightly like a caress.

"It is Christmas Eve. Let us forget the Kunas and the missionary and celebrate instead."

Ruiz insists that I open my presents from home. The first box I unwrap contains a jar of Mom's chokecherry preserves. We spread the wine-dark jelly on Ruiz's bread with our fingers. The next package has a framed photo of my family as kids—Ruiz recognizes me even with my overbite and ugly pageboy haircut. My parents also sent clothes—shorts and t-shirts. I peel the wrapping off one present and find a six-pack of white, department store panties.

Ruiz snatches the package out of my hand. "The underwear that you have on now is like this?"

"My mother must think that this is what I wear. But they're not even the right size."

He has slit open the plastic wrapper and unfolded one pair. "I should say not. This looks big enough for two of you!"

When I try to grab it out of his hand, he twists away from me. "You cannot possibly wear these, my Christmas angel. They will never stay in place on your slim hips. I will take these for someone who is the right size—my maid Felicity would love to have American underwear. And when I return I will bring you something more appropriate."

"Ruiz, you can't give me presents like that!"

"Why not? You need to have underwear and there is no place for you to buy any here in the jungle." He slides the package of underwear behind the log, rises to his feet, and offers me his hand. "May I have this dance?"

I decide not to protest the obvious—that there is no music—and instead try to follow his rhythm as he slowly sways around the fire.

His voice caresses my ear. "How old are you, my little love?"

"Twenty-five."

"The Kunas think that you are only twenty."

"They asked me my age the first day I was here but I was so spacey I couldn't think of the Spanish word for five."

Ruiz laughs. “Here I thought that you had lied about your age to make yourself more desirable to Kuna men.”

“You really thought I’d do something like that?”

“I know you better than you think. Inside of those men’s clothes, it is not your breasts but your heart that tells me that you are a woman.”

XXVI

When Ruiz gave me those two paperback books a few weeks ago, I assumed that he'd found them on the street or in a supermarket checkout, but once I looked them over I realized that he'd selected some serious fiction for me. By translating a page or two every night, I've gotten about a hundred pages into one of the novels. On the surface, the story describes an indigenous uprising in Peru, but on a deeper level the author addresses the difference between real events and fiction. Tonight by the single flame of the oil lamp, I read to the last page of the book. I read until my eyes burn, until the printing blurs, until those damn Spanish verbs dance meringues and *cumbias* in my head as I try to pin down their correctly conjugated translations.

I read to distract myself as I wait for someone from the island to appear at my camp, his brow knit with concern and his voice heavy as he questions whether I am hurt or sick. I wait for the Kunas to acknowledge my conspicuous absence from their town meeting. At first, I sit on my log chair by the fire pit and read in the half-light of dusk, and at every bump or sigh or whisper I glance toward the trail expecting to see a brown face and smiling white teeth. At dark I retire to the *nega*, light the lamp, and stretch out on my belly on the dirt floor. I leave the door open as a welcome. When I wake in the full sun of morning, the flame still flickers at my side.

Stiff from my awkward night, groggy from oversleeping, I try to make up for lost time by organizing my letters from David while my breakfast cooks. I get so absorbed with reading that I forget to stir the pot and everything that's inside ends up scorched. That thin corn gruel represented the last food that I have to my name. I'm tempted to toss everything—burnt gruel, pot, the four manila envelopes and all the letters inside—into the smoldering fire, but instead I collapse onto the log. A pulse throbs inside my skull.

In the distance, barely louder than the white noise of the surf, I hear a clear, liquid whistle: the call of a tinamou. The song reminds me of Ceferino and what he said about birds singing when they are around me. I wonder if it is true. I'm never quite sure whether I should believe what I hear from Ceferino, if I understand his garbled Spanish or if he understands mine, if he is teasing or maybe using metaphors that I mistake for facts.

The tinamou calls again, much closer, and I recognize the sweetness of Ceferino's whistle in the tremolo. After my lonely night of waiting and rejection, I have no desire to see anyone, least of all Ceferino. I consider bolting into the thin forest that surrounds my camp. I could hide behind a palm trunk so that when he comes up the path, the place would seem deserted. While he's occupied by looking for me inside the *nega*, I could pick my way down the ridge through the weeds, then hustle up the trail to the blind.

But before I can bring myself to move, I look up and see him step out from behind the *nega*—Ceferino with his easy, graceful stride and slim brown body—and my heart jumps into my throat. When I thought about hiding from him my muscles were too stiff and tired to move, but when I see his dancing black eyes I want to leap off the log and throw my arms around him. I try to control myself by rising formally and smiling, but my head hurts so much that my expression must resemble a grimace.

"I missed you last night." Ceferino's voice is low and intimate. "Without you sitting on the bench next to Iris, I didn't have anything to look at when I got bored by all the talking."

"I couldn't"—the words catch in my throat—"I couldn't go to the meeting last night because everyone's mad at me."

"Mad at you?"

I hear a smile behind his words and step closer but I'm too shy to touch him. "Because of what happened with that girl."

Ceferino flicks his finger across my cheek, then wrinkles his nose and grins. "You take everything too seriously."

"They are mad at me—they lectured me all the last meeting and fined me $35—it kept going up because they said I wasn't cooperating with them."

Ceferino raises his nose and makes a sniffing sound. "*Sulegoa*, what did you cook for breakfast this morning?"

"Nothing." My voice is sullen.

In less than ten minutes Ceferino has cleaned out all the burnt gruel and prepared a fresh meal of fried bananas and taro. He's brought other food, enough for several days: rice and corn, bananas and plantains and yucca. I ask, "Why did you bring all this food?"

"Romelio Rosterio—he owns the land closest to the place where you watch the eagles—yesterday he came from his farm and said that he was missing eight bananas."

"Monkeys must have stolen them."

"Romelio said that it was a funny thing: all around the banana trees were the tracks of a *sule*. How do you think a *sule* managed to climb those trees to steal bananas?"

"I'm not even a good thief."

"You should eat your food before it gets cold."

As I eat, Ceferino picks up the envelopes that I abandoned when he arrived. I watch him examine the writing. "You can't read, can you?"

By the way he turns his head away, I wonder if I've embarrassed him.

"This is my name." I point to the block letters of the address. "I always hope that *purbakan* can't read either, because if they saw this they'd know my name. That would give them power over me, right?"

"It is different where you are from?"

"There aren't as many spirits. Or maybe there are but we just don't feel them."

"You miss your name?"

"Not as much as I used to. I understand more about it now."

"But you are lonely?"

"I was this week. I felt like I had to avoid the island because I was afraid—" I catch myself and stop abruptly.

Ceferino sighs. "You are tired. You should not work today."

"Those eagle eggs could hatch any time."

"Not today. Probably Friday."

I look up from the food. "How do you know that?"

"A lot of ways."

"What ways? I need to know. It would really help my study."

He finally does what I hoped he'd do and slides closer on the log to cuddle me. "I'll tell you, but only if you come to the jungle with me instead of working."

"You'll give me the information that I need but only if I don't do my work?"

He looks a little confused by my construction but answers, "*Eh-yea.*"

"So by not doing my job, I'll actually be doing my job."

"*Sulegoa*, you think too much. Just come with me today."

In the jungle, he leads me straight to the lip of the waterfall. Before I know it, he is naked, the clothes falling from his body like scales from the eyes of a blind man. I look down into the canyon and shudder.

"You are cold?" His voice is barely audible above the rush of water.

"*Sully.*" I feel his nakedness next to me. I can't look at him.

"I used to come to this place often when I was a boy. To me, it seemed as far from the island as anywhere I could imagine."

The clouds above us must open because suddenly sunlight streams around us like water. "When you were a boy, did you jump off this cliff into the pool?"

"*Sully.*" He has moved closer to me: his breath touches my hair. "That time with you was the first."

I hug my arms to my chest to put a barrier between his body and mine.

His words are a whisper. "You were very brave to jump from here."

I twist my face away from the heat of his breath. "*Sully.*"

"You were not scared that day."

"I'm always scared. Ever since I got off the plane I've been scared."

"But you jumped."

"*Eh-yea.*"

"Why?"

At first I don't answer. With one finger, Ceferino guides my chin upward so that my face is level with his. When our eyes join, he repeats those two Spanish words, "*Por qué*?"

I shake my head free from his hand and look down the canyon. "Because the world at the bottom of this cliff seemed better than what I had up here."

"And now? You still think the world is better down in that canyon?"

I cannot look at him but feel him move away from me. A moment later, I hear a splash.

On the boulder at the edge of the plunge pool, our bodies dry slowly. For a long time we don't speak. Maybe I doze. My head on his shoulder, I ask, "Do Kunas kiss?"

"I don't understand."

"Your father and mother. When they are alone do they kiss—on the lips?"

"*Sully*. Only whites kiss."

"But you kiss. You kiss very well."

"I kiss like a white man?"

"Better. Where did you learn?"

"I don't know. Probably from my wife."

"You kissed her?"

"Sometimes. She liked it."

"Where did she learn about kissing?"

Ceferino doesn't answer.

"Is it hard to talk about her?"

His voice follows the river downstream. "*Sully.*"

"You loved her?"

He doesn't answer. I imagine his wife: young, slim, pretty, her short black hair fanned across Ceferino's chest. My voice is tentative. "I want to ask you more."

He sits up and pulls me onto his lap so that I'm looking straight into his face. "What do you want to ask?"

When I meet his eyes, I see a red fleck embedded in one of the irises. "You have a red mark in your eye."

"I hurt it when I was a kid. I couldn't see out of that eye for almost a year."

"What happened?"

"My father sent me over the mountains to cure it." Ceferino motions with his chin upstream. "There's a village at the beginning of this river where a woman who was a famous healer lived. I stayed there for a year while she cured my eye."

"And then you got your sight back?"

"*Eh-yea.*"

"How old were you?"

"Maybe seven."

"You were scared?"

Ceferino grins. "I was too dumb to be scared."

"You were alone, away from your family the whole time?"

"*Eh-yea*. But it was beautiful up there—the most beautiful place I've ever been. Even when I was a little kid, I loved being in the jungle. The healer woman would take me out every day and teach me about the plants. I felt like I was in paradise."

"How did your eye get hurt?"

"My brother poked it with a stick."

"Your brother? Eulogio?"

"*Eh-yea*." He chuckles. "We used to fight all the time. We were like—like those two jaguar kittens in the jungle, always rolling around on the ground to see who would end up on top. Our parents just let us fight because there wasn't anything they could do to stop us."

“Which of you is older?”

“I am, but not even by a year. Eulogio was always bigger than me. And smarter.”

“Not smarter,” I murmur.

“Much smarter.” He kisses me deeply.

When I get my breath back, I put my hand over his heart. “Tell me now about your wife.”

“Her father broke his leg and couldn’t work. She was their only daughter so she needed to get married to have someone to take care of her parents.”

“And?”

“She was very young. Very pretty.”

“And?”

“She was carrying a child.”

I reach up and run my finger along Ceferino’s smooth jaw. “Not yours?”

He kisses my fingertips but says nothing.

“Eulogio’s?”

He pauses before he speaks. “Disrelita had just given birth to their second daughter.”

“So your oldest son is actually Eulogio’s? But your younger son?”

“He may be mine.”

“But he might not be?”

“My wife was very young. And Eulogio is very handsome.”

I lean back to study his face but can detect no trace of bitterness or jealousy. “Where I come from, people kill each other over things like that.”

Ceferino’s smile is open and unaffected. “I guess it’s a good thing that we don’t live in the place where you are from.”

On the hike back from the falls, my feet feel as if they are weighted down by clunky old boots. I shuffle through the dust. Ceferino never turns his head, never checks over his shoulder to see how I am hiking, but he remains the same distance in front of me no matter how slowly I walk in the dead afternoon heat.

I'm panting and sweating freely when we finally arrive at the top of the ridge. "Now I will cook dinner for you," I declare.

Ceferino takes my hands and turns me so that I'm pointed toward the doorway of my *nega*. "Now you will lie down in your hammock while I cook your dinner."

"But I'm the woman—I'm supposed to cook for you."

"You are a white girl. White girls don't cook for Kuna men. Besides," he adds, "I saw what you cooked for breakfast this morning—remember?" He kisses me and I decide that some things are more important than pride.

I am dozing, the inside of the *nega* amorphous with dusk, when Ceferino enters with a bowl of stew. "*Nuedi*," I tell him. In the first spoonful, I taste meat and ask him, "What kind of stew is this?"

"*Sulegoa*, you need to realize one thing: eating is very serious business. Kunas never talk when they eat."

"I'm a white girl."

"But if you live here, you have to live like a Kuna. This is one of your lessons."

I wait until my bowl is empty before I speak again. "Now you will tell me how you know that the eagle eggs won't hatch until Friday?"

His hands work the hem of my t-shirt out from the waistband of my shorts. "No, *Sulegoa*, you are too sleepy now. I promise I will tell you everything another day."

"What are you doing?"

"Your clothes are wet from the hike. It will be better for you to take them off."

"Are you advising me now as a doctor?" I ask as I raise my arms so that he can peel off my shirt.

After my head pops free from the fabric, I comb the hair out of my eyes with my fingers. Ceferino stares straight at my face. The red scar in his iris flickers like a flame. He leans forward and kisses my lips as he guides me on to my back. "*Eh-yea*." He undoes the button and fly of my shorts and I lift my hips as he shimmies the fabric down my legs.

"Isn't that better?" he murmurs when I curl naked in his arms.

"*Eh-yea*." I run my hand along his arm. "All of that trouble I got into with the community was because of my clothes. Does it bother you that I wear clothes like these?"

He rubs his cheek against my shoulder but doesn't respond.

"You won't tell me?"

"Sometimes it takes a while for me to find the right words in Spanish."

I wait for what seems like a long time. Finally he answers. "You could wear the most beautiful blouse in the world but to me it would be ugly because it hides your body from my eyes, and your body is the most beautiful thing that I know."

My stomach quivers but his words embarrass me so much that I feel the need to argue. "Don't you think that my skin is too pale? And that I'm hairy?"

In the gloom, I see his white teeth flash. "*Nusa*."

"*Nusa*?"

"A *nusa* is an animal that lives in the jungle, about this big." He takes his hand away from my shoulder to measure the length of a finger. "She's very shy, always hiding under leaves, but if you catch her and hold her in your hand, then she lies still like she is happy. She has beautiful fur and when you run your hand across it, you feel her body shiver like a heartbeat or a pulse."

"So why are you telling me about *nusa*?"

"Because you have a *nusa* that lives between you legs." As soon as the words leave his mouth, he presses his lips into mine so that they muffle my surprised snort.

When the kiss ends, I tell him, "Your clothes are damp from walking, too. I think that you would be happier if you took them off."

"Are you advising me now as a doctor?"

"Actually," I bite my lip as I play with the hem of his shirt, "I'm speaking as a scientist."

"A scientist?"

"I was sent here to study the animals in the jungle. I think I need to learn more about this *nusa*."

"Stay here with me tonight. Please."

"You say that now but when I'm snoring and spread out over most of the hammock, you'll wish that you had sent me back to the island when you had the chance."

"I would never feel that way."

Ceferino's hand travels up my thigh to my hip. "How did you feel when you heard me call this morning? Why didn't you come down to meet me like you usually do?"

My breath catches in my throat and I cannot speak.

"You don't have to answer—I understand. You were afraid."

"I'm not afraid of you."

"But you are afraid of Anselmo, and Pedro, and the missionary, and of Eulogio, too. That's why you are a different person on the island than you are at the waterfall."

"Does that bother you?"

"Sometimes I think that you are not a woman at all, that you are a *purba*. A tree woman out to seduce me."

"Is that good or bad?"

"*An be sabe.*"

"*An be sabe?*"

"*An*," he says as he flattens his palm against the left side of his chest. "*Be.*" With his other hand, he presses the upper part of my breast toward my heart.

"*Sabe?*" I ask in a whisper.

His lips meet mine and for a moment I lose my breath.

"*An be sabe*," I whisper when he releases me.

XXVII

On New Year's Eve, I leave the blind early so that I can catch up on my paperwork: I haven't even begun the letter to my parents thanking them for the Christmas presents, much less composed David's year-end project summary. In my *nega*, I collect my notebook and a pen but the sight of two teddy bears—one pink and one blue—distracts me. Ruiz brought the toys, along with a beautiful emerald necklace, when he visited me on Christmas Eve. To preserve the charade of Flemming as the source of these gifts, I'm waiting until after tomorrow's mail exchange before I take them to Iris and her girls. I'm still smiling over Ruiz's choice of teddy bears when I step through the *nega's* doorway and straight into the rigid, upright form of the missionary.

The man doesn't move, he doesn't apologize for blocking my path. I don't like his eyes: they are as pale as the ice inside a glacier.

"You startled me."

He walks past my *nega* toward the fire pit. "What did you tell the Indians about me and that girl you saw at the river?"

The superior tilt of the missionary's head clenches my teeth. "I never said a word about you."

He snorts. "Why do you insist on lying to me?"

"I'm not saying that I wouldn't have sold you to the Kunas but they never gave me a chance. They were so busy lecturing me that I couldn't get a word in edgewise. Anyway, you have no right to act high and mighty with me since it's your own fault you're in this mess. It wasn't my idea to lure that girl into the jungle and then steal her clothes."

"I didn't steal her clothes!" His voice rises on the final word. "She couldn't very well be baptized wearing her heathen rags, could she?"

“If you want that wrap you gave her, I found it at the mouth of the river. You might want to rethink the location for your baptisms in the future: with all the red mud you two kicked up, the fabric looks like it’s been washed in the blood of the lamb.”

His hands ball into fists. I dart out of his reach.

“How dare you joke about the torture and death of the Lord Jesus!”

“I’m sorry if what I say offends you but I never asked you to visit me in the first place.”

When he doesn’t respond, I press him further. “Is there something specific that you want?”

The missionary opens his mouth—I get the feeling he was going to insult me but for some reason thought better of it. As I look at his face, the glacial blue eyes suddenly soften: I swear I see a sheen of tears over them. He plunks down onto the log and buries his face in his hands. “They say I have to marry her.”

I don’t know if I am moved by the desolation and hopelessness in his voice, his abject body language, or his tears, but when the missionary groans out this sentence I feel an ache of pity for him. “It can’t be as bad as all that.”

At the sound of my words, he jumps to his feet, his eyes blazing, and shouts, “You goddamned bitch—it’s worse than you can ever know!”

I leap out of his reach again, cursing myself for trusting him.

He throws his arms open in a dramatic gesture. “I’m married!” Tears and emotion make his face red and ugly. “I have a wife back home in Oklahoma—a beautiful, holy, Christian wife—and two blessed children. What will they say when they learn that I have been wallowing in filth with these sinful heathens?”

“It wasn’t filth—it was mud.”

“How can you make jokes at a time like this?”

“Your wife doesn’t know that you’re down here with the Kunas?”

His hoarse whisper is barely audible. "She thinks I'm building an orphanage in Caracas."

"And you're not in Caracas because—?"

"That's none of your business!"

"None of this is my business. All I want to do is study the eagles but you keep dragging me into this crazy soap opera of yours."

"The Lord's work is not a soap opera!"

"What do you want from me?"

The missionary draws a deep breath. Forcing a smile, he steps over the log to offer me his right hand. "The Kunas like you. They'll listen to what you say."

"They didn't hear a word I said last week."

"That was because—" he begins, then abruptly stops.

I'm thinking back to my trial at the meeting house, to the low male voice in the animated woman's narrative, to the lingering smile on Eulogio's face. "What did you tell them about me?"

The ice blue eyes are elusive. "Nothing. I didn't say a thing. And anyway they didn't believe me."

I'm silent for a minute, hoping he'll dig himself an even deeper hole trying to escape. When I realize that he is satisfied with his response, I decide to cut to the chase: "So the bottom line is that they say you have to marry the girl and you don't want to."

"I can't marry her—I'm already married. And even if I wasn't—"

"She's brown-skinned and a heathen. So who says that you have to marry her?"

"That one man who knows English on the island. The one who looks like a son of Satan."

I'm surprised at the accuracy in his description of Pedro. "Just him?"

"It's all of them. The whole island. They all decided that I have to marry her."

"They had a big meeting?"

He nods, his eyes averted.

"Once they've made a decision like that, they're not going to change it. You agreed to abide by their rules when you came to the island. You should have remembered that before you took that girl's clothes."

"I—I tried to get away. This morning. I went to the airport to catch the plane to Panama City."

"Running like a scared rabbit? That doesn't seem like a very Christian thing to do."

He shoots me a dirty look but surprises me by continuing in an almost submissive tone: "They wouldn't let me go. There were five of them, even that big one with the mustache who looks like he could be a boxer. They forced me to go back to the island with them."

"I don't see anything that I can do to help you."

"Please." His eyes soften and I'm afraid he's going to cry again.

"There's another airstrip about five miles up the coast. The planes from Panama City stop there first, before they come here. You could catch the plane there."

"How would I find it?"

"The airstrip? You just go west—"

"Through the jungle?"

"It's probably easier to take the coast."

His blue eyes open wide. "You expect me to walk five miles through the jungle?"

"No, I just said that you walk five miles along the coast."

"And what do I do when I get there?"

"I don't know. Whatever you want to do, I guess."

"But the plane doesn't come until morning."

"Yeah."

"So I'd have to spend the night there."

"Yeah."

"On the airstrip?"

"I guess that would be the safest place."

His face pales. "The safest place?"

I look at his bulging eyes and trembling lower lip. "You're afraid?"

His breathing sounds as if he's hyperventilating.

"What ever compelled you to come down here in the first place? Why aren't you in Oklahoma with that beautiful Christian wife of yours?"

"I had to come down here," he whispers.

"Why?"

"The Lord told me to."

I scribble a brief letter to my parents, then a note to David explaining that the eggs are so close to hatching that a year-end report on the Harpy Project would be incomplete without the preliminary results from the nesting. I load my knapsack with three bottles of drinking water, a few bananas, and a can of Brian's beans. The missionary stands with his hands hanging at his sides as if he is stunned. I lash my tent to the bottom of my knapsack and my sleeping bag to the top.

"You got something to sleep in?"

The man opens his mouth without speaking.

"A bedroll, some spare clothes, a Bible? Anything?"

His blue eyes are liquid. "I can't go back to get them."

"There's a thatch shelter at the airstrip. You can sleep in there."

"But the tent—?"

"That's for me. You ready to go?"

XXVIII

In the blind, I perch on the stool with my field glasses trained to the nest. The binoculars are Swarovski's and worth more than I am paid by the harpy eagle project in an entire year. The oversized lenses collect every glimmer of available light. So while my naked eye cannot separate the outline of the bird from the early morning gloom, when I peer through the binocular's eyepiece I see every gray feather, every black slash on the mother eagle's face.

She stands on a branch of the Maria tree and stares down into the nest. Her yellow legs—the first time I've gotten a good look at those since she began brooding—are scaly and rough, and two of her talons are cracked. Her feathers are rumpled like morning hair. On her breast, I see patches of bare, pink skin. As I watch, the eagle's black beak, so powerful it can crush the skull of a monkey, reaches down to her belly and tugs out a mouthful of down, then spits it into the nest.

She watches too, waiting like me. I sense her anticipation, her restlessness. The male is nowhere in sight. When I think back, I realize that I haven't seen him since before Christmas. The female must be hungry—starving—because as far as I know, she's hung tight to the nest. The only time I've seen her leave the tree was that one day I thought she had abandoned the eggs, the day before I met the fer-de-lance snake on the trail up from the river.

The eagle shakes her head as if she has an itch, then spreads her wings and flaps a few times, not trying to fly but simply stretching her muscles. On the nest, she's been so still, so stone-like that I had forgotten how magnificent these birds are. Harpy eagles are the largest avian predators in the world and although this eagle may only be a poor relation to the harpy, she moves with the power and confidence of a creature that knows that nothing in her world can threaten her.

After she has finished her stretch, she tucks her wings against her sides and settles onto the stiff ridge of branches that cups the nest. She stares down, motionless, for what must be an hour or more. By then, harsh sunlight has crept from the canopy of leaves and the wilted white blossoms of night to warm the nest and the scarred black trunk of the Maria tree, then swept down to the knotted vegetation of the forest floor.

The statue of the eagle moves. I jerk the field glasses back up to the crotch of the tree and focus in time to see the mother bird step from the rim into the nest. With her beak, she picks up something white. I wrench the binoculars off their tripod, focus wildly until I can confirm what I had hoped: the female is collecting fragments of broken eggshell. The first eagle chick has hatched.

My morning in the blind is divided between recording every detail of the imagined hatching—I still have not actually seen an eaglet—and carefully watching for any new development at the nest. The latter is conspicuously absent: after getting rid of the eggshell fragments by tossing them over the side, the female settled into her statue-like brooding position, upright and proud and vigilant.

As the afternoon wears on, I begin to wonder if only one egg survived incubation or if egg laying may have been staggered so that the other chicks will hatch at a later date. In the U.S., bald eagles often lay their eggs several days apart. If a food shortage develops during the nestling phase, the largest chick will eat its weaker siblings. Although appearing Darwinian and cruel, cannibalism among chicks has been proven to increase the brood survival rate in predatory birds.

The thought of siblings vying for supremacy reminds me of Eulogio, and Ceferino's casual acknowledgement of his brother's sins. I realize how lost I am among the Kunas, how in some ways they are more incomprehensible to me than these eagles. Maybe Pedro is right, maybe whites and Kunas should never try to live together. The missionary's stay on the island was a disaster for everyone. When the Kunas find out that I helped him escape to Panama City, they'll probably never allow another white person to set foot on their island. And I will be branded as the researcher who single-handedly ruined seven years of harpy eagle fieldwork and alienated not only the Kunas but the entire nation of Panama.

The eagle returns me to the moment: she has again stepped out from the nest to the supporting branch of the tree. I focus the binoculars, my hands shaking with anticipation. For an instant, I think I glimpse a flash of white, perhaps the head of an eagle chick. I feel a quiver in my body almost as deep as Ceferino's remembered caress. With my ragged exhale, I mutter a prayer for the eagles and their chicks.

Judging by the mother's position, another egg is hatching. The female eagle observes from above as before. She does not assist. In some species of wading birds, the mother will help the chick escape the egg, gently peeling the shell away from the struggling infant. This eagle mother exhibits no such consideration. Breaking out of its shell is the first in a lifetime of survival tests for this chick. Its mother watches and evaluates. If her offspring is weak, if it is deformed, if it is unable to survive, does she grieve or mourn? Can a creature that kills as readily as an eagle ever really love?

I've barely gotten comfortable with the binoculars when the mother eagle hops back into the nest and begins clearing the broken remains of an egg. This chick freed itself more quickly than the first, probably taking only twenty minutes to hatch. Does that mean that it is stronger than the other? These eaglets will share this nest for the next two years. By the time they fledge, the stronger chick may have killed the other. Certainly, one will have emerged as dominant, one will end up on top more often than the other as they wrestle in the nest for supremacy. And then, like Ceferino and Eulogio, the two siblings may be able to coexist in peace.

Her housekeeping complete, the female eagle settles back into the nest—to brood? I wonder if the bird cradles yet another egg. In many species, the mother will stay outside of the nest after all the eggs have hatched to give her offspring room to spread out. Sometimes she'll abandon the nest entirely, rejoining the chicks only if she senses that they need protection from weather or predators.

I jot more notes. I'm hungry but hate the thought of leaving the blind while there's still activity. For the sake of my job, for the sake of science, for the sake of my own personal curiosity, I don't want to miss anything important.

In the growing gloom of dusk, the mother eagle again leaves the nest and perches on the branch in what I have labeled her "hatching observation position." The movement is abrupt, as if she sensed the pecking of the chick's egg tooth through the brood feathers on her belly. Unlike the earlier hatchings, the adult eagle now seems impatient, fidgety: she jerks her head from side to side and frequently spreads and flaps her wings. I wonder what the two already-hatched eaglets are doing—do they instinctively peck and attack the helpless newcomer the way that domestic chicks will? I long to view the interior of the nest: I feel that all of the activity occurs behind a curtain and what I consider direct observation is only a combination of guesswork, intuition, and wishful thinking.

The female eagle stretches her neck down toward the hollow of the nest, and up pop two pink heads. The chicks must be nearly naked, their eyes sealed shut, helpless. Responding only to sensed motion, what will they find to eat? Do they peck at their mother's beak like seagull chicks? But the female cannot vomit a meal—she herself has not eaten in over a week. Where is her mate with food? Suddenly, I'm stuck by a terrible thought: what if the male eagle has been killed and I have to sit here, day by day, and record the gradual starvation of his family?

The image brings a sob, thick and convulsive, and then I'm crying uncontrollably. The eagle's obsidian eyes flash up, away from her babies. She must have heard me. A predator with hearing as acute as death: surely she can sense my weakness.

I bite my lip and swallow my sobs. The mother eagle returns to her vigil. When I glance away from the eyepiece of the binoculars, I discover that I can no longer read the writing in my notebook. The darkness in the blind is heavier, swifter than I expected. Under the dense canopy of leaves, there is no twilight.

In the blackness of a jungle night, unholy things rule. The jaguar, unseen mother to the kittens that wrestle for dominance, prowls the banks of the river, her steps silent as death. The fer-de-lance, twenty breath snake: if in daylight I could barely recognize his form, nighttime would render him more *purba* than reality. The tree women shed their hard, stiff skins and dance, smooth and supple in the starlight. The spirits that those women excite glide between the trees, seduced by the dancing and the lazy heat.

My belly grumbles. I sip from my canteen: my only dinner. My bed will be the packed dirt of the floor. But at least inside this blind I will be safe from the night. Damn that last eagle chick for taking so long to hatch. No matches, no lamp, not even a flashlight with dying batteries. I wad my shorts into a pillow, then curl on the floor and cover myself as best I can with my spare clothing.

Night passes slowly, the wind still and the stars clouded. Sleep eludes me: I feel—or imagine—that unseen creatures crawl across my skin. An owl wails as if it's perched on the ragged roof of the blind. I picture slotted yellow eyes studying me through holes in the canvas. Other noises defy identification by their vagueness.

Later, I am awakened by a deep, throaty cough. One of the papers on file at the research station, an elegantly composed essay from the last century, details a nocturnal visit by a jaguar to the compound's original site. All night long, the scientists were kept awake by a persistent cough outside their tents. In the morning they discovered three horses silently dead, the mauled carcasses circled by cat tracks as wide as a spread hand.

Is it my imagination or is it *purbakan*? Tonight everything is disturbed, tense, restless. For the first time, I hear howler monkeys in the hills close to the blind. A kingfisher—*sinna*, the bird of death—rattles his flight call to announce the blackest hour. Is he calling my soul to join him or are his laughing cries meant for another?

When I do sleep, I am frightened by what I dream. I see the missionary, his body dark and swollen with poison. I see blank eyes white as snow. I see undefined faces that grin like monkeys and skitter back and forth as if disembodied. I feel the hiss of expelled breath like a curse.

I shake myself awake. Outside, I hear rustling. Random noises resolve into footsteps that circle the blind once, twice. I want to call out: any animal would be frightened by the sound of a human voice. But I am still. What if my call sounds like a squeak of fear, the whimper of a victim? The footsteps resume their pace around the circumference of the blind—maybe only fifteen steps, the enclosure is that small. I listen with my mouth open, forgetting to breathe. Somewhere very near, I hear a cough.

XXIX

Saturday, January 4

Visual observation verifies three living offspring in the nest. I would guess that these are the three eaglets that hatched yesterday: two during daylight and one after dark. The offspring appear to be virtually naked and display very little voluntary motor movement. They spend the majority of their time nestled in the breast feathers of the female adult, who has assumed the same position that she did when she was brooding. When she sits in the nest like this, the bodies of the chicks are entirely covered by the mother's feathers, leaving only the eaglets' heads visible.

At approximately 10 AM, the male eagle arrived carrying a half-eaten sloth. The chicks exhibited no interest in the fresh meat or in the male, who stood in the nest while the female retreated to a neighboring branch and fed on the sloth. The male made no contact with the chicks. The female ate more rapidly than I have observed in the past, not harrying the meat in any way or pausing to take account of her surroundings. When the sloth was entirely consumed—including bones—she immediately returned to the nest. At this point, the male departed and the female settled in with the chicks against her breast. No exchange of food between the female and the young was observed during this feeding event.

As the day wears on, my eyes become too sore to focus, my mouth dry as death, and my stomach growling like something alive. The buzz of cicadas sets my teeth on edge. Sun beating down on the blind scrapes at my inflamed nerves. I'm so weak that I'm nauseous.

I leave the blind at midday and stumble to the river for a bath. I don't know how I'm going to deal with the meeting tonight. I should probably bring all of this month's pay with me when I go to the island, to cover the fines that the community plans to level on me for my role in the missionary's escape.

At camp, I stumble over two unexpected packages that lie just inside of the doorway to my *nega*. I drop to my knees to examine the paper-wrapped parcels. One is weightless—barely there—but the other gives off the seductive aroma of something baked. Without questioning the origin, I tear open the wrapping on the second package to reveal a loaf of rich, doughy bread. I devour it with the gulping urgency of a starving eagle.

When every crumb of the bread is gone, I lean my head against the smooth wood of the door frame and try to catalog the things I have to do this afternoon. My head throbs. I close my burning eyes and consciously unclench my muscles. Without resistance, I feel my body dissolve into the gray dirt of the *nega* floor.

I don't think that I slept for more than half an hour but when I wake I feel much better, strong enough to cook a meal under the harsh afternoon sun. At the fire pit, I discover a scatter of twigs across my log bench. Stepping back, I squint and the twigs resolve themselves into a message: "I was here. Where were you? R."

As the fire grows, I prepare a simple stew—sweet potatoes and smoked fish—one that won't take long to cook. Once the coals are ready, I slide the pot into the center of the fire and then, a banana in hand, retreat to the shade of my *nega*.

The other package that Ruiz left is almost weightless—it feels like nothing more than the wisp of brown paper that encloses it. When I untie the string, the wrapper parts like a curtain to reveal a shimmering rainbow. I isolate a turquoise as clear as the Caribbean and hold it up to the light: a pair of panties. Each color in the rainbow is a pair of silk panties. Bras, too—five panties and five bras. I had forgotten about the frumpy cotton underwear that my mother sent and Ruiz's promised replacements.

The silk is elegant and feminine. As I fondle it, I'm seized with a violent disgust for the clothing I have on: a dingy white t-shirt and a man's shapeless shorts. I slough them off like the bark of a tree woman. In the silk I feel breathlessly beautiful, like I am wreathed in flowers to seduce *purbakan* from the sky. I eat my stew wearing nothing but a turquoise bra and panties.

Sitting in the doorway of my *nega*, I open my notebook and laugh out loud when I think of what David would say if he knew that I composed the official report for the harpy eagle project clad only in a whisper of silk.

Nest Observation Study—Year-End Summary

I arrived at the site on September 13, replacing doctoral candidate Brian Geddes who left due to a medical condition. For information on the project prior to this date, the reader is referred to Mr. Geddes's notes, which he took with him in their entirety when he departed from the San Blas site on the morning of Sept. 14.

In my three-and-a-half months at the site, I have averaged 60 hours per week in direct observation of the nest from the blind, and an additional 10 hours per week in secondary research including interviews with several of the residents of the indigenous community on the nearby island who are very knowledgeable of the history and activities at the nest site and of the eagles in general.

I'm beginning to think that I can compose this entire report without once using the word "harpy" or revealing any of my doubts as to the proper identification of the subjects. I outline the observed behavior of the eagles during the breeding phase before launching into a description of what I have dubbed "the nesting event."

"*Na*?" On the other side of the bamboo wall, the man's voice holds a question.

"Just a minute," I squeak as I dart into deeper shadow to throw on my clothes. I emerge at the same moment that Eulogio steps around the bamboo wall. "*Na*."

He seems startled by my appearance. "You are okay?"

"I was writing. You startled me."

He studies my face. "You look very tired."

"I didn't sleep well last night."

"You were here?"

"No—I was at my work. The eagle eggs were hatching. They were still hatching when it got dark so I stayed at the blind the whole night."

"You work very hard, *Puna*."

"*Puna*?"

He bends over and picks up my notebook, then hands it to me. "You have a few minutes to talk?"

"Only if you tell me what *puna* means."

"It means sister. I have brought you something from my brother."

My face burns. The way Eulogio talks, his words and his tone of voice, I imagine that he knows every act Ceferino and I perform at the waterfall.

"You are okay?"

I realize that I'm still standing in the doorway of the *nega*, my eyes closed. "Yeah. I mean, *eh-yea*. Let's sit down on the log. It's shady there and I think the fire's gone down."

"You need a chair to sit on when it's too hot beside the fire."

"I'm never at camp much during the day."

"But you should have at least one chair. And you need a watch, too, so that you know what time it is. And a roof over your fire for when it rains."

"How about an airplane so that I can fly back and forth to Panama City?"

I speak lightly but Eulogio is serious when he responds. "You need to go back to Panama City?"

His tone makes me measure my words more carefully. "I don't have any reason to leave here. It's just this report that needs to get to the city."

"The report is for your work?"

"*Eh-yea*."

"Your work—it is hard?"

"It shouldn't be. I like watching the eagles and being in the jungle. It's just a few things that I have trouble with."

"The things that have to do with Flemming?"

I sometimes forget how quick and insightful Eulogio can be. "*Eh-yea.*"

"But he is in the U.S. Why would you have a problem with him now?"

"It's a long story."

"We're sitting in the shade."

His reply is so casual, so natural, that I laugh.

"It's good to see you smile and laugh again. You were very upset the last time I saw you."

"That's because everyone was mad at me."

"No one blames you for anything, *Puna*. We know that it was the missionary who had caused all the trouble."

"If no one blames me, why did you treat me the way you did?"

Eulogio looks down at his hands as if he doesn't want to meet my eyes. "Why did you help the *evangelico* get on the plane to Panama City?"

My stomach feels as if I've just been punched. "How did you know about that?"

"The air taxi pilot told Orestes that you picked up your mail at the airstrip near Usdup. When the missionary got on the plane."

"And Orestes told everyone on the island. So you're here now to make sure that I get to the meeting for the trial, right? Am I in for another fine or will it be something more serious this time?"

"*Puna*, everyone on the island wanted the missionary to leave. No one wanted him to marry Esmelia because then we'd be stuck with him forever. Everyone is glad that you helped him leave. Ruiz even paid your fine this morning. The only thing that you have to worry about now is your problem with Flemming."

I think I hear a hint of patronage in his voice. "You sound like an uncle."

His tone teases. “An uncle? Or a brother?”

I turn my face away to cover my embarrassment.

“And since I am your brother, you can tell me about your problem with Flemming.”

“It’s not really a problem with him. It’s just—this whole project was started because Flemming said the eagles on the nest here are a special kind of eagle, the biggest ones in the jungle. But the more I look at them, the more I think that these are not the kind of eagles that Flemming says they are.”

“You told this to Flemming?”

“I can’t. Flemming is the expert on eagles. I’m just a student. If Flemming says that these eagles are the biggest ones in the jungle, I can’t say that they’re not. Especially since I haven’t seen any eagles that are bigger.”

“Then how do you know there are eagles bigger than these?”

“It’s not just size. The different kinds of eagles look different too, like the difference between”—I cast around in my mind to find a suitable comparison—“the difference between a white man and a Kuna.”

“I understand,” Eulogio says quickly. He thinks for a moment before he asks, “There are people besides Flemming that you can talk to about this?”

“No. The people I work with, they wouldn’t believe me if I told them that Flemming might have made a mistake. They would just think that Flemming’s right and I’m wrong.”

“You are much smarter than Flemming.”

I offer him my notebook. “You want to write that down? Maybe my boss will believe it if he hears it coming from you.”

“The people you work with don’t respect you because you’re a woman?”

I shake my head to deny any gender bias but then remember David’s abrupt change after I slept with him. “You may be right on that.”

“Why do you work with people like that? Why don’t you get married and have a family?”

Three months ago, his question would have provoked a tirade on intellectual fulfillment and equal rights. "I guess I never met anyone I loved well enough to marry."

Eulogio says, "I have something for you." He reaches into his back pocket and unfolds two pages of notebook paper completely covered with cramped handwriting. "Ceferino had me write this up. It's all of the things he knows about the eagles."

I scan the papers eagerly. He has numbered the points from one to thirty-two, each a precise detail of eagle behavior. A few of the observations, like the one day "vacation" by the mother eagle, are things that I also noted. Other activities I either ignored or took for granted. Ceferino documents specific details and times, such as "For ten days before the eggs hatch, the male will avoid the nest entirely, sleeping during the night in a tree close enough to observe the nest and the female but not making any contact with her." Another: "Six days before the eggs hatch, the female will line the nest with feathers that she pulls from her own breast."

"My God." My voice is a reverent whisper. "This is absolutely amazing."

"You can use it for your work?"

"I've been watching those eagles every day for three months, but Ceferino knows more about them than I ever dreamed. He probably knows more about the eagles than anyone in the world."

"Ceferino has always been interested by life in the jungle."

"This goes way beyond interest. He's a genius. I learn so much from him every time we're in the jungle—" I catch myself, wondering how much Eulogio knows about our field activities. When I glance at him, Eulogio is smiling proudly.

"Ceferino is a *nele*."

"A *nele*?"

"A person who sees things better than other people."

"And how do you become a *nele*? Just by seeing things?"

"It's something you are born with. Some babies when they're born have a"—he pauses as if he's searching for the Spanish word—"a veil over their body. It means that they are gifted with special sight."

"And what does Ceferino see?"

"Everything!" Eulogio's eyes glow with admiration as he talks about his brother. "He sees what is happening in the jungle with the animals and snakes and trees and the river. But he also knows about people: he can read if a person is good or bad, or if they have secrets in their hearts. But most of all he knows spirits."

"*Purbakan*?"

"Did he tell you about *purbakan*?"

"Some. When Litos died."

"Ceferino is famous among the Kunas. He's the greatest *nele* alive."

"He uses his special sight to cure people?"

"He can see the spirits that hurt people and can communicate with them to balance out the good and evil. Most *nelekan* can only see problems, but Ceferino knows about curing too, and healing spirits. He often is called away from Sugatupu because people on other islands want him to come and cure them."

"So he's an important man?"

"*Eh-yea*." Eulogio looks straight into my eyes. "Ceferino is probably the most important man in all of Kuna Yala today."

I lower my gaze to the notebook in my lap, to the two pages that Ceferino and his brother painstakingly translated and transcribed for me. "Thank you for telling me those things about Ceferino." Eulogio shifts and I glimpse the face of his watch. "Oh my God, it's late! I have to get ready for the meeting!" I bounce off the log but as soon as I am upright, my head clouds and I feel my body sway.

Eulogio steadies me. "You are weak."

"I'm just dizzy. It was pretty bad sleeping in the blind last night."

He shepherds me toward the *nega*. "You need to rest."

"But the meeting—"

"No one expects you to come to the meeting tonight. I know now that you are okay. We were worried when Ruiz said that he came here last night and you were not in your *nega*. That's why I came here, to make sure that you are okay."

We're at the door of the *nega*. "And to give me Ceferino's notes."

Eulogio smiles. "You go inside and rest. You will be better after you sleep."

"Yes, uncle."

"Brother." He puts his arm around my waist—affectionately, not sexually.

"Oh—I just remembered. If I'm not going to the island, I need to give you the money for Iris." I dash into the *nega* and find the envelope from Panama City. Shuffling through the papers, I am careful not to pull out the entire wad of bills that David sent. Eulogio watches me but when I offer him the money—two twenties and a ten—he instead takes the entire envelope from my hands. Turning it over, I see him study the printed letters of my name. Without a word, he returns the envelope to me.

I push the bills into his hand. "The money from Flemming."

In an indulgent voice, Eulogio repeats my words. "The money from Flemming."

"Oh, there's something else, too." In the corner, I locate the teddy bears and jeweler's box that Ruiz dropped off on Christmas Eve. "These are for Iris and the girls."

"From Flemming?"

I figure if I don't meet Eulogio's eyes, he won't detect the lie. "Of course."

As gently as Ceferino, Eulogio takes my chin and twists my head so that I am forced to look at his face. "Those all fit into that little envelope?"

His smile is so much like Ceferino's that I have to close my eyes to keep myself from kissing him. "Amazing, isn't it?"

"Truly amazing," he says as he embraces me. His body is stiffer than his brother's, and as he hugs me I do not feel his heart. In my ear, he whispers, "I will be sure to tell Iris that these things are all from Flemming, just as my sister—my *puna*—tells me."

XXX

I try to rest as Eulogio—my brother—advised, but as soon as night falls the dreams return. The images are a compilation of every fear that has haunted me since I came to this place. I don't sleep. I am afraid to close my eyes, afraid of what I will see.

I sweat freely the next day in the blind. I strip naked but the lack of clothing does nothing to cool me. My head throbs. I want to watch the eagles—the mother bird has begun to feed the chicks by shredding bits of flesh from a dead sloth and forcing it into the babies' half-open, unreceptive beaks—but my eyes are so tired they'll only focus through the binocular for five or ten minutes at a time.

Back at the *nega*, I sweat and squirm through another sleepless night. Today instead of watching, I doze in the blind. I dread the western progress of the sun because as soon as light disappears behind the low, hazy hills, I know that the dreams will return.

At the river, I stretch flat and let the current rinse the brine off my skin. These last two days, I've sweated so much that my armpits and the back of my knees are chafed and raw. My clothes smell as sour as a receding tide.

I soak too long in the river. When I finally crawl out of the water, the sun has set and the evening chills. I'm so cold that my belly ghosts blue, so cold that my fingers can't clench to grip. I shake as if I have a palsy. Every time I try to step into my panties, I lose my balance and pitch forward. I forget about dressing and bolt naked up the trail, my clean clothes clutched to my chest, the dirty ones abandoned in a pile on the bank. I run as fast as I can, desperate to pump some heat into my chilled muscles.

At camp, I pull out my sleeping bag and spread it over my hammock. At first, even that doesn't warm me. My teeth chatter uncontrollably. I sob.

I wake in darkness, the flannel lining of my sleeping bag soaked with sweat. The air inside the *nega* is so heavy that I can't breathe. I tumble out of the hammock, slither from the sleeping bag like a moth emerging from a chrysalis. I drag myself through the doorway and into the moonlight. I lie flat on my stomach. My skin glows blue.

I must have dozed because the next thing that I am aware of is a soft, snuffling sound and the warm whisper of an exhale on the back of my neck. The sniffing continues: from its volume and resonance I can tell that the creature that scents me is large, as big or bigger than I am. Whatever it is, it does not touch me: only its breath ghosts along the nape of my neck. Or are those whiskers that tickle my shoulders?

In my mind, I list predator species and review the appropriate response to their threats. If a bear attacks, you should curl your body into a ball. For pumas, strike back. Make eye contact with wolves. At the small of my back, just above the swelling of my hips, I feel a sandpaper-like rasp. Instinctively, I glance over my shoulder.

The jaguar crouches beside me, his tongue gray in the moonlight as he lowers his head for another taste. When the creature catches my eye, he sits back on his rump—like a man—with his legs splayed in front of him. His genitals are naked and human.

I speak over my shoulder to avoid exposing the front of my body. "Who are you?"

When the creature laughs, he reveals long, cat-like canines. "I could ask you the same question."

I remember what Ceferino told me about *purbakan*, that if they know your name it's easier for them to control you, and say nothing.

"There's really no need for me to ask, though." His hand—it is a hand, with five long, graceful fingers—reaches out to stroke my naked flank. "Eagle has told me all about you: she watches, you know, even while you think that you are watching her. Fer-de-lance has told me about you too. You pass by him every day but he says that you seldom take the time to talk to him."

His palm is bare skin but I feel a fringe of fur around the edge as the hand caresses me. "What else do they say?"

The jaguar leans forward. His tongue, rough and dry, rasps upwards along my backbone to my shoulders. The creature's movements are lithe, sinewy, and sensuous. "They tell me that you have hair like the sun and flesh like the moon. But even that did not prepare me for your beauty. I have never seen a body that I wanted as much as yours. You put the moon to shame."

These last words are delivered directly into my ear as the jaguar's whiskers mouse through my hair and he stretches full length over my back. The fur that covers him feels like velvet. As he rubs against me, I abandon myself to the sensuality of his movements and arch my back like a cat in heat.

"You know about the moon, don't you, my pretty one?" his silky voice whispers in my ear. "The moon rides through the night so proud and lordly but he really is a coward. Sometimes when I think he's getting too full of himself, I paddle my canoe up into the sky and pretend that I am going to eat him. I even take a bite or two." His tongue explores the inside of my ear, then his teeth nibble at the lobe.

I fight to keep my hips from catting against his groin. "What happens then?"

His laugh ends with a cough. "Oh, the people on the island send their squinty pink ones out to shoot arrows at me. They think that scares me off. As if I would be frightened of a bunch of pale men who don't even go out in daylight to face the sun!"

His cat's tongue glides down my back, tracing every notch of every bone. I feel his weight shift. His tongue stops at the small of my back, then his whiskers brush along the skin of my rump. "Eagle, Fer-de-lance, even Toucan, they all have told me that you are afraid of nothing."

"I am always afraid."

"Even now, my pretty one? Even now as you lie beneath my body? You will have everything once you become my wife."

His hand explores the cleft between my legs. I shiver. "Oh, so beautiful you are, so warm and beautiful. You don't know what pleasure this brings me, my love, you don't know how long it has been since I have touched a real woman. Those dark women, they are all frightened of me. They flee to the island at night and cower in their houses behind locked doors. Not one of them will let me see her. Not like this, not like you are now, your skin glowing in the moonlight, your body open and ready. The only ones who will let me inside of them are the tree women."

His hands lift my hips so that I crouch on all fours like an animal. "Trees don't have blood, you know. They only have sap. The tree women pretend that they want to love a man, they dance and swing their hips, but when you touch them they're as cold as death. They have no blood to boil inside of them, nothing to spread the heat of passion through their bodies."

A sharp prick pierces the skin on my rump. "Ow!"

"I am sorry, my love. I am truly, truly sorry." His words are punctuated by pauses as his rough tongue laps the wound. "Your blood—it tastes as sweet as cane juice. I do not want to hurt you, I only want to love you. I will not bite you again as long as you raise you hips up just a little more, my love, just like that—yes, that's right—and now spread your legs wider, just a little wider, my love, my wife, just a little—"

He's off balance, leaning into my body, so that when I jerk away from him the jaguar man falls flat on his face. I dart into my *nega* and slam the door.

A moment later I hear him, snuffling outside the *nega*, his fingers probing the spaces between the upright bamboo of the wall. “I will return for you tomorrow night. You cannot run from me forever. Tomorrow I will make you my wife.”

On the beach at dawn a man—I don’t recognize him in the half-light—hauls his canoe up from the surf. I stumble against him, blinded by tears.

“Ceferino,” I gasp.

The man steadies me and says something in Kuna.

“Help me.” My mouth cannot form Kuna words. I gasp out, “Ceferino.” Tears stream down my face.

Another man appears. Ankle-deep in the sea, I collapse on to his chest.

“Help. Help. Ceferino.”

An arm slides around my waist. I am shepherded to shore. Men surround me, all speaking Kuna. I lean against one because I cannot stand on my own. Someone presses a gourd of fresh water to my lips.

I hear a voice I think I recognize. The words are Spanish. “What is wrong here?”

Orestes’s face floats in front of mine. “I need to see Ceferino.”

He says something in Kuna, then in Spanish, “You are sick?”

“Please help me.” I’m crying so hard that I can’t say anything else.

Another voice I know: “*Puna*, what is wrong?”

Eulogio’s arm winds around my waist, another under my knees. He carries me away from the beach, sets me down in the shade with my back against a tree. With the tip of his finger, he touches my forehead. “You’re burning with fever.”

“I need to see Ceferino.”

“He is coming.”

The Kuna voices around me continue. Eulogio presses a wet cloth against my cheek, comforting me with a soft singsong: “You’ll be okay. Ceferino will be here soon. Everything will be fine.”

Abruptly, he changes to Kuna and shouts a few words over his shoulder. A moment later, two hands slide down my forearms and twine through my fingers. When I open my eyes, I see Ceferino's face.

My voice barely escapes my throat. "A *purba*—a man in the skin of a jaguar—he found me."

When does everyone leave? Suddenly I am alone with Ceferino. He is shirtless. He sits on the ground beside me, puts his arm around my shoulders, and draws me into his chest. "Tell me what happened."

"It started Friday night when I slept in the blind. I had dreams, heard footsteps. I couldn't sleep. Every time I closed my eyes, I had horrible dreams. Every night since then has been the same. Then last night, it was so hot that I went outside."

"In the moonlight?"

"*Eh-yea*."

"And you saw him?"

"*Eh-yea*."

"Did he speak to you?"

"*Eh-yea*. He wanted—he wanted me to be his wife."

Ceferino pulls away from me and takes my chin in his hand to study my face. His eyes are so serious they frighten me. "Did he get inside of you?"

"*Sully, sully*," I repeat, shaking my head.

He doesn't say anything for almost a minute, still staring into my face. Then: "You are in great danger here. You must go to the island."

"I don't think I can."

"Eulogio will take you. But you must go soon, immediately."

At Mateo's *nega*, Irina fusses over me as if I'm a sick child. She feeds me hot corn gruel and gives me a sponge bath, then places a cool, damp cloth over my eyes and hums a soft lullaby while she strokes my arm. "*An mimi*," she murmurs as I fall asleep.

When I wake, Irina brings me water. "*An mimi,*" she says again, then leaves. In a moment, she returns with Pedro. I'm embarrassed: I didn't put on a bra this morning so when Irina stripped off my clothes, all she left were my panties. The thin wrap of skirt fabric that covers my torso leaves little to the imagination.

Irina takes my hand in both of hers. "*An mimi.*"

"Pedro, please, what is she saying? Why does she keep saying that to me?"

"*Mimi* is daughter. She is calling you her daughter." Pedro says a couple of words in Kuna. Irina strokes my hair protectively, then leaves.

Pedro draws a plastic lawn chair next to my hammock. "You are very sick. It could be malaria, dengue—anything. There's a hospital on Ailigandi, a western hospital. We'll have to leave soon to get there by dark."

"Is that what Ceferino thinks I should do?"

Pedro turns his head away from me when he speaks. "The Kunas believe—the Kunas don't know about viruses or penicillin or anything like that. They think that when you're sick, it's because something is trying to take over your soul."

"A *purba.*"

"You know as well as I do that's not what's wrong with you. You are very, very sick. You could die if you don't get proper treatment."

"Proper treatment meaning antibiotics."

"Proper treatment meaning whatever the doctor at the hospital says that you should take."

"And what about the *purba*?"

When Pedro looks at my face, his lips are a tight line. "You are feverish now. You're incapable of making decisions."

"Pedro, I don't have malaria or dengue. I've been taking malaria pills. And I haven't seen a mosquito in two months. I know what my problem is: a jaguar man found me in the jungle. His *purba* is haunting me."

"You're a Christian, a white person, a scientist. How can you believe that?"

"I believe it because I am a scientist. I've seen the evidence: it's happening to me. It's one of those things that Western medicine hasn't figured out yet."

In the *nega's* gloom, I can't tell if Pedro's smile is sympathetic or ironic.

"If I don't go to the hospital on Ailigandi, what will happen to me?"

"The Kunas will do their own medicine for you."

"Which is?"

"They'll take you to an island about half an hour from here. It's not an island really, just a little outcrop of coral barely big enough for a *nega*. They'll paint you black all over." Pedro glances down at my body and licks his lips as if they're dry. "You can't eat for four days, have to stay inside the whole time. They'll wash you in medicine water periodically. And Ceferino will be outside."

"Doing what?"

Pedro's lips twitch. "Performing the exorcism."

"You think I'm crazy?"

"I don't know. The way your eyes are shining right now, I don't know what to think."

"I'm sorry, Pedro. I know I'm a big pain in the ass for you."

Pedro reaches out to me and I'm surprised when he takes both of my hands in his. "You're not a pain to any part of my body except my heart. You make me realize how much of myself I've lost."

"I'm sorry, *anai*."

He gives my hands a squeeze. "They'll want to leave as soon as Ceferino gets back from the jungle. Irina will go with you, and Yarilista. Make sure that you eat something before you leave. You're so thin already that I can't imagine how you'll survive four days without food."

"I will, *anai*."

"And if you're not better when you get back, you'll come with me to the hospital?"

"I promise, *anai*. If this doesn't cure me, I'll do anything that you want me to."

XXXI

The black liquid, probably juice from some jungle plant, is watery—more like a wash than a paint—but it reacts with my skin to produce a deep, blue-black gloss. In the tiny *nega* on the isolated island, Irina uses her fingers to spread the dye over my legs and torso. She is careful to paint inside every crease and fold. By the time she finishes my lower body, daylight has faded and Yarilista, shorter and more frail than Irina, has me kneel. Irina holds a lit candle in her now-black hands while Yarilista paints my shoulders, arms, and face. In the candlelight, I see that the dye does not react with my hair: the down on my arms forms a startling halo above my glossy black skin.

The two old women appear to be arguing—Yarilista keeps pecking at my scalp and ruffling my hair as if she's looking for lice. Irina holds the candle so close that hot wax drips on to the top of my head. After she picks off the wax, she again examines my hair.

By the time Yarilista has finished with my face—she even dyes my eyelids and inside my nostrils—the women apparently have come to a consensus because they empty the contents of one of the gourds of juice onto my head and massage the liquid into my scalp. Three hands in my hair at once: Irina still holds the candle in their fourth hand, so close to my head I worry that a gust of wind might whip a stray lock into the flame. I shiver from the wind, from the movement of their fingers. I shiver at how I must look. They work at my scalp until they are satisfied, until, I assume, every inch of my white skin has been covered by the dye.

The women move away from me then, muttering and chatting. They rinse by dipping a gourd into a bucket and pouring water over each other's hands. The black stain does not wash off. I shift my position slightly. Yarilista waggles her finger, scolding me in Kuna.

Kneeling, I look down at my breasts and belly. The paint is deceiving: when I see the strange color on my torso I feel as if I am clothed. I remember the glide of Irina's fingers as she spread the paint everywhere—over every square inch of my skin—and conclude that I have never been so thoroughly handled in my life. I have never been as naked as I am now. I am naked but not threatened. I feel secure, cared for, even loved.

The candle burns down to a nub before the women allow me to move. Irina hands me an old skirt, stained black where past body paintings have bled into the fabric. I wear the cloth like a towel. Yarilista shows me a yellow bucket of water and pantomimes drinking from a dipper gourd. Another gourd will serve as my chamber pot.

Irina arranges my hammock, knotting the ropes to the wall supports of the *nega*. The hammocks of the crones block the doorway—to keep others out or me in? Yarilista blows out the candle.

"*Panni malo, mimi.*" Until tomorrow, daughter.

I wake often during the night. The wind swirls through the bamboo walls. The surf pounds heavily. The open ocean is rough: on the canoe ride out here, the waves were often ten or twelve feet high. The women maneuvered the tiny boat through the swells with an ease and nonchalance that would have amazed me if I hadn't been throwing up over the side of the canoe. Even now, the thought of those swells makes me queasy: we'll have to return to Sugatupu by the same route we came.

One of the women—probably Irina—snores as she sleeps. The *nega* is so small that I could reach out and jiggle her with my hand. My breath is jerky and convulsive. I wonder how long my skin will remain black. I have seen babies on the island painted this way. And teenage girls: one was forced to stand at the town meeting painted as black as I am now. That was after Litos died so I never found out what was going on. I assumed that the black paint was some kind of punishment.

I try to block out the sound of my own breathing, the sound of Irina's snores, the howling of the wind, and the pounding of the surf. Softly, like a whisper, like a breath, like a heartbeat, someone is singing. A man's voice. Ceferino is outside in the moonlight.

The sun hasn't crested over the ocean when Irina pokes me awake. I tumble out of my hammock. I'm dizzy and my skin feels as if it's burnt. I wonder if the black paint is making me sick. If my stomach weren't so empty, I'd probably be puking.

Irina gives me water to drink but I only wet my lips before she pulls away the gourd. She leads me to the wall of the *nega* opposite the door. A log hollowed into the shape of a canoe has been buried a foot deep in the sand floor. Irina steps into the canoe and faces the wall, then she climbs out. I assume that this is a signal for me to imitate her movements.

I climb into the canoe. Irina takes my right hand and presses it toward the wall: a short peg has been lashed to the bamboo, apparently to serve as a handhold. There's another for my left hand. Irina untucks the towel-like wrap and slides it off my body. I stand spread-eagle, feeling as though I'm about to be whipped. Instead, Yarilista empties a gourd of water over my back.

The splash of cold stops my heart. Instinctively, I try to escape by hopping out of the canoe, but Yarilista scolds me and Irina presses at my shoulders to hold me in place. She guides my fingers back to the pegs and fists her hands over mine for several seconds. "*An mimi*," she murmurs.

The women pour gourds of water over my head and back until the canoe is full. I keep my eyes sealed tight but taste an earthy musk on my lips. Tea-colored water washes down my chest, along my backbone, between my legs.

I'm so cold that I am numb. When the women finally stop bathing me, I stumble out of the canoe. I cannot walk: I collapse in the sand on the floor. My body tightens into a knot. I whimper like a sick cat.

I must sleep because it seems that only minutes pass before I am again poked by a bony finger. The water in the canoe is gone. Irina helps me stand in the hollow, helps me clutch the handholds. I hear myself scream when the water hits my back.

The second day is the same: I drink, I urinate into the gourd, I am bathed. By the third day I am so weak that I cannot stand. I slump in the canoe while the brown water washes over me.

At night, I do not dream. In the darkness, I listen for the heartbeat of Ceferino's song.

On the morning of the fourth day, I wake on my own before dawn. Even though I am weak, my head is clear. The burning in my flesh has cooled and I'm no longer nauseous. I slide out of my hammock and tiptoe to the water bucket. Slurping dipper after dipper, I try to ease the dryness in my throat, the emptiness in my belly.

On the other side of the wall, Ceferino's voice is so close that I feel the exhale of his breath. "*Sulegoa.*"

"Ceferino," the word catches in a sob of longing.

"You are better?"

"I need your heart."

"Put your ear against the wall, just above the row of lashings. Right here." He taps at the bamboo sticks. When I lay my head against them, I hear nothing except the surf but feel the warmth of Ceferino's body.

At midday I am allowed outside, Ceferino apparently having left the island. I lie in the sun and my black skin drinks the heat. When I feel that the sickness has been burned out of my bones, I cool in the ocean. On the beach, the old women join me: Irina lathers me with soap and Yarilista rinses the residue of the cure with clean, fresh water that has been warmed in the sun. The women wash my body as thoroughly as they painted it. When I am dry, they dress me in the fancy Kuna blouse that Iris gave me. The blue of the sleeves is startling against my black arms.

The sea is rough when we canoe back to Sugatupu but despite my weakness I am not sick. On the island, a Colombian boat is moored at the dock and half the town's population has gathered to trade coconuts for coffee and spatulas and hammocks and whatever else the Colombians have to offer. The boat is crewed by seven or eight rough-looking men who tower above the diminutive Kunas.

I duck my face behind my headscarf but it is no use: with my black painted skin, my incongruous blond hair, and my Kuna clothing, I must be the most bizarre sight the Colombians have ever seen. Every one of them stops what he is doing to stare.

"Red hot black mama," one of them calls to me in Spanish.

"Blond beauty."

I want to ignore them, to get away from the crowd around the boat as quickly as possible, but I'm so weak that I can't hoist myself out of the canoe. Before I know it, one of the Colombians has wrapped his arm around my waist and swept me up onto the dock.

"*Nuedi,*" I mumble, my eyes downcast. His body stinks as if he hasn't bathed for days.

"You're a Kuna?" he asks me in Spanish.

Yarilista, busy tying the canoe to the pilings on the dock, turns. When she sees the man next to me, she drops the rope and races at him as fast as her old legs can move. As she runs, she screeches in Kuna. Her excited momentum carries her headlong into the big man, like a bird smacking a brick wall. The impact stuns her for an instant but once she recovers, the old crone renews her attack, slapping at the man's massive chest with her open hand until he is forced to retreat to the deck of the trading boat. Everyone—Kuna and Colombian—laughs.

Once she's satisfied with her rebuff of the Colombian, Yarilista threads her arm around my waist. Irina shepherds me from the other side. We must be a laughable sight with my black face towering a good foot above my two withered companions as they direct my doddering steps toward the cool shade of a *nega* and the comfort of a hot meal.

After roll call at the meeting, Eulogio rises to speak. I notice that none of the women—not even the oldest ones—ever take their eyes away from his face. Eulogio speaks smoothly, glibly, without hesitation. Although I don't understand what he says, for some reason I am sure that he is talking about me.

To my amazement, Iris is the next person to claim the floor. She usually is so shy that she doesn't raise her voice above a whisper even in her own *nega*, but now she stands in front of the entire community holding her half-white baby in her arms and speaking haltingly, softly, but everyone in the building listens. Orestes is next: stiff and formal. In his speech, I hear the names of my parents, Roberto and Amelia, and I know for certain that the subject of this meeting is me. Eulogio's self-assured wife takes the stage and makes a couple of points. Irina when she speaks repeats the words "*an mimi*" almost continually.

Pedro rises, never glancing in my direction, and begins to talk. As I listen, I understand why the missionaries singled him out for schooling as a child. Pedro is a superb orator, masterfully varying his cadence and delivery, his rhythm and tone. At times he seems to be several people conversing and arguing among themselves. His words hesitate and stumble in places, then they flow and glide without effort. He seems to have a lot to say and the Kunas in the hall give him their undivided attention.

In my lap, Katrina Maria snores softly. She is heavy and so warm that I feel a thickness inside my lungs like the stale air of the midday blind. Maybe it's the exhaust from the Coleman lanterns. I swear I can taste gasoline, can taste the odor of the bodies that surround me.

I close my eyes. Pedro's voice becomes more remote. I wonder what he says about me. "Your ears are burning," my mother used to tease when I thought that someone was talking about me. My ears are burning. My whole head is burning, and pounding too. I don't know why I feel so weak and hot. It has to be cooler outside. I should go outside and get some fresh air. I lean toward Iris so that Katrina Maria can slide onto her mother's lap.

The next thing I know I'm surrounded by darkness. I seem to be moving although my muscles are slack. As I regain a sense of my body, I realize that thcrc is an arm behind my knees and another supports my back. Someone is carrying me.

"You are okay?" I recognize Eulogio because he uses the American word: "okay."

"I think so." I hate the helplessness of being carried. "You can put me down now."

"You're very weak. I'll carry you."

I must be weaker than I thought because instead of arguing I close my eyes. "What's your wife's name?" I murmur.

"What?"

"I always forget your wife's name. She's so beautiful and nice but I feel stupid because I can't remember her name."

"Disrelita."

"Like Benjamin Disraeli?"

"You shouldn't talk now. You should rest."

"Katrina Maria—is she okay?"

"She is okay. Everyone is okay except you. Here we are at Mateo's."

Irina fusses over me like a mother hen. Her withered hands spread the hammock and Eulogio lays me down. "*An mimi*," she murmurs as she smoothes my forehead with the tips of her fingers.

"Eulogio, what is the word for mother?"

"*Nana.*"

"*An nana,*" I whisper.

Eulogio and Orestes appear in the doorway just as Irina and I are serving breakfast. Orestes is as shy as ever: he won't even glance at my face. Eulogio takes a sip from the mug I hand him and asks if I made the gruel.

"Partially. Why, is it burned?"

"*Sully.* It's very good."

"*Yer goolege?*"

He takes another sip. "*Yer goolege.* You are better today?"

"*Eh-yea.*"

"You are very thin. Disrelita says this too, that you are too thin."

"I didn't eat much when I was sick."

"You will have to eat extra now. We don't want our *puna* to look half-starved."

Pedro sticks his head through the doorway. "*Na,*" I smile at him.

He doesn't return my greeting. In English he says, "When are you going back to the mainland so the rest of us can stop babysitting and get some work done?"

I bow my head to hide the quick tears that spring into my eyes. When Irina stands to serve Pedro, I touch her shoulder and whisper, "*Sully, Nana.*"

In the kitchen, I dip from the water barrel to wash my tears, then rinse out my mug and ladle in a serving of gruel. When I come back into the main house, I keep my eyes down as I hand the cup to Pedro.

"*Nuedi,*" he says, then in Spanish adds, "You practicing to be a Kuna?"

I kneel beside Irina's chair and bow my head.

"You've only got two weeks to learn everything you need to know about being a Kuna woman."

"I don't know what you're talking about."

"Didn't anyone tell you? They're going to have an *inna* for you, a traditional initiation ceremony. After that, you'll be a full-fledged member of our little community."

I glance at Eulogio, who smiles sheepishly. "You didn't understand anything we said last night?"

I shake my head. "*Sully.*"

Eulogio says something to Mateo. Mateo responds with a few sentences in Kuna.

Eulogio and Pedro both translate at once; Eulogio in Spanish and Pedro in English. I shake my head at Pedro.

Eulogio begins again. "All of us—everyone on Sugatupu—we are very concerned about what happened to you. It is not safe for you to live on the mainland. We have decided to make you a member of our community."

"But I'm not a Kuna."

Eulogio flashes a quick smile. "We noticed that."

"But isn't it wrong? I mean, an *inna* is so much a part of your culture—"

"You're the first outsider to come here who has respected our culture. You are the only one we have ever wanted to initiate into our community."

"You really like me that much?"

Eulogio says something in Kuna to Mateo. Mateo looks at me and smiles. "*Eh-yea, mimi.*"

Irina says, "*An mimi.*"

Orestes: "*An puna.*"

Eulogio continues. "Everyone on this island thinks of you as a daughter or a sister. You are very important to us. That's why we decided to do this."

"I hope that I won't disappoint you."

When Eulogio translates what I said into Kuna, Irina springs to her feet and embraces me. Kneeling, the top of my head brushes the sag of her breasts.

I glance at Pedro. "I'd better go now. I still have to pick up supplies and it's getting late. I'm sure you all have a lot of work to do."

Pedro says in Spanish, "You don't have to buy supplies."

"I've got to eat."

Eulogio and Orestes laugh.

"What's so funny?"

Eulogio answers. "You looked so thin last night, and then when you fainted everyone felt sorry for you. They've been bringing food for you all morning."

"So everyone thinks I'm pathetic."

"It's pretty hard not to."

I say in English, "I guess that's better than wanting to screw me."

Pedro lets out a surprised snort.

I don't want him to but he insists on walking with me to the point. I am silent until we are surrounded by mangroves. "You don't want them to have this *inna* for me, do you?"

"No."

"So what do you think I should do?"

"I think you should go back to the U.S."

"You can't expect me to give up everything I've been working for, not now when the research is just starting to result in some significant data. And with Mateo and Irina insisting that I can't live on the mainland, I don't know what I can do except stay here on your island. I'm sorry—I know that you don't like me."

"You are wrong, *anai,*" Pedro says softly. "I think that you are a very strong, brave, and intelligent woman. I want you to leave Sugatupu for your own good."

"You think it will be bad for me to become a member of your community?"

"Our cultures can never mix, *anai*. I have tried. It didn't work."

"You don't think that things might be different now?"

Pedro shakes his head. "I wish that they were. But with love and hate, nothing ever changes."

XXXII

When I duck into the blind, I'm surprised by a squeak—the sound like a startled mouse—and a quick flash of motion. As my eyes adjust to the gloom, I realize that I stand uncomfortably close to a teenaged Kuna boy.

"Who are you?" I can't think of anything else to say.

The boy tries to step backwards but comes up against the wall. "Samuel Lopez."

At least the kid seems to understand Spanish. "What are you doing here?"

"Eulogio told me to watch the eagles and write down everything that happens." As evidence, he offers me the open notebook.

I skim through the book, reading what I can in the poor light. Every entry is dated, and he has written at least four pages of observations for each day. "You've been here five days?"

"I came at noon on Tuesday. All the other days I was here at dawn."

"You've worked very hard. You are a good observer and you take detailed notes."

"I like learning about the eagles. Watching them."

"You can do a lot with what you learn when you watch things. You can become a scientist like me or a healer like Ceferino."

"Ceferino doesn't know as much as you do."

"He knows more—much, much more. I could study with Ceferino for years and still not know everything he knows."

The boy looks at me with wide, astonished eyes. "But Ceferino never went to school. He can barely speak Spanish."

"The eagles don't speak Spanish either."

"I thought that white people know everything."

"Who told you that?"

"The teachers at the school on Usdup."

"And they probably told you that what the Kunas know isn't important—that your language and traditions are all wrong."

"Yes." He doesn't even use the Kuna word, *eh-yea*.

"Samuel, a very wise white man once said that a fool thinks he is wise but the wise man knows that he himself is a fool. If someone tells you that you are stupid and they are wise, you can be sure that it's the other way around."

The boy's eyes are wide. "Really?"

"You are a very intelligent young man. You did my job as well as I could do it. And since you did the work that I'm being paid for, it's only fair that you be paid the way I am paid." Fortunately, I stopped at my *nega* on the way to the blind and picked up the latest envelope from David, the one with my pay. Inside, I locate a ten-dollar bill.

When I offer it to the boy, he's speechless. "Take it, Samuel. You earned every penny. And thank you. *Nuedi*."

"*Nuedi*." I'm glad to hear him drop the Spanish. The boy folds the bill into a tight square and centers it in the palm of his hand, then slides his fist into his pants' pocket. He's in such a hurry to leave that he accidentally shoves me as he bolts out the door.

In the five days that I have been gone, the eaglets seem to have doubled in size. Their eyes are still closed but fluffy white down now fully covers the crowns of their heads. Both parents are absent from the nest. During the course of the day, the father visits twice, the mother—obvious because of the still scraggly plumage on her breast—three times. On each visit, the adults bring food. The mother tears the flesh into bite-sized chunks that she feeds to the chicks. The father merely deposits the carcass in the nest and leaves.

I look over Samuel's notes. His Spanish is hard to understand at times—for example, he says that the adult eagle coughs when it arrives at the nest. I assume this refers to the mother feeding the chicks. Other than that, his observations are precise and detailed. When nothing is happening at the nest, I translate his notes into English. In the evening, I return to the island. The Kunas have decided that I will live with Mateo and Irina: the old couple already refers to me as their daughter.

After a few days, the rhythm of my new life becomes routine: in the morning, as a daughter I help with the cooking and serve breakfast to the men; but when I return from my work on the mainland I am allowed to rest while Irina prepares dinner. I learn more Kuna words during those lazy island evenings than I have in the past three months.

Late in the afternoon, I'm hurrying past the dock toward Mateo's when I am seized from behind and swung off my feet. My first reaction is fear but then a hand slides up my ribs to squeeze my breast.

"You're wearing a bra!"

"Ruiz, don't do that in town! Everyone will see it and they'll think—"

He's set me back on my feet and when I turn to face him, his jaw drops in a ludicrous expression of astonishment. At first I have no idea why he looks so shocked, but then I remember that my skin still wears a healthy sheen of blue-black dye.

"What the hell—?"

"It was for medicinal reasons."

"Really?" He seems distracted, as if he hasn't heard my words. "So you are black all over?"

"Yes."

"ALL over?" His eyes bug out of his face like he's having a stroke.

"Every square inch."

"Oh my God!" He closes his eyes, puts his hand over his heart, and rocks back and forth. "Oh—my—God!"

Out of the corner of my eye, I notice a handful of Kunas pretending not to watch us as they loiter in the street.

Ruiz demands: "You must let me see your body!"

"No!"

"Please?" he whines. "If I do not see you, the image will haunt me for the rest of my life. I will never be able to close my eyes without picturing how your beautiful white body would look if you were a black woman."

"It looks weird."

He sinks to his knees. "I will be your slave forever."

I finally agree to go with him to his boat, mostly to put an end to the scene he's creating in the middle of town. Fortunately, at that moment Samuel sidles past and I instruct him to tell Irina that I wouldn't be back until late.

"She will not be back tonight," Ruiz tells the boy in Spanish.

I shoot Ruiz a dirty look. "I'll be back tonight, but late. Tell her that I'll try to be quiet."

We take off in Ruiz's rubber dinghy, him at the tiller, me riding like a queen in front. The noise from the outboard motor makes conversation impossible. I rehearse what I'll say to him when we get aboard his boat.

As soon as I climb onto the deck, I turn to Ruiz, who is hoisting himself over the railing. "I'm not going to take off my clothes for you."

He plants his hands firmly on my shoulders and looks straight into my eyes. "What is going on? Are you all right?" His voice holds so much concern that I throw my arms around his neck and hug him. "You must not go back there."

"I'm all right."

"Where have you been? I went to look for you at your camp and you were nowhere to be found—"

"I was at the blind. The eagles were hatching. Oh, and thank you for the presents."

"You cannot distract me with your talk of presents! You are even thinner now than you were the last time I saw you. What did they do to you?"

"Nothing."

"Nothing except paint you black."

"That was because—"

"You will eat first. You will eat every scrap of food that I can find on this boat. And then you will tell me everything that has happened since the last time I saw you."

After a dinner so big that I can't swallow another bite, I tell Ruiz the story of the jaguar man's visit and of my exorcism. We sit at the table in the tiny cabin below deck, and Ruiz periodically downs shots of rum from a tumbler.

"So," he says after I have finished. "You are in love with Ceferino."

I hope that he doesn't see my blush through the black paint. "I didn't say that."

"You did not have to say anything," he says as he pours another shot.

I can't tell if Ruiz is angry with me. "Do you think it's wrong?"

"You could not have picked a better man, white or Indian."

"Pedro says—" my voice catches and I'm surprised to find a lump in my throat—"Pedro says that white people should never mix with the Kunas. That it's best to stay apart."

"You told Pedro that you are in love with Ceferino?" I hear hurt in Ruiz's voice.

I reach over and squeeze his big hand. "No, I didn't confide in Pedro. He just mentioned it in passing, talking about something else. But I thought maybe—I mean, he was married to a white woman. And it didn't work out. Do you think it was because of the difference in cultures?"

"I think Pedro's first marriage did not last because he was shooting up enough heroin to kill a horse."

"Pedro was a junkie?"

"He quit when he came back from England. Ceferino sent for me when the withdrawal symptoms started. I guess the Kunas figured that since it was about drugs, I would know what to do. We took him to an island—probably the same one you were on—and stayed there for two weeks while Pedro got all of the heroin out of his system. Ceferino did not close his eyes the whole time we were there."

"So you don't think it's wrong?"

"For you to love Ceferino? Of course not."

"What do you think I should do?"

He whispers in my ear, "You should do whatever your heart tells you to."

XXXIII

I arrive at the blind before the sun but Ceferino already waits for me. I haven't seen him in almost a week. For a few decadent moments, I embrace the smoothness of his body, the fresh river scent of his skin.

He turns his face away from my kiss. "We should leave soon. We have a long way to go."

I try to swallow my disappointment. "Where?"

"To the mountains. You're strong enough?"

"I don't know."

Ceferino does not walk fast—I think he tries for a pace that won't tire me—but he seems in a hurry. He doesn't stop to talk or show me things along the way. He leads me through the mountains along a faint game trail. At the crest of a heart-pounding climb, I double forward with my hands on my knees, panting.

"You can go on?" he asks.

"In a minute or two."

Ceferino's lithe brown body acts as a touchstone. I strive to match my movements to his. When I do, my preoccupation with my own body disappears and I'm free to concentrate on the jungle around me. Beneath my feet, the soil maps changes in vegetation and drainage. The bed of a small stream overflows with color, sound, and scent. Bird songs ring clear and distinct: tapaculo, ant wren, manakin. I become aware of breaths in the air, currents and eddies of warmth, pockets of life.

My mind blank, I concentrate on the few flecks of sunlight that have penetrated to the jungle floor. I blink the mottled, glowing patchwork into focus and realize that what I see is not random beams of sunlight: two clear brown eyes confront me from a fawn-colored face and behind that face, a white-spotted body crouches motionless among the low plants. The animal, as big as a fawn but chunkier, remains frozen except for its liquid brown eyes.

Beside me, I sense Ceferino's presence: the heat of his body, the tang of his sweat. We do not speak. I don't even look at him. But I am certain that he sees and recognizes the animal. I step backwards and whisper—maybe I just say the words in my mind—"*Con permiso.*"

I wait until I think that we are out of the animal's earshot, and when I speak to Ceferino my voice is soft. "*Sule?*"

"You felt him?"

"*Eh-yea.*"

"He must have called to you. I walked right past him and never realized that he was there."

We angle down a ravine to a stream. Ceferino lies on his stomach and drinks like a deer. I kneel and cup handfuls of water to rinse my face.

"I'm sorry I'm so slow."

"You are not slow—you're a very good walker. Eulogio tried to come up here once but didn't even make it this far."

"Eulogio had to turn back because he was tired?"

Ceferino laughs softly. "*Sully.* He said that he was afraid of the tree women. He thought that if they saw him walk by, they would be so overcome with lust they'd forget that during the day they're supposed to be sleeping."

From the bare, rocky outcrop, the jungle lies at our feet, undulating over the hills until it fades into a smoky, gray sky. "*Omekan.*" I say. Women.

"Kuna women never go very far into the jungle. I think they're afraid that the tree women are more beautiful than they are."

We look out over the unending, unvaried wilderness. "*Omekan yer dailege.*" The women are beautiful.

"You're afraid that they are more beautiful than you?"

"I'm certain that they're more beautiful than me. And if you say they're not, I'll know you're lying."

"But all of the women out there, all of those beautiful tree women—not one of them has a *nusa* as soft and warm as yours."

A light mist falls as we make love. After, I doze, my body curled around Ceferino and my head resting on his heart.

"Hist!" The sound is as quiet as a whisper but sharp enough to wake me. "Look!"

I try to sit up but Ceferino holds me firmly against his chest. When I peek over the slope of his body, I see a pair of gray wings. The wings beat with a slow, regal rhythm, defining a silhouette that flies outward from the sun. I straighten my head to focus my vision, then gasp. The most massive bird I have ever seen glides across the open valley, heading straight for our mountain.

Again when I try to sit, Ceferino smothers my movement. Details on the face of the bird are so precise that I wonder if somehow I've animated the stern profile of the harpy eagle from the sketch on page 104 of Ridgely's *Birds of Panama*. The diagnostic features that I have tried for months to reconcile with the eagle in the nest stand out on this bird in precise detail: the thick, powerful body and legs, the boldly banded wings and lighter breast, the collar of black plumage around the neck, the two-pointed crest at the top of the head, the massive beak fully twice as large as that of my nesting eagle.

The harpy eagle, now so close that I can see the yellow on its legs, continues to approach and I realize that its flight will take it directly over the rocky outcrop where we lie. I see the eyes—black shards of obsidian—and know that the eagle sees me. Naked, prone: does the eagle view us as equals or as prey?

As the harpy passes overhead, for a moment its darkness falls across the mountain. The shadow is large enough to cover both my body and Ceferino's.

I try to rise to watch the eagle out of sight but again Ceferino holds me. I resist and he is almost rough as he restrains me. "Wait," he whispers.

The word has barely left his mouth when I realize that a second eagle follows the first. This one flies even lower, on a level with the mountaintop so that it is close enough for me to hear the muffled "whup" of the wings as they pump. Almost as soon as I see it, the harpy is upon us. I feel the breeze born in the movement of its body through the air. I see the glint of white on the razor tips of its black talons, the scales on its naked yellow legs.

I don't know why I close my eyes at this point, when I am so near to something that I have lived so many months to see. Blind, I sense the hint of a touch shiver up my torso, bisecting my belly and ribs to sweep between my breasts. My breath catches: beneath me, Ceferino's body is still, the muscles in his shoulders inert. The whisper glides up the thin skin of my throat and then, abruptly, it ends. I open my eyes to a world gone gray: the body of the eagle so close that it becomes my only reality, so close that I feel muscles lifting wings skyward, primary feathers spread like fingers to channel the uplifting wind.

At the waterfall, we bathe and make love again. Despite the long shadows, Ceferino seems relaxed and languid. He tangles his fingers in my hair. "Your hair isn't golden now. It's brown like *nusa*."

"*Eh-yea*."

"Why?"

"It always gets darker when it's wet."

"Yarilista is making a lot of money from your *inna*."

"What do you mean?"

"Everyone wants some of *Olopuna's* hair. She's selling it."

I'm thrown by the word *Olopuna* until I put together the Kuna word for gold with *puna*—sister. "How can she sell my hair?"

"She's the one who's going to cut it."

I jerk upright. "What?"

Ceferino laughs. "I forgot—you've never been to an *inna* before. On the last day, Yarilista will cut your hair."

"How short?"

"She will cut off all your hair. So that your head looks like a coconut."

"You're kidding."

"I think you will look nice with your head like a coconut."

I put my hands on either side of his face so that I can look straight into his eyes: one brown and the other with the red-flecked scar. "You're teasing me now, right?"

He wrinkles his nose to make a face like a little kid. "*Sully.*"

I slump. "So at the end of the *inna* I have to get my head shaved like a coconut. What else?"

"Nothing."

"You're sure? No other surprises?"

Ceferino laughs. "*Sully.* You just have to sit by yourself in a little room for three days while everyone else gets drunk and has a good time."

"I have to sit all by myself?"

"Usually the mother stays with the girl. But Irina says you're old enough so you don't need anyone to stay with you. I think she's looking forward to getting drunk."

"Irina gets drunk?"

"Everyone gets drunk except you."

"Even Yarilista?"

"Especially Yarilista."

"But she's going to be cutting my hair!"

"You're afraid that she'll cut off your ears?"

"That would only improve them. They're way too big."

Ceferino gathers my hair tightly at the nape of my neck, tucking loose strands behind my ears. "You will not be able to go to the mainland while your hair is short."

"Is that one of the rules?"

"*Sully*. But if the monkeys see you with your ears sticking out like this, they'll be so in love with you they'll never let you come back to the island."

Before I can respond, Ceferino guides my face into his. In the passion of our kiss, I slide my tongue between his teeth. Ceferino moans and pulls his lips away from me. "What are you doing?"

"Don't you like it?"

"M-m-m." His lips rejoin mine. I coax his tongue into my mouth and suck on it. Ceferino shudders.

When we finally pull apart he says, "It doesn't matter how many times you kiss me like that—you'll still have to get your hair cut at the *inna*."

"There's no way around it?"

"You have to get your hair cut because when it grows back, that means you are a Kuna woman and can marry a Kuna man."

When he says this, my stomach lurches: from happiness or apprehension, I'm not sure which. "How long does my hair have to grow?"

With his finger, Ceferino flicks at a lock on my shoulder. "Long enough to cover your monkey ears."

XXXIV

As soon as I settle onto the bench in the meeting hall, Pedro slides onto the seat beside me. "I have to talk to you after the meeting."

"I need to talk to you, too. Something happened on the mainland."

"You're all right?"

"Yes, daddy, I'm fine. It's just something I need advice on."

"Uncle."

"What?"

"Uncle. *Kilu*. Kunas call men that they like either uncle or brother depending on how their age relates to yours."

"So you'd be my uncle? And Eulogio would be my—?"

"Brother."

"So if I called him uncle that would imply that he's an old fart?"

Pedro's face twists into a tight frown. "What are you talking about?"

"Nothing. It's just another of my social blunders. I'm getting really good at them. Pedro, *anai*—I mean *kilu*—could you do me a big favor?"

"Depends on what it is."

"I love your tone of unbridled enthusiasm."

Pedro's smile seems grudging.

"Could you stay here and translate for me? Litos used to do that and I had so much fun finding out all the gossip, but since he's gone I've been pretty much in the dark."

"There's not going to be any gossip tonight. Mateo and Ologuippa are going to chant."

"Oh, I love that!"

Even in the dim light, I read suspicion in Pedro's eyes.

"I was raised Catholic."

Pedro nods with a smirk. "That would explain it."

"Hey, I'm not the one who gets horny looking at pictures of angels." I pause for a minute, then add, "But those statues where Christ is wearing nothing but a loincloth—"

"The *evangelico* was right. You are a slut."

"Sh-h-h. Mass is beginning."

Mateo and his sidekick sit in their hammocks staring ahead, staring at nothing. The two men could be ventriloquist dummies, or mummies from some lost civilization. Their chant might be words from a thousand years ago, as old as Christ, as old as time. Mateo sings out the verses, the other man the refrain, a standard "We-oh" that serves both as a period to the words that preceded and an introduction to those that follow. The lines lap together like waves in the ocean.

"What are they saying?" I whisper to Pedro.

"Sh. You're not supposed to understand."

"Because I'm stupid?"

"It's like your Mass. The old Latin Mass."

Katrina Maria sleeps in my lap. I doze. Pedro pinches me on the thigh and I jump. Mateo sings his final verse and his sidekick hums out the standard response. The two men remain lying in their hammocks, impassive and still.

Anselmo rises from the bench closest to the center of the hall.

"Now he's going to talk?"

"He's the translator," Pedro whispers. "He'll explain the story that Mateo just told."

Anselmo glances at me, a quick flash of his clouded eyes, and begins speaking. Pedro listens for a few moments and then draws in his breath sharply.

"What's he saying?" I whisper.

"It's"—Pedro pauses, listens, and shakes his head. "I'll explain later."

Pedro's features are abruptly defined in the match's quick flare, only to disappear into starlight when he shakes out the flame. The moon has not yet risen.

"You going to tell me what was going on at the meeting?"

"Take a hit first."

"That bad, huh?" I hold the smoke in my lungs and hand the joint back to Pedro.

"Nothing like this has ever happened before." Pedro seems distracted and puffs at the doobie like a cigarette.

I smile stupidly, already a little stoned, and decide not to prompt him.

"Anselmo, at the meeting"—Pedro shakes his head, then continues. "The translator is supposed to explain the story that the *saylas* chant, to retell it in understandable terms. But tonight Anselmo just went ahead and told a different story. It didn't have anything to do with Mateo's."

"Why would he do that?"

Pedro stares out to the darkened sea. "I don't know. They've always had this rivalry, Anselmo and Mateo. Anselmo's a hothead—he loses his temper, always acts too quickly on everything. Mateo is a lot slower, too slow for some people. They alternate as *sayla*: for a while Anselmo will be in power then something happens that turns the community against him and they vote Mateo in. I always used to think that we were better off with Mateo."

"But now?"

Pedro shrugs.

"It's about me, isn't it?"

He takes a couple of quick hits, then flips the roach into the surf. "Of course it's about you. Everything's about you. The whole world revolves around you, doesn't it?"

"God, you can be mean sometimes."

He's turned away from me again, staring out over the rhythmic sigh of the waves. "Ceferino is in love with you."

"He told you that?"

"Everyone knows—even Eulogio."

"Is that what you wanted to talk to me about?"

"The *inna* starts Friday. If you go through with it, everyone expects you to marry Ceferino."

"When my hair grows back."

"You know about that?"

"Ceferino told me."

"He asked you to marry him?"

"He told me that we could go to the church on Ailigandi if I didn't want to get married Kuna style. What's Kuna style?"

"They throw the couple in a hammock and swing it three times."

"That's it? Sounds like fun."

Pedro rolls another joint. "I don't know what to tell you. I know you think that I'm—what did Ruiz call me?"

"A pissant."

"I just wanted to protect you from some of the things that I went through. What will your parents say?"

"I would hope that they can respect my decision. And I know that when they meet Ceferino they'll like him."

"You think that way because you're in love. And you were the one who said you didn't believe in love."

"And you, *anai.* You're the one who believes."

"I do. That's why I'm not going to clunk you on the head and drag you away to the Baptists on Ailigandi."

"I appreciate that, *anai*. I mean *kilu*."

Pedro looks away from me. "There are people on Sugatupu who don't like the idea of you marrying Ceferino."

"Anselmo?"

"Anselmo—and others."

"And you?"

Pedro sighs heavily. "Mateo likes you and he likes the fact that Ceferino is happier now than he's ever been before. But Anselmo—for Anselmo, I think it all comes down to power. I think everything he's done in his life was focused on getting power."

"That doesn't answer my question. I asked how you feel about me and Ceferino."

"What I feel is not important."

"It is to me, *kilu*."

Pedro lights the nearly-forgotten joint. "What is it you saw on the mainland that you wanted to talk to me about?"

"A harpy eagle."

"Don't you see those all the time?"

I shake my head.

"I don't understand."

"Flemming misidentified the eagles on the nest. They're not harpies."

"And you're sure of this because you saw a real harpy?"

"Ceferino took me up into the mountains. He must have known there were harpies there."

"So what does that do to your research?"

"It pretty much invalidates the entire study."

"What are you going to do?"

"I don't know. I don't know what I'm going to do about anything."

XXXV

At my feet, Orestes's astonishingly beautiful wife, Jacinta, sits on a low stool as she strings beads for my ankle bracelets. Bright seed beads—they remind me of colored balls of tapioca—are threaded onto a string that's spiraled around my leg until my entire calf from ankle to knee is completely covered with sparkling flecks of color. Jacinta works rapidly, without pause or plan, but when I study the beading I realize that she has created a repeated pattern of orange and yellow lines, a design my mother called a Greek key when she knit it into my mittens when I was a kid.

On the hammock beside me, Iris strings beads around my wrist. Disrelita, Eulogio's wife, started the bracelet but she put more energy into talking than beading. When Iris arrived at Eulogio's *nega* carrying three new blouses—one for each day of the *inna*—Disrelita abandoned the beads altogether, and without a word Iris picked up the thread and continued where Disrelita had left off.

Iris lifts my forearm so that she can tie off the end of the string. The completed band of beads is flawless. I am amazed that she has been able to maintain the pattern so perfectly along the swell of my arm from wrist to elbow.

"*Yer dailege,*" I whisper to her. "*Nuedi.*"

Iris smiles shyly.

Disrelita holds up one of the blouses that Iris brought, an intricate maze of leaves, animals, and birds that surrounds a female human form. The sleeves and trim of the blouse are ruby red. "You'll wear this tomorrow," Disrelita declares, speaking slowly and distinctly as if to a child.

"Me?" I say—or think I say. I'm still not comfortable with the Kuna language.

"Yes, you. Iris made this blouse for you, for your *inna*."

I look over at Iris as she measures the string to begin the bracelet for my other arm. "Thank you, my sister. It is beautiful. You are beautiful."

Iris scurries over to the hammock and throws her arms around me. I feel her tears against my shoulder. "*Olopuna*, you are beautiful. You are my sister."

I glance at Disrelita, who I've noticed wears an indulgent smile every time Iris opens her mouth to speak. "We'll have to find a pretty skirt to match this blouse, won't we, Jacinta?"

Jacinta grunts. The pattern she's beading on my calf has changed color, so apparently she needs to concentrate.

"And this blouse"—Disrelita holds up an elaborately decorated bodice with huge, flowing sleeves of burnished yellow satin—"We'll save this for the last day, the day of the haircutting. Without her hair, *Olopuna* will need to wear lots of gold in order to keep her name!"

I rehearse a sentence several times in my mind before I speak. "After the *inna*, I won't be *Olopuna* anymore. I will be No Hair *Puna*." I don't know if what I said makes sense but the women all laugh.

When Iris begins stringing beads on my other arm Disrelita, apparently bored with the blouses, settles on the hammock beside me. She continues to talk while she combs my hair although the other Kuna women are too absorbed with their work to respond and I only understand a fraction of what she says.

"No Hair *Puna*," Disrelita jostles my shoulder. "How do you think you will look without hair?"

"She will be beautiful," Iris asserts.

"*Sully*. I will be very, very ugly without hair."

Jacinta pauses in her beading to study my face and even by the dim light of the oil lamp I can see that she is astonished by my words. Iris whispers, "*Sully*," to me.

I'm so grateful to these women for accepting me, for giving me their friendship, that I feel an urge to confide in them.

"Ceferino says that I won't be able to go to the jungle after the *inna* because the monkeys will fall in love with my big ears."

The laughter is immediate and explosive. Disrelita is so overcome that she lies flat in the hammock and covers her face with her headscarf. After several minutes, still chuckling, she sits up and pulls my hair into a tight knot. She flicks the tip of my ear. "He's right," she sputters. "You do have monkey ears!"

Outside I hear a "hist!"—the sound urgent and sharp. I hold up my hand for silence. Now we all hear it: a beckoning, hissing whistle. Disrelita scoots out the door.

The rest of us are silent as we try to eavesdrop on the conversation on the other side of the *nega* wall: Disrelita's lilting whispers responding to a deeper, male voice. Disrelita comes back into the *nega* looking like the cat that swallowed the canary.

"That was Ceferino out there. Why does he call you *Sulegoa*?"

"It's a long story."

Jacinta's teeth are perfect and seem to light up the *nega* when she smiles. "We've got all night."

Iris raises her face and in the flickering flame of the lamp her eyes have a wistful, romantic yearning.

"I don't know the right words to explain it."

Disrelita slides onto the hammock beside me and takes my hand in hers. "We will help you. Please tell us."

"It's not a very good story. It makes me"—I don't know the Kuna word for "embarrassed"—"It makes my face hot."

Jacinta laughs. "Those are the best kind of stories!"

In my slow, garbled Kuna, I tell the women about my bout with the chiggers and Ceferino's unexpected visits. By the time I finish, Disrelita is laughing so hard that tears stream down her cheeks. She holds me in her arms as she falls back in the hammock, rolling and laughing. Even after she has regained some of her composure, she continues to hug me. "My sister," she whispers in my ear. "Ceferino told me to give you this. He loves you very, very much." She presses a mass of soft paper into my hand.

I peel apart layers of white tissue. Nestled in the center, a flash of gold catches the light from the oil lamp. I recognize the style of necklace that the Kuna women wear: a gold chain with a flat, hammered pendant. I hold the pendant up to the light and see that it is engraved with five elaborately scripted letters. Tears fall onto my cheeks when I understand the gift that Ceferino—a man who can neither read nor write—has given to me. The necklace proclaims a single word, a word that I haven't heard spoken since my arrival on Sugatupu four months ago: Jenny, my long abandoned and now nearly forgotten Christian name.

XXXVI

Under the ruby red blouse, I wear silk underwear of exactly the same color. My navy blue skirt is printed with bright orange flowers that match the beaded Greek keys on my forearms and ankles. Around my neck, a flash of gold proclaims my name to the four bamboo walls and low thatch of the closet.

I'm all dressed up with no one to see me. Early this morning—I barely had time to gulp down a mouthful of gruel—Irina and Yarilista shooed me into this closet and firmly slammed the door behind me. The room is barely large enough to accommodate a hammock. Its walls have no openings except the doorway that leads to the alley behind the party hall. I will sit in this room, alone, for the next three days while in the building across the way the entire adult population of Sugatupu feasts and drinks and parties. As the guest of honor, I will hear everything that transpires but participate in nothing until the last evening, when my head will be shaved by an ancient, drunken woman.

There's a bucket of water with a gourd dipper to use for drinking. There's the now-familiar chamber pot fashioned from another gourd. There's an oil lamp on a shelf and beside it a box of matches. There are two low stools, each fashioned from a solid piece of wood. One of the stools has been carved to resemble a crude animal, a pig or a tapir, with thick legs and a broad back. When I try to sit on this stool, I almost fall off—either the legs are uneven or the floor is. Lifting the stool, underneath I find my field notebook half-buried in the dirt. I open the cover and a loose sheet of paper spills out.

"Samuel is watching your eagles while you are here. I thought this book might help you pass the time. I will see you in three days, after you have become a Kuna woman. Your brother, Eulogio."

By sunset on the second day, the closet is an oven and the party across the alley is in full swing. They've even got music: pan pipes and drums and almost continual chanting. But most of the organized sounds are lost in a general babble: lots of laughter and random singing, loud voices, foot stomping, and—today more than yesterday—the occasional thud as a body falls to the floor. The air that filters into the closet is heavy with the scent of alcohol, cigarettes, and smoked food.

With my face against the widest crack in the bamboo wall, I can keep track of the comings and goings in the party hall. There's a lot of traffic, mostly people heading to the ocean to cool off or answer the call of nature. As he staggers out of the hall and into the golden sunlight, Orestes falls flat on his face. He lies in the sand for quite some time, laughing and singing to himself, before a couple of exiting men trip over his prone form. Without a word, the men hoist Orestes's limp body by the shoulders until he's nearly vertical. Orestes doesn't attempt to walk: his legs and feet trail behind him like a weird tail as the men drag him to the ocean and heave him in. He pulls himself out of the water shaking likc a dog, disappears, and returns a while later dressed in dry clothes.

Children sidle past: older girls with their hips cockeyed from the weight of bundled toddlers, boys with slingshots and kites. A few peek through the bamboo walls into the party house but most seem content to be living their kid lives without the usual interference from adults. Watching an adolescent girl mother a child almost as big as she is, I conclude that the kids right now are more mature than the adults. A loud "whup!" explodes from the party house followed by an eruption of laughter and the sound of bare feet slapping the packed dirt floor.

I'm so intent on the action in the courtyard—a broadly swaying woman helps another, dead drunk, negotiate the steps up the sea wall—that I almost jump out of my skin when two hands grab me from behind. I spin away, twisting to face my assailant, and encounter an extremely drunk Ceferino.

He says something to me in Kuna.

"I don't understand."

He repeats the words slowly, then when I still don't respond, he throws his arms around my neck and collapses, pushing me against the wall.

"I'm not supposed to be here." I finally understand what he's saying. "Irina would kill me if she found out." He giggles, then abruptly straightens and slaps his hand over his mouth. Behind his palm, I hear him hiss softly. He covers my mouth with his other hand and leans toward me. An instant before our faces collide, he pulls away both of his hands so that our lips meet.

His hands grope at my waist, then I feel a draft as he untucks my skirt and the fabric falls to my feet. Ceferino plays with the backs of my thighs and the smooth silk that covers my rump. He moans into my hair, his eyes closed.

"You're beautiful," he says in Kuna. "I love you."

He stops fondling me long enough to unzip his fly. His pants are so loose that they immediately slip down off his hips to his ankles. When he pulls me against his body, I feel his hardness. He slides his hands inside my panties to caress me, his lips working across my face, down my chin to my neck.

"*Yer goolege,*" he says to me. You are delicious.

Forgetting the tangle of pants at his feet, he tries to steer me toward the hammock and trips, falling heavily to the floor. I'm on my knees in an instant, fussing over him, but he seems totally oblivious to what just happened. He pulls me on top of his body and works my panties down until all I feel is his hardness against me, and inside me.

A blinding white light wakes me. I squeeze my eyelids tight but it's not enough to protect me from the glare. My hands, palm forward, spread to shield my face. Beside me, Ceferino must sense my movement because he shifts his hips and rubs his face against my breasts.

I hear a soft, masculine chuckle, then the light moves away from my face to focus on the sag of the hammock. Highlighted in the beam of light, Ceferino's body is entwined with mine. We are both naked.

"Who is it?" I demand in Kuna.

"Pedro says that in the Bible the angels all look like white women. Now that I've seen you, I know why so many Kuna men want to go to Christian heaven." Eulogio's Spanish is slurred but maddeningly understandable.

"Give me my skirt!"

Eulogio continues to spotlight my body with his flashlight.

"God damn it, give me my skirt!"

He clicks his tongue. "Such language for an angel to use." Squatting, he picks through our discarded clothing. The butt of the flashlight in his mouth, Eulogio examines my bra in one hand and my panties in the other.

"You pervert!" I slide out of the hammock and snatch my skirt from the floor, then try to establish some dignity by frowning sternly as I tuck the fabric above my breasts.

Eulogio still holds my underwear in his hands. He's drunk, but not as far gone as Ceferino was this afternoon.

"What are you doing here?" I demand.

"I'm looking for my brother." As if on cue, Ceferino moans.

"I guess you found him."

"He shouldn't be here. If anyone knew he was here, you'd both be in a lot of trouble." Eulogio points the flashlight toward the floor and now speaks in a hushed whisper as if he's trying to impress me with the gravity of the situation. I pluck my underwear out of his hands.

The voice behind me, speaking Spanish, is clear and sober. "Eulogio, you are a son of a bitch."

I spin around. Ceferino sits astride the hammock. "I'm sorry, Jenny."

When Ceferino says my name, my heart grows so big that I think my chest is about to explode. "What did you say?"

"I'm sorry that my brother is a son of a bitch."

"No—the other."

"Jenny? Does your name sound so bad coming out of my mouth that it makes you cry?"

"No," I sob as I throw my arms around his neck. "You say it perfectly."

Ceferino locates the seam where the two ends of skirt fabric meet. He parts them like a curtain, sliding his arms around my waist and pulling me into him so that the front of my body presses naked against his chest. "That's good, because your name feels beautiful in my mouth: Jenny. It sounds like the river sliding over your body when we're at the waterfall making love. Eulogio!" he raises his voice above a murmur. "Eulogio, you son of a bitch, do you know what Jenny calls—?" Ceferino uses a Kuna word here that I don't know. "She says that we are making love. It's so beautiful, that love is something that you can make and then hold onto later. I like to think that when I'm inside of her, I'm filling her up with love, that even after we've finished, she'll always have all of that love we made."

"You won't be making much of anything if Irina or Yarilista catch you in here."

Ceferino pulls away from me. "Jenny, I'm afraid the son of a bitch is right. I have to go now. Tomorrow at dusk Yarilista will cut your hair and then you will be able to join us for the last night of the *inna*. I will tell Yarilista to be especially careful of your monkey ears."

"But I'll be all bald. I'll be ugly."

"Jenny, you will always be beautiful. Your monkey ears will make you more beautiful than ever to this monkey man. And in the morning after the *inna* when everyone stays in their hammocks with a headache, we'll go to the waterfall together and the birds will sing about how beautiful *Sulegoa* looks with her monkey ears, and we will make so much love that the river beneath us will taste like the ocean."

Ceferino's shoulder abruptly jerks away from me. "Son of a bitch," he hisses.

Eulogio says something in Kuna that I don't understand.

"Jenny—*Sulegoa*—I am sorry. Please forgive me."

"Don't leave me now."

"I have to. That son of a bitch is right: if anyone found me here, you'd be in a lot of trouble. We both would be."

"Hist!" Eulogio hushes as he jerks him from the hammock.

"Hist yourself, you son of a bitch!" Ceferino manages to hop into his pants while Eulogio tugs him toward the door. "Jenny," he calls back to me in a stage whisper. "*Panni malo. An be sabe.*"

XXXVII

The plane floating down from the clouds seems anachronistic, like some kind of prehistoric flying reptile. Humidity dulls the roar of the engine as the plane taxis to a halt at the end of the runway. I swat at sand fleas that pepper my calves.

When the hatch of the plane is lowered and David unfolds himself through the doorway, I don't recognize him at first. He lurches stiffly onto the stairs, clinging to the guy wire, and hesitates before he steps down to the tarmac. The man who follows David is so massive that the plane visibly rebounds when it's released from his weight.

I approach the two men. David glances at me, then casts his eyes around the airstrip as if he's expecting someone else. "What did you do to your hair?" His voice has a flat indifference that I never noticed before.

Without waiting for an introduction, the other man—Flemming—sweeps both of my hands into his. The bulk of him eclipses the sky but a smile radiates across his fat face. "Congratulations!"

I must appear confused because he continues, "Your hair. When did they cut it?"

"About a month ago."

David snorts. "It makes your ears stick out."

"Like a monkey," I murmur. I can't take my eyes off Flemming—if he weren't so fat, I would almost describe him as handsome.

Flemming turns my hands palm upward and runs a sausage finger along my forearms. "And your beads have lasted all this time! I've never seen that color blue in one of these bracelets. It's beautiful."

"They told me it matches my eyes." Flemming's attention embarrasses me.

The pilot dumps the luggage on the tarmac beside us. I collect Flemming's—a surprisingly dainty knapsack—but leave David to haul his own bag. On the trail to camp, Flemming lumbers behind me. When his breath whistles harshly on the inhale, I stop to let him rest.

"This humidity's terrible when you're not used to it."

Flemming's voice is labored. "That's a polite way of saying that I'm as fat as a pig."

David rolls his eyes.

At camp, Flemming can't stop admiring my *nega*. I serve my guests raw bananas, and a gruel of corn meal and chocolate that David sips gingerly. Flemming's bulk, quiescent, dominates the log.

David fidgets restlessly. "We should go to the blind to verify the identity of the eagles."

"I'm sure that Jenny has verified their identity a thousand times by now. She wouldn't have jeopardized her career by challenging me without first making damn sure that she was right."

David opens his mouth as if to respond, then closes it and plunks down on the other end of the log.

"I think that since we're all together now, the thing we need to do is go through Jenny's proposal to enlarge the scope of the study. Jenny, maybe you could summarize what you had in mind."

"Well, like I said in the letter"—I focus on Flemming, who nods and smiles—"now that we know there are two distinct species of eagle nesting in the area, I thought that we could organize concurrent observations of both the cresteds and the harpies. That raw data could result in a comparative study of the two species. There's a boy from the island, a teenager, who's been helping me with the observations here. I was sick for almost a week around New Year's and he did a great job of recording the eagles' activities. I know that he could handle the observation of the cresteds. It would be cheaper to use a local person than a grad student, and it wouldn't disrupt the community the way it would if we brought in an outsider. The harpy nest is about five hours from here, in the mountains. With the boy observing the cresteds, I'd be free to concentrate on the harpies."

"You can't live that deep in the jungle without support, all alone like that." David's voice again sounds flat and dull.

"There's a small Kuna community on the river nearby. I could use that as a base."

Flemming nods. "Are the harpies nesting now?"

"There's an eagle—probably a grown chick—with the adult pair now. I think it's just about ready to go off on its own, and then I assume the mated pair will breed in the fall. That's all speculation, of course."

"How did you find the harpy nest?"

I hesitate. Flemming nods, smiling slightly, and I wonder how much he reads in my face. "One of the men on Sugatupu lived on the mainland when he was young. He has connections with the mountain community. He's the one who led me to the harpies."

"And he'll arrange your stay in that community?"

I nod.

David asks, "How much do you have to pay him?"

"Nothing. I mean, he goes to the jungle a lot on his own. And he's really interested in this whole study. He's doing this to help me—to help the study."

David persists. "I don't understand why this man would provide all of these services at no cost, while there's a woman on the island who—as far as I can tell—isn't doing a thing for you and you want to pay her $50 a month."

"That's—" I begin but Flemming cuts me off.

"You have never worked with indigenous people, Calabrese."

It's not a question but Flemming waits for a response.

"You haven't, have you?" Flemming's tone surprises me: curt and dismissive, almost arrogant.

"No."

"Then you know nothing about the way these people deal with outsiders, the way their community is organized, the proper etiquette in situations such as the one that Jenny is dealing with, do you, Calabrese?"

Again, he waits for a grudging, "No."

"Jenny has done a marvelous job of consolidating local interest and integrating members of the community into this study. I am very impressed with what she's accomplished here and her plans for expanding the research. And since she is willing to take a cut in her own pay to accommodate the additional expenses involved, I don't see where you can quibble with her numbers."

An awkward silence follows Flemming's rebuke. I squat in front of the fire pit and stare at the ashes.

When he next speaks, Flemming's voice has become conversational and light. "Since you're so eager to see the eagles, Calabrese, why don't you take a stroll down to the blind now before it gets too hot?"

"I don't know the way," David says churlishly.

"The path's obvious, isn't it, Jenny? Just follow it down this little hill."

"It turns right in a cornfield about half a mile down. If you miss the turn, you'll end up at the river."

"Is that Kuna boy in the blind?"

"Samuel—yeah. He speaks very good Spanish and can tell you everything that's going on with the eagles and the chicks."

Flemming waits until the sound of David's footsteps has faded. "I want to thank you for not denouncing me in front of Calabrese. I appreciate your restraint."

Astonished by his words, I try to keep my voice level when I respond. "I'm a scientist. I've been trained to avoid value judgments."

Flemming waits, and waits, until finally I'm forced to glance up at his face. "Your scientific training was very thorough. It allows you to be civil even to a son of a bitch like me."

"I have to depend on my training as a scientist to protect me in social situations. I've been told that I'm a lousy liar."

Flemming laughs until his belly jiggles. "Who told you that?"

"Ruiz."

"You know, when Calabrese said that he'd sent a woman out here to the site, the thing that most concerned me was Ruiz. I thought he might try to kidnap you or something like that. I even called Reilly and described Ruiz to him to see what he thought. Reilly said that you could chew up a man like that and spit out the pieces."

"Did he say spit or shit?"

Flemming's laugh could be Ruiz's.

"Ruiz was never a problem."

Flemming wipes his eyes: I can't tell if the moisture is sweat or tears. "Not like that fat white guy who abandoned his wife and daughter and was never heard from again."

"Iris has another little girl now. She must have been pregnant when you left."

"And you've been supporting the whole family out of your own pocket?"

"I told her it was from you."

"Why?"

"I didn't want her to think it was charity."

"So when are you going to damn me for being a fat-assed tomcat who can't keep his pecker inside his pants?" He is smiling, an open, pleasant, relaxed smile.

"I guess I don't understand you."

"There's not that much to understand, Jenny. When I first came down here I was trying to escape. I thought this would be the perfect place to hide from everything that was driving me crazy back in the real world. But you know what I found? All of those things that I was running away from, they followed me here. You can't get away from who you are. I was a son of a bitch in the U.S. and I'm a son of a bitch here."

"I don't think that's true."

"Just because I let you challenge me once with the eagles, don't think that you can get away with it again."

From where I squat, I look up over the fire pit to Flemming's face. He's still smiling, as if we're winding down over a few beers after a day of high-powered conferencing.

"That kid who was at this site before you—Brian what's-his-name—he never questioned my identification of the eagles."

"Ruiz told me that Brian spent all his time in a cathouse in Cartegenia."

"And I spent all my time screwing Iris." Flemming pauses, studying me. "That man from the island who you say has been helping you—it's Ceferino, isn't it?"

My face burns but I manage to respond with an even tone and a smile that I hope is as glib as Flemming's. "Are you planning to visit the island today so that you can catch up with your wife and two daughters?"

Flemming cocks his head to one side. "Jenny, how much of the Kuna language have you learned since you got down here?"

"Some. Not enough."

"Do you know how to say 'I love you'?"

"*An be sabe.*"

"*An be sabe,*" Flemming repeats. "You picked that up in five months. I lived here almost five years and never did learn how to say it."

XXXVIII

Moonlight transforms gaps between bamboo sticks into white stripes on the dirt floor. Wind breathes through leaves in the canopy trees, distant, and on it is the scent of rain. I raise my head to listen, trying to isolate the sound that abruptly wakened me.

One by one, the white stripes on the floor vanish, then reappear as a shadow passes between the moon and the *nega* wall. I hear a soft shuffle of footsteps, stealthy like a cat. The gait, however, is human: this cat walks on two legs. I close my eyes, my mouth open, my breath hushed. The footsteps pause. Abruptly, I hear a cough.

In the hammock, Ceferino shifts. His arms tighten to pull me closer. I relax my head on to his chest. Against my cheek, I feel the steady, strong beat of his heart.